LORI FOSTER

Bewitched

HQN™

ISBN-13: 978-0-373-77495-1

BEWITCHED

Copyright © 2010 by Harlequin Books S.A.

The publisher acknowledges the copyright holder of the individual works as follows:

IN TOO DEEP
Copyright © 2000 by Lori Foster

MARRIED TO THE BOSS
Copyright © 2000 by Lori Foster

Recycling programs for this product may not exist in your area.

This edition published by arrangement with Harlequin Books S.A.

For questions and comments about the quality of this book please contact us at Customer_eCare@Harlequin.ca.

® and TM are trademarks of the publisher. Trademarks indicated with ® are registered in the United States Patent and Trademark Office, the Canadian Trade Marks Office and in other countries.

www.HQNBooks.com

Printed in U.S.A.

CONTENTS

IN TOO DEEP

To Malle Vallik.

Though you'll no longer be editing at Harlequin Temptation, you'll be forever remembered as "one of the great ones." I take comfort in the fact that your Harlequin Temptation novels will go on, pleasing readers for years to come.

CHAPTER ONE

SHE HAD THE soft, sweet mouth of a woman. And as she bent slightly at the waist, peeking out the front window of the quaint grocery shop, he inspected her bottom—and found it equally sweet. His palms itched, and he wasn't certain if it was with the need to caress—or swat.

Maybe she was a cross-dresser. Or she just had really bad taste in clothes. But she was definitely female, of that Harry was certain. He hadn't even noticed her until she'd gotten too close to him, and then he'd picked up on her scent. It made him feel like a buck in mating season, it hit him so hard. He stared, unable to help himself, until she noticed he was staring. Then she gave him a sour look and moved away.

And still he stared. The battered brown leather jacket was a couple sizes too big, ripped at one shoulder seam. And the flannel beneath it was baggy and hanging loose over ill-fitting, patched jeans. Scuffed, low-heel boots with chains on the back gave the impression she was trying for a bad-boy biker look. *Absurd.* Even her slicked back, glossy dark hair, held in a short blunt ponytail at her nape looked more female than rebel male. She had only one pierced ear, a small spent bullet dangling from the tiny silver hoop.

She kept her hands in her back pockets and a sneer on her face. Harry wondered what she'd done with her breasts, for they weren't noticeable through the bulky clothing. Of course, maybe she was naturally small. He wouldn't mind. He was a bottom-man himself, and he liked petite women, he…

Harry drew up short, appalled at the direction his wandering mind had taken. He wanted nothing to do with the woman, absolutely nothing.

Whatever her excuse for aping a man, she didn't need to be here now, at this precise moment, possibly screwing things up for him, definitely distracting him.

Harry Lonnigan eyed the unfortunate female with annoyance, now dividing his attention between her and the two men working their way to the cash register. He had a job to attend to. Yet there she was, trying to saunter like a man, trying to sneer in a manly way. Harry snorted, then despite himself, he breathed deeply, trying to detect her sweet scent again. Not the smell of perfume, but the smell of warm woman, a smell proven to drive men crazy.

He wanted to ignore her, but couldn't. Who was she and what was she up to with her outrageous costume and bizarre acting? Only a complete imbecile would believe her to be male.

But just then one of the two men turned, eyed her, and gave credence to her costume by dismissing her without so much as a raised eyebrow. Harry was stupefied.

He came out from behind the rack of chips and strolled casually forward, in no hurry to draw attention to himself, but the female was getting entirely too close to the two men, trying it seemed, to keep surveillance out the front display window without being seen. Whatever she was up to, she apparently wasn't aware of the danger. Harry had no claims on being a hero, far from it, but he also wasn't callous enough to watch a woman get injured, not if he could stop it.

"Go away."

Harry halted, then blinked. The little imposter—she barely reached his shoulder—had hissed at him out of the corner of her mouth. How had she known he was behind her? He hadn't made a single sound!

The two men looked up. They were cocky and obnoxious

young men, overly confident because they'd been running their scam in this area for far too long, at least that's what Harry's friend, Dalton, had said. He owed Dalton, and stopping these ruffians from their petty extortion would be adequate compensation, but it was a nuisance. Especially if some stray with a weird agenda was determined to interfere and complicate matters.

One of the men turned to face them, propping his elbows on the counter and giving them both an assessing look. "What are you doing?"

Harry pretended not to understand. He stared at a shelf filled with canned goods, finally selecting some potted meat. He shuddered. Nasty looking stuff, potted meat. The little female remained frozen beside him.

After an extended silence where no one seemed willing to move, Harry looked up. "Hmm? You were talking to me?"

The guy pushed off the counter and started forward through the narrow, crammed aisles. His blond hair was long and greasy, like the rest of his body, and his eyes were a pale, washed-out blue, red-rimmed and with lashes so light they were nearly invisible. Scraggly whiskers dotted his chin, a discredit to every manly beard ever grown. His partner, heavier and darker, also turned to watch while the proprietor, a man close to seventy, seemed to grow more agitated by the moment.

"Yeah, you. Who did you think I was talking to? The kid?"

Harry smiled. So the guy was a dolt, believing she was a man. Or rather a boy. Was he myopic? Couldn't he *smell* her, for God's sake? Harry cocked an imperious brow. "I didn't hear the question."

Irritation flashed on blondie's face as he struck an insolent pose, one hip thrust out, his arms crossed on his narrow chest. "I asked what the hell you're doing."

Bells jingled as a customer started in, then jingled again

as the woman took in the situation in a glance and hurried back out. Obviously the denizens of this area were well aware of what went on. They were all simply too old or too wary to stop it on their own. Harry wasn't old or wary. He stared down at the man with utter disdain.

"I'm shopping. What concern is it of yours?"

Blondie's face darkened and he straightened slightly. "You've been hanging around since we got here. Why haven't you bought anything yet?"

Harry raised both brows. Pushy little bastard. "I'm selective."

The young man scowled, his pale eyes going even paler, then he obviously decided not to pursue it, probably given the fact that Harry stood a good six foot five, nearly half a foot taller than him. Though Harry dressed like a gentleman, few people ever thought of him as one. It was something, they said, to do with his eyes, though he tended to disregard such nonsense.

"Well, get done and get out. I don't like you hanging around."

Harry was willing to play along—up to a point. Right up until the punk turned to the girl and poked her in the chest with his finger, almost knocking her over. "Same goes for you. Beat it."

Harry wasn't a hero, he truly wasn't, but he detested bullies. Beyond that, he couldn't tolerate violence of any kind toward females, regardless of the fact the fellow was too dense to realize she *was* a female.

When he started to add an additional poke, snickering at the way she'd stumbled, Harry dropped the potted meat—no big loss there—and snatched the fellow's finger into his fist. Harry squeezed.

A loud wail of outraged pain filled the store.

Unconcerned, Harry asked, "Now, why would you want to inflict abuse on someone smaller than yourself?"

The guy's knees were starting to give way as Harry ruthlessly tightened his grip. Blondie stared up at him, his face pinched in a grimace. "He's almost as tall as I am!"

"Not an adequate excuse. You're obviously older. And moreover, I've decided I don't like you." Using a deft movement of his own hand, Harry twisted the hapless finger, attached to an equally hapless arm, until the man was forced to go on tiptoe, high-pitched curses winging from his mouth.

Pandemonium broke out.

The little female overflowed with umbrage. "I don't need your help, you pompous ass!" The men either ignored her, or didn't hear her.

The bully's dark friend rushed forward. "Floyd!" he called out, as he pulled a gun from his pants. His gaze lifted to Harry, narrow-eyed and mean. "Turn him loose before I shoot your head off!"

The hard nose of a gun barrel poked into Harry's ribs. He cast a wry expression on the friend. "Now, that'd be rather difficult, with you aiming there. My head's a bit higher up."

His ill-advised insult got the gun immediately raised, and now he felt the cold metal against his ear. This comedy of errors was getting out of hand. Slowly, he loosened his grip.

Floyd shook his hand and cursed, then shook it some more. He looked up at Harry with red-rimmed eyes. "Shoot him."

"What?"

"Damn it, you heard me, Ralph! *Shoot him.*"

Harry said a quick prayer. The girl, finally showing some small signs of intelligence, began inching her way nonchalantly toward the door.

"Get back here, damn it." Floyd wasn't about to let her, or rather him, get away. "I think you two are working together to distract us. Who sent you here?"

The little female blinked and her smooth cheeks were suffused with color. "No one sent me! And I never saw that guy before in my life."

Harry waited for a gasp, waited for the recognition because her husky voice had obviously been that of a female's, despite her efforts to lower it accordingly.

He waited in vain.

"We can't jus' shoot him, Floyd. You know what Carlyle said. Keep it tidy. Besides, it'll be easier if we jus' let him go. He's nobody."

"Then what was he buttin' his nose in for?"

Ralph lowered his brows in thought, all the while keeping the gun steady on Harry's head.

Trying to placate them, Harry shrugged and said, "I simply can't abide a bully."

The gun smacked against his head, making his ears ring. "You can *abide* anythin' Floyd tells you to! That's how it's done in these parts."

Floyd grinned, and Harry was amazed to see he had fairly even, white teeth. "So you didn't like me pushing the scrawny runt around?"

Knowing he'd handed Floyd his revenge on a silver platter, Harry almost groaned. Damn his mouth anyway. He started to speak, his brain searching for words to defuse the situation, and in that instant Floyd backhanded the woman. She went sprawling, landing with a clatter in a stacked display of canned tuna.

Harry growled, discretion forgotten, and lunged forward to grab Floyd by the neck. The proprietor shouted. Ralph, the only one thinking at this point, snatched the woman up and held the gun on her. "Stop now or the little bastard's gonna be in some serious trouble."

Harry stopped. The woman was dazed, he could see that, a bruise already coloring her jaw, but she was otherwise unharmed. Breathing hard with his anger, Harry slowly opened his hand and Floyd stumbled back two steps—and threw a punch. Harry caught the fist an inch from his nose, then made "tsking" sounds of disapproval. "I do believe your associate said to stop."

"He was talking to you, not me!"

Harry heaved an annoyed sigh. "Look, gentlemen, you obviously had business here and it's gotten sidetracked. Perhaps you should let us innocent bystanders go and finish up whatever it was you started?" Rather than observing, as he'd wished, Harry had managed to complicate things hideously. Now he only hoped to salvage what he could.

The proprietor nodded his head in frantic, disgruntled agreement. His low, scratchy voice was that of an aged sailor, used to taking command. "Yeah, take the damn cash. But put the gun away."

"Shut up, old man, and let me think."

Harry considered that an unlikely prospect given that Floyd obviously had very little brain to work with, but he held his peace. He didn't want to rile anyone further, especially the proprietor who looked ready for violence. That would be all he'd need to tip the scales into the never-imagined.

After a considerable amount of time, Floyd nodded. "I think you're a cop."

That straightened his spine. Harry blustered. "Don't be ridiculous."

A low whistle slipped past Ralph's drooping mustache. "Now that you say it, Floyd, he does look like a cop. Check out that coat he's wearing."

Rolling his eyes, Harry said, "You've been watching too much *Columbo*. It's drizzling today, therefore I wore a trench coat. I hardly think it's standard dress for the police force."

"Come to that," Ralph added, "you speak damn fancy for someone from these parts."

"I'm not from these parts."

Floyd jutted his chin forward. "Then what are you doing here?"

"I was in the area on business and I remembered I needed

to pick up something for my dinner. It's no more complicated than that, I assure you."

"I don't believe you."

Well, hell, Harry thought, eyeing the female who now remained blessedly silent, her eyes downcast. Was he to be done in by a damn coat?

"Just to be on the safe side," Floyd said, grinning, "I think we'll take the boy with us. You call the cops, or try to follow, and I'll kill him."

The situation had gotten completely out of hand. "No, you can't do that."

Ralph tilted his head, his smile taunting. "And why not?"

The woman began to struggle. "I'm not going anywhere with you two! If you want a hostage, take him!" Her slender finger pointed in Harry's direction, disconcerting him for just a moment.

"Somehow I think you'll be easier to handle."

She kicked at Ralph's shin and he neatly sidestepped her, but Harry could see he was nonplussed by her somewhat feminine, awkward reaction. "What the hell?"

She tried to run. Harry was helpless, seeing the gun held steady, knowing any move on his part could get her injured. He wanted to curse at her theatrics, since she only complicated things further.

Floyd made a grab for her, and after his arms circled her chest, he too stopped, stunned. He released her as if burned, his eyes wide, going over her entire body in a single sweep.

"Take off your jacket."

"Go to hell!"

Floyd began to laugh. "I'll be a son of a… He's not a boy at all."

Dryly, for he was tired of the whole thing, Harry muttered, "How very astute of you."

Floyd swung around to glare at Harry, his voice a sneer. "I suppose you knew?"

"Of course."

Ralph drew a deep breath. "I don't like you much, mister."

The woman crossed her arms over her chest. "I don't like him at all."

Of all the nerve! Here he was, trying to preserve her ungrateful slender neck, and she—

"I said take off your jacket. Now. I want to get a better look at you."

Ralph held the gun pointed at her chest while Floyd did his ordering. Gently, buying some time, Harry said, "Better do as they ask."

She glared at him. "Go to hell."

Trying to be reasonable, Harry said, "There you have it, gentlemen. Surely you can see you're wasting your time."

The elderly owner, fairly bristling in outrage, slapped an envelope down on the countertop, offering it like a bribe. "Here's your damn money. Forget the girl and get the hell out of my store!"

"Be quiet, Pops. Now, even if you don't take off the jacket, I won't shoot you. That'd be too messy and would probably ruin the fun of this. And Ralph and I do like a little fun every now and again, don't we Ralph?"

Ralph snickered.

"But if you don't take the damn thing off, and right now, I'll have Ralph shoot *him*."

The gun dutifully switched so once again it pointed at Harry.

After the briefest of hesitations, the girl shrugged, her chin elevated. "Go ahead, shoot him. What's it to me?"

Harry's chin hit his chest. Why that miserable little... "Now, see here!"

Enjoying himself, Floyd laughed. "So maybe you two

aren't working together after all. It doesn't change anything. I want to see what you have under there, girlie. What are you hiding?"

She seemed to calm, and her eyes, which Harry just noticed were a very deep, dark blue rimmed with thick lashes, held steady. "Touch me and I'll kill you."

Both men laughed at that. Even Harry felt a small grin. The girl was so tiny, she couldn't hurt anyone, yet she had her fair share of bravado. He shifted, moving a little closer to the front window. No one noticed.

"Maybe I'll just have you get naked."

The owner was outraged. "You'll do no such thing! I have customers who come in regularly this late. It's not a quiet time. You need to take the money and—"

"I told you to shut up."

Harry moved another few inches toward the window. Between the girl and the store owner, things were far too unpredictable. Was he the only one to realize how grave this situation had become? If he could just get in view and signal Dalton that things had gone wrong, they'd have backup in a matter of moments. Dalton's jewelry store sat directly across the street and was likely next on Floyd's list of stops.

He could see Floyd getting agitated, and besides being stupid and a bully, Floyd could well be trigger-happy. Harry didn't consider it wise to push him too far.

To distract the men from his subtle movements toward the window, he suggested, "You don't want my death plaguing your conscience, sweetheart. Remove the jacket. You can't have anything all that singularly special to hide."

"Huh?"

Floyd wasn't as confused as Ralph. "Yeah, it ain't like all of us men here, even Pops, haven't seen a woman naked before. And I really will have Ralph shoot him. Hell, I'm looking for a reason."

Her brows beetled down and her eyes narrowed. "It's no skin off my nose what you do with him."

At that moment Ralph looked out the window and cursed, then cursed again. "There's a couple of cops over at the jewelry store."

He was distracted for that moment, and Harry started forward, only to be brought up short as Ralph swung around, the gun moving wildly in his hand from Pops to the girl to Harry. "What do we do now, Floyd?"

But Floyd was already moving, snatching the envelope from Pops with a muttered warning, then pulling his own gun. He pointed it at Harry. "Out the back. You're coming with us."

Harry's first thought was, *Thank God, they're taking me instead of the girl.* Not that he was a hero, but he was trained for this, knew how to handle it. But then Floyd grabbed her, too.

Harry's muscles tightened all the way down to his toes. "Stop and think, Floyd. You don't need her. She'll just slow you down."

"If she tries that, she'll be sorry." And he sounded deadly serious, all fun and games over.

"One hostage is more than adequate."

"Be quiet, damn it. I've heard all I want to hear from you. Now move."

With guns at their backs, Harry and the girl were forced to exit out the rear of the store. Was Dalton still waiting for a signal? He wouldn't get one, not now. But why were the police there? Had Dalton somehow known things had gone wrong even without Harry's signal?

There were no answers to be found, and no more time to consider the circumstances as they were led through a light rain to a rental truck left parked in the dark alley. The sun was all but gone, and the mid-June air felt cool and thick. Floyd waved his gun, directing them into the open back of the truck. After hopping in, Harry turned to assist the woman, but she scrambled awkwardly in on her own, disdainfully ignoring his hand.

"You drive, Ralph. I'll ride in here with the little lady." His grin was more of a leer. "You two, into the corner. Sit and keep your mouths shut."

Harry took off his long trench coat and gallantly spread it over the dusty bottom of the empty truck floor, then signaled for the woman to sit. She gave him a furious look and perversely retreated into an opposite corner, slumping down and wrapping her arms around her bent legs. Her position pulled the jean material tight around her thighs and he could see she was slender, her bottom rounded. He forced his gaze to her face.

She looked dejected and in deep thought, but not, thankfully, as frightened as she should be. Her cheek was dark and swollen where she'd been hit, spurring his anger. Harry carefully lowered himself, keeping his eyes alternately on Floyd and the woman.

He hadn't counted on such a predicament when he'd agreed to take care of things for Dalton. He certainly hadn't counted on his attention being diverted by a woman. Any woman, but much less one who was trying to be a man and had an attitude problem. Out of all the female types in the world, headstrong, bossy, controlling women were his very least favorite. He'd had his fill of them long ago.

Yet he couldn't seem to keep his eyes off her.

Dim illumination filled the back of the truck as a small, battery-operated light came on. Ralph pulled the door down from the outside, sealing the three of them in. Harry knew he had to adjust his plans. He couldn't risk the possibility of being taken among the conspirators. The odds wouldn't be good and now he had an outsider to think about.

He eyed the woman again. Why was she involved? He didn't doubt for a moment that she'd been up to something, but his brain couldn't dredge up a single plausible motivation.

She hadn't been aware of what she'd blundered into until it was too late, of that he was certain.

Floyd paced the back of the truck, agitated, for a good fifteen minutes while the truck raced farther and farther away from the police. No sirens sounded in the distance; there was nothing but the gentle patter of the rain and the grinding of the shifting truck gears.

"Sit together," Floyd said as he slid down the opposite wall and propped the gun on a knee. "I want to be able to keep you both in my sights."

Harry merely raised a brow at the woman and with a muttered oath, she stood and came to him, then plopped back down. "Bastard," she whispered.

Taken aback, Harry said aloud, and with a good deal of annoyance, "I beg your pardon?"

Suddenly she turned and slugged him in the arm. "This is all your fault! They were paying me no mind until you drew their attention to me."

He rubbed his arm where she'd socked him, more out of indignation than actual hurt, as he eyed her furious expression. "How was I to know Floyd and Ralph were too ignorant to recognize a woman when she presented herself?" Unaccountable female hysterics. He knew he was frowning at her, knew his frown was enough to frighten most grown men, and didn't care one whit. If he scared her, it served her right.

She slugged him again. "I was disguised, you fool!"

He caught her fist and held it, careful not to hurt her, then leaned so close their noses almost touched. Through clenched teeth, he growled, "Obviously not well enough since I picked you out right away."

He heard her swallow. Her eyes shifted on his face, nearly crossing, then finally narrowed in suspicion. "How?"

Knowing he held Floyd's fascinated attention, Harry saw no reason not to explain. In fact, he relished the moment. "Actually, you have a woman's mouth."

He looked at her mouth again—now set in a mulish line—and felt his stomach muscles tighten. He swallowed. *Damn her.* His gaze came back up to hers and stayed there. "You have a woman's bottom," he said with a taunting smile, "despite the baggy jeans. You also move like a woman."

He grinned, pulling her slightly toward him, primed for his last tribute. "And you smell very much like a woman."

The hit was direct; she stiffened and sputtered. "Don't be stupid! I'm not wearing perfume."

He searched her face, amazed by his own reaction. He answered softly. "I know."

Floyd laughed, once again showing his perfect white teeth. "I hadn't looked at her butt." He shrugged. "I thought she was a guy."

Effectively distracted, Harry blinked and moved a little away from her, but maintained his grip on her punching arm. "Yes, well, she afforded me an unimpeded view. And since I'm a...*healthy* male, and I noticed, I knew she had to be female."

"Warped male logic," she accused with excessive heat, and tried to jerk her hand away. He held firm. "So why did you have to make my sex known to the other two idiots?"

"Careful." Floyd was no longer amused.

"That was unintentional." When she huffed, he added, "I was trying to protect you, you ungrateful child."

"I'm not a child."

"How old are you?" Floyd asked. It amazed Harry that Floyd could be so easily diverted.

"None of your damn business!"

The rain began to come down in earnest, sounding like gunshots on the roof of the truck. Gears shifted, throwing Harry slightly off-balance and completely toppling the girl.

Floyd stretched out his legs to brace himself. "I'd say you're young, but not too young." He frowned in consideration. "No one's following us and we have a ways to go yet. Maybe you should just get naked now so I can judge for myself. You look a little too flat for my tastes, but you never know."

The truck shifted again and they were all three caught scrambling for balance. Floyd crudely cursed Ralph's driving abilities. The woman landed on her hands and knees and, looking comparable to a rabid dog, she shouted, "For the last time you miserable worm, I am *not* taking anything off!"

Harry silently applauded her bravado, misplaced as it seemed.

Judging by the incredulous look on Floyd's face, he wouldn't be patient much longer, and with each mile that passed, their odds of getting out of this unscathed decreased.

They rode steadily uphill. From what Harry could tell they were heading out into the farming area. No residential homes there, and people would be scarce. He had to do something before they covered too much ground.

Harry got an idea. Risky, but he had to make an effort.

He bent a stern look on the woman and demanded, "Why not? For heaven's sake, your bosom can't be so spectacular that it's worth my life. Don't think I've forgotten you were willing to see me die to protect your dubious modesty."

She looked surprised, frozen, for only a heartbeat. Slowly, she turned to face him, her back to Floyd, her hands on her hips. Then to his shock, she gave him a wink, no smile, just that understanding wink that nearly floored him. At the same time she yelled, "I should have known you weren't really a hero! You're as bad as the other two."

He almost grinned. He did surge to his feet to tower over her. "Almost as bad? I'll have you know they're babies compared to me."

Floyd sputtered, no longer enjoying their show.

The woman leaped at him, the truck veered sharply left and they went down in a welter of arms and legs. Floyd yelled for them to stop, but they paid no heed. Their bodies rolled toward Floyd, twisting and fighting.

Harry made feigned attempts to subdue her while she did her best to bludgeon him with fists and feet. He caught himself alternately chuckling and struggling to keep from getting his nose broken. A sharp elbow in the ribs made him grunt.

Finally, finally Floyd got within reach, determined to end their scuffle. The woman neatly tripped him, and as he stumbled Harry snatched his gun hand and raised it to the roof, then clipped him hard in the chin.

He had very large, solid fists and Floyd went down without a whimper.

Breathing hard, the woman turned to him, stuck out her hand and said, "Thanks. I was starting to worry. My name's Charlie."

Harry laughed. "Charlie? I suppose that fits as well as anything else. You may call me Harry." He took her hand, noticing how slim and warm her fingers felt, then asked, "I didn't hurt you, did I?"

She snorted rudely as her eyes darted around the truck. "I say we toss his sorry butt out the back. I have things to do and they don't include going…wherever the hell it is we're going. Plus I have no desire to meet their pal, Carlyle."

Harry studied her, again stupefied. "You're not at all upset? You weren't frightened?"

"'Course I was."

She didn't look frightened. She looked determined to drag poor Floyd's body to the edge of the truck bed so she could throw him out. Never mind that it would probably kill him. Wasn't she squeamish about such a thing?

"Don't just stand there, give me a hand here. He's heavy."

Nope, not squeamish. Damn vicious female.

She could at least pretend *some* feminine qualities. He *really* didn't like bossy, overbearing women. Harry crossed his arms over his chest and studied her. "I'm sorry to disappoint you, miss, since you do seem rather set on your course, but I'm not up to killing a man."

"Coward." She heaved and pushed and dragged the body closer to the edge. "Besides, who says he'll die?"

"Now listen here—"

She jerked upright, her face flushed, one thick wisp of glossy black hair now hanging over her right eye. "No, you listen! You got me involved in this with your damn nosiness and misplaced heroism. This is all your fault. The very least you can do is...is..." Her voice dropped off and she covered her face with her hands. Her shoulders shook.

Harry had the horrible suspicion she might be crying.

Good God. He hadn't wanted her to be *that* female.

CHAPTER TWO

"DON'T YOU touch me." Charlie stared at the behemoth coming toward her, his expression now bemused. She drew a deep breath, absolutely refusing to give in to her tears, her disappointment. She felt humiliated and decided most of it was his fault. She lifted her chin in the air and said with disdain, "You've done plenty, already."

He held up his hands—very large, capable hands. "I'm sorry. But we don't have time for this." She started to speak, but then he put the gun in the back of his belt, and she wanted that gun, damn him. She didn't trust him, didn't trust anyone at this point, and needed to be able to protect herself. Whoever would have thought a simple Monday could get so dastardly confused?

After all her efforts to move Floyd—and she really did want to toss his body out—it took Harry only a second to heave him to the other end of the truck bed, well out of danger from falling out.

He pulled a knife from his own pocket, stripped off Floyd's jacket, and proceeded to cut it up. He used the cloth strips to tie and gag Floyd in record time.

"Now." He stood and dusted off his hands.

He seemed to have things well in control and that annoyed her anew. At first, he'd seemed too pretentious to get involved in a scuffle. But once he'd gotten involved, he'd been beyond impressive. It wasn't what she'd expected of him at all.

She was used to being the one in control, the one people

came to for help. This man acted as though getting kidnapped and held at gunpoint was a regular part of his workweek. "Now what?"

The truck shifted again and Harry braced himself before giving her a wary, probing look. "You're not going to cry?"

"No." Charlie almost laughed at his look of relief. She hadn't figured him to be the type to fall apart over female tears. She gave him a sideways look. "How about you?"

He paused, stared at her a moment, then raised his brows. "I'm holding up. Completely dry-eyed."

"Good, because I can't stand blubbering men."

He gave her a small smile—a very charming smile actually, and she was beyond shocked that she noticed. She ducked her chin to avoid looking at him.

"We're on an incline," he noted thoughtfully. He picked up his coat from the corner, shook it out, then slipped it back on. "Let me get the door open and see where we're headed."

Charlie bit her lip and mustered up a calm tone. Nothing ventured, nothing gained, she'd always heard. "Since you have the knife, I'll hold the gun."

"No."

She bristled at his blunt reply. "Why not?"

Harry carefully lifted the door a foot or so, then lay on his belly and peeked out. He kept looking at her over his shoulder, as if he expected her to push him out as she'd planned to do with Floyd. It wasn't a bad idea, except that it'd be impossible; he was twice as big as Floyd and very alert. Besides, she didn't particularly want to get that close to him.

His thick brown hair dripped with rain when he pulled his head back inside. "We're near the Wayneswood exit."

Charlie gasped. "Wayneswood!" She hadn't realized they'd traveled quite so far. Her heart started an erratic pounding. "I have to get home."

"Come here." Harry lifted the door a bit more and sat, hanging his legs over the edge. He took the time to overlap his long coat, protecting his trousers as much as possible from the pounding rain.

Once Charlie had settled beside him—accepting whatever his plan might be, because she had none of her own—Harry took her hand. She jerked and had to struggle not to pull away. She didn't want to look like a wilting ninny.

"As the truck travels uphill," Harry explained, "it will have to slow down even more. We can jump out then. Luckily the rain will help conceal us, in the event Ralph glances out his mirror."

"It's too dark for him to see us."

"Perhaps. But a flash of movement might draw his attention and we can't take the chance. So lie low as soon as you can. Just flatten out on the road and we'll hope the truck keeps going. I don't relish the idea of getting into a shoot-out."

"Coward. Give me the gun."

He grinned and shook his head at her. "Valiant try, but I don't provoke that easily, so you can hold the insults."

He completely ignored the rude sound she made.

"Besides, I have experience in handling guns."

His large hand felt so warm, and his muscled thigh pressed hard against her own. She shivered. Hand-holding with an appealing man was definitely not on the agenda for today. For the most part, it hadn't been on the agenda for her entire life. Raising her free hand, she flicked her earring with the flattened bullet attached. "So do I."

"You mean that trinket is real? And here I thought it was part of your costume."

She ground her teeth. He was humoring her, and she wouldn't put up with it. "It's real."

"Hmm." She was very aware of his thumb rubbing along her knuckles, and his close scrutiny. "Whatever could you possibly be involved in that would require a gun?"

To ease her own tension, and defuse his attentions, she said, "I own a bar. Usually it's as dull as dishwater, but one night things got too rowdy and there was gunfire. This particular bullet missed my head by an inch. I decided it was lucky. You?"

He watched her too closely and far too long before he answered. With an elegant shrug he said, "I'm a private investigator." And that was that.

With no more confidences forthcoming, Charlie turned her attention back to the weather. "We're going to be drenched." Already her jeans were wet at the bottom. Her legs didn't extend nearly as far as his, but the rain blew furiously in all directions.

"True enough. However, it's not all that cold yet and the rain helps to mask the noise we make in the truck. I'm grateful to Mother Nature for her assistance."

Charlie made a face at him, though he didn't see it. So calm, so sure of what he planned to do. She wanted to know what was going on, who he was and what he'd been up to, why Floyd and Ralph had taken money from the store owner and what a private investigator had to do with it. Her curiosity was pricked, even though she had no room for other mysteries, other ventures. And now definitely wasn't the time. First she had to get back to Corsville. All her plans, shot through.

"You'd truly have let them shoot me?"

She lifted her face to see Harry studying her. He was so sure of himself, so arrogant. *So damn good-looking.* "Of course," she lied, disconcerted with his stare and just annoyed enough to goad him. She evidently used enough sincerity because his fierce frown reappeared.

Despite his obvious polish, he looked almost demonic with that evil glare. His incredible light brown eyes seemed scorching hot and far too probing, as if he could see inside her. She shivered, then shook off the fanciful thoughts. He was just a man like all the others, bigger, definitely stronger and more eloquent, but still fairly basic and ruled by simple motivations. She could, and would, control him.

His gaze lowered to her chest. "I can't imagine why. You don't appear to have anything all that spectacular to conceal."

He was going for the jugular, but Charlie, having worked in a bar for the past seven years, wasn't even tempted by the familiar baiting. At least her disguise had worked well. She was wearing enough layers to keep her warm and conceal any feminine curves at the same time.

Harry squeezed her hand to regain her attention and his expression was still too intent. "It's not that I haven't been shot before, you understand, but—"

"You should be more careful with your gun."

His eyes darkened, grew hotter. "Not with *my* gun, you little—"

"Listen. Isn't he shifting now? And if I'm not mistaken, the truck is slowing."

Harry gave her a long look of promised retribution. "Yes." He pulled his long legs up against the bed of the truck, bracing himself. "Time for us to go."

Charlie gulped. She looked down at the passing roadway beneath her and winced. True enough the truck had slowed, but the road still flew by them.

"One…"

"Ah, maybe—"

"Two…"

"Wait a second!"

"…three."

"Harry!"

"Go." And with that, he gave her a shove while using his muscular bulk to propel them out. They landed together, their hands still linked, and somehow Harry managed to get beneath her so that he cushioned much of her fall, not that his hard body felt much more giving than the roadway. They tumbled before coming to a dead stop, her on top, their legs tangled together. But just as quickly he rolled to the left, putting her beneath him—and into a very large icy puddle. She sucked in her breath with the shock of it.

His enormous body covered her completely, unmoving, heavy and hard. For the moment she was unable to think with any clarity. It felt as though her teeth had been jarred loose and with his great hulking weight on her, she couldn't draw a deep breath. Rain struck her face, icy cold and stinging against her flesh.

After a moment he lifted his head and looked behind them. Rain ran in rivulets from his hair to her chest. "The truck lights are going around the bend. I do believe Ralph is totally unaware that he's lost his guests."

When she didn't respond, he looked down at her. Charlie stared at his shadowed features in the darkness, struck again by his perfect handsomeness. He seemed such a contradiction. A fancy-pants, but with a lumberjack's body. A gallant hero, but still a bit earthy. She couldn't help but be awed by him, and she hated it.

His head lowered until he blocked the worst of the rain from her face, until she could feel the warmth of his breath on her lips. Her chest constricted the tiniest bit more.

It was absurd! She'd long ago learned the truth about men and their deceptions. But now, at the most unlikely of times, her mind had gone wandering along wayward paths.

Still, she could feel him from breasts to knees, and he was firm and muscled and *big*. The wet ground and the danger seemed to fade for just a moment.

"Are you all right?"

His voice was low and deep and she wondered at it, even as she felt her belly curl in response to his tone. "I can't breathe."

His gaze dropped to her mouth and lingered for long moments. He closed his eyes and turned his head away. "My apologies." Gingerly, he removed himself, groaning every so often. He offered her a hand and together they sat there in the middle of the road. "I lingered in the hopes of feeling something worthy of my life, but you seem to be all pointy bones."

"What are you whining about?" As she stood, forcing her wobbly legs to support her, she squished. The puddle had seeped beneath her leather jacket to the layers of padding beneath. She was soggy as an old dishrag and probably holding about a gallon of water.

"Your breasts, sweetheart, those magnificent assets that are worth my life."

Oh for pity's sake. "Are you still harking on about that?" She looked around and saw nothing but darkness and endless stretching highway. The rain continued to fall, but luckily there was no traffic. None at all. "Where are we?"

"Yes, I'm still harking. It is my life, after all, though it obviously means little enough to you. And I'd say we're in the middle of the damn road, somewhere between Corsville and oblivion, getting more sodden by the second."

She started walking, leaving him behind. With every step, her boots, two sizes two large and now slick with the rain from the inside out, rubbed against her heels. It wasn't a pleasant feeling and she knew before long she'd have horrible blisters. But what else could she do? Stand around and wait for Ralph to return? Miss the grand performance she'd waited a lifetime to witness?

Probably, her thinking continued, she'd already missed it. That prospect angered her so much, she ignored Harry when he called to her.

"Hold up." His large hand closed on her arm and pulled her to a halt. "We can't just traipse down the middle of the road. In case it's escaped your notice, Floyd and Ralph are not nice men. They could double back looking for us. We need to get out of sight."

True enough, she thought, and nodded. "Yeah, and I suppose that means the woods." She glanced down at his dress shoes. "And with this downpour, it'll be a swamp." Her smile wasn't entirely nice. She started in that direction, and Harry followed. Both sides of the highway were lined with thick trees and little else.

"I can see by your snide expression you expect me to have a certain aversion to mud?"

She kept walking. "I hope not, 'cause big and heavy as you are, you'll sink up to your knees."

Harry turned up his collar and swiped the rain from his face, then shaded his eyes. "With all those trees acting as an umbrella, the ground might not be as saturated as you think."

"You hope."

He ignored her. "And likely the woods abut a farm or some sort of residential dwelling. We could get access to a phone."

She turned to face him. "All right, have you convinced yourself?"

His look of condescension had her grinning again. "I was attempting to reassure you, but I see the effort was wasted. Allow me to lead."

"Sure thing, Harry." At least his big body would block some of the rain. She stumbled along behind him in her heavy, soaked clothes, more miserable than she'd ever been in her life—not that she'd let him know it.

Harry took her arm. "You surprise me. I didn't expect you to be so agreeable."

She hunched both shoulders against the rain and trod onward, pulled along by his hand on her arm. "I'm easy."

His chuckle could be heard even over the rainstorm. "No grand confessions here, if you please. Not when I can't do anything about them."

She tried to stare at him, lost at his words, but he more or less dragged her behind him. "What's that supposed to mean?"

He grinned again; she couldn't see it, but she could hear it. "I appreciate an *easy* woman as much as the next man. But these conditions aren't exactly conducive to seduction."

Appalled, she forgot to watch her step and tripped over a tree root. Harry pulled her upright before her face hit the mud. *Of all the outrageous!...* "I wasn't talking about sex, you idiot!"

They continued a few more feet, and luckily, though the mud did suck at her too-big boots, it was drier, the rain not so blinding, filtered by the many trees.

"That's for the best, I suppose, since I don't as yet know what you have to offer. All I know is that you apparently think it's worth a man's life."

She rolled her eyes and decided to ignore him. Several minutes later, she was wincing in pain.

Harry stopped and turned to frown down on her. Without the rain lashing her face, her eyes were able to adjust to the darkness, and once again she found herself scrutinizing him.

He was by far the biggest man she'd ever seen, tall and thickly muscled, but with grace, if such a thing was possible. And he had the strangest eyes, a shade lighter than his medium brown hair, almost a whiskey color, but bright and thick lashed. Intense, bordering on wicked. When he looked at her, she actually felt it; she'd felt it even back in the store. That's how she'd known he was creeping up on her, intent on telling her something. She hadn't wanted his attention or anyone else's. She'd wanted to be able to concentrate on her first small victory in her private war.

But the plan had fallen through. Damn Dalton Jones.

Harry touched her chin, his fingers gentle. "What's the matter? I expected a tenacious little mug like you to keep up, not lag behind."

She sighed. Showing a weakness to this man, any weakness, went against the grain. He was the one out of his element,

yet he hadn't offered a single complaint. But there was no hope
for it. "My feet are killing me."

"Ah, I see. Well, since I may want to retain that pleasure
for myself—killing you, that is—why don't you explain to me
exactly what the problem is?"

The threat didn't alarm her. She was already used to his
wry sense of humor and didn't fear him at all. "My boots are
too big and now that they're wet they're sliding up and down
and I can feel the blisters on my heels. It hurts."

He stared down at her, those eyes of his bright in the darkness, like a wild animal surveying prey, making her shiver
with a strange and exciting feeling. But his voice, in comparison, was soft, inquiring. "Why are your boots too large?"

She scowled, attempting to ignore the fluttering in her
stomach. "Because I hadn't exactly planned on trudging
through the woods in them."

Coming down on his haunches in front of her, he said,
"Give me your foot."

"The bottom is covered in mud."

"I'll survive."

He lifted her foot and wiggled her boot, judging the size
while ignoring her cry of pain—the jerk.

"I have some knit gloves in my pocket. Do you think you
could stuff them into the heels as a little padding?"

Her sore feet loved the idea. "Yeah, thanks."

To her surprise, he picked her up.

To her further surprise, he cursed and hastily set her back
down again when streams of rainwater squished out of her
clothing to run down his chest. "What in the world are you
wearing? You feel like a sodden mop and weigh a ton."

She flushed, both from his initiated gallantry and his censure. She wasn't used to either. No man tried to schmooze her,
and they sure as hell didn't try to boss her around. Through
gritted teeth, she explained, "I have a few…layers on."

Though she tried to duck away, one large hand reached

beneath her jacket and clutched at the material over her rib cage. He squeezed, and it was like wringing out a rag. "Ah. I assume this is why your precious breasts are invisible?"

Overcome with embarrassment, ready to drown him in the nearest available mud puddle, she nodded. "And you can shut your mouth on any more questions because it's none of your damn business anyway!"

"My curiosity grows in leaps and bounds."

"I hope you choke on your blasted curiosity."

He laughed. "Come on, and no, I won't carry you regardless of how your feet hurt."

"I wasn't going to ask!"

He assisted her to a fallen log amidst tons of greenery. Charlie prayed it wasn't poison ivy vines twining everywhere. Harry crouched in front of her again and tugged off the boots.

"I'm sorry. I know it hurts." He pulled the gloves from his pockets, folded one in half and put it inside her sock. "Let's try this and see how it works." After both feet were repaired and her boots back on, she stood.

"How does it feel?"

The gloves were soft and thankfully dry. She took a few careful steps, then smiled. "Much better. Thanks. You're a handy man to have around, Harry."

He opened his mouth and she said, "If ever again I find myself kidnapped and then abandoned in a rainstorm on an empty highway bordering the woods while wearing boots that are too big, why then, you're just the man I'd want to…"

A beep sounded, interrupting her teasing, and they both jumped. Harry started to shove her behind him and she laughed. "I appreciate your efforts to save me from my pager, but I think I can handle it."

He muttered a low curse.

Charlie looked at the lit dial and added her own, more heated and descriptive curses to his.

He tsked her language, then asked, "An important call?"

"My sister."

"Will she worry about you and send someone to find you? Did she know where you were today?"

"Yes and no and no."

"I forgot the order of my questions. Care to clarify?"

Charlie felt like crying. Her poor sister. She hadn't wanted Charlie to go through with her scheme. She'd said it didn't matter. And now she'd be sick with worry.

"Charlie?"

It was the first time he'd called her by name and she liked the way his cultured tones made it sound. Everyone she knew called her Charlotte, despite her protestations. Her mother had set the example, and everyone had followed it. Except for her sister, but then her sister loved her.

"I hate to say it, Harry, but no, no one will look for us. My sister will worry when I don't call her back, but she won't know what to do, or where to check."

She fell silent for a long time, her thoughts dark and troubled, when Harry touched her arm. "Are you all right?"

That particular tone was new coming from him, and it surprised her. No one worried about her. "Of course."

"You're quiet and I don't like it." His hand touched her cheek, her ear. "I don't want you to turn too brooding on me. It unnerves me and won't help anything."

"So distract me."

She saw the flash of his grin before he tried to hide it. "I'd be glad to oblige you, even though you're too short and your assets are still rather questionable, regardless of the high value you've put upon them—"

"Harry."

"—but again, it's just too messy out here. Too much mud and too many weeds I don't recognize and don't want my more private body parts to come into contact with. Plus, I don't know anything about you, why you're dressed as a male, if you're possibly gay—"

"I'm not gay."

"Well, being that we're alone for who knows how long, that's a comfort of sorts I suppose."

Charlie stopped. She turned to face him, her hands fisted. "Will you stop blathering on. And what possible difference could it make to you if I'm gay or not?"

"We may never find civilization again. Or at least, it could take more hours than I'm willing to ponder. Feminine company might come in handy. Think about it. It's almost romantic. All alone in a dark woods, silence all around us. Only my body to keep you warm and protect you."

Though she knew he was being sarcastic, her stomach tingled at his words. She could almost feel his heat.

Men *never* flirted with her, if indeed that's what he was doing. Men threw lewd comments her way on occasion, but she doubted Harry could sound lewd if he tried.

She dredged up her own sarcasm to mask her response. "All we need is candlelight and wine?"

His voice lowered to a sexy rumble. "I never imbibe when with a woman. It dulls the senses, you know, and I prefer to feel everything as it's supposed to be felt."

Despite herself, she drew in a long breath of surprise.

He laughed, then flicked her nose. "Also a flashlight is more economical. Candlelight is far too vague." He pulled a small penlight from his pocket, dangling with his keys from a key chain. "I think I'd like a nice sharp beam of light so I can fully explore things. Especially these mysterious breasts of yours." A skinny beam of light flashed over her shoulders and she jerked around, giving him her back. She saw the light coast lower.

"Harry," she warned.

"Hmm?"

"You're being outrageous." She started walking again, no better reply forthcoming.

"Thank you." When she snorted, he said, "I did manage to distract you, didn't I?"

She paused in her stride, but just for a moment. "I suppose. Now tell me why you were in that store, what a private investigator has to do with Floyd and Ralph. And, oh yeah, who's Carlyle?"

"If I tell will you tell?"

"Kind of like, show me yours and I'll show you mine?"

"I'm willing if you are. Of course, I don't have the added pressure of having to produce something worth a man's life."

Charlie laughed, she couldn't help herself. For several years now, she'd disdained men, her supposed father especially, though she didn't remember the man all that well anymore, the long ago memories and her mother's words mixing together in confusion. Today might have been the day to end the confusion, but everything had gone worse than wrong.

As to the others, the men who sat in her saloon night after night, drinking themselves into a stupor, claiming their wives were responsible or irresponsible or dull. And her mother's old boyfriends, no accounts without a future or the urge to motivate. They were all jerks and users and she had nothing but contempt for them all.

Harry was different. He was outrageous, true, but he made her laugh and his outrageousness wasn't a threat or an insult, but rather a game, a certain charming wit that he employed with skill. She had no fear he would force her, or that he'd actually try to humiliate her as Floyd had. He was big and brave, and something of a hero, a fact she couldn't deny since she'd seen herself the efforts he'd made to try to protect her, even with a gun to his head.

"How old are you, Harry?"

"An odd question, coming out of the blue like that, but why

not? As a conversational gambit, it beats the obvious chitchat of weather, and it's as good as any other. I'm thirty-two. And you?"

"Are you a good private eye?"

"Meaning?"

"Do you make much money at it?"

He cleared his throat. "Less of a gambit, but yes, I support myself nicely if that's what you mean."

He was probably expensive, too expensive, but maybe she could figure something out. "How long have you been in the detecting business?"

"Detecting? Well, let's see. About six years now."

"Are you kind to animals?"

He laughed. "There's a purpose to this interview? All right, I'll trust there is. I have two dogs and a cat and they love me or at least they pretend to in order to get me to do their bidding or sometimes when I find a chewed up shoe or a mess in the corner. Does that answer your question?"

"Are you married?"

"Did you have an unemployed dog in mind that you're hoping to foist off on me?"

A small lump of dread formed in her stomach and she struggled to keep her tone light. "So you are married?"

"Divorced, actually, not that it should concern you."

She turned to face him. He was big and gorgeous and funny and a hero. He might well be the man she needed. God knew her level of success on her own hadn't been anything to boast about, especially given today's incredible fiasco. "I think I like you, Harry."

"Look there," Harry said, pointing over her head and studiously ignoring her last statement. "A building of some sort. I do believe salvation is at hand."

Charlie looked in the direction he indicated. They'd wandered completely through the woods to another road. A small

block building, bludgeoned by the rain, sat close to the road,
looking indeed like salvation.

Harry, his face averted, plodded onward and Charlie gladly
let him lead the way, content to follow behind. To say she
trusted him now would definitely be going too far, but he'd
made her laugh and that was a huge accomplishment. As to
the rest, she'd just have to wait and see.

CHAPTER THREE

"WELL WHAT DO you know, it's an abandoned gas station."

Harry stood in a spot of grease, thankfully out of the rain, and studied their little Eden. He'd had to kick in the door, which had proved remarkably easy given the rotting wood and rusty lock. Likely inhabited by any number of critters, it was still dry and safe and a block against the growing breeze. The rain finally began to taper off, but with that concession came a chill that sank bone-deep. The temperature had dropped by several degrees and he could see Charlie's lips shivering. Nice lips, sort of pouty in a seductive way, especially for a woman who wasn't all that attractive and seemed to have a problem with cordial behavior. Would she have really let them shoot him?

Damn her, he just didn't know.

"How long has it been empty do you think?"

She stood huddled in the middle of the floor, her arms wrapped tight around herself, her knees knocking together, determined not to utter a single complaint, as if admitting to the cold was a weakness. Strange woman.

A growing puddle formed around her. Her hair had mostly come loose from the rubber band and was starting to curl just the tiniest bit.

"Perhaps from the time they put in the highway some five years ago. This is the old county road. No one travels it anymore which is, I presume, the reason this particular station closed up."

"The road must still lead somewhere though, to a house or two."

"No doubt, but we won't be finding any help in this storm. You're the picture of misery, half-frozen and too tired to budge. Time to get as dry as possible." He looked at her, saw her staring back wide-eyed, and added, "That means removing your ridiculous costume."

She froze in the process of rubbing her arms, sluicing off more water. "Is that the only tune you know? All right, damn it, I lied. I wouldn't have let them shoot you, not if I could help it. But I knew if they thought I cared, they'd think we were together. I wanted them to take you and forget about me."

Well, that was brutal honesty of a sort. Not quite what he'd had in mind, but… "Believe it or not, Charlie, it was my wish as well." He found a crate, tested it for sturdiness and sat down with a deep groan of pleasure. "I had no desire to be responsible for you, and in fact I could have defused this entire situation if you hadn't screwed things up."

"It was you—"

He held up a hand. "No more bickering. And no more ridiculous modesty. Your belated concern for my safety has nothing to do with anything. I don't want to be lugging a half-dead woman back to town tomorrow, and that's what you'll be if you don't make some effort to warm yourself. It has nothing to do with my curiosity over your precious body parts."

"You have only my welfare in mind?"

"Quit sneering." He felt a smile tug at his lips and firmly repressed the urge to grin at her. "Come now, you must be in your mid-twenties at least. Surely you can't claim all that much modesty. I promise not to be impressed no matter what you unveil."

She looked ready to strike him, so he quickly added, "I'll make the grand sacrifice. My coat is still fairly dry on the inside, given that it's made for this weather and water repellent. You can wrap up in it after you've gotten out of your wet clothes."

She chewed her lips, thinking of heaven knew what, and finally shaking her head. More hair slipped free and clung to her forehead and cheeks. She didn't look like a boy now; she looked like a drowned rat. A wide-eyed, nervous rat. "No."

"What if I insist?"

She went stiff as a poker. "Insist all you want! I'm not taking anything off and I'm not—" Her voice dwindled into a very ratlike squeak when he started toward her. "Don't you dare touch me!"

"You're being unreasonable, Charlie. I hadn't thought you the type to submit to hysterics, but what else can it be? You can't be comfortable and if there was enough light to see, I have no doubt you'd be a pale shade of blue." He caught her arm and she tried to jerk away. He easily caught the neck of her jacket and stripped it off her, despite her efforts and the volume of her rank curses. The woman had the vocabulary of a sailor. "It's too dark in here for close observation anyway. What exactly do you suppose I'll see?"

"You'll see nothing because you're going to take your hands off me right now."

That calm tone of hers should have given him a warning, but he was too intent on forcing her to accept his benevolence. He was wet also, yet he'd offered her his coat, which would leave him with only his dress shirt and undershirt. Contrary to popular female opinion, men were not impervious to the cold. She should be thanking him, not cursing his ancestors. Why were women always so stubborn?

And then he felt the gun press into his ribs. He almost laughed. She'd done nothing but surprise him since he'd first spotted her. It was entertaining when it wasn't so annoying.

"Ah, you're fast. Don't tell me. You were a pickpocket once, weren't you, as well as a saloon girl? No, don't lie to me."

"I wasn't going to lie! I'm not a *saloon girl,* I'm the owner, and no, I was never a pickpocket. It's just that you weren't paying attention." She pressed the gun harder against him. "And you're *slow*."

In the next instant he jerked up her wrist and snatched the gun from her hand. In the process, it fired, the sound loud and obscene, sending particles of ceiling plaster to rain down on their heads. They both heard a flurry of scurrying from around them.

The shock left them still as statues. "Good grief, what was that?"

Harry was aware of her uneasiness, even her breath held. "Rats. And at the moment, they're the least of your worries." This time he stuck the gun a good distance inside his pants, then dared her with a look to try retrieving it. "Now."

She quickly regained her aplomb. "You're lucky you didn't shoot me!"

"I'd say you were luckier, being that you would have been the one shot." He took a firm step toward her.

"All right." She held up her hands. "Give me your coat, then turn your back and close your eyes."

"No." The silly woman persisted in her belief that he was an idiot.

"You're not going to watch, Harry."

"In case it's escaped your notice, it's exceedingly dim in here. What miserly moonlight there is can hardly penetrate the rain and the dust on the broken windows. I can't see my own hand in front of my face." That was an exaggeration; he could see just fine, but she didn't need to know that.

"I'll give you the coat, and if you'll promise not to do anything else foolish, I'll try to find a propitious spot for us to nest in until this storm completely blows over."

She curled her lip at him. "Your diction is astounding."

"Thank you." He handed her the coat and turned away, kicking debris with his feet as he carefully walked.

"It wasn't a compliment!" she called out, her voice heavy

with sarcasm. "You're what the regulars at my bar would call a *fancy-pants*."

"I'm wounded to my soul by their censure." The station stunk, literally. He could smell oil and rotting vegetation and heaven only knew what else. He preferred not to ponder the possibilities. He retrieved his tiny flashlight, flicked the light around in a wide arc, avoiding Charlie's dark corner, then settled on an area that would have to do.

"I've found a spot that's fairly dry and empty, and there's an old car bench seat. I suppose it'll support us and keep us off the cold cement floor."

He heard a "plop" and knew she'd dropped part of her disguise. He smiled in the darkness. "What exactly did you have on under your shirt?"

"Some old linen, pinned in place." Another plop. "Why don't you sit on the bench just to make sure nothing else is nesting there. I'm not keen on sharing with rats."

"I'm sure they feel the same about you." He kicked the seat with his foot. Nothing happened. Holding the flashlight in his teeth, he lifted one end and dropped it. And then did it again. "Nothing but an abundance of dust."

Another plop.

He turned off the flashlight before the temptation became too overwhelming. His eyeballs almost itched with the urge to peek. "Exactly how many layers did you have on?"

"Enough to get rid of any lumps or bumps, which was easy since my femaleness isn't all that noticeable anyway."

Temptation swelled. He looked toward her voice, but could only see a vague outline. He felt cheated and stared harder, but still only got shifting shadows and a stinging sense of guilt.

A wet length of toweling slapped up against his face. "You can use that to wipe off our nest."

Grumbling, he did as instructed then turned to her again. "I beg to differ. About your femaleness, I mean." He noticed her voice shook when she talked, more from cold now than anything else. His concern doubled. "If you'll recall, I knew right away that you were a female sort of person."

"I don't understand that. No one else noticed."

He could hear the chattering of her teeth. Definitely the cold. "Come here, Charlie. Let me warm you."

Not a sound. Not a movement. The irritating little twit.

"Oh for pity's sake." Though he tried to hide it, his irritation came through. "Charlie? Come on, I've proven myself by now, haven't I? We may have the entire night ahead of us, with nothing but the rain and the rats for company. Regardless of how stoic you might be, I don't mind admitting I'm cold. Let's at least make the attempt to get warm."

She took a step out of the shadows and he could see her vigorously rubbing her hair with her discarded shirt. His coat covered her from neck to ankles, enormously big on her petite frame. "What, exactly, did you have in mind?"

"A little cuddling." He smiled, already feeling the anticipation which was surely odd considering she really wasn't all that attractive and she had a penchant for insulting him with every breath. It was a unique feeling for him, being insulted by a woman. Even his ex-wife had refrained from that, at least until the very end. Before that, she'd been cajoling and sweet, even as she tried to manipulate him. Unaccountably, Charlie's bluntness piqued his interest. There was no understanding the workings of male hormones. "I'm willing to sacrifice myself by being on the bottom. You can sit on my, ah, lap and with our combined body heat we should stay warm enough."

"I don't know."

Her hair was a tousled dark mass of shining black, some locks hanging down to her eyes, other flipping around her ears. She looked almost cute, in a disheveled, bedraggled way. "Charlie, did you take everything off?" Now *his* voice shook. Damn it.

"No, of course not! My jeans are wet, but that can't be

helped. I did remove those muddy boots, though, so you don't
have to worry about them."

"My gratitude knows no bounds."

"What about you?"

He cleared his throat. "Just damp around the collar. Except
for my pants, which are soaked."

"Leave them on."

He grinned again, but kept his tone mild. "I have no intention of lacerating your dubious sensibilities by strutting around
naked. Now come here."

The stillness was palpable.

Harry sighed. "If you're hesitating because I said you
smelled nice, well, keep in mind I feel the same about new
leather and burnt sugar, but neither has ever inspired me to
levels of uncontrollable lust."

He heard her grousing and mumbling, heard her shifting,
then she moved a little closer. And damned if he didn't catch
a whiff of her elusive scent again, now mixed with the dampness of the rain and the fresh outdoors. With his eyes closed,
he breathed deeply.

"Why burnt sugar?"

She'd sidled close, near enough that he could see her clearly,
could reach out and touch her. He did, his fingers first landing
on her narrow shoulder, and when she didn't bolt, he let them
slide down to her slender wrist. His coat sleeves had been
rolled up but still hung down to her fingertips. She'd buttoned
up all the way, but the coat was so big on her, the neckline
hung disturbingly low. All in all, she looked adorable in his
coat, all wet and stubborn and mulish. *Only, he didn't like
stubborn, mulish women.*

He sat on the bench and tugged her down to his lap, giving
her a moment to get used to the feel of that and giving himself
a chance to calm his stampeding heart.

Ridiculous. There was absolutely no reason to react so
strongly to her. She was just a woman, caught up in the

same bizarre circumstances as he. Masculine interest hadn't prompted his offer to share body warmth. No, his motives were altruistic, they were—

"Harry?"

He could feel her breath on his throat when she spoke, feel her shivers. His awareness of her as a woman was acute. Slowly, wary of getting slugged at any moment, he wrapped his arms around her. "A friend of my father's used to make me this candy. He called it burnt sugar, and I suppose that's exactly what it is. He puts plain white sugar in a small buttered metal dish, melts it in the oven until the edges are dark brown, then lets it cool and harden. It's sort of like a sucker without the stick, and has a different taste since it isn't flavored at all. As a child, I forever had sticky fingers from eating burnt sugar."

She relaxed slightly, her body settling more closely into his and he could feel her heartbeat, could hear her breathing. "I can't imagine you as small, or with sticky fingers. You're so big now, and you seem so… fastidious."

"Yes, well, we all must grow up." Hoping to catch her off-guard, he asked, "What were you doing there, Charlie? And why the cross-dressing costume?"

She turned her face inward, doing the cuddling he'd suggested. Moments before he'd been cold and uncomfortable. But now he felt abundantly warm, almost too much so. He wouldn't be at all surprised if his damp clothing started to steam.

She was a very soft, very feminine weight nestled into his lap. And he really did enjoy her scent; something about it hit him on a gut level, very basic and primitive, forcing him to react in spite of himself. Overall, it was the kind of thing men fantasized about. Except for the kidnapping and the irritating storm.

"I was there to spy on someone."

He hadn't expected that, and the immediate conclusion he

came to had a volatile effect on him. He stiffened, his voice sounding cold and hard even to his own ears. "A lover? A husband?"

She chuckled. "Nah, I have no interest in either of those, thank you very much." There was a heavy silence, then she added, "I suppose you could say I was actually spying for someone else."

"A friend?"

"Mmm. I didn't want anyone to recognize me."

"Well, you blundered into a mess and now I have to rescue you."

"Just like a fabled hero?" Her hair tickled his chin as she shook her head. "Not likely. I can take care of myself."

"I'm the first one to admit I'm not hero material. But I am bigger and stronger and I know the situation, whereas you're small and weak—"

She punched him in the stomach and he wheezed, then immediately flattened her against him so she couldn't retaliate further.

"—and you obviously don't know what you've gotten yourself into."

"Okay, so tell me. Who are these clowns who grabbed us and what are you going to do about it?"

He twisted to look down at her, and she lifted her face at the same time. Their noses bumped. Harry's thoughts scattered, and he struggled to bring them back to order. It wasn't easy.

"First I'm going to get you home and safe and out of my way. Then I'm going to get Floyd and Ralph, on my own ground, and pound some sense into them." He hesitated, pondering his own words and the probability of enacting them. "Maybe. I still have to weigh my personal vendetta against a promise I made to get them both legally stopped."

"A promise to who?"

"The friend who makes burnt sugar. He owns a shop in the area. Floyd and Ralph work for Carlyle as petty extortioners, and my friend refuses to pay. He's been threatened, and I don't take kindly to that sort of thing."

"What had you planned to do today?"

As she asked it, her gaze dropped to his mouth and one small hand opened on his chest. She looked vaguely confused, as if dealing with unfamiliar feelings. Harry understood completely, since he was in a similar predicament.

He forgot to answer her for the longest time. He could feel that small palm, warm and still, like a brand against his flesh. It aroused him, and surely that was insanity.

"Harry?"

He forcibly shored up his flagging wits. "Today I was just sizing things up." He touched her cheek where the bruise was visible, along with a little swelling. His tone lowered with regret. "Damn, I'm sorry you got hit."

"I've had worse."

Given her backbone and courage, he didn't doubt she'd led a hard life, but hearing of it made him want to hold her closer, to protect her. They stared at each other while Harry's fingers gently coasted over the bruise. If for no other reason than this, Floyd deserved to feel his fist, Harry decided.

"Answer me something, Charlie." His hand cupped her cheek and she didn't protest. He smoothed wet tendrils of hair away from her face, marveling at how soft her skin felt. Surely all women were as soft, but he couldn't seem to remember.

She didn't move away and he felt his heartbeat thud, felt his muscles harden. "Did you mean what you said about not being interested? Not at all?"

Her gaze met his, so close. "Interested in what?"

"A lover."

"I don't know." She frowned, then looked at his mouth again. "I've never given it much thought."

He drew a slow breath, filling himself with her scent. "And now?"

She looked away, then back up again with a sort of daring grin. "I admit I'm thinking about it."

She was so bluntly honest, he smiled. Charlie might be demanding, but she would never be manipulative.

Her arms looped around his neck. "You know, Harry, this is turning into a romantic moment after all, isn't it?

Harry gently kissed the bruise on her cheek, his lips just grazing her skin, his nose nuzzling her temple. "Hmm. And I don't even have my flashlight out."

She chuckled. "I'm starting to like you, Harry."

It was the chuckle that did it, low and husky. He turned his face and she met him halfway and their mouths met, open and hot and devouring. *Oh damn,* Harry thought with some surprise. He hadn't expected this, hadn't thought she'd be this way, avaricious and hungry, clinging to him as if she'd never been kissed before or was starved for it. He was the starving one, and the hunger had come on him so suddenly…. It turned him on so much he groaned.

Sweeping one large hand down her back, he fondly cupped the adorable backside he'd admired earlier. Soft and sweet, the feel of her made him want more.

But before he could allow things to progress, he felt he owed her a measure of honesty. "Charlie, honey, listen a minute. I have to tell you something."

Her eyes narrowed. "Getting discriminating on me again, Harry?"

He swallowed hard. Did she actually think he'd want to back out when he was shaking with lust? Not likely. "I'm not interested in a romantic relationship."

She blinked at him in surprise. "Okay." She tried to kiss him again, her hands clutching his shoulders.

He held her back with one hand, putting breathing space between them. "Charlie, I can't make you any promises."

She blinked twice, then frowned at him. "What are you talking about?"

She looked so confused he wanted to shake her. He realized his hand still held her bottom and he gave her a gentle squeeze, then shuddered with the effects of that caress. Damn, he wanted her. *Insane.*

"Marriage." He cleared his throat and managed to explain. "All those questions earlier. You were hinting about marriage and I want you to know, my plate is full right now. I have no intentions of getting even mildly involved with a woman."

One side of her mouth quivered, and she bit her lip. *Oh God, don't let her cry,* Harry thought, his body so tense he hurt, his mind feeling like mush.

She covered her mouth with her hand and a chuckle escaped. Harry frowned. In the next instant, her chuckles turned to uproarious laughter. "You," she said between hiccups, "thought I was sizing you up for marriage material?" She laughed some more, not dainty feminine laughter. No, this was boisterous, unrestrained hilarity. "Good grief, I hardly know you!"

Disgruntled with her misplaced mirth and his unabated lust, Harry demanded, "Then why all the questions?"

"Actually, if you must know," she said, trying to get herself under control and failing miserably, "I had thought to *hire* you."

"Hire me for what, damn it?"

"To find out more information on my father." She wiped her eyes, perched primly on his lap with her midnight hair hung over one eye giving her a seductive look. "That's what I was doing there today. Spying on him. I haven't seen him in almost eighteen years."

Harry wanted explanations and he wanted them now. Who was her father? And why the long separation?

His arms were still around her, one hand still splayed over perfect buttocks. When she smiled, her dark blue eyes seemed to smile, too.

He wished now that he'd kept his big mouth shut.

She traced his mouth with a delicate fingertip. "You really are a wonderful kisser, Harry."

Hope rose that he might be able to salvage this debacle, but then car lights hit the window of the gas station, and every thought other than protecting her slipped from his mind.

He shoved her off his lap and onto the dirty floor. "Stay there and don't make a sound." In the next second he was gone.

CHAPTER FOUR

CHARLIE SAT ON the floor, her backside bruised, her lust squelched. Where had Harry gone? On hands and knees she crawled to the window to peek out. Just as her head lifted, Harry snatched it back down.

Hissing close to her ear, he asked, "Is there a particular reason you want to offer up your brains for target practice?"

"Where did you go?" Her words were muffled against his fly, and while there, she noticed he'd suffered quite a reaction to their kisses. Heaven help her, the man was hard.

"I was surveying our options, of course. Now be still."

She quit squirming and sighed. Having her cheek pressed to an erection, her nose smashed against a muscled thigh, with no hope of any loveplay, seemed like a terrible waste, especially since this was the first time in ages she'd been interested in such a thing. "Do you have any suggestions?"

"Yes, as a matter of fact, I do."

At that moment, Floyd called out. "You might as well come on out of there!"

Charlie whispered, "He certainly sounds furious."

"Yes, well, maybe he knows you planned to toss him off the truck."

"Ha! I think it's probably his aching jaw where you slugged him that has the bastard madder than hell."

He tsked. "Your language is a disgrace."

"You have my face buried in your lap, but you're worried about my language?"

Harry groaned, and his fingers contracted on the back of her head. "This is no time for your unregulated tongue, so keep quiet if you please."

"We know you're both in there!" Floyd growled. "There wasn't no place else for you to go. Now come on out and maybe we won't shoot you. We'll just take you to Carlyle."

Harry kept one large hand mashed against her head, forcing her to stay low, as he yelled out, "I have your gun, remember? Come anywhere near here and I'll be obliged to put a bullet in you! At the moment, the thought doesn't distress me at all."

Curses exploded from outside the garage.

"He really doesn't like you, Harry."

"The feeling is mutual, I assure you."

Unable to help herself, she nuzzled slightly into his lap. Harry jerked away. "Keep your head down, and no, don't say a thing. In case you've failed to notice, we're in something of a situation here. I need to keep my wits collected." When she dutifully remained silent, he nodded. "Good. Now, I'm going to draw them to the back of the garage. There's a door back there, and when they think we're escaping out the back, we'll make a run for the truck. Understand?"

He was all business, his eyes bright, his voice low, his body hard, poised for action. He impressed the hell out of Charlie, being so urbane one minute and so lethal the next.

"How can I help?"

"By not getting yourself killed. Now, do you understand everything I told you?"

"I'm not an idiot."

He sighed. "I suppose I'm to take that as a yes." He started to move away, then suddenly leaned forward and grabbed her by the neck. His mouth landed on hers, hot and hard, for the briefest second, and then he disappeared into the shadows. He managed to move without making a sound, causing her admiration to grow.

Charlie plopped down onto her backside and waited. She

didn't like waiting. She felt ineffectual and cowardly and the feelings didn't rest well with her at all. She was used to taking action, to controlling things.

Floyd evidently didn't like waiting, either. "I'm losing patience!" he shouted. "I'll give you to the count of ten, then we're coming in and shooting any damn thing that moves. Carlyle would rather have you dead than loose."

Hurry up, Harry, she thought, listening as Floyd started a loud, monotonous recitation of his numbers.

Glass shattered at the back of the garage, followed by the sound of running footsteps. Cautiously, Charlie peeked over the edge of the window above her head. Floyd and Ralph stood frozen in the moonlight for a single heartbeat, then they cursed and ran hellbent for the back of the garage.

She waited until they were out of sight before she slithered toward the door Harry had kicked in, proud of the fact that she, too, made no discernible noise. She'd barely edged outside before a rough, hot hand clamped over her mouth and a steely arm closed tight around her waist. She would have panicked if it hadn't been for Harry's height, assuring her he was the one who'd accosted her.

Without struggling, she got dragged to the truck and roughly thrust inside through the driver's door. Harry slid in beside her.

Seething, Charlie restraightened the huge coat she wore, holding the throat closed with a fist, and leaned close to whisper, "What? You thought I'd refuse your rescue and opt to stay with my buddy Floyd? Is that why you felt you had to manhandle—"

"No keys, damn it."

She squeaked. "What do you mean, no keys? How the heck are we going to—"

He thrust the gun into her hand. "Watch out for the two stooges while I hot-wire this barge."

Bemused, Charlie looked down at the gun in her hand, then

to where Harry bent low beneath the dash, then dutifully out the window.

Hmm. There was something innately sexy about a man who could hot-wire.

It took him mere seconds. He'd just managed to fire the engine when Floyd and Ralph came stumbling back around the garage, their curses so hot Charlie's ears felt singed, and that was surely impressive given she'd been raised hearing curses all her life. The two men literally jumped up and down in rage as gravel and mud slung off the spinning tires, embellishing Harry's daring getaway. Ralph fired, and Charlie thought she heard a bullet or two hit the side of the truck bed, but it didn't slow Harry. She waited, wondering if, because of the gunshot, he'd feel it necessary to put her head back in his lap.

She was slightly disappointed when he didn't.

Harry didn't say a word, concentrating instead on finding the main road and figuring out how to turn on the lights, the wiper blades, the heat. Charlie was just about to tuck the gun into her pocket when he retrieved it from her without a word.

She knew a struggle for the gun was useless, and she scowled. "Now what?"

Harry rubbed the back of his neck, glanced at her, his gaze moving over her from head to toe, then cursed slightly. "I think we'll abandon this truck outside town. No sense in taking a chance that Carlyle or one of his cronies will recognize it and want to pull us over. We'll grab a taxi to my apartment."

"Why your apartment?" Not that she'd complain. Her curiosity over Harry grew more rampant with every moment she spent in his company. From his place, she could call her sister, and then maybe they could finish what they'd started at the garage. She glanced down at Harry's lap, but the interior of the cab was too dark to tell if he still reacted to their little interlude. She liked it a lot that she'd turned him on. In all her life, she'd seldom had the opportunity, or the desire, to indulge in lust. But with Harry, well, she was more than a little intrigued.

"I think we need to talk, to figure out what we're going to do."

Charlie sighed, then carefully ventured a suggestion. "I don't think we should call the police."

Harry stilled for a moment, smoothly switched gears, then nodded. "Okay, I'll bite. Well, not really, not unless you wanted me to, and then it'd be more appropriate to say nibble—"

"Harry."

"Why don't you want to contact the police?"

"Because I can't see any way for you to explain this without telling them I was there, dressed as a guy, spying. And I'd just as soon no one knew about that."

"I can see where that would be a tale you'd hesitate to broadcast. But as it so happens I don't relish involving the police, either."

"And your reasons are?" When he only slanted her a look, she poked him in the side. "No way, Harry. I told, now it's your turn."

"You told very little, actually."

"I'll get into more detail once I'm warm and dry and have time to reason a few things out."

"I suppose that'll have to appease me."

"Give it up, Harry."

He didn't want to, she could tell that. He gave her a grudging look that almost made her smile. "I promised my friend I wouldn't involve any of the other people in the area. They're older proprietors, like Pops, and they aren't excessively fond of the police right now."

"You mean Pops—the guy who runs the store we were in before Floyd decided to play kidnapper?"

"That's right. They've contacted the police a few times in the past over other situations—loud music, loitering, things

like that. They were pretty much told that since they're in
a run-down, high-crime area, they have to expect a certain
amount of that sort of thing. The police offered more surveillance, but the elders didn't think that was enough. They were
determined to take matters into their own hands, which of
course would be dangerous."

Even as she nodded, Charlie wondered if her father was
one of the men being bothered. It seemed likely. She felt a
moment's worry before she firmly squelched it. Her father deserved nothing but her enmity, and that's all he'd ever get. He'd
never been there when she needed him most, but she'd found
him now, and he could damn well pay. What she wanted from
him—financial assistance to get her sister through college—
had nothing to do with emotions or family relationships.

The rain started again, and they settled into a congenial
quiet. Harry reached over and pulled her to his side. It wasn't
quite as nice as his lap, but he was warm and firm and secure,
and she took comfort from his nearness, though she'd never
have admitted it.

As they neared the outskirts of town, Harry nudged her
with his shoulder. "It's regretful things got interrupted back
there."

"Yeah."

He cleared his throat. "If you're interested…"

"Yeah."

Laughing, Harry pulled the truck up to the curb and turned
the engine off. He tilted Charlie's face up and kissed her softly.
"There's nothing coy about you, is there?"

She raised a brow. "Should I pretend I'm not interested?
That'd be dumb, Harry, since I don't get interested all that
often."

Harry fought a smile, and lost. "So you're telling me you're
not easy after all?"

Charlie snorted. "Most of the men that frequent my saloon
could tell you I'm usually damn difficult."

"No! You? I'll never believe it."

Charlie smacked his shoulder. "Smart-ass."

Chuckling, Harry said, "Wait here. I'll call us a taxi."

He left the truck and trotted to a pay phone across the street. Charlie watched him go, admiring his long-legged stride, the way he held his head, the natural confidence and arrogance that appeared as obvious as his physical attributes. He was a strange man in many ways, his lofty wit and cultured diction in opposition to his easy acceptance at being kidnapped, shot at and holed up in a greasy garage. He'd stolen a truck as easily as if such a thing were a daily occurrence. Though it was apparent to Charlie he'd led an expensive, well-bred life, he hadn't so much as sniffed at her admission to owning a saloon, or the fact that for the most part, she was an obvious gutter rat, born and bred on the shadier side of life.

And he didn't hesitate to call her Charlie.

Most of the regulars at her saloon called her what she told them to, wary of getting on her bad side. They weren't, however, great examples of masculine humanity, so their concessions counted for very little. She had a feeling Harry, with all his grins and arrogance and stubbornness, was a true hero, even if he'd chosen to deny it.

He watched her from the phone booth while he placed the call, alert to any possible danger. With a smile, Charlie turned away to view their surroundings. They were near a park, but not one she recognized. Of course, she had little time or interest for dawdling in parks, so that wasn't a surprise.

Seconds later, Harry returned. His wet dress shirt clung to his upper torso, showing a large, smoothly muscled chest and shoulders, and even through his undershirt, she could see a sprinkling of chest hair. The shirt opened at the collar and his strong throat was wet, a couple of droplets of rain rolling down into the opening. Charlie swallowed.

His damp hair stuck to his nape and one brown lock hung over his brow. His light brown eyes, framed by spiked eyelashes, darkened as he watched her inspect his features. Harry leaned back on the seat and the corners of his mouth tipped in a slight smile. "Have I sprouted horns?"

Charlie shook her head. "You're a real looker."

One brow lifted as his smile turned into a grin. "Thank you."

"I bet you hear that a lot."

"Seldom enough to keep me humble."

She choked on a laugh. "There's not a humble bone in your big body, Harry, and I bet women fawn over you all the time."

He didn't deny it. He did tilt his head to look at her, then slowly reached out to touch the top button of his coat, where it rested low on her chest. "I don't suppose you'd want to pass the time by appeasing my curiosity over these mysterious breasts of yours, would you?"

Charlie gaped. She should have been used to his boldness by now, especially since his brain did seem to stay focused on her upper assets—or lack thereof. "You expect me to just flash the coat open for your entertainment?"

He shrugged, shifted to his side to face her. His finger trailed over the deep V at the neck of the coat, tickling her skin, raising her body temperature by several degrees. "I'll admit I'm vastly interested, and while you're indulging in more temperate humors, I thought this might be the ideal time. Besides, what else have you got to do right now other than model for my delectation?"

He certainly had a way with words. And his gentle touch and tone, compared to the coarseness she was accustomed to, was a major turn on. But she shook her head. "I'm not putting on a show for you, Harry, so forget it."

Harry fought his grin. "Ah, well, you do like to vex a man, don't you?"

Before she could answer, headlights flashed against the windshield of the truck. For a second there, Charlie panicked, thinking somehow Floyd and Ralph had found them. But then Harry leaned forward, gave her a swift kiss, and said, "Our ride is here. Faster than I'd anticipated, but evidently the cabbie was in the area. Come on. Other than seeing your elusive bosom, dry clothing is the most appealing thing on my mind."

The cabbie, a seasoned veteran, made no comment on her lack of shoes or bedraggled appearance, much to Charlie's relief. Harry somehow managed to be imperious, despite their circumstances, and the driver gave him due deference.

Harry held her hand all the way to his apartment, which wasn't all that far, taking a mere fifteen minutes. But it was long enough to make her edgy, to make her ponder several different things, mostly how enticing the thought of having an affair with him seemed.

He paid the cabbie, refusing to let her dig money from her own pocket to pay half. In fact, he seemed insulted by the very idea. Charlie shrugged. She needed her money, and if he wanted to play the gallant, that was fine by her.

Harry led her to the first floor of an exclusive complex, and Charlie wasn't at all surprised to see, once he'd gotten the door unlocked, that his apartment wasn't an apartment at all, but rather an expensively decorated, immaculate and beautiful town house. She couldn't help herself, she felt intimidated.

Then the barking began, startling her half out of her skin.

Harry relocked the door and switched on more lights. A miniature collie and a small, stocky, mixed-breed mutt darted out around a large, beige leather sofa. The collie's entire body quivered with happiness at the sight of Harry and he laughed as the dog jumped up and down in near berserk joy. The mutt, a little more subdued, ran circles around Harry and howled. Harry immediately knelt to rub the dog's scruff. He glanced up at Charlie. "Meet Grace and Sooner. Grace has been with me a long time, but Sooner has only been in the family a couple of years."

She stared at the dogs, who stared back, one sitting on each side of Harry, heads tilted, expressions alert, like sentinels guarding the king from a scourge. She grinned, and the dogs seemed to grin back.

"I can understand the name Grace, since she looks so re-fined. But Sooner?"

Harry shrugged. "He'd 'sooner' be one breed as another."

"Ah."

Harry patted the dogs. "She's entirely acceptable, guys, so you may as well present her with the royal treatment."

Once he said it, both dogs trotted over to sniff her, lick her hand, bark a few times in a doggy greeting. Then they each gave Harry a quizzical look, as if her presence made no sense at all, and retreated. Grace leaped up to lie on the sofa, resting her head on a black and beige motif throw folded over one end. Sooner went over to flop onto the floor in front of a white stone electric fireplace. He gave a loud groan and closed his eyes.

The town house was very sleek, and as Charlie looked around, she saw marble-topped oak end tables, bare wood floors with thick area rugs, and windows with streamlined blinds rather than curtains. All in all, she thought the room was gorgeous and suited Harry to a T.

She was afraid to move. Her bare feet were muddy, grime from the garage between her white toes. Water still dripped from her hair, her nose, Harry's coat. She felt like a flea-ridden squirrel turned loose in a palace.

No wonder the dogs thought her curious.

"Make yourself at home. I'll locate us some dry clothes. Would you like something to drink?"

All the social niceties. Charlie shook her head, fighting the urge to fidget. "I'd really like to call and check in with my sister, if you don't mind."

He went to a desk situated in front of a long window that looked out over the backyard. It was partially separated from the living room by a wide arched doorway. Charlie could see oak file cabinets and office equipment. She heard Harry curse.

"What's wrong?"

"The electricity evidently went out with the storm. My answering machine is dead, meaning I've missed any calls that may have come in."

"Were you expecting an important call?"

"Several, actually." He walked back to her. "You'll have to use the phone in my bedroom. The portable is out."

His bedroom?

Harry crossed his arms over his wet chest and frowned at her. "Surely that look doesn't mean you're afraid of me? Not the woman who challenged Floyd and Ralph, the woman who did her best to bait two miscreants. I assure you, you're safe enough with me."

"Me, fear you? Ha!" She was more afraid of herself at the moment. She felt like tossing his gorgeous self to the floor and having her way with him. But she would never do such a thing in front of the innocent dogs. "It's just that my feet are dirty. The dogs are cleaner than I am. I don't want to track mud all over the place."

Harry looked down, took in her bare feet and growled. "I forgot you'd removed those hideous boots. You could have cut yourself on something when we ran for the truck. I can't believe I didn't notice sooner. Well, actually I can, given my attention was somewhat fractured by other things, but not so much so, I shouldn't have noticed naked feet. I am a P.I. after all, usually very alert to small details."

"Uh, Harry?"

He still stared at her feet. "Hmm?"

"The phone?"

"Oh, yes, of course. Okay, no help for it. I suppose I'll have to play the martyr."

"No! Don't you dare... Harry, put me down."

"You're really very slight, now that we've rid you of your ridiculous waterlogged costume." As he made his way up a flight of carpeted stairs, he looked down at her, their noses almost touching, and the smile he gave her made her catch her breath. His gaze dipped lower, and Charlie glanced down to see the coat had slipped some and she had a modest amount— all she possessed really—of cleavage showing. She tried to make a grab for the coat, but then Harry lowered her, and she realized she was in a taupe and black tiled bathroom, more specifically, he stood her in the black tub.

"Don't move. I'll play lady's maid and get you a towel and dry clothes and you can clean up just a bit before we progress any further."

Progress to what, she wondered? Another part of his home, or another level of intimacy? She knew where her vote would be, but she didn't say so. She did need to clean up, and dry clothes sounded heavenly.

Harry reappeared with two plush white towels, a long polo shirt, and silky boxer shorts. He grinned as he laid the items on the marble vanity. "The thing is, you're something of a squirt, so nothing I have would be small enough to fit you. However, I wear a "tall" so my shirt should make do for a dress, only I couldn't bear the thought of you being naked beneath it, not if you expect me to exhibit my more civilized tendencies, so I determined the boxers would serve as well as anything." He lifted his hands. "I'm fresh out of ladies' panties."

She drew a blank, except to ask, "You wear silk boxers?"

"Actually no. They were a gift from a friend."

"Ah."

He headed for the door. "Go ahead and wash up. You can

hang the coat on the back of the door and I'll take care of it later. There's a hamper under the cabinet where you can stick your muddy jeans. I'll be in the kitchen making coffee after I've changed."

The second he was out the door, Charlie rushed through her bath. She stripped off the coat, praying it wasn't ruined, and then spent several minutes working her wet, worn jeans down her legs. She didn't know what to do with her panties—no way would she put them in his hamper for him to find later. After giving it some thought, she washed them out and hung them on the side of the tub.

She disdained a full shower for simply cleaning herself off. Calling her sister was a priority.

Once she'd pulled on the dry clothes Harry'd brought her, she found his comb and worked the tangles out of her short hair. The polo shirt hung almost to her knees, looking, as he'd predicted, like a dress. It adequately covered her, but the silky boxers tickled. Rather than toss her dirty jeans in the hamper as he'd suggested, she folded them, put her panties in the pocket along with her money, and left the bathroom.

Harry sat on a corner of a colossal bed, head bent forward while he towel-dried his hair. He had on clean khaki slacks, and nothing else. His back was broad, muscled, lightly tanned. His feet were long, narrow, braced apart on the thick carpeting. Charlie stood there gawking, appreciating what a spectacular sight he made.

Oh yes, she definitely wanted to explore these unique feelings he inspired. She'd been around men all her life, but she'd never, not once, felt this much interest in one.

Her sigh caught his attention. He lifted his head, surveyed her tip to toes, then slowly stood. "You are an adorable sight, Charlie..." He paused, looking much struck. "I just realized I don't know your last name."

"Jones," she squeaked, breathless over the way he watched her. She cleared her throat. "Charlie Jones."

He held out his hand in the formal, time-honored tradition. "Harry Lonnigan." Smiling, she stepped forward, shifted her wet jeans to one arm, and took his hand. With a mere glimpse of evil intent, Harry tugged her forward. He took her small bundle from her and dropped it to the floor. His hands lifted to cradle her face, she caught her breath, and then he kissed her.

HARRY COULDN'T believe the way she made him feel. It was a simple kiss, damm it, and heaven knew he'd kissed plenty of women in his time. And among those women, Charlie was likely the least proficient at it. So her lips were soft? So she smelled incredibly sweet?

She looked like a rumpled child in his shirt, the shoulders bagging almost to her elbows, the hem skimming her knees—very sexy knees actually, followed by shapely calves. He shook his head. She'd combed her hair straight back, evidently not the least interested in impressing him with her feminine attributes. She'd made no effort at all to make herself more appealing. Yet he already had an erection and he practically shook with lust. All because of a simple kiss.

It was so unexpected, he almost grinned.

That happened a lot with her; hell, he'd grinned more since first spotting her in that small grocery, all decked out like an adolescent thug, than he had in the past six months.

Beneath his palms, her skin warmed and she felt so incredibly silky, so vibrant, he wanted to devour her. *He never devoured women!* He was suave and controlled and applauded for his technique.

She had him so turned on, he couldn't even remember his touted technique.

His thumbs stroked over her temple, her jaw. He kept the kiss easy, letting her lead, though he wanted badly to taste her, to slip his tongue into her mouth, to feel her tongue on his.

With a groan, he pulled back the tiniest bit and looked at

her. Eyes almost closed, she swayed toward him, her pale, flushed skin in striking contrast to her glossy black hair and dark blue eyes. Her lips were slightly parted, and unable to help himself, he kissed her again, this time giving in to the urge to explore. He licked over her lips, and when she gasped, he slipped inside, coasting over her teeth, mating with her soft tongue.

He pulsed with need, he was so aroused.

Charlie's hands opened on his naked shoulders. She moved against him, and he could feel her stiff little nipples, could feel the plumpness of her breasts, small, but very feminine and sweet. He started to lift a hand, to cup her, tease her and himself, and his honor came knocking, just barely nudging aside the need.

Unspoken invective filled his brain. He wanted so badly to feel her breasts, but...

Once he got started, he knew good and well it would be hours before he got his fill. He should be getting in touch with Dalton. He had no doubts the man would be worried, wondering what had transpired, whether or not Harry had been able to make any headway. He owed Dalton that much.

"Charlie."

"Hmm..." She nuzzled his throat, took a small nip of his chin.

"Sweetheart, we need to talk."

She blinked up at him, her look dreamy. "You called me sweetheart."

Sighing, he said again, "We need to talk. Now."

She stiffened, her gaze searching his. "Oh good grief. Please, don't give me the old 'you're not that kind of guy' routine."

He took two steps back, and commended himself for accomplishing that much when he wanted so badly to feel her flush against him.

"I'm absolutely that kind of guy," he assured her, staring

down into her sweet face. "I'm the kind of guy who is nearly desperate to strip you to your very sexy naked hide. I'm the kind of guy that once I got started, especially on the unveiling on these stupendous breasts of yours, I wouldn't want to stop until we were both insentient and without wit. I wouldn't stop until you begged me to. Unfortunately, what happened tonight probably has several people worrying about us."

The changing expressions on her face were almost comical. She went from openmouthed surprise, to blushing, to wide-eyed with realization. "My sister!"

"Yes. And I have a friend to contact. They deserve to know that we're still alive and kicking."

She rudely shoved him aside to snatch up the phone, and Harry admired the smooth rounded lines of her delectable backside. Nobility was surely a curse.

"I can't believe I forgot about my sister." She sent him a grave look of accusation and dialed the phone, muttering how it was his fault for distracting her, leaving off his shirt, showing his bare feet.

His bare feet? Harry shook his head. There was no accounting for her strange twists of reason. "I'll finish dressing while you make your call."

She'd barely finished dialing when Harry heard a shouted, frantic "hello" through the earpiece. Her sister had evidently been waiting for the call.

"Jill…I know, and I'm so sorry. I'm fine, really— *Jill, I'm fine,* I promise. Well, it's a long story. I met a guy… No, Jill, it's not *that* long." Charlie glared at him, and Harry took the hint. He grabbed the rest of his clothes and left the room with a salute.

As he bounded down the stairs, he could hear the animated conversation, along with the occasional hushed, whispering tones, which he assumed meant the two women were discussing him. He entered the kitchen and because he was distracted, he almost tripped over his cat, Ted, now twisting around his bare ankles. It didn't matter where Ted might be, if Harry entered the kitchen, Ted showed up.

He smiled down at the cat as he added some fresh food to his dish—always the first order of business. "I wonder how much Charlie will actually tell of our adventure."

The dogs heard him talking and sauntered in. Harry reached for the back door which led to a tiny yard with a privacy fence. "Hey, why don't you guys go out and run around a little, maybe give me some privacy?"

Doggy tails wagged, but actual bodies didn't move.

The cat looked thoroughly indignant at such a suggestion and continued to eat.

"So it rained a little. Don't you have to go?"

Sooner woofed an agreement and ran out. Grace took a little more coaxing, until she heard Sooner bark again and trotted out to investigate. Ted, with a look of disdain, licked his whiskers clean and leaped up to sit in one of the kitchen chairs.

Harry had the coffee ready, two cups poured, when Charlie came striding in. Harry handed her a cup and motioned for her to sit at the round table. Unfortunately, she tried to sit in Ted's chair.

Ted could be very theatrical when it suited him. He made a horrid hissing sound, arched his back, fuzzed out his tail and made a general threatening display until Charlie had backed up a good five feet.

"What the hell's wrong with your cat?"

Harry smiled fondly at his pet. "That's Ted. He doesn't like females."

"Ted? How'd you come up with that name?"

Shrugging, he said, "He's just Ted. Here, use this chair."

Cautiously, keeping her gaze on the cat, Charlie circled to the chair Harry held out. "Is he always so mean?"

"With women, yes. He behaves well enough for me. Or

maybe I behave well enough to suit him. Whatever, the arrangement works." Harry smiled at her.

"The dogs don't bother him?"

"Actually, they all get along fairly well. On his first day here, about a year or so ago, Ted explained things. We haven't had a real ruckus since."

"You've only had him a year? He looks older."

"He is. I found him in an alley while I was on a job. He saved me by making a grand distraction when he objected to our invasion of his private space."

"He threw a hissy like he just did to me?"

"Exactly, which effectively distracted the fellow who'd been holding a gun on me. I was able to…get the upper hand. So I brought Ted home. The vet treated him, despite Ted's vicious complaints, and as long as I keep him well fed and his litter box clean, he doesn't destroy my home."

"A fair enough trade-off, I suppose." She still eyed the cat warily, but Harry was pleased to see there was no dislike in her eyes. She understood, and he liked that.

"Cream or sugar?"

She snorted at such a suggestion, then took a healthy sip of her black coffee.

Harry scrutinized her as he liberally sweetened his own. "So you drink yours like a trucker, hmm? Now why doesn't that surprise me?"

After another sip, she asked, "For the same reason that seeing you turn yours into syrup doesn't surprise me?"

"Your insults are getting sloppier. You must be tired." He glanced at the clock, saw it was after midnight, and wondered if he should call Dalton after all. He hated to wake the older man if he'd already gone to bed. And Dalton did know Harry could take care of himself, so perhaps he hadn't been worried at all. "Is your sister appeased by whatever story you told her?"

She frowned at that. "I told her the truth, and yeah, she's

appeased, but far from happy. She told me she's going to wait up for me."

Charlie offered that last small tidbit with a wince, which told Harry the night was going to get a whole lot shorter. "I assume this means you want to head home soon?"

"I'm afraid so. Jill is only eighteen, and she worries more than she should."

That brought out a snort, which appalled him. Good God, he was beginning to pick up her less discriminating habits. Harry cleared his throat. "More than she should? With a sister who muddles into extortion and gets herself kidnapped, I'd say she's justified."

Charlie shrugged. "She wants me to give it up, my spying that is, but I'm determined."

"Charlie—"

"No, before you start any lectures, I have a few questions for you."

"Please, don't keep me in suspense."

"I know you said you wouldn't want to see me again—"

Before he could correct her, because at this point he had every intention of seeing her, all of her, as many times as was necessary to get the fever out of his system, she held up a hand and continued.

"Don't worry. I'm not going to get clingy. A little hanky-panky would have been…nice. But the night has gotten way too complicated, and I can see why you wouldn't want to get involved with me beyond the night. I mean, we're hardly two peas from the same pod." She tried a smile that looked more like a grimace. "But… Well, I was hoping we could work out a different arrangement."

Harry leaned back in his seat, positively prostrated. "You think a rendezvous with me would be merely *nice?*"

She looked startled by his tone. "*Very* nice," she clarified, as if that made it better.

He felt smote to his masculine core. Here he'd been dredging up pagan images too erotic to bear, and she'd relegated the possibilities to merely *nice.* "I'll have you know—"

"I'd like to hire you, Harry."

That effectively put the brakes on his righteous diatribe. Hire him? Did she consider him a gigolo? Did she dare think she could afford him if he *was* for sale? The nerve.

But in a lusty sort of way the idea genuinely appealed to him. His body tensed until his muscles cramped. He was so hard, he could be considered a weapon.

Carefully, in case he misunderstood, he asked, "Hire me for what?"

"Detecting, of course. What else would I mean?"

Disappointment flowed through him. Nevertheless, he contrived to look merely curious. "Of course. And what would you need a P.I. for?"

"I told you." she said with exaggerated patience. "To find out information on my father. He abandoned my sister and me ages ago, and that's fine by me because from what I know of it, we were better off without him. Except now I think it's time he accepted a few responsibilities. I figure since your friend has hired you to look into the extortion, and my father is one of the proprietors in that area, it shouldn't really be too much trouble for you to find out a few things for me."

A sick feeling of dread started to choke him. He remembered their most recent introduction, when she'd given him her last name. His belly churned, and he forced the question out. "Your father is?"

"Dalton Jones."

CHAPTER FIVE

HARRY STARTED TO choke, picked up his coffee to take a large gulp, then choked some more. Coffee spewed out his nose and Charlie jumped up to pound on his back with surprising force. The cat hissed and loped out of the room. Harry fumbled for a napkin, and while Charlie tried to drive his ribs through his chest, he cleaned his face.

"You okay?"

Wheezing, he said, "If you'd quit bludgeoning me, it's possible I'll survive."

She quit. In fact, her small hand opened, and rather than pounding, she smoothed her palm over his back. Harry stiffened. "What are you doing?" he asked carefully.

"You feel nice. Hard. And real warm."

He started to choke again, and Charlie reseated herself. "That was the strangest damn thing, Harry. I've never seen coffee shoot out someone's nose before. And it was still steaming." She looked vaguely impressed when she added, "That had to hurt."

"You frightened Ted, attacking me that way—"

"Yeah, right." She gave a hearty snort. "Nothing would scare that beast."

"—*and* you don't sound the least bit sympathetic, so just be quiet." His brain throbbed not only from her interested, caressing touch, but with ramifications of her admission. Dalton Jones, his best friend, the man who'd always been there for him, emotionally supported him, got him through his divorce-from-hell, was Charlie's father? And she didn't appear to have any fond feelings for the man. No, she literally sneered when she said his name, leading Harry to believe her feelings bordered more on contempt than anything else. Harry dropped his head to a fist and sighed.

"Sheesh. What's got you so all-fired dejected, Harry?" She lounged back in the chair, at her leisure. "If you don't want the job, just say so. It's not like I was trying to coerce you or anything. I just thought since you'll be checking things out there anyway, it'd be no big deal to let me know if you heard anything."

Feeling himself duly cornered, Harry sighed again. "Let me get this straight. You want to get reacquainted with your father?" It was a shock, but Dalton would certainly be thrilled. Harry knew he'd spent a good portion of his life chasing after his ex-wife, doing his best to locate his children, to reclaim them, but the woman had always eluded him for reasons of her own.

Charlie bristled like an offended porcupine. "Hell no! I personally don't want anything to do with him. And if I had any other choices, he could rot for all I cared. But...well, my mother passed away not too long ago and between her never-ending medical bills and the funeral, I'm flat broke. I need some cash to get my sister through college. The bar is mortgaged through the roof, and I can't handle another personal loan."

Harry started to tell her that Dalton would gladly help her in any way he could. But he held back. It wasn't his place to make promises for Dalton, so he decided to talk to him first. Besides, Charlie's attitude was less than promising, and explaining away the past was a chore Dalton could better handle.

Still, Harry felt he had to soften her just a bit, to perhaps suggest she modify her assumptions until the facts could be

presented. "I'm sorry to hear about your financial difficul-
ties, but—"

Her fist smacked the tabletop, causing him to jump. "Why
should my sister have to settle for less than the college of her
choice, just because my father was too low, too deceitful to
own up to his responsibilities? Why should he get off leaving
the entire burden to me...I mean, my mother?"

Harry heard the slip, of course, but he let it pass. All he
knew about Charlie's mother was what Dalton had shared,
and he imagined from what he'd heard, Charlie's life hadn't
been an easy one. That had been one of the biggest motiva-
tors for Dalton, the main reason why he'd refused to give up
the search. He'd worried endlessly for the well-being of his
daughters.

The dogs chose that propitious moment to want in, giving
Harry a few minutes to think. He automatically went into
his laundry room first to get an old towel, then opened the
back door and knelt down. The dogs, well used to the routine,
waited while Harry cleaned their muddy paws.

Charlie gawked at him. "Do you do that every time they
go out?"

"When necessary, yes. I have fastidious dogs."

"Gee, I wonder where they get it from?"

There was just enough sarcasm in her tone to tell Harry
she was nettled. Very slowly, he looked up at her. "You're not,
perchance, making fun of my animals, are you?"

Her brows lifted.

"Because while I'll accept aspersions thrown at me, I don't
take kindly to insults of my pets."

She rolled her eyes. "You're defending an old collie, a mutt
and an alley cat?"

His eyes narrowed and she muttered, "All right. Sorry."

She didn't look overly sincere. In fact, she still looked
angry. Well, there was nothing he could do about it, not yet
at least.

Harry reseated himself. Sooner lay on the floor, resting his head on Harry's feet. Grace went to her dish to eat. "Perhaps your father has a legitimate excuse—"

"Ha! If he does, then he can damn well keep it to himself, because I'm not interested in hearing it. Years ago I might have…" Her voice trailed off and she looked away. Sooner stared at her, picked up on her distress, and abandoned his master to go lick her hand. Charlie smiled and scratched his head.

After an audible swallow, she continued. "All I want to know is if he's got any money, if I can count on him to do the right thing. He owes it to my sister to help her, to give her the opportunity to do her best in this world."

Harry saw her stubborn pride, her visible struggle to keep herself together. Something inside him softened, and that tender feeling made him uneasy. "What about you? Doesn't he owe you, too, Charlie?"

She stared him straight in the eye and said, "If it was just me, I'd gladly survive in the gutter with the moldy rats before giving him the time of day."

Well. Harry leaned back in his seat, nonplussed. She certainly had a visual way of getting her point across. "Things aren't always as they seem, you know."

She stood, and both Grace and Sooner flanked her. "If you don't want to help out, that's fine. But spare me the lectures on goodwill. My charitable attitude died a long time ago."

She turned away and the dogs followed, forming a small parade. Harry felt abandoned and left his seat to hurry after them. Since his legs were so long, he only had to hurry for two steps. "Where are you going?"

"To call a cab. It's time for me to head home."

"Charlie." He caught her arm and turned her back around to face him. But she looked up at him, and her face was so innocent, despite her bravado, her eyes dark and searching, he felt that damn tender feeling swell up again. It seemed to explode inside him, filling him up, choking him when he hadn't even touched his cursed coffee.

He released her and backed up. The dogs frowned at him, but with the facts of her parentage dropped at his feet, all carnal tendencies would have to be forgotten. He couldn't see her as a sexual being, as a woman he wanted so badly his muscles ached. No, she was the daughter of his friend, a man who'd always been like a father figure to Harry. Touching her would mean betraying Dalton, and he couldn't do that.

Charlie was definitely off-limits.

That little truism annoyed his libido and gnawed at his control, but he stiffened his resolve.

He shook his head, verifying to himself, if not to her, that he couldn't, *wouldn't,* be tempted. Not now. "I'll drive you home. You can't very well get into a cab alone this time of night, especially not dressed like that."

She summoned a look of such scorn, he felt his ears burn. "I know how to take care of myself, Harry. I've been doing it most of my life. You can rest easy. Your duty is over."

He looked down his nose at her, being deliberately intimidating, which sent the dogs slinking off, though the effect on her seemed minimal. "Your shoulders are too narrow to support such an enormous chip, Charlie. No, don't flog me with your insults. I *am* taking you home and that's all there is to it. Since I'm of a greater size, and you're rather piddling in comparison, it stands to reason I'm more capable of carrying through with any threats, veiled or otherwise. It'll be better for both of us if whatever you're thinking remains unsaid."

She rolled her eyes. "Half the time, Harry, I have no idea what the hell you're saying."

"And…," he added, knowing he was jumping into a muddy creek when he had no idea how deep it might be, "I will check into things for you."

There, he'd committed himself. But even as he'd reluctantly uttered the ill-fated words, Harry wondered what else he could possibly have done. He couldn't just let her leave; Dalton would never forgive him. He'd looked for his children, spent a small fortune on the chore, for a great many years. Now here was his daughter, despising Dalton without knowing him, resenting him on hearsay, condemning him without knowing all the details, and Harry had the chance to find out where she lived, to assure Dalton that his daughters were alive and thriving.

He thought of everything at stake, and added softly, "Please, Charlie."

It was the "please" that did it, causing the rigidity in her shoulders to relax, her attitude to soften enough that she could agree. "Oh, all right," she muttered, without an ounce of feigned graciousness. "I suppose it doesn't make sense to give up what I want just because I'm pissed off."

She was certainly direct. "Ah...exactly." He retrieved her jeans and found her another jacket to keep her warm on the ride to her place. They both said goodbye to the dogs, who wanted badly to go along but Harry explained to them there wasn't room. "Just guard the place until I come home."

The dogs went back to sleeping in their self-appointed spots.

Ted was nowhere to be found.

"He sulks when it's dark," Harry explained, "because more than anything, he likes lazing around in the sunshine. When there is none, Ted hides. Which is good, because when he doesn't hide, he makes his discontent known to everyone."

Charlie gave him a soft, feminine look that took him completely off-guard. "You're very good to them, Harry."

He didn't like that look, didn't want her thinking soft, feminine things about him, not when he couldn't do anything about it. So he hustled her out to the parking garage where he kept his car before temptation could get the better of him, or before she could start disagreeing with him again. She truly was a most contrary woman.

He worried about her being barefoot, but he certainly had no shoes that would stay on her small feet, and she'd disdained the socks he offered her. Luckily, the complex was kept tidy, with nothing strewn about the grounds to injure her tender skin. No broken glass or debris.

She had very cute feet.

"You know, Harry, I figured you'd left your car at the grocery today."

Distracted from her pink toes—hardly a source of sexual stimulation, even if his body tended to disagree—he looked up at her and made a face. "My car wouldn't have survived three minutes parked at that curb. I took a taxi. What about you?"

"The bus. Cabs are a little out of my price range."

As he stopped next to his car, a shiny black Jaguar convertible, she dug in her bare heels, stiffened up again, and whistled low. "*These* are your wheels?"

"Yes." He noticed her horrified expression and patiently asked, "Now what's the problem?"

She turned to him, beautiful blue eyes wide, jaw dropped. "I can't afford you! First that luxury town house, and now this. You must make a killing as a P.I. to afford this car. I mean, these suckers go for over fifty grand a pop!"

Her phraseology alternately amused and irritated him, but her meaning was always quite clear. After another heartfelt sigh, Harry opened the door and practically thrust her inside. "Put on your seat belt." He closed the door, circled the car and slid behind the wheel.

Her frown was ferocious. "I mean it, Harry. We need to reevaluate here. I thought it'd cost a few hundred bucks at the most to get your help. I had no idea—"

The car started with a throaty purr. "I'm not charging you, Charlie."

He was in the middle of backing up when she opened her

car door and literally leaped out. He slammed on the brakes. "What in the name of—"

She leaned in and growled across the seat, "I don't take charity, Harry Lonnigan!" He opened his mouth, and she said, "And before you bother sighing again, let me tell you, this is *not* negotiable!"

Since Harry had lost all semblance of patience, he barked, "Fine. Have it your way. But a few hundred will more than cover it, so get your sweet little posterior back in the damn car!" He ended on a shout, and shouting was something Harry had seldom done since his divorce. He liked it that way, liked his life calm and orderly, dished up to his specific design, without interruptions and disturbances and ill-mannered females throwing things into a whirlwind and stirring up unaccountable lust.

He sucked in a deep breath, sought for lost control, and continued in a forced icy-polite tone, "I have inherited money from my father, and that's how I bought the car. Now, will you please quit making a spectacle of yourself and let me drive you home?"

She gingerly reseated herself, as if the leather seat could bite her. She also looked around the garage, then snorted at him. "I can hardly be a spectacle when there's no one here to see."

"I'm here, and your show is beyond distressing. A little decorum wouldn't kill you, you know."

She relatched her seat belt, then waited until they'd entered the nearly abandoned roadway before saying, "So you come from a rich family, huh? I could have guessed that."

Harry looked at her with acute dislike. His father had been rich, and he'd also been unfeeling. He'd given Harry very little during his life, certainly no real emotion or pride or concern. Taking his wealth after his death had been beyond difficult. At first, all Harry'd wanted to do was give it away. But Dalton convinced Harry to accept his father's legacy, to acknowledge and use the one thing his father had been capable of sharing.

He didn't discuss his father with anyone but Dalton, certainly not with a woman he'd only known a day, a woman who seemed to take pleasure in pricking him, both his mind and his body. "You're an irritant, Charlie. Now would you like to give me directions or should I try guessing?"

"Go to the corner of Fifth and Elm. You can see my bar from there. It's called the Lucky Goose. There's a big sign hanging out front, painted in lime green."

That description alone was enough to make his stomach queasy. "You must be joking."

"Nope." She sent him an impish smile and added, "Lime is the dominant shade in our decorating scheme. Not too long ago, I had to replace several things, and I found a lot of stuff at an auction, real cheap."

"Whenever something is 'real cheap,' there's usually a viable reason why."

She laughed. "You're right about that. The lime is almost enough to make you toss your breakfast, especially with so much of it. But the men who frequent my bar aren't out for the fashionable ambiance. They're there to drown their supposed woes, and as long as they have a stool to sit on and a glass in front of them, they can forgive anything else. And to be real honest with you, the color's kind of grown on me. I figure if I ever get far enough ahead, I'll add some black accent pieces. That'd look good, don't you think? Sort of classy? Black and lime?"

Harry shuddered with the image. *I'll tell Dalton how witty Charlie is, how spunky, how energetic. I'll simply leave out her appalling lack of taste.* When she continued to stare at him, waiting for his response, Harry forced a smile. "Yes, charming."

She beamed at him.

"Tell me about your sister."

"What about her?"

"I don't know. Anything, everything. Does she help you in the bar, things like that."

Charlie turned to look out the window. "Jillian just turned eighteen. She's beautiful, so intelligent she scares me sometimes, sweet, giving. She's also naive and a worrier." Charlie turned back to face him, her expression earnest. "And no, I would never let her work in the bar. That's why I need the money so she can go to college. She's gotten some partial academic scholarships, but not enough to foot the whole bill. If I left it up to her, she'd put off going for a year and save the difference herself, and even then, she'd have to settle for a less expensive college, and she'd lose the partial scholarships. I don't want her to have to do that. She's worked too hard all these years, keeping her grade average up, excelling in all her classes. She deserves the best, and one way or another, she's going to have it."

It was that *one way or another* that had Harry worried.

They rode the rest of the way in companionable silence. The late moon was partially hidden by clouds, not a star in sight. The near empty roads were still wet and the tires made a slick hissing sound that could lull a turbulent mind.

And then that damn glaring green sign jumped out at him. Charlie hadn't told him it was framed with a neon green gaslight. The color was so bold, it seemed to throb in nauseating waves through the darkness. Cautiously, surveying the area, Harry pulled up to the curb. He swallowed hard, not wanting to ask but knowing he had to. "So, this is the bar. But where do you live?"

"Upstairs." She unhooked her seat belt. "When I bought the place, the second floor was empty, so I converted it into an apartment. My mother was already sick then, so I needed to work close to her and Jillian. The setup is great, though I wasn't crazy about having Jillian at a bar. But the stairs leading up are just inside the door, so Jillian doesn't have to come all the way into the bar unless she wants to. There's a door at both the bottom and top of the stairs, and they're kept locked. Only Jillian and I have keys. Anybody I see messing around with the door gets tossed out and isn't welcomed back. Since the Lucky Goose is so popular, nobody wants to test me on it."

That strange tenderness swelled in his chest again, making him warm and fidgety. "You're a real tough guy, aren't you, Charlie?"

He said it softly, working the words out around the lump in his throat, but she took him literally. She shoved the door open and climbed out. "I have to be."

She looked surprised when he turned off the engine, stepped out, and activated his car alarm.

"What do you think you're doing?"

Harry grinned. "A gentleman always sees a lady to her door."

She looked nearly frantic with consternation. "I'll agree you're a gentleman, Harry, but I'm hardly a *lady*. You can save your gallantry for someone who'll appreciate it. I don't need to be seen anywhere."

Her denials made that strange tenderness more acute, almost like a pain. She was so used to taking care of herself, with no help at all. She was a small woman, but she gave the impression of being an amazon with her stubborn, forceful attitude. It hurt to think of all she'd been through before perfecting that attitude.

Shaking off the feeling, Harry took her arm and began ushering her reluctantly forward. "You look more than feminine to me." Especially since he knew she wore his silk boxers beneath the long shirt. His palms itched with the need to smooth that slippery material over her sweetly rounded bottom. *No, no, no. Dalton's daughter, Dalton's daughter...* He mentally repeated that litany until his heart calmed.

As they stepped inside the heavy wooden doorway he was

met with dim light, cigarette smoke and a low hum of noise. He looked around with feigned casual interest, when in truth, he felt appalled. He cleared his throat. "I'd very much like to get a peek at your establishment, and to meet this paragon sister of yours, if you wouldn't mind."

"You want to meet Jillian?"

"Is that a problem?"

"No, it's just…why?"

He shrugged, trying to fetch forth a logical excuse that wouldn't make her more suspicious. *So I can describe her to Dalton.* "Because she's your sister, and I'm vastly curious."

Charlie looked doubtful, but just then the door to Harry's left burst open and a tall, slender, very young girl bounded into the hallway. "Charlie!"

Harry had already thrust Charlie behind him and taken a fighter's stance. The girl's eyes widened as she stopped dead in her tracks, one hand lifting to her throat. From behind him, Charlie snickered in a most irritating way.

And Harry muttered, "Ah, hell."

Peeking from around him, Charlie said, "Harry, meet my sister, Jillian. Sis, this is Harry Lonnigan. You'll have to ignore his chivalry, but you did bust out like a tornado. You see, Harry has these odd heroic tendencies, and he was trying to protect me, in case you were a threat."

Harry pulled her around to the front of him and growled, "I am not a hero."

"No? Well, Ted or the dogs might disagree. And you saved me from a pager today, remember? And now you just protected me from my sister." She snickered again, and the sound grated along his raw nerves. "You're either a hero, or you're nuts. Take your pick."

CHARLIE CONTINUED to smile as Jillian cautiously stepped forward, her eyes huge, staring at Harry with absolute awe. Charlie knew the feeling. It seemed every time she looked at him, he impressed her anew. He was just so…big. And so manly and hard and solid. Despite the fine clothes, the immaculate haircut, Harry Lonnigan had an aura of savagery about him.

She liked it.

Harry reached out and gently took Jill's hand. "Never mind your rather disputatious sister here. She seems to take immense enjoyment in plaguing me for no evident reason." Jillian stared, and Harry added, "It's a pleasure to meet you, Jillian."

Jillian licked her lips, glanced sideways at Charlie, and whispered, "What did he say?"

Charlie laughed. "Who knows? He always talks funny, but it seems to be getting worse as the night goes on. I think he needs to get some sleep and recharge his wits."

Jillian nodded, then turned back to Harry. She clasped his hand with both of hers. "Thank you so much for bringing my sister home safe and sound. She tends to get herself into trouble awfully easy, but from what she told me, she topped herself tonight."

Harry nodded. "Hmm. Her intentions are good, but she appears to be misguided by too much pride and bravado."

"Yep, that's Charlie. I tried to talk her out of doing something so stupid, but—"

"Jill."

Jill smiled. "Would you like to come up for a drink? I was just making some hot chocolate."

"Jillian…"

"Thank you, I'd love to," Harry said, cutting off Charlie's protest. "Hot chocolate sounds like perfection."

Charlie rubbed her head. "Harry, don't you think it's getting kind of late?"

He glanced at his wristwatch. "Very. What time do you close the bar?"

"At two. And as soon as I change, I have to check on things. So really, it'd be better—"

He gave her his back. "Jillian, if you'd like to lead the way, I'll drink my hot chocolate and then head home. Charlie's absolutely correct that it's been a rather full day."

Jill smiled. "Follow me."

Eyes narrowed, Charlie stomped along behind them up the silent stairwell. When they reached the top, Jill used the key hanging from her wrist to unlock the door. She said over her shoulder to Harry, "The doors automatically lock when they shut."

"Good idea. Are you ever bothered by the noise downstairs?"

"Not at all. I'm used to it."

"And the patrons respect your privacy?"

"Patrons?" Jill giggled as she headed down another hall and into the kitchen, the first room on the left at the top of the landing. Water already boiled in a softly whistling teapot, so Charlie got down three mugs and the tin of chocolate powder. Jillian dug three spoons from the drawer. "I'd hardly call the guys who hang out here 'patrons.'"

"No? Then what would you call them?" Harry seated himself at the Formica table and crossed his long legs. He looked entirely too much at his leisure to suit Charlie, especially when she noted him looking around, surveying their small but tidy kitchen.

Jill shrugged. "I don't know. Regulars? I suppose that's the nicest thing I can come up with. Oh, really, they're not all bad. But as Charlie has always told me, we attract a certain clientele here at the Lucky Goose, and it doesn't include anyone who's too discriminating."

Charlie finished stirring in the chocolate and handed Harry his cup. He sipped, made appropriate sounds of approval, then leaned back in his chair. "Do you ever go into the bar?"

"Are you kidding? Charlie has fits if I even peek in there

after four o'clock. Before that, it's pretty tame, just a few guys hanging around, usually getting a sandwich and a beer. She doesn't mind if I'm in there then. But the rowdiest crowds don't start until after seven."

"What time do you open?"

"Charlie opens it up from two in the afternoon to two in the morning. She's got things pretty organized and we get a pretty steady crowd."

Harry made a pretense of drinking his chocolate, but Charlie could easily see the crafty interest in his gaze. "Those are long hours to work. What other employees do you have?"

Waving a hand, Jill commented, "Charlie likes to keep things simple, so she doesn't hire in much help. She does almost everything herself, which means she works much more than she should."

"So it seems."

"The only relaxation she gets is in the tub. I swear, she'll soak for hours. There've been a few times she's fallen asleep in there—"

"Jill." Charlie could feel the heat pulsing in her face.

Twin dimples showed in her sister's cheeks when she grinned, proving Charlie's warnings did little good.

"We have a bouncer, of course, who also serves as a bartender on occasion. Then there's the regular bartender, and two women who help serve drinks during the busiest hours. Other than them, we have a few part-timers who fill in every now and then."

"Do you have need of the bouncer very often?"

"Nope." Jill leaned forward and dropped her tone to a conspiratorial whisper. "If you saw the guy Charlie hired, you'd know why. He's a real sweetheart, but no one seems to know that, and given his handicap and the way he always—"

Charlie interrupted, thumping her mug of chocolate onto the table and spilling a bit. "That's enough, Jill." She didn't want Harry getting the idea she had an overly soft heart, but if Jill had her way, she'd start telling stories that could give anyone the wrong impression. Her sister had a way of slanting the perspective to always put Charlie in a very rosy light.

She narrowed her gaze at Harry. "Okay, give. Why the third degree?"

After another long drink of his chocolate, Harry pretended confusion. "I have no idea what you're talking about. I was only making idle chitchat."

"Chitchat? Is that what you call it?" She glanced at Jill, who looked horrified by her sister's sudden rudeness, and explained, "Harry's a P.I. Snooping is his business."

Fascinated, Jill stared.

Harry raised a supercilious eyebrow. "Actually, I investigate. I do not snoop."

"Uh-huh. So why snoop here? I'm paying you to check on my father, not to pry into my personal life."

Jill groaned. "Oh, Charlie, you didn't? I thought we agreed! There's no reason—"

"Don't start being dramatic, Jill." In an aside to Harry, she explained, "Jill is prone to melodrama, no doubt because of her age."

Harry made a rude sound to that. "More likely due to her sister's penchant to get into trouble."

"Harry—"

"No, don't berate me. My brain is tired and I really do need to head home." He finished off the chocolate, stood, then took Jill's hand once again. "It's amazing your hair is still brown and not gray. I swear, while I was with her today, I could feel the gray hairs struggling to sprout."

Jill giggled. "She has a way about her."

"Indeed."

"She's also the very best sister in the world."

"I got that impression."

"That's enough out of both of you!" Charlie circled the table and stood toe to toe with Harry. She had to bend her head way back to meet his gaze. "When do you think you'll know something?"

He cocked a brow. "I know an abundance of things, Charlie. Can you be more specific?"

She ground her teeth together. "When, exactly, do you think you'll be able to give me some info on my father? I don't mean to rush you, but I don't want to wait too long, either."

"Patience," Jill muttered as she put Harry's mug in the sink, "is not one of Charlie's strong suits."

She was ready to refute that when Harry touched her cheek with two fingers. "I'll get back to you just as soon as I can. Try not to worry, okay?"

She gulped, feeling that simple touch all the way to her bare toes and back up again. "Can you…maybe give me a ballpark guess?"

He smiled. "I'll tell you what. Give me your phone number and I'll call you tomorrow evening. By then I should be able to have a better idea, okay?"

Charlie hurried to a drawer to pull out a pen and paper. "I'll give you our personal number, for here in the apartment, and the number for the Lucky Goose. You should be able to reach me at one or the other."

Harry slid the slip of paper into his back pocket. "Jill, thank you for the drink."

"Thank you, Harry, for bringing Charlie home in one piece."

"That was my pleasure. Well, at least part of the time. There was the occasional moment when—"

With a shove, Charlie started him on his way. She knew he was laughing, but she didn't mind. She walked him down the stairs and with every step, her heart thumped heavily. She was so acutely aware of him beside her, tall and strong and warm. When they reached the end of the stairwell, Charlie still one step above him, putting her on more even ground, she caught his arm before he could open the door.

He turned to face her, his look questioning.

She cleared her throat. His biceps were large and thick and she knew even both her hands wouldn't circle him completely. She lightly caressed him and her breathing hitched. She was so damn ignorant about this sort of thing. "Harry, I really do appreciate all you did tonight. Not that I couldn't have handled it on my own—"

"But it was nice to have the company? My sentiments exactly."

She tilted her head, searching for the right words. This entire situation was awkward for her, because she'd never really wanted anyone before. "I know you said you don't want to get involved, and I feel the same way."

His entire expression softened. "Charlie—"

"No, you don't need to explain. I understand. But…"

"But what?"

His voice was low, the words gentle. She could feel him looking down at her, and so she mustered her courage, looked him straight in the eye, and said, "But I want you. There. I said it."

He stared, shock plain on his face, and she took advantage of it, throwing herself against him. She felt his arms automatically catch her, and she kissed him while his mouth was still open in surprise. He was motionless only a moment, then he turned, pinned her to the wall, and with a low deep groan, proceeded to kiss her silly.

CHAPTER SIX

HARRY ENTERED the hospital with his heart in his throat and his pulse racing. The day, which had begun with no indications of a catastrophe, continued to slide rapidly downhill. Actually, he thought, he was well into a new day. Surely things would begin improving, surely Dalton would be all right.

A nurse directed him to the CCU, or coronary care unit, and the name alone made Harry break out in a sweat. *A heart attack,* Dalton had suffered a heart attack. He felt sick with anxiety and throbbing guilt.

It took him mere seconds to reach the right room, and as soon as he was close enough, he could hear Dalton complaining. He increased his pace, rushed into the room, then came to a standstill.

Dalton, pale and obviously agitated, was in a sterile white bed, oxygen hooked up to his nose, other apparatus connected in various places. He fought to sit up while a nurse struggled to keep him still. Harry drew himself up and said, "What is going on here?"

The nurse looked at him with utter and complete relief, then asked hopefully, "Harry Lonnigan?"

"Yes." He stepped forward and nudged her out of the way, giving Dalton a glare. "Be still."

Dalton rested back with a smile.

The nurse heaved a heartfelt sigh of relief. "He needs to be resting, but he was insistent on seeing you. I told him we'd left a message for you, but when you couldn't be reached, he wanted to get out of bed and try calling you himself—"

"I'm sorry for the delay. The storm knocked out my answering machine and I didn't receive any message." He frowned at Dalton. "I called your house and the housekeeper told me what happened. I got here as quickly as I could."

Dalton gripped his hand. "She contacted me, Harry."

Harry looked down at the man he loved like a father and winced. Dalton was still good-looking at fifty-nine, tall, lean, with only a smidge of gray mixed in with his dark hair. He'd always looked so vital to Harry, but now, he looked shrunken and frail. "Who contacted you?"

"My daughter."

Everything in Harry jolted. His wits jumped about hither and yon, his heart thumped. He cast a quick glance at the nurse, then squeezed Dalton's hand. To the nurse he asked, "Can I speak with you in just a moment? I'd like to be updated—"

She patted Harry's arm. "Get your father settled, then come out. I'll be at the nurses' station. But please—" and she bent a warning look on Dalton "—he needs to be still and calm."

Harry nodded. "I'll see to it. And thank you."

The nurse went out, closing the door behind her. Harry hadn't bothered explaining to her that Dalton wasn't his father. In all the most important ways, he'd been the only father Harry knew.

The room was silent, with an acoustical ceiling and floor, good lighting, and a variety of electrical, suction, and other outlets. Monitors were hooked up to Dalton, and other assorted machinery sat at the ready. Overall, it should have been a distressing sight, but to Harry, it showed the competent level of emergency care available, giving him a sense of security. Dalton wouldn't die. He was well cared for here.

Harry scooted a narrow chair closer to Dalton's bed and seated himself. He had a feeling a lot had happened that he wasn't aware of.

Dalton gave him a shaky smile. "I got a letter from my daughter today. The oldest one, Charlotte." His smile widened. "She's a gutsy little gal. Do you know what she said? She said I owed her a lot of back child support and she wanted to claim it. She said she *would* claim it. What about that?"

Harry winced, both at the name Dalton called his daughter, and the irony of the situation. So Charlie had sent her father a letter. That was likely her reason for being in the store in the first place. She'd been waiting, Harry remembered, peeking out the window on occasion. And Dalton's jewelry store was directly across the street from the grocery. The little witch. Had she hoped to see her father's reaction?

Would she be happy with the results?

He no sooner thought it than he shook off the disturbing notion. Charlie wanted what she considered her due, but she didn't strike him as the type to wish actual harm on anyone. Well, except maybe Floyd.

Dalton cleared his throat. "The girls...they're alone now. Charlotte told me in the letter that her mother recently passed away."

"I'm sorry, Dalton."

"It was a hell of a shock, reading that letter and knowing in my gut what my girls have gone through. Rose wasn't much when she was around, but she was still their mother. Damn, if only I could have found them."

Harry wondered where to begin, but before he could finish formulating his thoughts, Dalton actually laughed. "Here I was, watching for a sign from you, then that damn letter arrived. I could hardly believe it—liked to stop my heart."

Oh God. "From what your housekeeper told me, it almost did stop your heart."

"Ha! Now that I know I'm this close to getting my girls back, there's no way I'm going to let a little heart trouble stop me."

Harry stared at Dalton, that *ha!* sounding all too familiar.

He wondered if Charlie had inherited the blunt expletive from her father.

"No sir," Dalton continued, full of vehemence. "I'm going to make it up to them, everything they missed out on because I wasn't there. But Harry, I still don't know where they are. The letter didn't say. So I was hoping you could…"

Harry decided before he could say anything, he needed all the details on Dalton's condition. He patted the older man's hand, then slowly stood to pace. "Everything will work out, Dalton, you'll see. As soon as I find out about you, we'll talk about the letter and what to do next, okay?"

"Damn right we'll talk about it. It's all I can think about."

"You need to rest, you know, if you want a chance to meet Charli—Charlotte." He barely caught himself, then shook his head. "Promise me you'll sit there quietly until I get back."

Dalton made a face. "What choice do I have? They've got me connected to so many wires, they know if I'm going to burp before I even do it!"

"Good. I like it that way. Now sit tight and I'll be right back."

It took Harry about ten minutes to find out that Dalton had suffered a mild heart attack, although *mild* wasn't really descriptive of the condition. Dalton had evidently suffered some discomfort through the night, including dizziness, but being the stubborn cuss Harry knew him to be, he'd ignored the problems, determined to be at the shop that day to observe Harry's meeting with Floyd and Ralph.

The nurse didn't know what had upset Dalton, only that a customer had called the paramedics when he'd turned deathly pale and grew nauseous. They took an EKG as soon as he reached the hospital, and then had to insist that Dalton not leave when they found evidence of a heart attack. He kept claiming he had important things to do.

Harry had to shake his head. What rotten timing for Dalton.

The nurse explained that a cardiologist on call had been in to see Dalton, and that they would continue monitoring him throughout the night. He had no prior history of problems and was basically a healthy man. In the morning they'd check his cardiac enzymes and see how his heart rhythm had done through the night, which would tell them more.

Though the nurse was reassuring, Harry still worried. It took him another five minutes to figure out what he wanted to say to Dalton about Charlie, censoring it in his mind so as not to upset him further. Such an awful situation. He could almost be angry at Charlie, except that her life hadn't been an easy one, and she'd obviously been led to believe her father hadn't cared. Under those circumstances, she could hardly be blamed for her actions.

Dalton's face was turned away, staring out a window when Harry returned. He immediately turned to face him, and that damn smile was back on his face. "You need to read the letter, Harry. It's in my pants pocket, over there in the cabinet. Take it home with you for safekeeping."

Harry retrieved the letter and stuck it in his pocket. "I'll take care of the letter, Dalton, don't worry about that. But first I need to tell you something."

Dalton blinked. "Well, damn, I'd forgotten all about Floyd and Ralph and those other idiots. How did it go? You didn't have any trouble with them, did you? I got that damn letter, had the attack and the next thing I knew I was in here and no one would listen to me when I said I had to call you."

"I'm really sorry about that. You know if I'd gotten the message, nothing could have kept me away."

"Of course I know it. That's why I was worried about you when you didn't show up right away."

Harry swallowed hard. "I have to tell you something, Dalton."

"Out with it. I'm not so delicate I'll swoon, you know."

"Well, to come right to the point, I met your daughter today."

Dalton lurched, he was so surprised, and Harry rushed to soothe him. "Settle down now before they throw me out of here."

"But I don't understand! You met her? Where?"

"In the grocery. She was there, evidently waiting to see your reaction to her letter, though I didn't know she'd sent a letter. I didn't…ah, find out she was your daughter until much later."

"This is incredible!"

"Yes, I know." Harry didn't mean to sound facetious, but the whole situation was too ironic. That last kiss that Charlie had forced on him—forced, ha!—had damn near killed him. He'd forgotten himself, and within a heartbeat he'd had her pressed against the stairwell wall, her small hands clutching him, her hips squirming against his, inciting his lust, making him hard. Damn. Even now he gasped with the pleasure of it. Never in his adult years had he been hit by so much uncontrollable lust. He'd tasted Charlie and wanted to go on tasting her, everywhere, all over her small sweet body. He could have spent hours doing just that.

He shook, remembering.

He'd been a hairsbreadth away from taking her right there in the stairwell, and probably would have if a commotion in the bar hadn't jolted him out of his lust-induced stupor.

After that, he'd all but run from her. And she'd actually had the gall to laugh at his predicament.

He shook his head, wondering how he was ever going to be able to handle this absurd situation. A reluctant smile caught him unawares. "She's something else, Dalton. A little bitty thing, barely reaching my shoulder."

"Everyone just barely reaches your shoulder, Harry. You're what we average people call *tall*."

"She's shorter than most, though. But you're right about the guts. Ralph and Floyd tried to intimidate her, but she easily got the best of them. Calling her fearless would be a gross understatement."

Dalton shuddered. "Thank God you were there to keep her safe. If those hoodlums had hurt her…"

Harry had a feeling she might have done just fine on her own. Under no circumstances would he tell Dalton that she'd been dressed as a boy—or that he was the one who'd inadvertently blown her cover.

Dalton drew a slow breath. "When I last saw her, she was nine, missing a few teeth, skinny as a twig, and loved football much more than dolls. Her mother kept her hair cut short so she wouldn't have to spend time working the tangles out. If I remember it right, Charlotte begged her to do the cutting. She was the epitome of the American tomboy. Of course, she's a young lady now, so none of that matters.

"I worked too many long days back then, and I missed out on so much. Then I caught her mother cheating, found out it wasn't even the first time, and when I sued for divorce, the witch ran off with my kids."

Harry left the chair to sit on the side of the bed. He clasped Dalton's shoulder. "You can explain it all to her now, Dalton. She'll understand. From the time I spent with her, I can tell she inherited her father's intelligence."

"Did she mention me at all?"

This was the tough part, but Harry didn't see any way around a few truths. "As a matter of fact, she wanted to hire me to find out more about you."

"No fooling?" Dalton seemed pleased by his daughter's curiosity.

Harry nodded. "I didn't say I already knew you. I wanted to give you the chance to tell her everything yourself."

"Did you…you know, get a feel for what she thinks of me? What her mother might have told her about me?"

Harry hesitated, unsure just how far he could stretch the truth.

"Out with it, Harry." He grinned. "From her note, I'm already assuming she has a healthy chip on her shoulder where I'm concerned. And knowing her mother the way I did, I can easily guess at how she probably lied about me."

Helpless, Harry admitted, "I think that's more the case than not. Charlie seemed under the impression you'd abandoned them."

"Charlie?"

"That's the name she goes by."

"Ridiculous! She has a lovely name."

Harry kept his opinion in check. By his way of thinking, *Charlie* suited her much better than the too reserved *Charlotte*. Of course, Dalton wasn't reacquainted with her, so couldn't yet know that.

"Did she mention Jillian at all?"

Ah, safer ground. "Actually, I met her. It's a long story, and no, get that look out of your eye because I'm not telling it right now. You've had enough excitement for one day."

"Tyrant."

"I promise to fill you in on all the details tomorrow. But as to Jillian, she's a lovely girl. Eighteen now, and the opposite of Charli—Charlotte. Tall, light brown hair. But the same blue eyes."

Dalton's blue eyes crinkled at the corners with a huge smile. "I have an idea, Harry."

Harry rubbed his forehead with a sigh. The past several hours had depleted him sorely. He needed some sleep, he needed something to eat.

He needed Charlie.

His head snapped up with that errant thought, and he coughed. "Dalton, I'm sure if I go to her now and tell her what's happened—"

"No! You can't do that. Why, she might blame herself for

my ill health. Finding out the truth, that I didn't leave her, is going to be enough of an adjustment. She'll know her mother lied all along, that she kept us apart out of sheer spite. That'd be tough for any young lady to accept, especially now that Rose is gone and can't admit the truth."

"Dalton, this particular young lady is tougher than shoe leather. Really. I don't think—"

"No. I tell you, it'd be too much. And if she thought she caused my heart attack—which of course she didn't—"

"Of course not," Harry agreed with wry cynicism.

"—she just might run off again. I can't take that chance, now that I'm so close to being reunited with her. She just might leave without giving me time to explain."

From what Harry knew of Charlie, she wasn't going anywhere without enough money to get her sister started in the college of her choice. The woman could vie with a herd of mules and come out ahead on stubbornness.

"No," Dalton continued, thinking out loud, "a better idea will be if you pretend to work for her."

"What?"

He rubbed his hands together. "You can soften her up for me, Harry. Leave little hints about the past, pretend to uncover clues about how much I do care for her, to let her know I wasn't just another neglectful father. Then she can get accustomed to the idea little by little. When she's ready, you can arrange a meeting between us."

"You want me to lie to the girl?"

Dalton managed a supreme look of affront. "Not blatant lying, no. Just little white lies, for the good of all of us. Besides, you've already lied to her by not admitting you know me, so don't get sanctimonious on me now."

"Dalton, you're not in the best of health. You've had a really rough day and you're not thinking straight." Besides, Harry wasn't at all certain he could maintain a facade of indifference to Charlie. He wanted her, and being around her while resisting her would be an undeserved hell, especially as she seemed determined to seduce him—when she wasn't doing her best to irritate him.

Dalton slammed his fist down on the side of the bed. "I'm thinking just fine!"

His actions reminded Harry so much of Charlie, how she'd slammed her own smaller fist down on his table, he almost grinned. Stubbornness definitely ran through the genes. Charlie had come by her obstinate nature legitimately. "Okay, so you're impervious to health concerns, wise beyond your years and immortal to boot. I still don't think it's a good idea."

Dalton fell back against his pillows, and Harry again noticed how pale, how drawn he looked. He frowned in concern. "Dalton—"

"No, never mind," Dalton sighed in a pathetically weak voice. "I shouldn't have been such a bother. You're already working on the extortion case for me, and heaven knows that's more than I should have asked of you. Though those young punks are idiots, it could still be dangerous."

Harry could attest to that.

"And now this, dragging you into the middle of my personal affairs." He sighed again, closed his eyes, and looked forlorn and dejected. Even knowing it to be a ruse, Harry couldn't stand it.

He came to his feet and propped his hands on his hips. "You don't play the martyr worth a damn, Dalton, so spare me the theatrics."

Dalton peeked one eye open. "I know that tone. It means you're ready to relent. Right?"

"Yes," Harry said, then groaned. "I suppose I have no choice, given you're lying there in a sickbed and you're not above using it to make me toe the line."

Dalton beamed at him. "You're a real hero, Harry. I don't know what I'd do without you."

"I am not a damn hero!" He felt mired in conflicting

emotions. Regret, because Charlie was now off-limits and he was honor-bound to keep his hands off her delectable little body and his thoughts away from lascivious ventures.

Anticipation, because despite being off-limits, he'd be seeing her again and her spunk and wit never ceased to amaze and amuse him.

He also felt anxiety, because he had no idea how he'd placate her infatuation with him while still keeping her a discreet arm's length away. She seemed determined to seduce him, given that last scorching kiss, and he'd have to find a way to feign disinterest without hurting her.

It was enough to boggle the mind, and Harry's mind, at present, was already overtaxed and sluggish. "I'm a stooge maybe, but never a hero."

"Yeah, well, right now, you look like an exhausted stooge. Why don't you go on home and get some sleep? My God, it's nearly dawn. And with all this excitement, I'm suddenly pretty tired myself."

Alarmed, Harry started forward, only to have Dalton wave him away. "It's not my heart, son, only my age and the excitement. Honest. We'll talk later and go over what you should tell Charlotte. We need a plan of action."

"You think I might have forgotten all your sterling qualities? You think I might not be able to make you sound a veritable icon among men?" Harry tsked. "You should know better, Dalton. I'll sing your praises until she cries mercy."

Somber, Dalton took Harry's hand and squeezed it. "I can't tell you how many times I've wished you were my own son."

Harry felt a lump in his throat that could strangle an elephant. "In all the ways that matter most, you're the only father I've ever had. And a damn good one to boot."

Dalton wiped his eyes, then said gruffly, "Aw, get the hell out of here. You look worse than I do."

Harry laughed. "That's saying a lot." On impulse, he leaned

down and gave Dalton a hug, then straightened and headed for the door. "I'll be back, but in the meantime, I'm giving my home number, cell phone number and pager number to the nurses in case you need me for anything."

"You sure you don't want to leave your social security number, too?"

"If I thought it necessary, I would." He heard Dalton grumble and had to smile. "I mean it, Dalton. If you need me for anything, even conversation, simply call, all right?"

"Don't rush back just to hold my hand. Take care of business instead. I'd rather know you were seeing to my daughters and protecting my friends. Besides, there's a few cute nurses here willing to keep me company. If you hang around, they'll all be looking at you, instead."

Shaking his head, Harry said, "I'll let you know what your daughter thinks of my investigative skills. Even she should be duly impressed, given I'll have found out several remarkable things about you within half a day."

"Make me look real good, son."

"No problem. It'll be a piece of cake."

Or so he wanted Dalton to think. He couldn't abide the idea of causing him undue worry, but he knew from experience that nothing with Charlie would be easy, and she'd be the hardest person in the world to impress, especially where Dalton was concerned.

A reluctant grin curved Harry's mouth as he made his way to the nurses' station. *He would have to spend more time with her.* The decision was out of his hands, his motives altruistic and pure...

It would be a struggle to keep his hands to himself, to keep his thoughts on the straight and narrow. Charlie was just so damn...*cute,* in a perky, twisted, Annie Hall kind of way. He couldn't remember ever being so intrigued by a woman.

He wondered what she'd look like in regular clothes, how she'd dress, how she'd wear her hair.

He also wondered how anyone in his right mind could possibly call such a unique, independent, headstrong woman *Charlotte*. Absurd. Charlie suited her far better. He only hoped Dalton would realize that, to avoid any disappointments.

CHARLIE KNOCKED, but when that didn't bring forth a response, she leaned against the buzzer. Judging by the commotion on the other side of the door, at least the dogs were at home. She really wanted Harry to be in, too, so she could share her news. She needed...

Oh, who was she fooling? She simply wanted to see him again, and when such a good excuse presented itself, she couldn't resist. It was almost noon, so Harry surely was up, despite the late night they'd had. She was amazed she'd managed to wait this long.

Keeping one shoulder on the buzzer, she smoothed her hair, then caught herself and dropped her hand. She was not a prissy person and damn if she'd start acting like one now just because she had the temporary hots for a very urbane gentleman with outlandish diction.

Charlie grinned. Actually, she'd sorta grown used to the way he talked. It was smooth on the ears, certainly not something she was used to when the men at her bar tended to slur and used very crude language.

When the door suddenly opened, she was caught with that outrageous grin still on her face. And Harry, all six feet five inches of him, looked disgruntled. He was—she gulped—wet, and wearing only a towel. The dogs were now quiet, peeking around Harry's bare knees.

His eyes narrowed when he saw her. "Perhaps you're not aware of it, but you're leaning on my doorbell."

Charlie, never to be confused with an idiot, widened her eyes and quickly stepped away from the bell. "Oops! I'm sorry. I didn't realize."

Harry stilled, then slowly looked her over. His gaze lingered on her hair, her breasts, then skimmed down to her feet. She stared back. He stood there blocking his doorway, wearing only a towel, clean shaven. Droplets of water clung to the hair on his chest and trickled through the silky line of hair leading from his navel downward. He smelled of delicious male scents that made heat bloom and curl in her belly. She delicately sniffed the air, breathing him in, then sighed.

His voice was gruff when he said, "You certainly look different out of your male apparel."

Charlie glanced down at her slim-fitting, well-worn jeans, her lace-up brown work boots. Donning a soft, cream-colored sweater was as far as she'd been willing to go to try to impress him with her less than apparent femininity. Anything more, anything as ridiculous as a skirt, would have been too obvious. She wasn't altogether certain she even owned a skirt.

Besides, any efforts to make her look more ladylike would have come across as asinine. She just didn't have the heart for it.

Harry reached out and touched her hair, tugging one curl through his fingers. His cheekbones flushed and he whispered, "Like silk. Warm silk."

Charlie wanted to melt. Oh, the man had a way of saying things that hit the pit of her stomach and radiated out to make her shaky and hot and... She sighed again. If he'd wanted her to, she'd have stood there all day letting him play with her hair. But then his fingers touched on her bullet earring and he suddenly stiffened and stepped back.

"Good heavens. Come in before someone sees you."

"Me? You're the one who's nearly naked."

She walked in, thoroughly greeted by the dogs who went all out by jumping and shaking and appearing happy to see a new face. Harry, however, was already stalking away. He waved vaguely toward the kitchen. "Go make yourself at home and I'll be right back."

Charlie admired the view of his retreating backside. His

shoulders were wide, hard, his spine straight, muscles evident all over the place.

She'd have admired the view even more if he'd dropped the towel. "Don't dress on my account!"

"Brat." He galloped up the steps without looking back. She heard a door slam.

Well, well. He certainly was grouchy this afternoon. Charlie slipped off her lightweight jean jacket, laid it over a chair, and went to investigate the kitchen. The dogs followed on her heels and their nails tapped-tapped on the kitchen tile floor as they danced around her.

She wasn't surprised to find coffee just finished brewing. Remembering how Harry had taken his, she fixed his cup as well as her own. Then she spotted Ted, glaring at her from his seat at the table. She shrugged. "Don't mind me. I'll sit way over here. You won't even know I'm around."

Sooner howled, as if he found that hilariously funny.

Harry returned only seconds later wearing suit pants and buttoning up a blue dress shirt with one hand. In the other hand he carried shoes, socks and a tie.

Charlie raised a brow. "What? You didn't trust me alone in your kitchen? Or did you think Ted and I would be brawling? You had to rush back half-dressed?"

He slanted a frown her way and picked up the coffee cup for a healthy sip. "At least allow the caffeine to penetrate my brain cells before you start sniping. I've had very little sleep, certainly not enough to counteract yesterday's adventures." As if by rote he opened the back door and the dogs darted out.

She hadn't gotten much sleep the night before, either. She'd spent most of the evening staring at the ceiling and thinking of that last kiss. She doubted he'd done the same. Maybe he just slept late when he needed to. She, however, didn't have that luxury, not with the bar to run. "Uh, Harry, are you on your way out?"

"As a matter of fact, yes, so perhaps it would be auspicious for you to explain this unexpected visit?"

"Auspicious, huh? All right, don't get red in the face. I found out some info on our villains."

He froze with the cup to his lips, then slowly lowered it. "I assume you're referring to Floyd and Ralph?"

"Aren't they the only villains we know jointly?"

He frowned, took a large drink as if to fortify himself, and she continued.

"They're going to drop in on Pops again today, so I figured I'd follow them when they leave, just to see where they go, and I wondered if you'd want to tag along to keep me company—"

Coffee spewed across the table, making Charlie jump back a good foot. She growled. "Damn it, Harry, you do seem to have a problem with coffee, don't you?"

He thunked the coffee cup down and took two menacing steps toward her. Ted raced past her with a vicious hissing complaint, but since Harry seemed the bigger threat, she didn't dare look away from him. She widened her stance, braced herself and waited.

Through gritted teeth, he said, "You're not to go anywhere near them, Charlie, is that understood?"

She fetched forth her most direct, intimidating look, and must have succeeded, given his stormy expression. "Uh, Harry. You're not trying to give me orders, are you?"

He stepped closer still, until her neck felt like it might cramp from the drastic angle it took to meet his gaze and his breath hit her face with the force of a puffing bull. "Yes," he said succinctly. "I'm giving you an explicit directive to stay the hell away from anything and anyone that has to do with Ralph and Floyd."

He was so close, she couldn't resist, and leaned just a scant inch closer to smell him, her nose almost touching his chest.

Harry leaped back as if burned. "What do you think you're doing?"

"You smell so good, Harry. If I could bottle you, I'd make a fortune."

He flushed, blustered for a moment, then started in frowning again. "You're trying to distract me, damn it."

Actually, distracting him had never entered her mind. Charlie examined her nails. "They kidnapped me, Harry. They threatened me. You can't expect me to just let them get away with that."

"I told you I'd take care of them."

"Terrific. I'll go along to see that you take care of them right. I haven't forgotten you're the one who was too chicken to push Floyd off the truck."

He looked nearly apoplectic. "You bloodthirsty little... it would have killed him! I do believe I can handle things without resorting to murder."

Charlie sniffed. "He's too mean to die. He'd probably have just gotten his hard head bruised a little."

"Charlie." He clasped her shoulders and shook her lightly. "You don't know what you're playing with."

She wanted to play with him, but he didn't look overly receptive to the idea at the moment. No, he looked like it took all his restraint not to choke her.

"Forget it, Harry. If you're too much a sissy to go with me, I can go alone. No problem."

Choking became a distinct possibility.

After several moments where she held her breath, waiting to see which way the chips would fall, Harry finally released her and stepped away. He picked up his coffee.

She eyed it warily. "Careful. I don't want you to drown yourself."

He drank the rest of the cup in one long swallow, glaring at her over the rim all the while. After he finished the cup, his expression grew crafty. "I have a deal for you, Charlie."

"I'm listening."

"Remove yourself from my business with Floyd and Ralph, and I'll tell you what I've discovered concerning your father."

Her breath left her in a whoosh and she gripped the edge of the table. "You've found out something already?"

He looked down his nose at her. "Quite a few somethings, actually, which is why I didn't get to bed until the early hours of the morning, and why I was just rising when you arrived. Now, do we have a deal or not?"

Charlie weighed her options, decided lying would be the most expedient way to go, and said, "Whatever you say, Harry. Now tell me everything you know."

CHAPTER SEVEN

HARRY STARED AT her hard, but she didn't so much as flinch. Still, he knew without a shadow of a doubt she had no intention of backing away from Ralph and Floyd, despite her rapid agreement.

With a sound of disgust, he dropped into a chair and bent to pull on his socks. "You're lying through your teeth and you aren't even doing it well."

"That's absurd!" She pulled out a chair and sprawled into it. "I'm an *excellent* liar!"

He looked nonplussed for a moment, then laughed. "You're something else, you know that, Charlie?"

He sounded…affectionately exasperated. But then what did she know? She'd never heard honest affection from a man before. And she'd certainly never known a man like Harry. "I like watching you dress, Harry." He glanced up at her, startled, and she smiled. "I think I'd probably like watching you undress, more."

A shoe dropped from his hand, thumping onto the floor. Harry swallowed, made a strangled sound. Charlie eyed him. "Thank God you're not drinking coffee, huh?"

He stared, then jerked his gaze away from her. Furious, he yanked on the rest of his clothes, including a silk tie, then began pacing the kitchen. Glancing at her, he accused, "You've traumatized my cat."

"I'm not the one who can't swallow coffee."

His eyes narrowed. He looked downright harassed, and

he kept checking his watch. The dogs scratched to come in, and again he went through the chore of cleaning their feet. Afterward, the dogs cuddled up to him and got thoroughly petted. He even whispered to them, though she couldn't hear what he said.

Charlie loved watching him with the animals. He was so big, so strong, but so incredibly gentle, too. She remembered the way he'd touched her, how he'd kissed her, and she was instantly jealous of the attention he lavished on his pets.

When Harry stood, Sooner and Grace came over to her for a few pats. Harry watched, his brows down, and he warned, "Don't try to ingratiate yourself with my dogs. I already explained to them how conniving you can be."

She gave each dog an extra hug. "Yeah, well, since they know you, they've probably realized you're just being unreasonable." The dogs didn't agree or disagree, they just went off to sleep.

Charlie crossed her legs and waited. He had news to tell her, but she did her best to look indifferent despite the churning in her belly and her anxiety. She couldn't give him the upper hand.

"Okay, are you interested in knowing what I've discovered or not?"

"What a dumb question! Of course I'm interested." Then in the coolest tone she could manage, she asked, "Do you think he has any money? Will he be able to pay what he owes?"

Charlie watched, fascinated, as Harry's lean jaw hardened, as his muscles bunched and flexed. For a second there she thought his eyes turned red, but then he stepped around her and headed out of the kitchen.

"We'll have to discuss this in transit. I'm late already."

Charlie hustled after him. "Late for what?"

The look he gave her wasn't promising. "I was intending to tail Floyd and Ralph."

Grinning, she skipped to keep up with his long-legged stride. "Then you already knew—"

He held her jean jacket while she slipped it back on, causing her thoughts to jumble. It was a first for her, that small courtesy, and it amused her that even while he was so obviously irritated with her, his unrelenting manners came through.

She leaned back against him as he settled the coat over her shoulders, and he jumped away, grumbling, cautioning her "Charlie…".

"Hmm?"

He frowned, blinked at her, then shook his head. "Come on, let's get going."

Charlie had to hide a smile. He fought her, but he was tempted. Maybe she'd be able to work on that.

Looking decidedly perturbed, Harry pulled on a suit coat, then his raincoat. The dogs stirred themselves enough to look up as Harry said goodbye to them, then they went back to sleeping peacefully. He led her out the door, locking it behind him.

"So, Harry, you did know about the visit Ralph and Floyd have planned?"

"Of course I knew. I'm the P.I., if you'll recall."

"Well, I only found out late last night from a regular. When I went in to close the bar, I overheard two guys talking and I recognized part of what they said. I asked a few questions and found out Ralph and Floyd have been trying to drum up some assistance."

Harry led her to his car and opened her door. "You shouldn't be asking questions, Charlie. What if it gets back to Ralph or Floyd and they figure out where you live? Is that what you want?"

"Of course not. I'm not an idiot, I know what to say and not say. I was careful."

"You don't know the meaning of the word *careful*." He

looked at her long and hard, then touched her cheek. "I don't want to have to worry about you."

Contentment bubbled up inside her. "I don't want to worry about you either, Harry. That's why I thought it'd be nice if we did this together. I mean, considering you're so squeamish about actually hurting anyone." And it'd give her a good excuse to spend more time alone with him.

He dropped his hand and sighed. "Get in the car, Charlie."

"I brought my own transportation. Will you drive me back here?" She'd almost taken the bus today, then realized leaving her truck behind would provide a good excuse to return to his apartment. Her plans weren't exactly orthodox, but then, neither was she.

Her life had never been easy, and she'd learned to be hard and brazen and forceful by necessity, to take care of her mother, to protect her sister. Now, for the first time that she could ever remember, she really wanted a man. She didn't know how to deal with that except to give it her best shot.

Harry rubbed the back of his neck, cursed softly, then asked, "I don't suppose you'll go on home and let me take care of things?"

"Ha! Don't be stupid, Harry."

"No, I didn't think so. All right, yes. I'll bring you back here. But Charlie, promise me you'll do as I tell you. I don't want to drag you along only so you can act recklessly again and end up hurt."

She slid into the stupendous car with the butter-soft leather seats and the smell of money. "I'm never reckless. Quit worrying. You're starting to sound like Jill."

He slammed her car door.

They were five minutes on the road before Charlie said, "All right. Are you waiting for me to beg or what?"

He glanced at her, clearly distracted.

"Harry, what did you find out about my father?"

"Oh, sorry. My mind wandered."

"Where did it wander to?"

He stared hard at the road. "Never mind. Besides, you seemed so disinterested, I wasn't sure you even cared."

She scooted closer to him. "Didn't you sleep well, Harry? You're awfully snide today."

"I slept fine for the short time I had in bed."

Very casually, she touched his thigh. It was hard and warm and the muscles flinched under her palm. She smiled. "Now who's lying?"

He growled, gripped the wheel, then blurted, "By all accounts, your father didn't abandon you."

That was *not* what she'd been expecting to hear. She was so surprised, she sat back on her own side of the seat, releasing Harry. The old resentment rose to the surface, and her tone was sharper than she intended when she said, "No? He had amnesia and forgot he had children? He was taken prisoner in a foreign country and only just got free? It's been eighteen years since I've seen him or heard from him, Harry. I'd pretty much call that abandoned."

Harry sighed, then incredibly, reached for her hand. "Honey, he tried to find you. He really did."

He called her *honey*. She felt all warm and mushy inside again. Clearing her throat, she asked, "How do you know that?"

"He's worked at that same jewelry store for some time now, so a lot of the other proprietors are familiar with him. Many of them told me he's spent years looking for his daughters, that even now he hasn't given up hope of finding you."

She tried to pull her hand away, but he held her tight. "Charlie, he cares about you and Jill."

Charlie swallowed down the unfamiliar lump of emotion in her throat. Even if what he said was true, it didn't matter. "Concern and caring from a father back when I...I had to work two jobs and my mother was so sick and Jill got cheated out of Christmas twice would have been real nice. But I don't care anymore about that. All I want from him now is enough money to get Jill through college. Does he have money, Harry?"

Harry sighed, and she snapped, "Oh, stop that! You're forever sighing, like you're so put-upon whenever we're together."

He fought a smile. "I'm sorry. I suppose it's just that I expected that answer from you, and I'll admit I'm disappointed. Charlie, your father can't help it if your mother took off and he couldn't find you."

She snorted. "How hard did he try? True, we moved around a lot. I remember that, mostly because it made it so damn difficult for me to get Jill settled. But even so, a single woman with two children should be easy enough to track down. The school records alone—"

"Did you go to public schools?"

"Yeah, well...come to think of it, we almost always settled in real small towns."

"How small?"

She forced a casual shrug. "Almost nonexistent. The schools were independently run by the townsfolk, since there usually wasn't more than a handful of kids attending." She felt a twinge of doubt, but ruthlessly shoved it aside. She would not be suckered that easily. Dalton Jones had a lot to account for. "We chose small towns because the housing was generally cheaper, not because it was a good way to hide!" She hated her own feelings of defensiveness, and added, "It made finding an after-school job almost impossible. At least, until I got older."

His large thumb brushed over her knuckles, gently, soothing. "Where did you work, Charlie?"

She stared at their linked hands and marvelled that such a simple touch could make her feel so funny. Funny in a very *nice* way. "When I was twelve, I got a job helping out at a market stand. It was seasonal, but I loved it. Being outside, meeting so many people. And I didn't have to dress up. In one town, my mom got me a job helping this old lady out at her boutique. I hated it. She expected me to wear dresses."

Harry laughed. "You're not into female frippery?"

"Can you imagine me in a dress, Harry? It's ridiculous." She stupidly blushed just thinking about it. But whenever she talked about that time of her life, she felt vulnerable. She'd been out of her element, and it had been the first time she'd realized just how different she was, and what a disappointment she was to her mother.

He sobered, then pulled up to a red light. "I think you'd look very nice in a dress, but no more so than you do in those snug jeans."

Her heartbeat tripped. "You…uh, like my jeans?"

He kept his gaze deliberately on the road. "You're very attractive, Charlie, regardless of what you're wearing. Surely men tell you that often?"

She wrinkled her nose. "I work in a bar, Harry. Men tell me a lot of things, but I don't pay much attention to slurred words and suggestive innuendo."

"Will you pay attention to me?"

She felt flushed and drew a slow deep breath. "Since you haven't been drinking all day, and your words are coherent, then sure. I suppose so."

He looked undecided for a moment, then turned to face her. "You're beautiful." Their gazes locked, and Charlie felt drawn in, surrounded by his attention. His hand released hers, but then lifted to her cheek. He smoothed the back of his knuckles over her cheekbone in a very tender gesture, tucked a curl behind her ear. She could get very used to being touched so tenderly. "You don't need any frills to turn a man on, Charlie."

"Really?"

He continued to touch her, small touches that elicited so

many feelings. "I think you're one of the sexiest women I've ever met."

"Then…"

"But I'm not going to get involved with you. It has nothing to do with you, and everything to do with me. Okay?"

"No."

"Charlie—"

She laughed, because he looked so frustrated. She decided a dose of honesty couldn't hurt. "I want you, Harry. That's pretty unique for me, so I can't just forget about it. Besides, I'm used to fighting for what I want." When his eyes nearly crossed, she said, "Go ahead and sigh if you really need to, but it won't change anything. Consider yourself forewarned."

A horn blared, prompting Harry to drive now that the light was green. He shook his head, then chuckled as he stepped on the gas. "Only you, Charlie, could make a seduction sound like a threat."

She lifted her nose and tried for a seductive look. He didn't laugh, so she considered herself more successful than not. "I prefer to think of it as a promise, Harry."

HARRY FELT strung too tight. It was absolute torture, sitting next to Charlie while knowing she was smugly plotting his salacious downfall. He could tell by the way her dark blue eyes slanted in his direction every so often, or the way she looked him over, as if sizing him up for a meal. It was possibly the most erotic thing that had ever happened to him.

And he couldn't do a damn thing about it.

He shouldn't have shored up her confidence by admitting he found her sexy. But he couldn't help himself. The second she started speaking of her past, she'd looked…uncertain, not her normal indomitable self. Her eyes, usually so forthright, had filled with reserve and he'd wanted nothing more than to reassure her.

Now she knew he was susceptible to her, and he could almost hear the wheels turning in her head.

He needed a distraction, but he was hesitant to pursue the topic of her father. Maybe after she considered things, she'd soften just a bit. She was bullheaded, but not cruel. He decided on the next order of business. "Are you at all nervous about seeing Ralph or Floyd again?"

She gave him a double take. "Nervous?"

"Yes. It would make sense, you know. Yesterday was fairly tempestuous, what with being kidnapped and held at gunpoint."

Strangely enough, her expression softened. "We were shot at, too."

"Yes."

Suddenly she scooted closer and hugged herself up to his right arm. "Harry, I think it's wonderful that you're still determined to protect those old people despite being scared."

"What?"

"It's nothing to be ashamed of. As you said, yesterday wasn't easy. It even rattled me a little."

"Well, gee. That makes me feel so much better."

She patted his shoulder. Then rubbed. Then squeezed. "You have very nice muscles, Harry."

"Stop that!" Her voice had gone all throaty and warm. "Return to your own seat and put on your seat belt."

"Sheesh. I was only trying to—"

"Comfort me? This may come as a shock to you, Charlie, but I wasn't unduly upset by what happened. I was, in fact, mostly just concerned for you."

"What? Now why would you be worried about me?"

"Why, indeed?"

Her lip curled and she gave him a look fraught with disgust. "Because I'm *female?*"

Hiding a smile, he added, "And small. It's the truth, honey, you're on the…short side."

She stretched out her spine, managing to look an inch taller. "What the hell does that have to do with anything?"

Now she looked more inclined to punch him than kiss him. He felt relief—and other things he didn't even want to ponder. "My wife was a small woman. Not as small as you, but still considered petite. She hated it that I chose to be a P.I. In fact, she flatly refused to have anything to do with it."

"How could she be married to an investigator and not have anything to do with it?"

"Ah. Good question."

"Oh, you're divorced." She winced. "Is that the reason you broke up? Just because of what you do?"

"I had other options. My father had recently passed away and he'd left me a small fortune, as well as the opportunity to get involved in his business ventures. But I had no interest in such things." He lifted one brow. "She was adamant that I toe the line, that I give in to her will, but as it turns out...I didn't. And she couldn't stand it. She said my job was too dangerous, and if I didn't give it up, she'd leave me."

"And she did?"

He nodded. "Without much reluctance, but with a lot of dissension. She's remarried now, very happily. And she controls her husband with a velvet glove."

"I think your job could be exciting, although so far it's been kind of dull."

"Is that so?"

"And Harry? I don't own any velvet gloves."

He glanced at her, then grinned. "I wasn't drawing a comparison, brat. Well, perhaps I was, in an obscure, peripheral manner. You may not own velvet gloves, but I'll bet you own leather ones—maybe boxing gloves. Or possibly even brass knuckles?"

She blushed, giving herself away. "One of the men at the bar had a pair of those. I confiscated them when he kept causing trouble."

Harry raised a brow, wondering exactly how she'd accomplished that. "You're unlike her in many ways, Charlie. But you're even more controlling." It dawned on him that he could use this argument to turn her away from her seductive course. He truly had no intention of getting involved with any woman who wanted to call the shots.

"Harry, this may come as a shock, but I didn't ask for your hand in marriage. I just want to try out this…um…"

Knowing Charlie and her penchant for boldness, he decided to help her out before she said something too descriptive, too luring, that would push him right over the edge. He cleared his throat and offered, "Chemistry?"

"Yeah!" She beamed at him. "This chemistry we have going. I like it. I've never felt it before."

He gulped and almost swerved off the road. He shouldn't ask, because the less he knew, the better, but he couldn't seem to keep the words contained. He *had* to know. "Never, as in…?"

"As in never. The men I've known weren't the type to inspire illusions of lust. It's the truth, and I hope you won't hold it against me, but I'm pretty much inexperienced in this kind of thing."

He closed his eyes briefly, not enough to wreck his car, but enough to suffer a moment of silence. When he opened them again, he realized nothing had changed. He still could barely breathe. How did she keep doing this to him? "Charlie, when you say inexperienced, do you mean—"

"I'm almost a virgin."

His head throbbed. "How does a woman remain *almost* a virgin?"

She shrugged. "Once when I was nineteen, I felt rebellious and gave in to this total dweeb who lived close to us. What a mistake that was! I ended up punching him in the nose he was so inept. I mean, I *was* a virgin then, and he was twenty-two years old, and supposedly experienced, but even I knew more than he did. And he was so obnoxious about it, blaming me." She snorted in renewed righteous indignation over the slight.

"Good God."

"Then, when I was twenty-three, I got engaged to a guy I thought was nice. And even though I didn't really want him particularly bad, I figured I should know if we were compatible in bed or not before I shackled myself to him."

"And?"

"It's a good thing I didn't marry him." She shuddered in revulsion, then twisted in the seat to face Harry, full of confidences. In a stage whisper, she said, "He peeled off his clothes, and Harry, he had hickeys that I hadn't given to him in the strangest damn places!"

Harry bit his lip.

"Ooh, it was disgusting." Her voice lowered even more. "And his body wasn't all that great, either. Nothing like yours. He didn't have any hair at all on his chest. Slick as a baby's bottom. Can you imagine?"

Harry, who had a nice covering of chest hair, sighed. Well, hell. "You know, you really could benefit from just a pinch of discretion."

"I shouldn't have told you?"

"I might have suffered less not knowing." Her admiration had the ability to fully arouse him from one heartbeat to the next. He could already envision her fingers tangled in his chest hair, smoothing, stroking...

"Why should you suffer? I'm the one who's had to contend with fools and abstinence."

He choked on a laugh. "Charlie—"

In a mournful tone worthy of the divine, she said, "It really has been rough, you know."

Dalton's daughter, Dalton's daughter, Dalton's...

She peeked up at him, a study of feminine adoration. "If he'd looked anything like you, Harry, I might have been able to ignore the hickeys, even though they weren't mine, and even though I can't imagine anyone putting their mouth on him *there*. But he wasn't you and he'd been with someone else. And if I wasn't going to marry him, and of course, after knowing that, I wasn't, then I didn't think I should have to sleep with him."

Harry didn't think she should have to, either. He didn't particularly want to think of her sleeping with anyone, certainly not a man with a hairless chest, not a man who'd been with someone else and gotten love bites in unlikely places. *What places?* No, he didn't care what places. He didn't want her with any man, except maybe himself, and he was out of bounds.

He pulled up to the curb across the street and a few doors down from where their human targets would be making mischief. "Promise me that no matter what, you'll keep your cute little bottom in my car. I don't want you to start—"

"You think my bottom is cute?"

He bit his tongue. "It's a figure of speech used whenever addressing female bottoms."

"Oh."

"Promise me."

She shrugged. "I don't intend to start a brawl in the middle of the street, if that's what you're worried about."

"You're unpredictable. I worry about a lot of things." He glanced at his wristwatch. "We have some time before our neighborhood psychopaths are due to exit. There's a pattern to their visits, and they have the timing down. It's my hope to do nothing more than follow them today, see where they go, then perhaps I can turn the authorities on them without involving the proprietors."

"Why don't the proprietors want to be involved?"

"They want to be involved. Badly. If it was left up to them, they'd have set a trap already and, like vigilantes, exacted their own sort of justice, which I have a feeling is as bloodthirsty

as your own. But my…friend, fears retribution against them
if they do so. Being the stubborn cusses they are, they refuse
to involve the police. They've called on them a few times, for
less serious issues—minor vandalism, loud music, loitering,
that sort of thing. And the police were unable to do much
more than offer to drive by more frequently. It injured their
pride."

"And so they've given up on the police?"

Harry nodded. "I can understand them. They're older, but
resistant to the idea of being frail. All their lives they've been
independent, able to handle all situations. They're settled and
productive and happy. Then a few months ago the extortion
began, and they can't tolerate it, but their pride insists they
don't need the police now, not when they couldn't help them in
the past. My friend is concerned, of course, but he did promise
them he wouldn't contact the law. And actually, I'm concerned
that if they did, especially without rock solid evidence, things
could become worse. Ralph and Floyd are only minions. They
answer to Carlyle."

"So it's Carlyle you want?"

"Yes, I want him. Badly." Harry rubbed his hands together,
imagining what he'd do to Carlyle. "I detest a bully, but a bully
who picks on the elderly ranks right up there with the devil
himself. With any luck, once I find out where they gather,
I'll be able to link them with more than extortion. They're
criminals, and I hope to find them with illegal firearms, drugs,
anything that will implicate them with the law, without involving the extortion."

He happened to glance over at Charlie, and caught her
staring—worshipful lust in her big blue eyes. He scowled.
"Stop that."

Her smile was almost sappy. "You're incredible, Harry. A
real—"

"Don't say it!"

"But don't you see? You are a hero."

He bent a severe, utterly serious look on her, determined to make her back off before his control snapped. "I'm not a damn white knight, Charlie. I'm not the man you've been waiting for, even though I have a hairy chest and no unseemly love bites. I'm doing a job, that's all."

"I saw the way you looked, how eager you are to get hold of Carlyle. You're a good man, Harry. And good men are few and far between. Believe me, I know."

She looked warm and soft and admiring, and he liked it. He responded to it. She was such an enigma, so strong, so outspoken and confident, yet still so very female. She was quirky, rough around the edges, but so brutally honest she took his breath away. And unlike his ex-wife, she seemed to thrive on the excitement of his job. She actually admired him for what he did, rather than disdaining his choices.

Of course, she also thought he was afraid, and as much as that rankled, he supposed allowing her to believe in some flaws would only add to his efforts to push her away.

He clenched his muscles and forced his honor to the forefront of his brain, nudging the lust aside. "Your father is a good man, by all accounts." She stiffened immediately, but he pressed on. "Wouldn't you like to meet him? I could arrange it, you know."

"That's not necessary."

"You should be pleased, Charlie," he said gently, knowing this was difficult for her, glimpsing again that damn vulnerability that squeezed his heart. "He can assist you financially, and he can be a friend, if you'll let him."

He saw it in her eyes before she even moved. The determination, the cunning. He braced himself, both distressed and anxious, and then she was against him, her hands gripping his shoulders, her body as close as she could get it.

"I don't need a friend, Harry. Right now, I need a lover. You." She kissed him.

Harry tried to resist, he really did. But as he kept telling people, he was far from a hero. Mortal men couldn't be expected to withstand such provocation. He made a desperate effort to recite all the reasons he shouldn't kiss her back; it didn't work.

He felt her breath on his jaw, the silkiness of her hair on his temple when she slanted her head. Her tongue stroked tentatively over his closed lips and he groaned.

"Harry, please…"

Before he knew it, his hands were on her body, under her blue-jean jacket, cupping her small, perfect breasts through her sweater, and there was nothing mysterious about them. They were soft and firm and her nipples burned against his palms. *"Damn."*

Charlie panted. She bit his jaw, nuzzled his neck and kissed his throat. Somehow she managed to get one slender thigh up and over his and he helped her, smoothing a hand over that luscious, resilient bottom and cuddling her closer, letting his fingers probe and explore and entice. She straddled his lap and he could feel her feminine heat from the juncture of her thighs against his abdomen, and it made him nearly wild with need. He wanted her naked, in this same position, riding him gently, then not so gently. He groaned.

With her breasts pressed to his chest, her heartbeat mimicked the furious rhythm of his own.

Then he heard a shout.

He opened his eyes, trying to orient himself and his fogged brain. He saw Floyd scurry out of the meat market, his last stop of the day. Harry stiffened.

Ralph had already gotten in on the passenger's side of a blue sedan, and two seconds later, just as Floyd got the driver's door open, the proprietor, Moses, came out swinging a fist.

All hell broke loose.

CHAPTER EIGHT

CHARLIE WAS shocked when Harry suddenly tossed her into her own seat with the growled order to buckle her seat belt. The convertible ripped away from the curb, leaving the smell of burnt rubber in the air and a number of interested folks on the sidewalk. Charlie managed to say, "What the hell—" before Harry grabbed her head and forced it down in the seat.

"Stay down."

Furious and confused, she tried to lift back up, but his hand remained locked in her hair, keeping her immobile. She thought about punching him, but the car was going too fast, swerving, then pulling away again with a vicious squeal of tires. Harry released her, using both hands to turn the wheel sharply, and when she sat up, more than a little ready to commit murder, she found he had a look of grim satisfaction on his face.

Charlie huffed. Her body was still tingling all over, her mind sluggish, her heart beating too fast. As she smoothed her hair out of her eyes, she decided to give him a chance to explain before she extracted revenge for his high-handedness. "You care to tell me what that macho display was about?"

He cast her a quick glance, then brought his gaze back to the road. "We're distracting Floyd, before he hits Moses and I have to kill him."

"Moses?"

Harry nodded while constantly glancing in the rearview

mirror. They were doing about seventy-five and still gaining speed. "A grouchy old relic who's evidently gotten tired of being robbed. His shop is part of the lineup Floyd hits. Moses took a swing at Floyd as they left the store, but when I cut close to him, he leaped out of the way and forgot about retaliating in favor of trying to catch us."

Excitement bubbled up inside her. She whipped around and sure enough, there was a blue sedan trailing right behind them. "Does he know it's us?"

"I have no idea. Not that it matters. Hold on."

She barely had time to grip the door handle before the car took a sharp turn onto a side street, without slowing down much at all. Charlie fetched up against the door, then just as quickly found herself thrown against Harry.

"I told you to hold on!"

"I'm trying!" Readjusting her position, she again looked out back. "I don't see him."

"That was the point. Now that we've lost him, we'll circle back around and still be able to follow him."

"That won't be risky?"

His lips firmed in a calculating smile. "Are you getting nervous on me, Charlie?"

He sounded downright hopeful and she scowled. "No way. I just want to know what we're doing."

"I'm tracking. You're just along for the ride." The car slowed a tiny bit as Harry maneuvered in and out of side streets. "And this is the last time. I work much better alone."

"Suit yourself. I can work alone, too."

He growled, surprising her with the suddenness of it. "You're not going to work on this, Charlie. Promise me, or I'll pull over right now and toss you out."

He sounded serious, but she didn't think he'd actually do it. He'd lose too much time in trying to catch up with the Bumbling Boys. "Go ahead. I can make my own way home, or rather, back to your place. Then I'll get my truck and start my own surveillance."

Whatever he said was mumbled low enough that she couldn't hear, but his inflection was plain enough. He was beyond frustrated and likely wishing a curse on her head. Then his expression sharpened and a slow smile appeared. "There he is."

Charlie realized with a start that he was enjoying himself. It amazed her that someone so polished could have such an evil smile. Harry pulled into the main flow of traffic, now going a moderate speed that wouldn't draw attention. Charlie looked around, but didn't see a single familiar thing. "Where?"

"About twelve cars up, enough that he probably won't notice us."

"Probably?"

His look was smug. "Even if he does, my car could outrun his any day."

Aha. So there was a reason for the expensive wheels, besides great looks and the expression of wealth. "There's a wild side to you, Harry Lonnigan."

He didn't bother to answer, and she used the quiet moment to study his profile. That last kiss had filled her with unfamiliar tension that still throbbed and teased and kept her edgy. When she'd climbed over his lap, being deliberately brazen in her efforts to seduce him, she'd felt his erection and it had thrilled her.

She smiled, then tilted her head and asked, "Did you like kissing me before?"

His jaw flexed, but he didn't look at her. "Any red-blooded male would enjoy kissing you. It didn't mean anything."

"Because I'm too bossy, like your ex-wife?"

"That's part of it. And no, I'm not up to a barrage of questions right now. Let me concentrate, will you?"

A few minutes later they entered a commercial district where old and new warehouses stood together. Harry slowed the car even more, and eventually pulled up behind an abandoned building. He checked his watch, cursed, then turned to look at Charlie. He chewed his upper lip a moment, his expression both weary and considering. Eyes narrowed, he asked, "Do you think you could handle my car?"

It was the kind of question that never failed to rile her because it pricked her pride. Her spine stiffened and she said, "I can drive anything, including a semi."

"I'm sure that accomplishment will look sterling on a résumé." He held up a hand when she would have replied, and only the seriousness in his gaze kept her from being insulted. "I'm going to go take a look at where our thugs are headed. I'd like you to slide behind the wheel. If anything strange happens, if anyone approaches you, just drive away."

She tucked in her chin and stared at him in disbelief. "Without you?"

"I'll be fine. But not if I have to worry about Floyd getting hold of you again. Believe me, honey, he won't take any chances with you the next time. And his interest isn't only in revenge."

She really liked it when he called her honey. "You think because of my disguise, he's as interested in my breasts as you were?"

Harry drew in a quick breath. His gaze darted to her chest, and then quickly away. His hands tightened on the wheel and he looked ready to snap it in two. "It's possible, but I don't think you'll enjoy his interest."

He looked so furious, she decided against baiting him further. Though she had absolutely no intention of going anywhere without him, she nodded agreement. "Fine."

He studied her face, looking for the deception, but as she'd told him, she was a good liar. He spared her one brisk nod. "Lock the doors as soon as I get out. I should be back in a few minutes. If it takes me more than that, leave."

Then he leaned forward and cupped her chin. Charlie held

her breath, hoping for a kiss, but all she got was a threat. "No matter what, don't you dare get out of this car. Do you understand me?"

She especially loved it when he touched her. His hands were always hot, a little rough, and it excited her. She probably would have agreed to anything when he was touching her. She forced air into her lungs and whispered, "I understand."

His gaze dropped to her mouth, and with a slight curse, he pushed himself away. He was out of the car in the next instant. She watched him crouch low and race around the building, keeping to the shadows. More than anything, she wanted to follow him, to protect him, but what if they got separated and he came back to the car? What if Floyd chased him, but she wasn't where she was supposed to be? Though he expected her to run like a coward, she knew Harry would never leave without her. He was naturally protective of anyone or anything smaller than himself. He wanted to help the senior proprietors, he'd willingly tried to shield her from Ralph and Floyd before he'd even known her. And just seeing him with his animals, the way he took care of them, even surly Ted the cat, reaffirmed in her own mind how special Harry was. He could deny it all he wanted, but he had the makings of a true hero.

Waiting was one of the hardest things she'd ever done.

It seemed an hour had passed, but she'd checked the car's clock every minute, and knew it had been less than a quarter of that time. When she saw a shadow fall across the pavement, coming from the direction Harry had disappeared, her shoulders started to sag in relief.

Then the man stepped around the brick building and he looked as shocked to see her as she was to see him. He wasn't Harry, no, not even close. This man was shorter, heavier, and he had an aura of menace about him. Even when he smiled, she wasn't encouraged, because there was no comfort in his baring of teeth or the tilt of his thin lips. Charlie felt her senses scream an alert.

Where the hell was Harry?

The car was still idling, so she put it in gear, undecided on what to do. The man approached as if driven by mere curiosity. He tapped on the window, and Charlie, nervous but not wanting him to know it, lowered the window a scant inch.

The man looked her over. "Is everything okay, miss?"

"Fine, thank you."

She started to roll the window back up, and he quickly asked, "Can I help you with something? This isn't a good place for you to be loitering around alone. Or are you alone?"

She tried to think, but her worry for Harry had doubled and she didn't know what to say. "I'm just…lost."

"Where did you want to be?"

"Um…" *Where?* She had no idea. She hadn't even been paying that much attention while Harry drove, choosing instead to look at him.

The man grinned again, one brow lifted. "If you'll just roll this window down a little more so we can talk—"

Of course she had no intention of doing any such thing, but then it became a moot point anyway. The man suddenly swung around, but not in time. Harry, who'd crept up with neither she nor the man knowing it, landed a powerful blow against the man's jaw, driving him hard against the car. Charlie jumped.

But the man didn't stay put. In half a heartbeat, he'd pulled himself together and lunged at Harry. Charlie stuck the car in park and would have gotten out to help, but the two men again fell against the car, blocking her door. She tried to climb over the seat and keep watching at the same time. The shorter man hit Harry in the eye, making him curse and duck, then grabbed up a piece of pipe lying on the ground and swung it at Harry's head.

Frozen in very real fear, Charlie screamed.

She struggled with the door, but she'd forgotten it was locked, and by the time her frantic hands got it unlocked and open, Harry was there, cursing her and shoving her back in. "Damn it, I told you to leave!" he roared, and then he slid in beside her, forcing her to move, to climb over the controls to the passenger side while she tried to assure herself his head was still where it was supposed to be.

"Oh my God, are you hurt?"

Harry pushed her away, jerked the car into reverse and stepped on the gas. The car shot backward, and Harry jerked the wheel, spinning the car in one fluid motion so it faced forward, then speeding out of the lot.

Charlie came to her knees beside him and touched the swelling bruise already visible around his eye. "Harry—"

"Put your seat belt on, damn it."

She ignored him. "What happened? I…I thought he was going to hit you with that pipe and—"

"And you screamed." He looked at her, his injured eye swollen almost closed. "I never thought to hear such a female sound from you."

That gave her pause, but she shook the discomfort off. "You weren't even looking. I thought he was going to split your head open."

Harry grunted. "I kicked it out of his hand. The fellow was a totally pathetic fighter, slow and inept, and I'll thank you to have a little more faith in me, if you please."

Charlie sank back on her heels, nonplussed. He was actually insulted that she'd worried for him? "You, ah, handled that very well."

"You didn't." Without looking at her, he began the same tedious drive in and out of side streets, making it difficult for anyone to follow, though he didn't seem overly concerned with the prospect. "I think I could be happy if even once you'd follow my instructions. What were you waiting for? For him to open the car window with the pipe he tried to use on my head? What would you have done if I hadn't shown up?"

"I don't know. But it was dumb of you to tell me to leave without you. I'd never do that."

In a burst of temper, Harry hit the steering wheel with a fist. "This is exactly why you should have kept your stubborn hide at home instead of dogging my heels!"

His tone was vicious, not loud, yet twice as intimidating for the low tone. Charlie swallowed, more hurt than alarmed by his anger. Guilt gnawed at her because she knew he had a valid point. He'd obviously had everything under control, but for the first time in her life, she'd panicked. The realization was so new, so alien, she couldn't quite fathom it.

Of all the stupid things, she'd fallen in love with Harry Lonnigan.

"That was one of Carlyle's henchmen, you know. He'll tell him we were there. If you hadn't blundered, I could have looked my fill with no one the wiser. But now, they know we know where they're at, and odds are they'll move. Tracking the idiots will be twice as difficult after this!"

She had no idea what to say. They'd been through a lot together already, and not once had Harry sounded so fed up, or so disgusted with her. Slowly, she sank into her seat and relatched her seat belt. She stared out the window, hoping to collect her thoughts enough to offer an excuse, a reply of some kind. But how could she tell him that she cared, that she was worried about him? Obviously the man was big enough, tough enough, to take care of himself without her questionable assistance, so she surely couldn't use that excuse. And mentioning love, or any type of emotion, was out of the question. Harry had been very clear on his feelings for her. He didn't even want her anymore and did his best to fight her off. She was such an uncouth yokel compared to his sophistication and background. She hadn't thought of it before, but now she had no choice.

The ride home was made in painful silence. Several times Charlie glanced at him, wincing in sympathy over his swollen, bruised eye. But the mulish set to his mouth, the hard glitter in his eyes, kept her from commenting on it.

After Harry had turned the car off in the parking garage he drew a deep breath and faced her. "Where's your truck?"

She shrugged, doing her best to look cavalier. "I parked on the street."

"Charlie…"

That sympathetic tone of his made her spine stiffen. She didn't want his pity, especially when he refused to share anything else.

Various emotions seemed to bombard her, wearing her down, but she was made of pretty stern stuff, not one to wilt when things went sour. So she wanted him? It was in her nature to fight for what she wanted, but this situation was different, wanting a man. She knew he desired her, and that had strengthened her resolve, but it was also obvious he didn't want to desire her, and she could understand his reasonings very easily.

Pride forced her to give in graciously, to salvage what she could of her self-respect. She worked up an icy smile, then opened her car door before looking at him. "I've decided to let you off the hook."

The swelling black eye seemed obscene on his handsome face. He didn't move, just sat there staring at her. "What the hell are you talking about?"

She lifted one shoulder. "I won't pester you anymore. I've decided to quit playing spy and get back to my own business. The bar doesn't run itself and I've neglected it these last few days. If you want to send me a bill for what I owe you—"

His good eye narrowed, giving her pause.

"—for the info on my father, I mean. I'll get the money to you right away."

"I haven't finished telling you what I know of your father."

Though she wasn't a coward, had never been a coward, she

wanted to leap out of the car and run away. She didn't want to continue sitting there, chatting like everything was fine when she'd just had the most astounding realization of her life. There were very few people she'd ever loved, and other than Jill, they'd all been mistakes. She hated to think of Harry that way.

"That's all right. You said he hadn't completely abandoned us, so I'm assuming he'll pay what he owes. That's all I really need to know. I can have a lawyer contact him. Or maybe I'll just send him a letter..."

Harry reached for her and she slid quickly out of the car, dodging him. If he touched her, she'd want to touch him back, and she was determined not to make a bigger fool of herself. "Thanks for the help, Harry. I can handle it from here."

He, too, left the car and slowly stood to face her. The slamming of his door echoed around the empty garage. She closed hers more carefully. When Harry started around the car toward her, she began back-stepping to the entrance. She tried an airy wave. "It's been...fun."

His growl reminded her of a rabid animal. He kept coming, his narrowed eyes looking more lethal than ever with the dark bruise and the swelling. He was large and imposing and some-how all his sophistication seemed to have melted away under his basic masculinity. "You're coming inside with me."

Her spine stiffened. "No thanks. I need to get going."

"I'm not asking, Charlie. I'm giving an explicit mandate. We have things to talk about, and I'm fed up with your unac-countable stubbornness and scurrility."

"I don't even know what that word means, Harry." He looked like he might lunge at her any minute, so she kept backing up. Unfortunately she didn't look behind her, and she fetched up against a concrete wall, clunking her head. "Ow."

While she rubbed her head, he closed in on her, using his long muscled arms to cage her in, stepping so close she could feel his warmth and breathe in his hot scent. He stared at her face, at her eyes and her mouth. She felt the gentle touch of his breath, and the blast of his temper, in sharp contrast.

"It means," he said succinctly, "that cutting wit of yours which you dispense with no thought to consequences and without evident remorse."

She forgot she wanted away from him, or even that her head hurt. Her own temper snapped and she leaned closer to taunt, "Oh, poor baby. Have I said something to hurt your feelings?"

His jaw worked. They were so close her nose bumped his chin. Then he took her arm in an unbreakable grip, stepped back, and headed for the town house. She got dragged in his wake. "No, but I do believe you prodded me into hurting yours. And for that, I'm sorry."

"What nonsense! I don't need an apology from you. Really… *Harry,* let me go!"

"No."

He tugged and pulled and coerced her along until they reached his door. Losing a fight really went against the grain, so she doubled her efforts. She didn't want to hurt him, so she was at a distinct disadvantage. She tried going limp, hoping her weight would throw him off-guard, but he managed to control her by the expedient method of wrapping one arm around her and lifting her off her feet. Mortified, Charlie went perfectly still.

He unlocked the door with his free hand and stepped inside to the sounds of excited barking. With a laugh, Harry released her to relock the door, and Charlie, seeing red, gave up on trying to get away from him. Instead, she launched her own attack. She took Harry off-guard and he stumbled and with the dogs flying around their feet and Ted screeching out a raucous complaint, they went down on the floor, hard.

Unfortunately, Charlie was on the bottom.

HARRY DODGED A tight fist aimed for his bruised eye. He'd
expected no less of Charlie, especially since he was well aware
of her more bloodthirsty tendencies. But for a moment there,
she'd seemed too withdrawn, almost sad, and the thought that
he might have hurt her feelings with his temper had been a
squeezing pain in his heart. When he'd seen that thug leaning on the Jag, talking to her... He never wanted to feel that
possessive, that protective or enraged again.

She swung at him again, demanding his immediate attention. Laughing, he captured her hands and pinned them over
her head. The dogs were going crazy, taking the struggle as
a free-for-all game. Sooner jumped close enough to stick a
wet snout in Harry's ear, then dodged away again, howling
maniacally. Charlie got a gleeful lap across the temple from
Grace, and she struggled even more, cursing Harry and trying
to discourage the dogs.

Her wriggling body had a very basic effect on him. He
looked down at her, seeing the way her short, glossy black hair
tumbled around her head, the way her cheeks flushed with her
efforts. She lurched up against him, her head thrown back, her
teeth catching her bottom lip, and he nearly groaned. Damn,
she looked like a woman in the throes of a climax.

Her legs were caught under his and she tried to kick one
free. Harry used his knee to spread her thighs, then settled
between them. This time when she lunged upward, there was
no way she could mistake his state of arousal. He had a throbbing erection and she froze.

The dogs moved in, taking advantage of the inactivity,
whining and barking and nudging the humans. Harry barely
noticed. Charlie had opened her eyes and locked her gaze on
his, and the emotional connection was so strong, so powerful
compared to anything he'd ever felt, he couldn't move. It was
like he was inside her already.

She gasped for breath and he raised himself slightly, not

enough to let her get away, but enough so she could breathe. She immediately lifted herself to press against him again. She could drive him crazy, he thought, even as he settled his hips against hers, giving in to her silent demand. His pulse raced, his muscles drawing tight. It felt so right to be with her like this.

Her knees bent, and she slowly moved her pelvis against his in an unpracticed, voluptuous sway. Mesmerized, he watched her face, saw the trembling in her lips as she drew in a shaky breath, saw her beautiful blue eyes darken, saw her skin heat.

Sooner howled again and without looking away, Harry commanded, "Go lie down." The dogs complained, but they finally obeyed.

Charlie tried to pull her hands free, but he held tight. "No you don't. I like you like this," he whispered. "You need just a little controlling, someone to keep you in line."

Though her eyes were heavy lidded and filled with sensual need, she lifted her chin. "You have to let me up sometime."

As far as threats went, it held no weight. Harry leaned down and nuzzled the soft skin beneath that raised chin. "Who says?"

Her eyes drifted shut and she hooked her feet behind his thighs. "You feel so good, Harry. Will you make love to me now?"

Everything righted itself in that instant and his brain cleared. With a vicious curse he released her and sat up. She didn't. She remained sprawled on the floor beside him, offering the most delectable temptation man could imagine. He tried not to look at her, but he couldn't help himself.

"Damn, I'm sorry."

"I'm not," she whispered.

He ran a hand through his hair. "How do you keep doing this to me?"

"I didn't do anything except try to let you off the hook. You're the one who dragged me in here."

After a calming breath, he forced himself to say, "I don't want off the hook. And I'm sorry I yelled at you."

"All things considered, I'd kinda forgotten all about that."

He looked at her, lying there so sweet and submissive—surely a first for Charlie—and his muscles cramped in rebellion of what he knew he had to do. "Honey, this is all wrong. I brought you up here to talk about your father, not to…ravish you on the damn floor."

"I rather liked being ravished on the floor."

He couldn't help but laugh, she was so persistent and candid and honest. There wasn't a single ounce of guile in her expression, and the fact that she was as free, as unreservedly sexual as himself, made him crazy. She hadn't minded their rough play in the least, and wasn't offended at being debauched on a floor. She would be his sexual equal, and knowing it made his arousal even more keen.

But she was Dalton's daughter, and Dalton would be appalled to know just how low Harry had sunk.

He stood, caught her arms, and pulled her to her feet. She stared up at him and he cupped her face. "Tell me you'll at least give your father a chance, okay?"

To his surprise, she seemed to be considering it. "Why is it so important to you, Harry?"

With complete and utter honesty, he said, "Because I think he's a good man and he loves you. I think he deserves a chance to tell his side of the story. And because I was never able to connect with my own father. It's something that bothers me still, something that every so often vexes me because now the man is gone and more often than not I don't even mourn him. I don't want you to ever suffer that, to wonder if only you'd softened a bit you could have had a wonderful relationship.

For Jill's sake, for all it will mean to her, why don't you at least try?"

Harry held his breath, praying she'd relent. With any luck at all, Dalton would be getting out of the hospital today. Harry didn't want him under unnecessary stress, and he knew Dalton would stew endlessly about the situation until he was reunited with his daughters. If Charlie would agree, it could be taken care of within a week. That would give her time to prepare and give Dalton time to rebuild his strength.

Also, Harry's control was almost at an end. For his own sanity, he had to tie up loose ends so he could distance himself from her before he made a mistake he'd live to regret. Dalton deserved his loyalty, and Charlie deserved a man who would love her forever.

Unfortunately, the thought of her with another man made his system revolt, so he quickly shoved that thought aside.

Harry had no idea which part of his discourse convinced her, but after several moments of deep thought, she nodded. "All right." She hesitated, then stepped close and embraced him. "Will you...go with me?"

Harry wrapped his arms around her and held her tight, too tight, judging by her laughing, mumbled complaint. He didn't understand the near desperate urge to hold her, but he knew her embrace hadn't been designed to seduce him this time. Rather, it was the need for emotional comfort, and it touched him to his very soul. She willingly showed him her vulnerable side, something she normally kept well hidden, and he'd never felt so gifted in his entire life.

Though he knew it would be incredibly awkward, he kissed her temple and nodded. "Of course I'll be there."

She leaned back with a relieved smile. "When?"

He couldn't make her any promises until he found out how Dalton had fared. He'd called the hospital when he first got up, and the nurse had told him all seemed well. Dalton had been in high spirits, anxious to know what Harry had planned—a tale Harry related with precise discretion, leaving out any reference that might upset Dalton. He hadn't spoken to him again since the doctor's visit, and now he was anxious to do so. He led Charlie to the door, though he was equally reluctant to let her go.

With a last kiss on her forehead, which was a habit he desperately needed to break, he said, "Try not to worry, honey. I'll arrange everything as soon as I can, and then I'll let you know."

She smiled up at him, her eyes big and soft and filled with gratitude. "Thanks, Harry. I know it's stupid, and if you ever tell anyone I'll deny it, but it's kind of a relief that I don't have to do this alone. I owe you."

As she left, his guilt doubled until it nearly consumed him. Damn it, what would she think when she found out he'd known Dalton all along? Would she understand? Or would she likely feel betrayed by the one person she'd started to trust? The worry gnawed at him, making him angry with regret, until the phone rang.

It was Dalton, and he was ready to come home.

CHAPTER NINE

THE SECOND Harry stepped through the barroom doorway, he could tell Charlie was nervous. He'd spent the past week with her, and her mannerisms and mood were very familiar to him now. He picked up on the small frown, the way she repeatedly swallowed. She was behind the thick, scarred wooden bar, a clipboard clutched tightly in her hand, taking some kind of inventory. Beside him, Dalton looked around in horrified disbelief.

"My God. She can't actually work here?"

Pulling his gaze from Charlie, Harry said, "She does, and she manages quite credibly. I don't think it's been easy for her, but she's the type of woman who once she sets her mind on something, it gets accomplished one way or another." Harry knew there was a wealth of pride in his tone, but he couldn't seem to help himself. He *was* proud, and he wanted Dalton to be, too.

The bar wasn't yet open. Charlie had insisted they meet there, partly, Harry assumed, because she felt it gave her an advantage to be on her own territory and in familiar surroundings. She wouldn't admit it, not even to herself, but she was very uncertain about meeting her father.

Her insecurity, and the need to hide it, endeared her to Harry all the more. He smiled toward her, though Charlie was still unaware of them. They were early, but keeping Dalton away any longer had proved impossible.

Harry had convinced Dalton to wait a week, to give himself

plenty of time to recover. He refused to let Harry tell Charlie about his heart attack, so there was no telling how Charlie would react during the meeting, but Harry thought it a safe bet she'd be antagonistic and stubborn. She had a lot of past grievances to get through before she'd be able to fully accept Dalton.

Harry found himself very ambiguous about the meeting. He worried for Dalton, though the doctor had said he was fine. Other than routine checkups and a warning to take life easier, Dalton was free to do as he pleased.

Harry also worried for Charlie. This wouldn't be easy for her, having the foundation of her resentment pulled out from under her. Today she would find out her mother had been a bitter, vindictive woman, and Harry would have done just about anything to shield her from that.

But he had another motive for putting the reunion off until today.

Over the past week he'd spent nearly every day with her, arguing, doing his best to protect her when she insisted on forcing her way into danger. Whenever he tried to accomplish something without her, she threatened to go off on her own. But despite her interference, he'd learned quite a bit about Carlyle, while keeping Charlie in the dark. She might suspect a few things, but thankfully, she had no solid evidence of his plans. If she had, she wouldn't have agreed to meet her father today.

Harry was counting on the meeting to keep her busy until everything was finally resolved.

Dalton was still looking around, his expression appalled. Harry had been in the bar many times, however, and the bar was empty with the lights turned up and no cigarette smoke to cloud the air. True, the lime green was almost blinding. But the place was tidy, and comforting in a lived in, relaxed sort of way. The wooden floor wasn't highly polished, but it was immaculately clean, and though some of the round, mismatched tables looked less than elegant, they were sturdy and in good repair. The walls were bare except for the occasional unframed poster, curling at the edges.

She'd obviously done the best she could with the bar, and Harry hoped Dalton would see that. Charlie had been given too much responsibility and too few breaks in her young life, and Harry was more than a little relieved to introduce her to her father, knowing Dalton would offer her new opportunities.

"Damn it, I wish Jill was going to be here. Charlotte's just being stubborn."

It was an unending refrain, and Harry sighed. They still hovered in the doorway, preferring to survey the bar and Charlie without notice. With a hand on Dalton's shoulder, Harry reminded him, "She doesn't yet know you, and she's fiercely protective of Jill. Until she's certain you won't disappoint or hurt her, I think you'll just have to be patient. In a way, that should reassure you, because you can tell Charlie's taken excellent care of her sister."

Dalton's hands fisted. "Damn Rose. None of this was necessary. If only the woman hadn't tried to punish me by running off."

"True, but go easy on what you say today," Harry advised. "Rose is the only parent Charlie knows, and I have a feeling her stubbornness would force her to be defensive even about that. And remember, I'm just a P.I. I don't want her to have to deal with my deception today, on top of everything else."

With that last reminder, Harry determined to get the whole thing going. He wanted to see Charlie and Dalton settled, so he could attend Carlyle's little surprise party.

He stepped forward and cleared his throat.

Charlie jerked her gaze up, then stilled. Harry could see the near panic in her beautiful eyes, and it smote him clear down to his masculine core. He wanted to hold her, but of course, he couldn't. "Hello, Charlie. I'm sorry we're early, but your father was a bit anxious."

Very slowly, her gaze shifted from Harry to her father. She looked like a small animal caught in the headlights of an oncoming car, but only for a moment. Harry saw the resolve stiffen her spine, saw her summon that indomitable courage. He felt emotion expand inside him, and though it scared him spitless, he smiled.

Charlie plunked down the clipboard, skirted the bar, and started toward them with a swanky, confident walk. Her clothes were even more disreputable today, her jeans well worn and a tad frayed at the hem, her boots scuffed. She wore a T-shirt with a suggestive beer logo on the front. It was at least two sizes too big, tucked into her snug jeans, and Harry thought she looked adorable.

Judging by the expression on Dalton's face, he didn't.

All nervousness had disappeared from Charlie's mien. She stood within a few feet of them, hands on her slim hips, feet spaced apart. She could have been facing Floyd and Ralph again for all her arrogant bravado.

"So." She glanced at each of them, then focused on Harry. "I had a delivery this morning I had to deal with. Usually I'm not even up till ten, given the hours I'm open, but the delivery guys always come early. I'd almost forgotten about them after the week we've had."

Harry didn't even want to think about that and cast a quick glance at Dalton to see if he'd caught the insinuation. Dalton had no idea Charlie had involved herself with the embezzlers, and he'd be twice as upset if he found out. But Dalton still stared at Charlie, and thankfully, looked unaware of the conversation.

Harry had tried refusing to let her accompany him as he continued checking into things, partly because he'd feared for her safety, and partly because he didn't trust his dubious control around her. It boggled the mind the way she could push his buttons, but damn if she didn't manage it every time she got near. She laughed and he wanted her. She stuck her stubborn chin in the air and he went hot with lust. And her eyes—when she looked at him with her sultry, bold expressions, it took all he had not to give in to the urge to have her.

Over the past week, he'd twice found her snooping on her own. The urge to put her over his knee had been overwhelming, and had dampened his carnal appetites. Yet when he'd offered that threat, she'd merely laughed, proving she knew he'd never hurt her. To his chagrin, *she* was the one who discovered Carlyle hadn't moved his operation at all. Evidently the man was so cocky he was totally without caution, disregarding Harry's interference as a threat.

After today, Carlyle would have to rethink that.

Harry looked at Dalton, who remained mute, and decided he'd have to get the ball rolling before Charlie disclosed things better left concealed. "Charlie, this is your father, Dalton Jones."

She tilted her head at Dalton, studying him closely. "You don't look as old as I had you pictured."

Dalton smiled nervously. "Did your mother show you any photographs of me?"

"Sure. But they were years ago. Eighteen years ago to be exact."

Dalton's eyes closed briefly and he nodded. "Eighteen years that I regret more than I can ever tell you."

His words and tone were so heartfelt, Charlie wavered. Harry could see her expression shift, the uncertainty come into her eyes. He took her arm and said gently, "Why don't we sit down? You two have a lot to talk about."

Once they were at a round table toward the middle of the floor, Charlie looked at Harry with a slight smile. "Your eye is healing—the bruises are only green now instead of black. But you still look wiped out. If you can keep from strangling on it, I'll go get some coffee from the back and we'll see if that can revive you."

He smiled, too, pleased to see the appearance of her

wit. "I promise to only sip, to cut back on the chances of strangulation."

She glanced at Dalton and hesitated before asking, "Would you like some, too?"

He nodded. "Actually, Charlotte, I'd love some. Black, please."

Harry winced at the name, but quickly forestalled the storm he saw brewing on Charlie's face by saying, "Isn't that just how you take yours, Charlie? Black?"

Her smile turned sickly sweet. "Just." She walked away without another word.

When she was out of sight, Harry turned to frown at Dalton. It wasn't his place, but still he said, "She prefers to be called Charlie."

Dalton pulled out a chair and sat down, prompting Harry to do the same. With his back to the kitchen doorway Charlie had gone through, Dalton whispered, "It's a horrid nickname, probably her mother's doing, which is a good reason for me not to follow suit."

"God." Harry rubbed his face, unsure how to convince Dalton he should back off. Charlie definitely wasn't a woman you wanted to push, and especially not when she felt cornered emotionally.

Dalton stared around the bar with a grimace. "Don't you see? She deserves better than this, and it's my duty to see to it. She's wearing grubby clothes and working in a dump, when I want her to be free to be a young lady. I'll worry myself into an early grave if I have to think about her being here every night. I can help her now. She can sell this place and get a respectable diner or something instead. Or she could work for me at the jewelry store." His face brightened with the prospect. "You know I'd love to have her there."

"You're jumping the gun, don't you think?"

"Ha! She deserves a lot better than working in a place like this."

The sudden stillness in the air was palpable and Harry jerked around to see Charlie frozen behind them, a tray with coffee, mugs, cream and sugar in her hands. Her jaw was positively rigid, her face pale. There was such a wounded expression in her eyes, he knew he'd never forget it as long as he lived.

He and Dalton both stood. Dalton, fidgeting nervously, took the tray from her and put it on the table, then held out a chair. As she sat, Harry touched her arm, but she shook him off. Dalton poured coffee while she stared at him.

"You know, Jill looks a lot like you."

Her calm, controlled tone reassured Dalton. But it didn't fool Harry for a single second. She was up to something, and he knew it wouldn't be pleasant. He cleared his throat. "You all have the same blue eyes."

Dalton grinned. "I'm anxious to meet Jill. Though from what Harry has told me, she's lovely and doesn't look a thing like me."

Charlie shook her head. "You've got the same color hair, the same smile. And you both look the same when you feel guilty." She ignored Dalton's searching glance. "I look more like my mother."

"Yes, you do. And she was beautiful."

"Not toward the end she wasn't. She'd led a hard life, always drinking too much, smoking, never getting enough sleep. We found out she had emphysema and she had to go on oxygen. She hated it, because dragging the oxygen around made her feel old, but she was always tired, so she used it when she absolutely had to. One day she got pneumonia and just died."

Charlie recited the facts as if it had been a play, something unreal that had happened to someone else. Without even realizing his intent, Harry took her hand. She clutched at him, but her gaze never left Dalton.

"This *dump* paid for her funeral. It's also kept my sister clothed and fed for the last few years when I had no idea where you were." Charlie tilted her head, and her grin was without an ounce of humor. "And of course, it's given me the opportunity to be free."

Dalton, already looking stricken by what she'd said, asked cautiously, "Free?"

Charlie shrugged. "I'm my mother's daughter. Did you think she hadn't told me? I knew she'd cheated on you and I heard all her excuses for why you should have forgiven her. She blamed you completely, you know, because she said you weren't around often enough. Even if she hadn't told me, her character was pretty plain to see for anyone with eyes, much less a daughter who lived with her. So what makes you think I'm any different?"

Dalton blustered. "Well, I never thought… I mean, that wasn't the indication I was…"

Charlie pulled Harry's arm over and hugged it to her breasts. Harry, taken off-guard, gawked at her.

She laughed. "Harry didn't tell you that? Well, of course he didn't. Harry is a gentleman, and gentlemen never kiss and tell."

She leaned over and lightly kissed Harry on the jaw, and he stiffened. When he got her alone, he planned to throttle her. "Charlie—"

"I appreciate your efforts on my behalf, Harry. But whether Dalton likes it or not, the bar suits me. I'd go nuts in a nine-to-five atmosphere with rules and restrictions and you know it. Besides, the men here are always so complimentary—when they're not too tanked to get the compliments out."

Harry locked his jaw and struggled to think of a way to get her off-track. He understood her, knew exactly what she was doing, but he didn't like being used.

"Now Harry, he's such a smooth talker, he never runs out of compliments." At Dalton's unblinking stare, she added, "You didn't think he only *worked* for me, did you? No, Harry and I have gotten real close."

Harry cursed when Dalton looked at him, brows raised in question.

At a momentary loss, Dalton swallowed hard. Finally he shook his head. "I understand how difficult your life must have been, Charlotte, believe me. But I'm here now and—"

"And I've been doing as I please too long to start restricting myself at this late date." Her tone was hard, uncompromising. "If you hoped to step in and play father by correcting all my faults, forget it. I happen to revel in my faults."

Dalton directed a commanding look at Harry, then slowly stood. "I… Could you excuse me a moment?"

Charlie nodded, watching him with narrowed eyes. "Sure thing. Boy's room is in the back, down the hallway and to your left."

Harry, having correctly interpreted that look, started to follow, but Charlie didn't let him go.

He turned on her, as furious with the situation as he was with her absurd theatrics. "What the hell are you doing, making him think you're…we're…"

"Lovers?" She made a face and sipped her coffee. "Why not? He obviously thinks I'm lacking and has some hare-brained idea of reforming me. This way, he'll know right off it's a lost cause and not start meddling in my life."

Harry sank back into his seat. Dalton could wait for the moment. He turned Charlie's hand so he could lace their fingers together. "He thinks no such thing. He's very proud of you, he just wants to help."

"Ha!"

Harry grimaced. He was getting damn sick and tired of that expression.

"I heard what he said, Harry. He wants to help me get my life straightened out, but it's the truth, I enjoy my life. Other than wishing I could give more to Jill, I wouldn't change a thing."

Harry knew that wasn't merely pride talking. The bar was

home to her, and she wouldn't give it up easily. He sighed. "All right, so tell him that, but don't start pretending there's something going on between us—"

"Isn't there? Well, okay, not as much as I suggested, but I was on your floor the other night, Harry, and I enjoyed what you did to me. I'd like us to do it again."

"Damn it, Charlie…."

"You're working for me, right? So consider this a side assignment—with bonus pay."

Harry narrowed his eyes. "You're pushing me."

She leaned toward him with a wicked grin. "I like pushing you." Then the grin was gone, replaced by a stubborn set to her mouth. "But this is important. And since you *are* working for me, I figured you wouldn't mind helping me dupe him just a little bit. I know it pushes the boundaries of reality to think of us actually involved in anything more than a quick fling, but Dalton can't know that. So what's the big deal?"

Harry groaned.

"If he really does care, which I have serious doubts about, it won't matter to him what I do or who I am. And if it does matter, well, then, he can give me the money for Jill's education and get lost for another eighteen years. The money is all I really care about anyway."

Harry stared at her, knowing she lied. He could see it in her eyes, how much her father's apparent disapproval had hurt her, and he decided to give Dalton a piece of his mind.

"I'm going to check on him. Stay put, okay?"

"Did you think I'd run off and hide? Not likely."

Harry found Dalton standing in the tiny gray bathroom. The walls were painted brick and cement, the ceiling light a bare bulb. Dalton looked at Harry with bleak eyes. "She can't really like this place."

Harry crossed his arms over his chest and leaned against the door. "You know, Dalton, I've gotten to know Charlie— and *yes,* she is Charlie whether you like it or not!"

Dalton subsided, biting back his complaint.

"I've gotten to know her beyond what she presents to most of the world."

Dalton quirked a brow. "So she said."

Harry waved that off. "That's just her way of getting even for your censure. She wanted to hurt you, the way you hurt her."

"But I didn't mean to hurt her! I just wanted her to know she has choices now."

"I know that, but she doesn't. She's a wonderful, caring, independent woman who prides herself on those qualities. I have the feeling she's never asked anyone for anything, and coming to you now for money really rubs her the wrong way."

"It shouldn't. I'd gladly give her anything I have."

"But don't you see? She's always been able to get by on her own through gumption and strength of will. She turned this run-down dive into a favored local saloon, and she's supported her sister and ailing mother by doing so. I've watched her working here. From the regulars to the occasional drop-in, Charlie deals with them all in her own special way, protecting herself, but not really offending, being friendly, but never letting any man get too close." *Except for himself.* He shoved that thought aside and continued. "She's rightfully proud of this place and what she's accomplished. When you insult it, you insult her."

Dalton rubbed his face. "It's just so—"

"Not what you'd expected? What you'd want for her? I never thought to say it, but you remind me of my own father, Dalton."

That got his attention, his head snapping up and he frowned.

"She has to lead her own life, not the life you'd choose for her. All you can do now is be there for her. She's twenty-seven years old, a grown woman, and frankly I don't think she needs to change."

Dalton drew back, both brows shooting high. "You sound like you care about her."

Through his teeth, Harry said, "I like her as a friend."

"Hmm."

Harry decided it was time to change the subject. "Dalton, she has this crazy idea of making you think we're lovers. I have to tell her the truth."

"No! I think this might be the perfect opportunity. I screwed up, I admit it, but maybe I can fix things." He began pacing back and forth in front of the sink. "I never meant for her to hear me, it's just that I'm anxious to help. But now I can prove to her that I do care. As long as she's only acting with you, I'll know she's safe. I'll be able to show her that I accept her, that I..." He swallowed hard, his eyes misty. "That I love her no matter what."

Harry's insides cramped. "That's an asinine plan."

"No, don't you see? She's doing this to shock me because she thinks I'll walk away repulsed. But now I can show her I'll never leave her again, no matter what."

Harry muttered a crude curse that had Dalton blinking in surprise.

"All right. But I'm telling you, I don't like it. You'd better prove yourself to her and fast because I can't take too much more."

Harry stomped out of the bathroom without explaining what it was he couldn't take, and almost ran over Charlie, who'd come to see why it was taking them so long. He caught her to keep her from falling, and she landed against his chest with a thud. She saw Dalton behind Harry, and that was all the encouragement she needed. She threw her arms around his neck, plastered her body up against his, and kissed him so thoroughly he thought he was having his own heart attack.

"I just got off the phone," she whispered against his mouth. "I found someone to cover for me so I could have the night off. I guess we've got a date after all."

CHAPTER TEN

CHARLIE ALMOST laughed at the look on Harry's face. He went from heated response, to shock, to chagrin. Luckily her father was still behind him and didn't see that variety of reactions. She kissed him again for good measure, and as he removed her arms with a chastising frown and started around her, she patted his butt.

Harry jumped, looking like a man who'd just been stung, then took her hand and literally dragged her to the table. Dalton came along, smiling like a damn Cheshire cat, though what he had to grin about, Charlie had no idea.

When they reached the table, Harry pulled a chair out for her. She laughed, pushed him into his seat and dropped onto his lap. She was prepared to put on a real show, not only to prove to her father she was beyond redemption, but because this gave her the perfect opportunity to be close to Harry. Very soon now, their time would be over. He'd brought her father to her, and he planned to wrap things up that week with Floyd and Ralph. He wouldn't share his plans in that regard, but she'd come to know Harry very well and knew he was up to something. Just the fact that he'd been hanging out in the Lucky Goose all week told her he wanted to keep an eye on her, to make sure she didn't blunder into whatever plans he had in mind.

It didn't bother her. She was so at ease with Harry, she could enjoy his company while being herself.

To her surprise, Harry didn't try to push her away. He

sighed, then looped his arms around her waist. In her ear, he whispered, "There's always retribution to be paid, Charlie. Don't forget that."

She ignored this threat, just as she ignored all his others. Harry wouldn't hurt her and she knew it. She turned to Dalton, to judge his reaction to the scene, and saw him staring toward the doorway. With an inkling of dread, she whipped about and there stood Jillian. She had a shopping bag clutched in her hands and a frozen expression on her face.

"Oh hell." Charlie started to scramble off Harry's lap, but he tightened his hold.

"Ah, ah. Don't turn cowardly on me now."

"Harry, I don't want Jill—"

"To meet her father?" He gave her a gentle hug. "Honey, relax. It'll be okay."

"Not with me on your lap! What will she think?"

"That you're up to mischief again, no doubt."

Dalton came to his feet like a sleepwalker. "Jillian?"

Jillian's smile trembled the tiniest bit, and then she walked forward cautiously. She glanced at Charlie, and her eyes widened when she saw how her sister was seated. Charlie groaned. "It's not what you—"

Laughing, Harry interjected, "I'd stand, but you can see I have a vexatious burden in my lap."

Jill nodded politely. "Is there, ah, any reason why?"

With a smile that was pure wickedness, Harry said, "We're passionately involved, don't you know."

Charlie's elbow came back hard enough to make him grunt, then she smiled at Jill. "I was going to tell you later, after... well, I wanted to make sure everything would be okay..."

Jill glanced at Dalton, then back to her sister. "I understand. Would you like to introduce me now?"

"I suppose I don't really have a choice, do I? Jill, this is our father, Dalton Jones."

Jill caught her breath and dropped her bag. She blinked

hard, trying to fend off tears. "I thought…I mean, you look exactly as I imagined, but I just wasn't sure…"

Dalton, his own eyes wet, reached out to her. "I never gave up hope of finding you."

Jill took his hands. "I have so many questions."

"Me, too."

They seemed to be in their own little world and Charlie, disgusted and a tad jealous, shook her head. Her sister was so much more accepting than she could ever be. She leaned back against Harry and whispered, "Don't start looking smug. If he does one thing to insult her or upset her, I'll toss him—and you—out."

Frowning, Harry appeared to consider that. "I don't think you can just toss a lover out. No, a lover gets to stick around through thick and thin."

"You're enjoying yourself, aren't you?"

"I'm beginning to."

Charlie looked at his totally shameful grin and had to smile herself. He did enjoy matching wits with her, that had been apparent from the first. She enjoyed it too, along with a great many other things.

She forgot about provoking Dalton and leaned forward to kiss him. Jill cleared her throat.

"Oh." Charlie straightened, flustered, while Harry looked sublimely unaffected.

"Don't mind us," he said, "she just can't keep her hands off me."

With a smothered laugh, Jill said, "I'm going to run upstairs and put my stuff away, then I'll be right back down."

Dalton stepped forward. "You live upstairs, is that correct?"

"Yes. Would you like me to show you around?"

Charlie stiffened, ready to refuse despite Harry's gentle stroking on her back, when Jill added, a touch of warning in her tone, "Charlie won't mind. She never lets men upstairs—well, except for Harry, but he's different."

"So I understand."

Jill laughed. "Charlie is rigidly uncompromising about how she handles having our home above the bar. She's never wanted any of the men here to get the wrong idea. She won't admit it, but she's something of a mother hen most of the time."

Dalton glanced at Charlie with a smile. "I realize that. And it soothes me to know what a wonderful job she's done handling everything."

Charlie's mouth fell open in surprise at the praise, and Harry started to laugh, tempting Charlie's elbow again. She gave in to temptation, and at the same time prompted her sister with, "I thought you were going to put your things away."

Jill rolled one shoulder. "I don't know why you're so shy about being a good sister. It's not like it's a bad thing."

Dalton took Jill's arm to start them on their way. "Maybe you can tell me more about…Charlie, during our tour?"

"I'd love to!"

As they disappeared through the doorway, Charlie dropped back against Harry with a groan. "Jill and her big mouth."

Harry smiled against her temple. "If I laugh, will you poke me with that sharp elbow of yours again?"

"Absolutely."

"Then I'll content myself with telling you how childish you're acting." She started to pull away, but he locked his arms around her, just below her breasts, and held her secure. "Allow your lover just a little leeway, please. It's my right as such to point these things out."

"Okay, so pretending we're involved was a bad idea on my part. You can quit punishing me for it."

"Is that what I was doing?"

"Yes. You've made your point. I've acted like a total idiot."

"I never said any such thing and I'll thank you not to put words in my mouth."

She twisted to face him, bracing her hands on his shoulders. "All right, so what would you say?"

He smoothed her hair away from her face and his expression grew serious, his golden brown eyes intent. "That you're fighting yourself more than anyone else. Dalton's reaction wasn't one of disapproval, but guilt. He doesn't know you well enough yet to know you wouldn't be taken advantage of. He doesn't know how strong and capable you are."

"But you do?"

His hand cupped her neck, caressing. "You're the strongest person I've ever met."

"Too strong?"

His brows lifted in admission. "Sometimes. You plow your way through life assuming sheer determination will get you what you want."

She wondered if he was talking about himself. True, she'd been coming on strong, but that was the only way she knew. Sheer determination *had* gotten her everything she wanted—with the exception of a responsible mother or an available father.

She looked down at his chest and toyed with a button on his shirt. "Today...well, this was just for show."

"I wasn't talking about us, Charlie. I was talking about this unreasonable assumption you have that you can handle men like Carlyle, or even Floyd and Ralph."

"Oh." She waved that away. "I'm not worried about them, even though you're keeping secrets from me." She slanted him a look. "I know something's going on, and I'll figure it out sooner or later. Now, don't look like that, Harry. You know I will! I'm not dumb, and despite all your warnings, they don't scare me."

His sigh was exaggerated. "I know, and that's what worries

me. I have enough appreciation for their malevolent capacities for both of us."

Charlie grinned. "I love it when you talk like that. *Malevolent capacities*. It sounds dirty."

He shook her slightly, but she could see the amusement in his eyes. "I'm serious here, Charlie."

"Yeah, well, I'm seriously starting to wonder what's taking them so long. Our apartment is pretty small. You could walk the whole thing in under two minutes."

"You're incorrigible."

"Tell my father that." Harry grew so solemn, she sighed. "All right, I'm sorry."

He grabbed his head and weaved in the chair, almost toppling Charlie. "I must be delirious. Surely you didn't just apologize? Not Charlie Jones, the toughest—"

"My elbow hasn't gotten any softer you know." She stifled a chuckle as she made the threat, drawing her arm back in warning.

Harry grabbed her close and kissed her mouth, laughing against her lips. It was a ticklish kiss—at least at first. Then his mouth softened, slowed with awareness. She was on his lap, feeling his heat, his strength. At first the closeness was a game, but now it struck her how cozy it could be.

She'd never sat in a man's lap before meeting Harry.

They both remained motionless for a long moment, and Charlie could hear the thundering of her heartbeat in her ears. Her lips parted, and with a groan, Harry tilted her back over his arm. His mouth was suddenly hot, hungry, his tongue stroking past her lips, tasting—

"Maybe we should leave the lovebirds alone."

Harry jerked back so fast he made Charlie lose her balance. She almost slid off his lap. He managed to catch her arms, saving her the disgrace of falling on her behind. To her disgust, she could feel her face heating.

"Ah, Jill, we were just…"

"I'm young, sis, not stupid." Jill shook her head at Harry, then continued. "Father and I have decided to go to dinner. He said you two had a date, so we'll just use the time to get better acquainted."

Charlie felt her temper start to boil, but then Dalton stepped closer and said, "That's if it's okay with you. Harry drove here, but we can catch a cab. I thought after dinner, I could show Jill the jewelry store I own on the other side of town. I'd love for you to see it as well, but of course, I don't want to interfere with your personal time."

Momentarily stuck in her own deception, Charlie said, "Uhhh...."

Harry had no such problem. "That's fine. I'm sure we'll manage without you."

Charlie stood and stared hard at Dalton in warning. "Where are you going to dinner?"

He didn't look the least put off by her tone, or her question. "I thought we'd go to Maria's. It's a nice little Italian restaurant not too far from my store."

It was a restaurant she'd never been to, a very ritzy, expensive place well above her budget. She glanced at her sister and saw that Jill had changed into a dress and looked very excited by the prospect of dining there. Charlie didn't want to let her go. Old protective instincts clamored inside her, reminding her of all the years she'd spent looking out for her sister's well-being. But Jill was eighteen now, a young woman, and it was time to give her some freedom.

It went against her instincts, but Charlie nodded. "All right."

Jill stepped forward and gave Charlie a tight hug. "Thank you."

She waved her off. "Don't thank me. I'm not the one taking you."

"But we both know I wouldn't go if you asked me not to."

Uncomfortable with Dalton and Harry listening in, Charlie

made a face. "Yeah, well, I'm assuming Dalton will take good care of you."

Dalton's mouth twitched at the malice in her tone. "Absolutely." Then he, too, stepped forward for a hug, taking Charlie by surprise. In a low voice meant only for her ears, he said, "I can't tell you how pleased I am to finally meet you. Pleased, and so damn proud."

Charlie was still mute after they'd walked out the door. Harry, with a twisted grin, waved a hand in front of her face.

"Are you all right or did Dalton put a trance on you?"

She shook her head as if to clear it, then looked at Harry, but she didn't really see him. A jumbled mix of emotions made her shaky inside. *Her father was proud?* She swallowed hard and tried to digest that information, but every stubborn, fighting instinct she had rebelled against it. Accepting any accolades from him would make her weak, would detract from the foundation she'd built over the past months and alter her goals completely. It was too much to take in all at once, and so she did what came naturally instead.

With a determined look that made Harry draw back, she walked around him and started out of the bar.

He hustled after her. "Where are you off to, brat?"

"I'm going to follow them."

"What?"

"He can visit with my sister all he likes, as long as I'm close enough to take care of her if anything goes wrong." Using her key, she unlocked the bottom door and rushed through it. Harry caught it in time and went up the steps with her. "I'm going to change, then I'm leaving. If you want to come along, fine, but I don't need you there."

He tried to catch her arm, but she shook him off to unlock the door at the top of the stairs.

"Charlie, this is insane."

"Think what you like. I'm still going to do it." She went

down the hall to her bedroom, aware of Harry right behind her, and of his shock to her decorating scheme. He'd been upstairs many times, but never in her bedroom.

He stood there with his mouth open, his face blank. "Good God. You have ruffles."

Belligerent, she said, "Yeah, so? It's my room and I can decorate it any way I want." She pulled out a clean pair of newer jeans and a white button-down oxford-cloth shirt. It was the closest thing she had to "dressier."

Harry touched the fluffy white quilt on her bed. "I like it, so don't sound so defensive. It's just that I pictured you with…"

"Barbed wire? A bare mattress?" She snorted. "The quilt is warm and the bed skirt hides all the stuff I stick under my bed."

Harry bent and looked. "There's nothing under your bed."

"Go to hell, Harry."

He laughed, but when she pulled off her T-shirt to change, his humor died a quick death. Sounding strangled, he asked, "What are you doing?"

"Changing. I can't very well go unnoticed if I wear what they've already seen."

"Charlie." With his gaze glued to her upper body, bare except for her bra, he clasped her shoulders. "Don't do this to yourself."

She tried to shrug him off, but his large hands held firm. "I have to hurry."

"You're not going anywhere, sweetheart."

Turmoil exploded inside her, making her hands shake and her stomach pitch. In a voice that was less than steady, she growled, "Don't start with me now, Harry. I *have* to go."

"Shh." Despite her resistance he pulled her close and his big hot hands smoothed up and down her naked spine. "I

know, babe, I really do. This is so damn hard. But you need
to indulge in a little trust."

"Trust a man I barely know?"

He kissed her ear, still making those "shushing" sounds.
"You know me, and I've told you the man is safe. And you
should certainly trust your sister. What responsibilities did
you have at eighteen?"

The trembling became worse and she leaned into Harry,
for the moment letting herself relax, letting his heat seep into
her. "None that I want Jill to have."

"You've done an incredible job with her, Charlie. She's an
intelligent young lady and an excellent judge of character. She
has enough sense to call you if anything should go wrong."

She bit her lip, trying to sort out her thoughts. "Why should
I trust you when you don't trust me?"

His hands stilled.

"Something's going on with Carlyle. I can feel it."

A look of alarm passed over his features and his frown
turned fierce. "That has nothing to do with you."

Flabbergasted, she leaned back to look at him. "And my
personal life has nothing to do with *you,* but I noticed that
hasn't slowed you down any!"

Her new posture pushed her pelvis closer to his, while
baring her upper body. His gaze again lowered to her breasts,
and he remained silent.

Tension radiated off him and she shifted. "What? No
answer to that?"

His hand coasted down her spine to her backside, cuddling
and stroking. In a near rasp, he said, "We're standing in a
bedroom, you're taunting me with these luscious little breasts
of yours, and I'm so aroused I can barely think. Did you really
expect me to indulge in conversation?"

Her own arousal hit like a tidal wave, stealing her breath
and filling her with undulating heat. All her confusion, all her
nervousness, magically transformed into sexual awareness.

She could barely get a whisper past her constricted throat. "Harry?"

Shaking his head with a denial she didn't understand, he closed his eyes. "I can't do this anymore."

The heat of his hard chest beckoned her, and she braced her palms flat there. "Do what?"

Startling her with his suddenness, he lifted her, walked the two steps to the bed, then dropped with her to the mattress. He caught her hands and lifted them over her head, then groaned as her breasts pressed to his chest.

The weight of his body both appeased and intensified the ache, making her squirm. "I love how you feel, Harry. So hard and hot and strong."

The low gasping of his breath tickled her ear. "I'm glad you think so, because I'm in no hurry to move."

"I don't want you to move. Let my hands go."

"No."

"What do you mean 'no'?" When he didn't answer, she tried to pull away.

"Not this time, honey. This time we finish it. *My way.*"

Charlie felt both excited and slightly alarmed by his uncompromising tone, uncertain how she should react. Then she realized she really had no choice. Harry wasn't letting go, and that meant she'd have to accept whatever he had planned.

Her eyes narrowed sensually. She'd wallow in every second of his dominance.

RAISING HIMSELF slightly, Harry smiled and transferred both her hands into one of his own, then cupped her jaw. "You're just filled with demands, aren't you?"

"I wasn't…"

"Hmm. Yes, you were. It's part and parcel of who you are. But I like it. Most of the time. Right now, I like you soft and submissive beneath me." He kissed her gently, pulling back when she tried to deepen the kiss. "Do you like it too, honey?"

"Yes."

That soft whisper shook his resolve. Harry closed his mouth over hers, felt her lips part and immediately stroked his tongue inside. Her slender thighs tightened restlessly, her body shifting in subtle, erotic moves. His free hand slid down her side, then to her soft breast. Damn she felt good. Her nipple was already puckered, pressing against her thin cotton bra, and with a low curse, he caught the cup with his fingertips and pulled it down until her firm breast came free.

Harry tore his mouth away from hers to look at her. He leaned back and to the side, keeping her hands firmly clasped, watching in heated appreciation as she strained toward him.

Her breast was so white, the nipple a soft pale pink, and he wanted her. He leaned down with no forewarning and drew her into his mouth.

She gave a stifled scream.

"Hush. Someone downstairs might hear you."

"Harry…it's too much."

"Nonsense," he said, taunting her with his assurance. "You'll like this. Just be still."

She didn't even try. As he licked and gently sucked, she struggled against him, moaning, twisting. She kept trying to pull her hands free, but he didn't think she was even aware of it. She didn't want to be free, it was just in Charlie's nature to fight any type of restriction. He felt provoked by her reactions, and grew all the more determined to control things.

From the day he'd met her, she'd made him crazy with her take charge ways, even while his admiration for her courage grew. Little by little she'd seduced him, not just sexually, but emotionally as well. He wanted her, and he was tired of denying himself. Unlike his ex-wife, who tried to manipulate with tears, Charlie fought fair, with upfront demands and honest compromises. He enjoyed his battles with her, rather than feeling guilty over them. She excited him on every level, and he couldn't resist any longer.

Later, he'd work through the problems. But now, in this precise moment, all he cared about was making her his own.

He loved the taste of her, her hot reactions, and he wanted more. Coming up to his knees, straddling her hips so she couldn't scoot away, he tugged the bra completely off. Charlie froze for an instant as the heat of embarrassment colored her face and throat. "You're looking at me."

"Yes." With one finger he touched her exposed nipples. "You're wet from my mouth, tight and sweet."

Her eyes closed again and she made soft sounds of desire. Her breasts were plump, offered up by the way she kept straining toward him. The mere sight of her aroused him as much as an hour of foreplay. "You're right, sweetheart. These are very special."

"You're embarrassing me, Harry."

His mouth tipped in a small smile. She didn't sound embarrassed. She sounded excited. Her breasts shimmered with each breath, her diaphragm expanding. Her abdomen was silky smooth, narrow. The waistband of her jeans curled out away from her skin and he deftly flicked the snap free. He could hear her rasping, anxious breaths as he slowly tugged down the zipper. Her belly was taut, her hips staining upward. He dipped one fingertip in her navel, then followed the line of her zipper downward, gradually parting the material until he came to the elastic waistband of her bikini panties. Because he'd already seen her bra, he wasn't surprised that these were also white cotton.

"You have very conservative taste in underclothes," he murmured.

His finger continued to tickle up and down just inside her zipper and her voice shook when she replied. "No one sees them but me."

Her words filled him with satisfaction, and the possessive

urges no longer alarmed him. "I think this one is jealous," he said of the breast he hadn't yet tasted.

"Harry…"

Her tone was a whimper in anticipation of what she knew would come. He wanted her to understand that she couldn't always control him, that some things were better left in his hands, especially the sensual things.

With that in mind, he bent and carefully kissed her breast, avoiding the erect, puckered nipple and ignoring her soft cries. Relentlessly he teased, always staying just out of reach no matter how she turned or tried to coax him to take her into his mouth. She cursed him softly, then moaned, her thick lashes drifting down over her eyes, her body going utterly lax, with no fight left at all.

Harry tried to stifle the overwhelming feeling of triumph, but knowing he'd won with this one particular woman—and that she'd enjoyed letting him win—filled him with primitive instincts. He loosened his hold and whispered close to her ear, "Don't move, sweetheart."

"Harry…*please*."

His heart tripped. He'd never thought to hear that word from her mouth. She'd not only given over to him, she trusted him enough to show her full need. Releasing her hands and sitting up, Harry pulled off her boots and socks, then hooked his fingers in the waistband of her jeans and tugged them down to her knees. She helped him by kicking them off the rest of the way.

Charlie watched him through dazed eyes. Her soft mouth was slightly open, her hands resting above her head, the palms up and vulnerable. He shook he wanted her so badly.

Coming down on his elbow beside her, he kissed her hungrily and she groaned in relief. Impatient, he stroked his hand down her belly and below, cupping his fingers over her mound, feeling the heat of her, the dampness of the cotton panties.

He could hear the race of his blood in his ears, and the sexy little sounds Charlie made.

She was already so close, and he'd barely begun. He leaned away from her and saw her hands were now fisted tightly, her chest heaving, her pale thighs clenched. He pushed his hand inside her panties and with his middle finger pressed and stroked. "You're so wet, honey. Do you like that?"

"Yes."

She didn't hesitate in answering, though her reply was an almost incoherent hiss. He'd always loved watching a woman climax, but seeing Charlie, her head pressed back, her neck muscles straining, her pretty breasts heaving—it was more than he'd ever expected. More than he likely deserved. Very slowly, he worked one finger inside her. Though she was silky wet and very excited, she clenched his finger tightly. He groaned, imagining how she'd feel squeezing his erection. His heart pounded.

"Ah, Harry, I…"

"Does that hurt?" he whispered. His free arm was beside her head and he smoothed her silky dark hair away from her face.

She shook her head, then said, "A little. But don't stop."

"No, I won't stop." It pained him to smile, he was so aroused, but he felt full to bursting with love and contentment. He kissed her cheek, her nose, then used his thumb to find her small clitoris. He touched it lightly and she jerked, her reaction very telling.

He found a rhythm, using her own wetness to slick the way, to make the friction sweeter. He could tell she held her breath, her entire body tensed in expectation, and when she suddenly lurched and cried out he kissed her, swallowing the sound, taking it into himself. She forgot his instructions and wrapped her arms tightly around him, gripping him as if needing an anchor, as if she needed him as close as possible. Harry continued to kiss her, his tongue stroking in her mouth just as his finger stroked inside her. Her climax was long and full and she held him, her thighs rigid, her inner muscles trembling. She was so explosive, so *real,* he nearly lost control.

Making love to her, actually being inside her, might well kill him. But he was more than willing to take the risk.

As she quieted, he tenderly kissed her trembling lips. "You okay?"

She mumbled something he couldn't hear and burrowed a little closer.

"Should I take that as a yes?" He wanted to tease, but his voice shook and he knew he wouldn't last a minute longer.

For an answer, she bit him. He jumped, then rubbed his chest, though the small nip of her teeth hadn't really hurt. "Your vicious tendencies never cease to amaze me."

She gave him a scorching look and smiled. "My vicious tendencies will explode if you don't get on with it."

"Impatient wench." But he stood beside the bed and began unbuttoning his shirt. Charlie watched, lying on her back at her leisure, unashamed of her nudity or the sensual pose she presented.

Impossible as it seemed, her gaze grew even warmer and she breathed more deeply as he tossed his shirt aside and unbuttoned his slacks. He removed his wallet and pulled a condom from it, tossing it onto the nightstand beside her bed. She smiled.

Holding her gaze, he toed off his shoes, then pulled down his slacks, removing his shorts and socks at the same time. He straightened, then stood there, letting her look her fill.

She took a leisurely perusal of his body, from his shoulders all the way down to his feet. Once that was done, her gaze lifted to focus on his erection. He throbbed painfully, feeling her attention like a tactile touch.

"Well?"

With warm cheeks and hot eyes she nodded. "You'll do."

The laugh emerged as a bark, relieving a bit of his tension. He climbed back into bed with her. "Merely satisfactory, huh?"

"On the contrary." She crawled over him, lying along his length, propping her elbows on his chest. Her voice turned low and husky as she stared down into his eyes. "You're so incredibly sexy there are no words."

The breathless compliment pushed him right over the edge. "Charlie." He turned her beneath him and kissed her deeply, groaning at the acute sensation of her nakedness beneath him. With her arms free this time, she explored him, her small palms coasting over his shoulders, down his spine to his buttocks. He groaned again, then reared back. "Damn it. I'm sorry, but I can't wait. I wanted to make this last, to glut myself on you—"

"How romantic."

He shook his head, unable to banter with her at this moment when his need was so great. "I'll explode if I don't get inside you right now."

Her smile was pure female satisfaction. "So explode. I'm not stopping you."

Muttering another curse, he leaned over to the nightstand and grabbed the condom. Charlie watched in fascination as he put it on, then squealed when he quickly tucked her beneath him. "Put your legs around me."

She obeyed. He reached between their bodies, touching her, opening her for his thrust. "You're small, honey."

Her eyes were huge, watchful. "And you're not."

"No." He ground his teeth together while his fingers again explored her. Her feminine flesh was swelled, hot. And she was wet from her release. He closed his eyes. "I don't want to hurt you."

"It's all right, Harry. I won't break."

He wanted to laugh. Even now, she was full of bravado, unwilling to show any weakness. He wanted to wait, to ease into her gently, but she kept touching him and her hips squirmed against him. His control snapped. With a harsh curse, he entered her.

She caught her breath, but didn't fight him.

"Easy, sweetheart." He saw her through a red haze of overwhelming lust and tenderness, emotions that when mixed became volatile. She quivered, and her eyes closed, her neck arched. She gave a small moan, of pain or ecstasy, he couldn't tell. Then her legs tightened around his waist and her fingers tangled in his hair, and he was gone.

He rode her as gently as he could considering every muscle in his body strained for release. He felt sweat on his shoulders, felt her uneven breaths on his throat. And he felt Charlie, soft and inquisitive and delicate, despite the impression she liked to give the world.

Sliding one hand beneath her hips, he tilted her pelvis to allow him a deeper penetration, driven to bind their bodies together, to make her a part of him. She cried out, and her inner muscles clamped down on him.

"Come on, sweetheart," he ground out through his teeth, thrusting harder, faster, his control a distant memory. "Come for me again. I want you with me."

He felt the spasms in her legs first, then the way her entire body tensed. She caught and held her breath, her eyes squeezed tight, and she climaxed, holding him, whispering his name. Tears seeped past her lashes and as he joined her, his own release strong enough to steal his strength, the truth hit him. He loved her. Damn, how he loved her.

Now the real trouble would begin.

CHAPTER ELEVEN

"OH HARRY. That was…indescribable."

She heard a grunt that could possibly pass for a reply, and grinned. Harry at a loss for words? What a novelty.

Her hands coasted over his slick shoulders and she kissed his throat. He tasted good. He smelled good. She admitted he *was* good. Her body still tingled pleasantly in very interesting places. "I wouldn't mind doing this again."

The grunt turned into a groan. With obvious effort, Harry raised his head. His light brown eyes were soft and sated and filled with some emotion she didn't understand.

He touched her hair, her cheek. "Insatiable, are we?"

"A tribute to your skill."

"Hmm. I suppose I could be convinced—in about an hour."

She laughed, then pushed at his shoulder. "In that case, you need to move. I have things to do."

Obediently, Harry rolled to the side, sprawling on his back like a vanquished warrior. When she started to crawl over him, he made a sound of appreciation and pulled her flat to his chest. "Don't you know lovers are supposed to talk after sex? It's callous to just use me and then leave the bed without any soft whispering and cuddling."

Toying with the hair on his chest, she laughed. "Callous, huh? I wouldn't want to be accused of that. But maybe we can talk later? I need to get going."

A frown appeared where before he'd been all smiles. "Where is it you think you have to rush off to?"

She tried to get up again, but now he had both hands cupping her bare backside, anchoring her in place. "I told you, I want to go keep an eye on Jill."

Harry closed his eyes with a soft curse. When he opened them again, she was struck by the cold determination there. "You don't need to do that."

"So says a man who doesn't have a little sister. Look, Harry, I know you said you checked up on Dalton. But how much could you have really found out? There could be all kinds of skeletons in his closet, and until I'm assured—"

"There aren't."

"You sound awfully sure of that." She watched him skeptically, knowing that particular tone and look.

With a sigh, Harry lifted her to the side of the bed and sat up. "We need to talk."

Charlie scrambled for the sheet and pulled it over her. "And we will. Later."

Resignation darkened his features as he glanced at her over his shoulder. "I know your father."

A strange foreboding made her stomach pitch. She pressed a fist to it and said logically, "Of course you do. You brought him here."

He waved her logic away. "I knew him before that. I've known him for years." He turned to face her, still naked, his powerful shoulders gleaming in the lamplight, his dusty brown hair rumpled. His gaze never wavered from hers but tension emanated off him, pelting her with his resolution. "Dalton Jones has been like a father to me."

Feeling unsteady and sick, she moved away from him. She needed distance; she needed to be off the bed where they'd just made love. Backing up until she bumped into the dresser, she watched him. Harry never so much as flinched. "I don't understand."

"Dalton has looked for you for years, honey. He's suffered more than any one man ever should."

"You know him?" That one fact wouldn't quite penetrate.

Harry stood, too, but when she clutched her sheet tighter, he went still, making no move toward her. "My father was a cold, distant man who barely knew I existed. Dalton stepped in and did all the things for me that a father should do. He supported me in my decisions, and helped me get through my divorce from hell. He encouraged me and—"

"And did all the things for you that he didn't do for me." She felt lost, wounded to her soul.

"Not because he didn't care! He's spent a small fortune trying to locate you and Jill."

Not for anything would Charlie let him see how he'd hurt her, how her heart felt ready to break into pieces. She clutched at the sheet and tried to order her thoughts into some decipherable rationale. "Why didn't you tell me?"

Locking his jaw, Harry paced away, giving her a distracting view of his muscled backside. It angered her that even now she was drawn to him, finding him irresistible.

He turned to face her and propped his hands on his hips. "I didn't know what the hell to do when you asked me to find your father. At the time, I felt my loyalty was to Dalton. It was his responsibility, his *pleasure,* to get to explain that he hadn't abandoned you. But you were so hostile about the whole thing, so…detached. You'd sent him that damn letter—"

"You knew about the letter?"

He gave a small nod. "I knew. Dalton told me that very night at the hospital. And he asked me not to tell you the truth yet, because he wanted a chance with you. He thought if I pretended to investigate him, I could give you a few facts that might soften you toward him."

That word *pretend* felt like a slap, bringing home just how much of her relationship with Harry was based on lies and manipulations. "So you played along?"

"Honey, I didn't know what else to do. I tried to talk him out of it, but he was afraid of losing you again."

"And of course, what he wanted is the only thing that mattered. I mean, you hardly know me really. I'm just…" She stopped in midsentence because she had no idea what she meant to Harry. Obviously not much or he couldn't have deceived her so easily. Needing something to do before she fell apart, she went to the closet and pulled out a T-shirt.

The bed creaked when Harry sat back down. "I'm so sorry, Charlie. I swear I never meant to hurt you."

She pulled clean jeans from the dresser, fighting off the tears the best she could. "I understand. I don't like it, of course." The laugh, sounding close to hysteria, took her by surprise and she quickly suppressed it. "I feel pretty damn foolish, too. I can just imagine how the two of you must have been snickering. Especially after my stupid display tonight."

"No."

He started to get up, to come to her, but she warned him off with a bleak look. If he touched her, she'd sit down and cry like a baby, and that was something she hadn't done in too many years to count. "Don't even think it, Harry. The pretense is over."

Eyeing her rigid stance, he said carefully, "It wasn't all a pretense."

"No? Well, some day you'll have to tell me which parts came close to the truth. Right now, I'm just not interested. I'd like you to leave."

He swallowed hard, still watching her. "No."

"I need to get dressed!" The panic was real, making her voice too loud, too high. She needed to be alone. Already her hands were shaking and her legs were following suit.

"Charlie." Despite her warnings, he started toward her.

She shook her head, but he looked more determined now than ever. "We have to talk about this."

"About how you used me? How you played along so Dalton wouldn't be disappointed?" His hands reached for her and her temper snapped. Without really thinking it through, she slapped him. Hard. The loud crack of her palm striking his handsome face sounded obscene. For an instant, they both froze. Then she covered her mouth, appalled.

Harry fingered his cheek, his brows up in surprise. "I didn't see that coming. Knowing you as I do, I was watching for a fist, or maybe a kick. Not a feminine slap."

"Don't you dare tease me now."

"I'm sorry. But Charlie, there's more I have to tell you."

"Oh?" Her stomach clenched, but she forced herself to be flippant. "Did you maybe just fake what we did in bed?"

Incredulous, he stared at her a moment, then laughed. "Honey, men can't fake a thing like that."

Her teeth ground together. "You know what I mean. And don't call me honey."

He hesitated for the briefest moment. "No, I didn't fake it." His gaze softened, turned intimate, and he whispered, "I love you."

Her chest hurt so much she gasped. She felt raw and exposed, and she almost hated him. *Almost.* "Did Dalton tell you to say that? To do whatever was necessary to appease me?"

"No."

In a burst of temper, she snapped, "Will you at least put some damn clothes on!"

His expression didn't change. "Dalton had a heart attack the day you sent the letter." He caught her before she dropped to the floor, then led her to the bed. He spoke quickly now, rushing his words together. "I was so worried about him, it's part of the reason I let him talk me into this harebrained plan, because I didn't want to see him disappointed again. You've been so hurt, I couldn't guess how you might react to the truth, if you'd even give Dalton a chance. And if you didn't, with his health in danger—"

She was back off the bed in a flash, no longer worried about her sheet or keeping her body covered. She jerked on her jeans and pulled the T-shirt over her head, then stepped into a pair of sneakers.

"Charlie—"

She rounded on him. "You bastard!" Stepping close so she could shake a fist in his face, she yelled, "My father could have died, and you didn't tell me?"

He caught and held her fists. "He's fine now, Charlie. He only needs to be more cautious."

She shoved him away then turned for the door. Harry grabbed her shoulder. "Where are you going?"

"To see him. I want you out of my place." She picked up a key off the dresser and flung it at him. "Let yourself out."

"Wait!" He started rushing into his own clothes. "I'll go with you."

"Ha!"

"It's not safe, Charlie! Damn it, you don't know what's going on!"

But she was already hurrying down the hall. Harry tried to follow after her, and she barely slipped through the door in time. She heard his fist hit it with incredible force, and he yelled her name again. She ignored him. She knew by the time he got the key and unlocked the door, she'd be gone. And if she never saw him again, it was only what she deserved.

CHARLIE CHECKED first at Maria's, the restaurant where they'd planned to eat, but Dalton and her sister weren't there. She assumed they had gone on to Dalton's jewelry store, so she headed in that direction. At the moment, she had no idea what she planned to say to her father, but she needed to reassure herself that he was okay. Whether he cared about her or not, he was her father, and that mattered. It mattered more than she'd ever thought possible, and she now regretted all her plans for revenge. It made her almost sick to think she might have played a part in his ill health with her hurtful letter.

All her concentration was centered on the problem with her father. She couldn't think about Harry. If she did, she might start bawling like a baby. She loved the arrogant, obnoxious jerk, and yet he'd used her. The really sad part was, she could understand his reasons for the deception. In his position, she might have done the same. And if she hadn't pushed so hard, their relationship probably wouldn't have become intimate. She had only herself to blame. She'd been a complete fool—and she'd behaved like her mother. The truth hurt so bad she didn't think she could stand it.

She trudged up the sidewalk to the jewelry store, lost in thought. At first she didn't notice when a car pulled up beside her. Absently, she turned to look, and was stunned to see Floyd in the passenger seat, grinning at her with evil intent. The car stopped and she broke into a dead run, but she'd only gotten a few feet before he caught her arm and jerked her back. She stumbled, going down hard on one knee. She groaned at the jarring pain.

The car pulled alongside and Ralph got out. "Get her in the back seat."

Hearing that cleared the pain from her knee enough to allow her to fight. She started kicking and shouting, doing anything she could to fend them off. Somehow she knew if they got her in the car, she might never get out again.

Floyd managed to drag her as far as the curb, using her arm and her shirt collar for leverage. Even in her struggle, she saw the unfamiliar man in the front seat. She had the brief impression of a polished businessman before shouts sounded behind her. Her blood nearly froze when she recognized Dalton's voice.

"No!" He couldn't get into a skirmish because of her, not with his heart condition. If anything happened to him... She doubled her efforts, and caught Floyd low in the stomach with a fist. He grunted and loosened his hold. She tried to roll away, but Ralph reached for her.

"Let her go!" Dalton leaped onto Ralph's back, knocking him down, all the while cursing so vividly Charlie couldn't help but be impressed. The third man in the car got out and started toward them with a purposeful stride.

Suddenly other men were there, leaving their shops in a rush, leaping into the fray, crowding together on the sidewalk. It became a chaotic free-for-all with the elderly swinging canes and brooms and fists. Vile threats filled the air from both factions. Charlie was tossed aside and landed on her butt, but she was back up in a heartbeat when she saw the man from the car reach inside his jacket. *Oh God, a gun!*

Dalton threw himself in front of her, and no matter how she tried, she couldn't get around him. The brawl ended, no one daring to move. Floyd and Ralph, with a lot of blustering, brushed themselves off and straightened their jackets. Six older men and two gray-haired women stood in a circle, their hands in fists, their faces red.

"What should we do with them all, Carlyle?"

Carlyle. Again, Charlie strained to see around Dalton's shoulder, curious about the man Harry wanted so badly. After being kidnapped and harassed, she owed Carlyle much, and now with him threatening her father her rage grew.

She ducked under Dalton's arm, but before she could take two steps Harry was there. In a flash, he was around the parked car, jerking Carlyle's hand up so the gun fired in the air with a loud crack of sound, and wrapping one long muscled arm around his throat, squeezing tight enough to make Carlyle's eyes bug. Sirens whined in the distance.

Ralph and Floyd started to back up, but they were quickly subdued by the older folk. Floyd screeched like a wet hen when his arm was twisted high, and Moses, with a look of disgust, muttered, "Sissy."

Pops stepped forward and wagged a fist. "Shoot 'em!"

Harry's gaze met Charlie's, and he smiled. "He's as blood-thirsty as you are, brat."

Carlyle lurched, trying to break free, and without a single hesitation, Harry punched him the jaw. The man went down like a lead balloon. Very slowly, Charlie applauded.

The police showed up in two patrol cars and a plain sedan. The detective in charge appeared to know Harry. With the men subdued in cuffs, the trunk of Carlyle's car was opened and Charlie glimpsed a variety of weapons, rifles and guns and ammunition. There were so many of them, it looked like an arsenal.

One of the officers whistled low.

"They're dealing in illegal and stolen weaponry." Charlie noticed Harry didn't mention the embezzlement, keeping to his promise not to involve the older proprietors. "I can give you an address of an abandoned warehouse where you'll find more of the same, as well as evidence of other illegal activities."

The detective clapped Harry on the shoulder and they spoke quietly for a few minutes. The officers were questioning everyone and to Charlie's surprise, the seniors loved it. They fairly crowed in their excitement. Charlie used the moment to go to Dalton.

"Where's my sister?"

He was still catching his breath, but he looked relieved. "Inside. My assistant is practically sitting on her. She wanted to rush out with me, but seeing you threatened was more than enough." He touched her face and his hand trembled. Charlie took his arm and hustled him to a shop stoop to sit. Even as he did her bidding, he asked, "Are you okay?"

She smiled. At the same time big tears welled in her eyes. "That was my question to you."

"Now that you're safe, I'm fine. But I don't mind telling you, seeing that bastard put his hands on you nearly stopped my—"

"Your heart?" She knelt down in front of him and took his hands. "Are you sure you're all right?"

"You know?"

"That you had a heart attack? Yes. Harry finally came clean."

Dalton sighed heavily. "It wasn't your fault, you know. Your letter didn't distress me. It thrilled me and made me so proud I wanted to dance up and down the street."

"It was a hateful letter."

"It was a letter filled with guts and courage and pride. I knew the moment I read it you were an incredible young woman. I was right."

The tears trickled down her cheeks and she impatiently swiped them away. "That was a dirty trick you played on me, having Harry lie about everything. But under the circumstances I suppose I understand."

"Do you? I couldn't take the chance you'd shut me out. I'd waited too long to get my girls back." His own eyes teared up, breaking Charlie's heart. "I'm so sorry I hurt you earlier today."

She shook her head. "It doesn't matter."

"That's not what Harry said. I've known him since he was a boy, back when his father and I were friends. We've always been as close as two men can be, and that's the first time he ever raised hell with me."

Once again, her temper rose. "Harry yelled at you?"

Scoffing, Dalton shook his head. "Harry never yells. He just gets glib and lectures. He told me what a wonderful woman you were, and he insisted there wasn't a single thing about you that needed to be changed."

Charlie was absorbing that when a voice from behind her said, "What I didn't tell you is that I love her."

She jerked around so fast, she landed on her rump. Since that particular part of her anatomy was already sore from the skirmish, she scowled at Harry. He didn't give her a chance to grumble, reaching down and grabbing her under her arms, then lifting her completely off her feet until she was eye level, dangling in the air.

Charlie gulped, eyeing Harry cautiously. His shirt was untucked and only half-buttoned, and he had on shoes but no socks. He'd obviously dressed in a rush.

Shaking her slightly, he shouted, "You scared the hell out of me, taking off like that!"

Charlie glanced over at Dalton, who sat there grinning, and she said, "I thought he never yelled."

Dalton shrugged.

Harry shook her again, making her feet swing. "In the normal course of things, when not unduly provoked, I *don't* yell! But you have a way of pushing me on everything."

Despite her ignominious position, she lifted her chin. "Good. Because you push me, too."

That vexed him for a moment, and he growled, "Damn right! And I'm going to continue to do so. I love you, damn it. Doesn't that matter at all?"

Pops leaned in to say, "It should matter."

Moses nodded. "Always used to matter in the good ole days." The rest of the seniors offered mumbled agreements.

An elderly woman with gray hair escaping her bun patted Charlie on the arm. "You should listen to him, honey. Harry's a good man, and he packs one helluva punch."

They all nodded, even the officers. Moses stepped forward and he looked sheepish. "Harry convinced us we couldn't handle those punks on our own. We should have trusted the cops. Even outnumberin' 'em two to one, they almost got away from us."

Harry, still holding Charlie off the ground as if her weight were totally negligible, said to the hovering group, "I couldn't have done it without your assistance."

Charlie frowned. "It was a plan?"

"A very sound plan. I knew Carlyle would be with Ralph and Floyd today, and I knew they'd have the guns."

Charlie gasped. "This is the news you refused to share with me! I suspected something was going on, but you wouldn't tell me a damn thing, and you kept sneaking off without me—"

"Which wasn't easy, I'll have you know. You're too nosy for your own good."

Dalton blustered. "*Charlie* was involved in that?"

Harry didn't answer, however his eyes glittered. "After picking up the money, they were going to make a deal—and the police would be ready." He glared at Dalton. "Things would have gone as planned if people didn't throw wrenches into the works, skipping dinner and coming here first."

"I had no idea!" He frowned at Harry, then shrugged. "I needed a reservation, so we were going back in an hour."

"And," Harry added, drawing Charlie so close she could see the fiery specks in his light brown eyes, "if stubborn women would only listen when given a heartfelt declaration of love."

"It really was heartfelt?"

"Haven't you been listening?" He shook her again, then hugged her tight. "It was extremely heartfelt."

Charlie looped her arms around his neck. "I haven't forgiven you yet for lying to me."

Harry pulled her slightly away and he looked at Dalton. "I compromised your daughter."

Dalton started in surprise. "You did?"

"Yes. But I'm willing to do the right thing."

The old people cheered all the more.

Charlie, enjoying herself now that she no longer doubted her father—or Harry—pretended to think things over. "I'm going to keep my bar."

"Fine. As long as you live with me."

"What about Jill?"

"She's more than welcome as long as she doesn't object to Ted, or Grace and Sooner."

Dalton stood. "Or she could live with me!"

Jill appeared, dragging the assistant in her wake. Several of the young officers looked at her with interest as she forged a path to her sister. "I'm going off to college, remember? But it's nice to feel so wanted. Who're Ted and Grace and Sooner?"

Harry brought Charlie close again and kissed her. In a whisper, he said, "I do love you, Charlie. So damn much. Please don't ever scare me like that again."

Those stupid, ridiculous tears threatened, but they were happy tears now. "If I marry you, can I help in all your investigations?"

He pretended to stagger with the mere thought, making her laugh. But that was the thing about Harry. Even from the first, he'd managed to bring fun and laughter back into her life. He'd even given her back her father. And now that she had those things, she couldn't imagine letting them go.

She pressed her face into his throat and said, "Since I love you, I suppose we should get married."

"That's a yes?"

"That's an absolute."

Sirens from the retreating patrol cars mingled with the shouts from the seniors and the happy shrieks from her sister. Dalton just sat there grinning—like a very proud papa.

* * * * *

MARRIED TO THE BOSS

To Emily Toerner,
A gem for a gem. I couldn't have chosen better myself,
and that surely puts my mother's heart at ease.

CHAPTER ONE

As soon as R. J. Maitland turned into the sweeping drive of Maitland Maternity Clinic, he saw the mob. Not a rioting mob, but every bit as bloodthirsty. *Reporters.*

They wouldn't destroy property, but they were certainly doing their best to destroy his reputation and that of the clinic. As president of Maitland Maternity, he felt responsible for its good name.

As a man, he felt a red-hot rage.

His hands tightened painfully on the wheel of his Mercedes, the only sign he allowed of his inner turmoil. Damn Tanya Lane for naming him as the father of the abandoned baby. And damn himself for having ever been involved with her in the first place.

Hoping to go unnoticed by the milling, impatient crowd, he drove to the parking lot around the corner. It turned out to be a futile effort; his car was spotted, and the mob rushed his way, flashbulbs popping, video cams zooming in, reporters with microphones extended, running to reach him, hoping for the first damaging quote of the day.

Since the baby had been discovered on the steps of the clinic in September, it had been like this, but now the focus had changed. He was the target.

Though his anger was near the boiling point, he remained outwardly aloof, ignoring them all and walking with an unhurried stride to the door. A security guard stood there, ready to block out the unwelcome press, but it wasn't easy getting past them. Questions were shouted at him, questions he couldn't honestly answer, and that made the rage all the worse.

"R.J.! Are you the father of the baby?"

"What do you intend to do about your child?"

"How does your family feel about this unexpected turn of events?"

He'd been asking himself the same things over and over again, ever since the basket with the little boy had been left at the clinic with a note claiming that he was a Maitland. Now, of course, the situation was worse.

Tanya Lane, an ex-girlfriend, had deliberately labeled him the father.

He forged onward, his jaw locked, his hands curled into fists. Just as he stepped through the polished brass-and-glass door, another reporter shouted loudly, "R.J., do you think you and Ms. Lane will reconcile now?"

R.J. stopped in midstep, then turned with fatal deliberation, jaw set, eyes hard. He sought out the reporter, who blinked owlishly in response to his visible fury, and with icy disdain said, "No."

A hush settled over the reporters with the finality of that single word, then they quickly erupted with more questions. Damn it, he knew better than to respond to the press at all. It was best to simply ignore them, to claim *no comment*. But he was sick and tired of their barbs, and he was fed up with being labeled as the type of bastard who would walk away from his responsibilities. He was used to controlling his life, to adjusting events, plans and people to suit his purposes. But in this, he had little control at all. It was intolerable.

Turning his back on the throng of reporters, R.J. headed into the clinic while the doorman struggled to close the door behind him. *Reconcile with Tanya?* he thought with acid disgust. *Not in this or any other lifetime.* He hadn't seen the woman for months. If it hadn't been for that TV reporter Chelsea Markum, offering a paltry bribe to get the negligent mother to come forth, he probably still wouldn't have heard from Tanya. Their parting hadn't been particularly pleasant, but it had been final.

At the time, Tanya had accepted his decision, taking the farewell money he offered her and walking away—as he'd known she would. She'd said nothing about a baby, not even about the possibility of a baby. Yet a baby had been left, alone and unprotected, on the clinic doorstep, and that sickened him as nothing else could.

If Tanya Lane was the mother, R.J. thought viciously, she would be wise to stay the hell out of his sight, and well out of his reach.

The elevator was thankfully empty as he rode to the second floor, where his office was located, giving him the few necessary moments to reign in his temper. He wanted, needed to shut himself inside and concentrate on work, on getting back on track. He hoped to find the usual relief in his daily routine, but he doubted he would, given his dark mood.

The second he stepped through the office door he saw Dana Dillinger, his longtime secretary, preparing a cup of coffee. Dana was quietly efficient, totally competent and a balm to his escalating frustration. Somehow, Dana always seemed to know exactly when he would walk in, and she continually found ways to make his work environment as comfortable for him as possible. Today he appreciated that more than ever before.

He eyed her prim back for a moment, watching her economical, graceful movements. "Good morning, Dana."

She looked up at him with a commiserating smile as she stirred just the right amount of creamer into his coffee. As usual, her dark blond hair was neatly swept into a sophisticated twist at the back of her head, and her light gray suit was tailored, perfectly pressed and eminently suitable for the secretary to the president. "I guess you saw the reporters outside?"

"They'd be damn hard to miss."

She didn't so much as flinch at his sarcastic statement. Instead, she followed him into his office with the coffee in one hand and a bagel in the other. "You probably haven't eaten today, have you?"

As well as being a top-notch secretary, Dana had the tendency to coddle. She was, in fact, the only woman he let get away with it. "I'm fine," he said as he sat in the black leather chair behind his desk.

"No, you're not." Never one to be affected by his moods or surly temper, she set the steaming coffee at his elbow then insistently pushed the bagel in front of him. "Eat. You'll feel better."

He stared at her in disbelief. Feel better? Is that what she thought, that he merely needed to *feel better?* Everything he'd carefully constructed—his reputation, his standing in the community, his contacts and associations—was threatened by the recent scandal. And the reputation of the clinic was undergoing critical speculation.

"Dana," he growled, not bothering to regulate his tone now that he was away from the press, "I seriously doubt a goddamned bagel is going to do much to repair the damage from all the vicious gossip."

She bit her lip, then sighed. As usual, she took his moods in stride, never backing off, never flashing her own temper in return. That, too, was a blessing, allowing him the total freedom to be himself, without having to concern himself about the impression he might give.

At moments like this, she positively amazed him.

"R.J., anyone who knows you realizes you'd never abandon a woman just because she got pregnant. You're far too conscientious for that. Miss Lane's ridiculous story that you got her pregnant and then refused to marry her is just that—utterly ridiculous."

Her overwhelming belief in him made his stomach muscles

tighten in response. He watched her, his expression deliberately impassive. "She was no more than a casual, ill-advised fling, Dana. Available for what I wanted, which sure as hell wasn't marriage. I'd hardly rush to the altar with her, regardless of the situation."

Though a blush brightened her fair complexion and her eyes wouldn't quite meet his, she muttered stubbornly, "Maybe not, but you wouldn't abandon her, either. You wouldn't leave her to take care of the situation on her own."

He gave her a hard look, judging her earnestness, then shook his head. In a low, nearly imperceptible whisper, he muttered, "You sound pretty sure of that."

Her chin lifted resolutely. "I am."

R.J. wasn't given to self-doubt or worry, but then, this was a unique situation. No woman had ever dared to try manipulating him as Tanya had, and never before had his honor been questioned. He found himself moving the bagel from one side of the plate to another as he considered his very limited options. A sleepless night had done little to help resolve the issues. He wanted—needed—to talk, to sort out his thoughts, and right now his family had more than enough to deal with. That left Dana as his only sounding board.

Without an ounce of apology, he met her steady gaze and admitted, "It's possible that I could be the father."

Dana stared at him, her expression blank. He'd noticed her wide green eyes before, of course, since they were a focal point of color against her fair skin. But never before had he seen them look so wary. She stood there before him for a frozen moment in time, then suddenly launched into a flurry of efficiency, straightening books on a shelf, putting away a file. When she spoke, her hands nervously and needlessly tidied the subdued twist in her blond hair.

"That's absurd." She didn't meet his gaze, but rather stared at his tie clip as if fascinated by it. "I seriously doubt Miss Lane is even the baby's mother, so how could you be the father? She just wants the five thousand dollars that TV reporter offered, that's all."

R.J. saw the way her straight shoulders had stiffened inside her suit, how her hands, with their short, unpainted nails, were clenched tightly together, turning her knuckles white. Her distress was plain to see, and for one ridiculous moment he wanted to soothe her. He shook off the aberrant sensation.

"I hope you're right," he said quietly, still watching her. "But I did some calculations last night, and the timing works."

Dana closed her eyes and let out a long, shaky breath.

She looked so distraught, he felt a frisson of uneasiness. He grimly tamped it down. "Dana?"

Shaking her head, she turned away and stalked to the window behind his desk. She wrapped her arms around herself in a strangely defensive gesture that he didn't understand, and when she spoke, her voice emerged as a rasp. "You didn't… didn't use protection with her?"

An instinctive flash of anger took him by surprise. He was far too old, and far too private, to be explaining himself or his actions. No one—family, business associates or friends— dared to take him to task. Under normal circumstances he would have responded to such a question with contempt.

But he supposed he'd invited the query by bringing up the topic. He almost grinned as he considered her question. Never would he have imagined having such a discussion with his professional-to-the-bone secretary. Dana was so straitlaced, so proper, R.J. doubted she understood the most basic aspects of hot, gritty lust. But he certainly did, and he'd long ago learned to utilize his icy self-control even during the most heated moments, refusing to be drawn in by any woman, refusing to take unnecessary chances. His sense of responsibility and his natural inclination to have the upper hand had always kept him safe from any long-term commitments—and fathering a baby would definitely be considered long term.

Though he was half amused, he also resented Dana's lack

of faith. "Of course I took precautions," he said coolly, letting her feel his displeasure over her implications. "In this day and age, only an idiot wouldn't, and I promise you, I'm not an idiot."

She looked startled. "I never meant—"

He cut her off, not wanting to hear her clarify her doubts. "Nothing is foolproof, Dana, you should know that. But if Tanya did get pregnant, this is the first I've heard about it."

The tightening grip of rage he'd been experiencing ever since the baby had been found threatened to break his control.

Damn it, he didn't want his reputation trashed just because he'd made an error in judgment. He should never have slept with Tanya, but he hadn't realized what a conniving bitch she was at the time. She'd claimed to want the same things as he, and that damn sure didn't include being a parent. But if a baby had been conceived, she should have known him well enough to realize he would never disregard his obligations.

R.J. came to his feet, hating the look he'd seen on Dana's face, one of disappointment, when all he'd ever seen there before was admiration and respect. He wouldn't tolerate it. He clasped her shoulders and turned her to face him, aware suddenly of how small she seemed. If she leaned forward, she'd be able to nestle against his chest perfectly.

That errant observation took him by surprise, and he ground his teeth together. He wanted to shake her, more out of anger at himself than at Dana.

"If I am the father, she never bothered to tell me. All that garbage about me refusing to marry her, to acknowledge the baby—it's all lies. I'd *never* turn my back on my responsibilities. You know that, Dana."

His statement demanded that she agree. She looked at him, her eyes liquid, as if she were on the verge of crying, which didn't make a damn bit of sense. Dana never showed excesses of emotion. She handled his office and his business affairs with a remarkable competence that sometimes left him awed, but she never got emotionally involved. In all the time he'd known her, he'd never seen so much as a hint of her personal side. When she was sick, she stoically denied it. When she was tired, she hid it. If she'd ever been hurt, or if she'd ever grieved, he knew nothing about it. Even though his sister Abby and Dana were longtime friends, Dana's personal life was a mystery to him.

Which was how he'd always wanted it.

As if it had never been there, Dana's tearful expression disappeared. She visibly drew herself together and mustered a shaky smile. R.J. felt as if he'd just taken a punch to the gut. Without meaning to, he tightened his hands on her fragile shoulders.

"I know, R.J.," she said, her gaze unwavering. "You're the most dedicated, reliable, professional person I know. You just... just took me by surprise."

Struck by some unnameable emotion, R.J. released her and stepped back. The urge to pull her closer, to see just how well she might fit against him, had nearly overwhelmed him and he didn't like it. The whole situation was getting out of hand, taking its toll on his lauded control, which he assumed could explain his sudden need for her trust and understanding. But he'd be damned if he let things get to him that much.

With a deceptive calm, he added, "Since she's lied about so many things, I'd be willing to bet Tanya is making every bit of it up. I doubt she's the mother because we have similar acquaintances and someone would have mentioned her being pregnant. And I can't believe I'm the father or she'd have been after me long before now, demanding I pay, if nothing else."

"Which you'd have done."

He gave one sharp nod of agreement. Oh, yeah, he'd have paid, all right, and more. "All I'm saying is that I want to be sure. I want proof."

Dana touched his sleeve. "And until then you can't deny

a thing. I understand. Is there anything at all I can do to help?"

R.J. found his first smile of the day. Though Dana was clearly troubled over the possibility that some of the gossip could be warranted, she still managed to be supportive. Outside of his family, she was the one person he'd always been able to count on, and having her trust now lightened his burden. "I should give you a raise, you know."

She smiled, too, looking vaguely smug despite the lingering shadows in her eyes. "You just did two months ago."

"Which obviously proves I'm an intelligent man."

"I won't argue with you there."

She touched him again, just the light press of her fingertips to his wrist, but R.J. felt an unexpected, almost acute pleasure from the small caress. The look on her face went beyond admiration and regard, bordering on something he'd never quite noticed before. He studied her expression before admitting he wasn't sure how to deal with it, or his reaction to that look. He felt an all too familiar tightening in his body—*for Dana?*

"Is there anything I can do to help?" she asked again.

He was still caught up in wondering why she was suddenly affecting him this way. Thinking it through, he decided it could be because his thoughts and emotions had been thrown off base by all the outside turmoil surrounding the scandal. He was likely imagining things where she was concerned, or grasping at any safe line available. And Dana had always been very safe.

Either way, he didn't like it. He stepped away from her with the pretense of getting back to his desk again to eat the bagel. With a casualness he didn't feel, he said, "You've done more than enough, Dana, just by being yourself."

After he said them, it struck him forcefully how true those words were. He twisted to look at her again, trying to decide what it was about Dana that made her so different, so easy to be with.

She wasn't an unattractive woman, he thought, taking note of the soft gray business suit she wore, which made her skin look very pale and luminous, emphasizing the vivid green of her large, almond-shaped eyes.

Her hair, a silky dark blond, was probably long, though he'd never seen it out of its elegant French twist. He started to wonder further about her hair, trying to imagine it hanging loose, a sleek fall around her breasts. Quickly he drew his thoughts away from that direction and the heated images it conjured. He didn't want to be that curious about her.

Her features were pleasantly balanced, a slim nose, softly rounded cheekbones, a high, smooth forehead. Her ears, which he felt absurd for even noticing, were small and, as usual, adorned with tiny gold studs. Dana wore very little jewelry. In fact, she wore very little adornment of any kind. R.J.'s gaze skimmed her ringless fingers and her smooth throat, where he realized he'd never seen a necklace. She wore a simple white silk blouse buttoned to the top. There were no clasps in her hair, no bracelets on her delicate wrists, no bows or buckles or frills of any kind on her clothing.

If she wore any makeup, he'd never been able to detect it. But even without mascara, her lashes were slightly darker than her hair, a dusty brown, long and feathery. Her eyes, he decided, bordered on erotic, though he'd never noticed that before. Her lips, without the shine or color of lipstick, were soft and full and damn appealing.

His scrutiny apparently unnerved her. As he watched, her lips parted on a shaky, indrawn breath. His thighs tightened, and his eyes narrowed the tiniest bit in speculation.

When his gaze met hers, she blushed, not a dainty, pretty blush, but an amusing splash of color that made her skin glow and look heated from within. He meant to tease her about what she was thinking, but swallowed the words instead. His own thoughts didn't bear close inspection, and teasing her about what was going on between them could affect their business relationship. That was something he didn't want, even if he was suddenly noticing things about her that he'd never noticed before.

What really drew him, he thought, feeling relief at the sound and reasonable revelation, was her almost eerie sixth sense of what he wanted and needed, and when. She was the perfect secretary, always one step ahead of him, and he intended to keep her solidly in that role.

Dana shifted slightly as the silence dragged on. "R.J.?"

"I'm sorry." He turned back to his bagel and took a healthy bite. "My mind is a little preoccupied today," he said after he'd swallowed.

The tension she'd felt could still be heard in her breathless tone, giving credence to his need for discretion. "No wonder. But it will all work out. You'll see."

"I intend to make sure that it does." He leaned back in his chair, watching her as he finished off the bagel. Silently, he admitted she was right about him being hungry. He'd just been too annoyed to realize it. "I've tried calling Tanya, but either she isn't answering her phone, or she's moved again. I didn't bother to leave a message."

Dana flashed him a look of wry amusement. "Perhaps since she's fabricated this whole absurd situation, she's decided it's best to avoid any confrontations. Especially with you."

He nodded. "The more people she talks with, the better her chances of mixing up her story."

Dana came hesitantly closer. "Have you considered explaining to the press that this is the first you've heard about Tanya's possible connection to that poor little baby?"

"Mother doesn't think it's a good idea, and since she's the CEO—and basically I agree with her—I'm deferring to her. For the moment, it's best if I keep the lowest profile I can. Tanya will trip herself up soon enough, especially with Chelsea Markum and 'Tattle Today TV' helping her along."

The phone on Dana's desk rang, and she glanced at the

outer office with annoyance. "So in the meantime, it's work as usual?"

"I don't see that I have a lot of choice. Besides, I refuse to let those vicious witches or the nosy press totally disrupt our schedule."

She hesitated a moment more, then hurried to the door. "All right," she said on her way out, "but remember, R.J., if you need anything, anything at all, all you have to do is let me know."

The door closed behind her with a quiet click, and R.J. leaned back in his leather chair, thoughtfully considering her words. Given the circumstances, it was a very generous offer. Anyone getting close to him risked being dragged into the limelight, as well.

But to be honest, he'd expected no less of Dana. In the years she'd worked for him, she'd been as loyal and supportive as any person he knew. He could always count on her.

Which was why admitting the truth to her had been so important. He didn't think he was the baby's father, but on the off chance that at least that much of Tanya's story proved to be true, he'd wanted Dana to know about it up front. She deserved as much.

He hated the fact that she might have lost a modicum of respect for him. Having been abandoned himself as a child, and knowing his father to be irresponsible and uncaring, R.J. valued his reputation above all else. He'd always protected it with savage determination.

Seeing his integrity questioned in the press was painful enough. Having Dana doubt him would be unbearable.

CHAPTER TWO

Dana was typing up correspondence for the day, getting ahead of herself before R.J. showed up for work in case he needed to talk. She wanted to be there for him in any way she could.

The last few days she'd gladly listened as he'd ranted and railed against the world. The press was having a field day with him, splashing the story across every newspaper in the state. He wasn't sleeping well, she knew, and her heart ached for him. That he needed her now both troubled and appeased her. She hated seeing R.J. in such an untenable situation, knowing how much he valued control. She'd gladly have done anything in her power to make things right for him.

But for the first time that she could recall, he needed her as more than a competent secretary, and her heart swelled with the satisfaction of being the one he turned to.

She'd loved him forever, it seemed.

Not that he knew of her love. Dana had far too much pride to expose her feelings like that. On the rare occasions when R.J. got involved with a woman, if fleeting affairs could be termed as involved, he'd gravitated to the type of sophisticated, sexy femininity that Dana could never achieve. The women he was seen with were elegant and beautiful and confident.

They were everything Dana was not.

R.J. had always treated her with full respect for her abilities in the office, and he was generous to a fault, showing his appreciation for her dedication with raises and hefty holiday bonuses. He gave to her, but never in the way of a personal gift.

Not once had he looked at her as a man looks at a woman he desires. And she knew he never would.

As president of Maitland Maternity and a member of Texas's wealthiest families, R.J. was considered a prime catch. He had money, status and connections—all qualities that drew women in droves.

But Dana knew that even if he'd been dirt poor and unknown in the community, women would have flocked to his side. At thirty-nine, R. J. Maitland was a handsome man in the prime of his life.

He stood easily six feet two inches tall, all of him hard and strong and capable. He had broad shoulders and a lean physique that looked equally gorgeous in a formal tux or well-worn jeans. His hands were large and sure, and he possessed an innate virility that overrode his sophistication, making him seem almost primitive on occasion—just often enough to keep any woman around him slightly breathless and filled with anticipation.

Dana understood that feeling firsthand, because she'd been close to him for many years now as his personal secretary.

She closed her eyes and sighed, picturing him in her mind. R.J.'s straight sandy hair and probing hazel eyes set him apart from the other Maitlands, who tended toward darker hair and blue eyes.

Dana's love for R.J. meant she'd never even been tempted by another man, though there had been a few times when she'd tried. Dating had been a severe disappointment, and she'd long since decided it was easier to skip it altogether than to suffer the dissatisfaction of being held or kissed by a man she didn't want.

Talking quietly with R.J. about his problems, having him

listen to her opinion helped soften the pain of his usual aloofness. Knowing he was upset and that she'd been able to make him smile for just a bit had filled her with conflicting emotions. She felt guilt for enjoying this time with him when he was so obviously burdened with frustration and rage. And she worried because no one could predict how this entire mess would be resolved, or how badly the Maitlands, R.J. in particular, might be hurt in the bargain.

R.J. was a man used to taking charge. In both his work and his personal life, he controlled the people and events around him. But always with a velvet glove, and with the best of intentions. In many ways, he controlled Dana, too, though she fought him on it often, and she knew he respected her for it.

However, in this instance, there was little he could do. He was virtually helpless against his former girlfriend's spite and the gleeful condemnation of the press, and Dana knew how impossible that would be for R.J. to accept.

She also felt sick with the fear that he might prove to be that little baby's father. She didn't think she could stand it if that happened, but what could she do? She had no claim on him, and reality told her she never would.

Her thoughts were interrupted when R.J. stepped into the office, his face dark with anger after forcing his way through the crowd of reporters who'd been camping outside day after day.

Dana was on her feet in an instant, going to the coffee pot and pouring him his customary cup of sweetened coffee. She shouldn't have let her thoughts get away from her like that. Before she could finish, R.J. growled, "Have you seen the morning paper?"

His tone warned her it wouldn't be pleasant, and she turned warily. "No. I came in early to get some things taken care of. I haven't looked at the paper yet."

R.J. tossed a section of crumpled newspaper on her desk. "There's an entire exposé in there on how wealthy Maitland

Maternity president R. J. Maitland has deserted his poor pregnant lover. The suggestion is that I was more than willing to sleep with her, but walked away the second she found out she was expecting. They make me sound like the coldest bastard alive."

The wash of anger took her by surprise. "Those vipers!" Dana set the cup of coffee down with a hard thunk, and some of it sloshed onto the cabinet. She ignored the spill. Snatching up the paper, she quickly read the article, and her temper began to simmer. She felt fiercely protective of R.J., and the unfair way he was being treated was more than she could take. "This is awful—all speculation and innuendo. Pure slander. I think you should sue!"

In an uncharacteristic snit, she viciously wadded the paper into a ball and jammed it into the metal trash can.

R.J.'s brow rose. "I think you may be taking this worse than I did."

Hearing the sudden amusement in his tone, she whirled to face him. "How can you joke right now?" She was nearly strangling with outrage on his behalf, easily imagining how that report had made him feel. "They're saying terrible things about you!"

The minute the words left her mouth, she wished them back. R.J. cared a great deal about his reputation; Dana, who watched him give everything he had to the clinic, knew that better than most. She'd learned long ago that R.J. had been abandoned by his father, Robert, after his mother's death. He and his little sister, Anna, had been adopted and raised by Robert's brother, William, and William's wife, Megan.

William and Megan had loved R.J. as their own son, but R.J. still suffered over the shame of knowing he'd been discarded, left for someone else to raise. He worked hard to prove he was different from his disreputable father, and Dana understood the toll the gossip was taking on him.

Her heart ached, but she knew better than to approach

him, to try to hold him. R.J. didn't want that from her. He was satisfied that she be his assistant—so she'd always been the best one possible.

Scrubbing at his face, R.J. turned away. "They're not cutting any corners, I'll grant you that. Every new story gets a little uglier, with a little more speculation thrown in." He muttered a curse just under his breath and shoved his hands into the pockets of his slacks. When he faced Dana again, his eyes were glittering dangerously. "Fifty invitations to the party have been returned with lame excuses."

"You mean people are giving their regrets."

"I mean people are bailing out, plain and simple."

The party, scheduled for March, was to celebrate Maitland Maternity's twenty-fifth anniversary. Five hundred invitations had gone out, and the event was supposed to be a huge success. But now, with invitations being returned… "What are you going to do?"

"I'm not certain yet, though Mother has a few ideas." There was a fleeting smile on his mouth. "She loves that baby, you know."

Dana nodded. Megan Maitland was a friend, and one of the most generous women Dana knew, both with money and with her heart. She had created Maitland Maternity Clinic, with her husband's blessing, out of a need to help all pregnant women, rich or poor. Because of the caring atmosphere Megan cultivated, the clinic in Austin, Texas had quickly become world-renowned.

The family had been announcing the anniversary party to the press the day the baby had been discovered. The timing couldn't have been worse, with so many cameras and reporters already on hand. Megan had shielded the infant as much as she could, and at that moment she'd started to care for him. Dana smiled softly. "I knew when she was given permission to take the baby home as a foster mother, she'd get emotionally involved."

R.J. gave a brief nod. "I think if the note hadn't been there, claiming the baby was a Maitland, she'd still have felt the same." He worked his jaw a moment, then added, "She has in the past."

"Yes." Dana wondered if R.J. was thinking about his own circumstances, or the other children Megan had cared for. But R.J. *was* Megan's son, even if Megan wasn't his birth mother. "She's a very special woman."

"That she is." R.J. tilted his head, and another rare smile touched his hard features. "And speaking of special women..." He withdrew a long velvet box from his inside jacket pocket.

Dana stared at the box. "You bought Megan a gift?"

This time R.J. laughed, startling her with the sound of it. R.J. was rarely given to moods of joviality. A workaholic, he took life seriously and molded it to suit him. That didn't leave a lot of room for laughter, and lately, there'd been no reason for it at all. "When I said a special woman, I was talking about you, Dana."

"Me?" Her voice squeaked, and she quickly cleared her throat. "What—?"

At her surprise, R.J.'s expression warmed with masculine satisfaction. He stepped closer to her. "Dana, you've always been the perfect secretary, taking care of things before I can even tell you what needs to be taken care of."

"You would expect no less from an employee."

His smile widened. "True. But these last few days you've gone above and beyond the call of duty."

Dana stared at him wide-eyed, her heart thumping heavily in her chest, her legs feeling suddenly weak. He held the box out to her, but she pressed her hands behind her back to avoid touching it. "I don't understand."

She knew she sounded a bit panicked, but she was so afraid to think more of the gesture than what it really meant. She didn't want to do or say anything awkward, anything to make herself look foolish or make R.J. regret—

R.J. reached behind her and caught her hand, drawing it forward. Rather than giving her the box, he enfolded her fingers in his own. Dana felt the incredible heat of his touch, the roughness of his fingertips and palm proving he was more than a desk jockey, that he enjoyed working outdoors and using his hands. He was strong and rugged and thoroughly masculine. She grew warm from the inside out, her skin flushed, her pulse racing with excitement and anticipation.

R.J. moved his big thumb over her knuckles and smiled. "I've been in a black fury all week, thanks to Chelsea Markum. With her promise of a five-thousand-dollar reward, she's practically begging for frauds and trumped-up lies, knowing people will do damn near anything for a lump of cash. I've been made to look like the center attraction in a three-ring circus."

Dana forced aside her own misgivings and nervousness to curl her fingers around his, giving him a reassuring squeeze.

His hazel eyes, glittering with intent, stared into hers. "People who've known me forever are starting to wonder just how accurate the gossip might be."

"That's not true…" she started to say, but R.J. tugged her just the tiniest bit closer, and she swallowed the denial.

"Yes, it is. None of them trust me right now, but you've never wavered."

"Of course not."

His smile this time was self-mocking. "You've made it all bearable, Dana, and I want you to know how much I appreciate that."

She didn't want his appreciation, but what she did want, she couldn't have. "I know you too well to suffer doubts about your character, R.J."

His expression tightened for one timeless moment, then she felt the velvet box placed in her hand. "I want you to have this."

Thinking she finally understood the gesture, she shook her head. "It's not necessary."

"I know." Some vague emotion flickered in his eyes before his dark lashes dropped to hide the expression. "That's why I got it for you."

With a smile of pure giddy delight, she carefully opened the box, then drew in a startled breath of wonder. Inside, nestled in more velvet, was a dainty, exquisite emerald and diamond pendant. It wasn't ostentatious, but tasteful, the green stone perfectly cut with a border of small shining diamonds, hanging from a delicately woven gold chain.

Dana swallowed, unsure what to say as she stared at the jewelry. She'd never had anything like it. Her mother would have claimed it was wicked, particularly since it had been bought by a man. But then, her mother had hated any type of artificial decoration. She'd taught Dana that proper women didn't indulge in such frivolous advertisement. Her mother thought it looked tacky, and as she'd explained to Dana many times, the artificial beauty wouldn't do her any good. Dana would simply end up looking ridiculous.

As a plain woman, she was best off just accepting her appearance, rather than making a fool of herself trying to improve upon it.

R.J. leaned down to see her face, his brows lowered slightly in a frown. "You don't like it? You can exchange it for something else..."

Oh, God, she liked it *so* much. "It's...it's beautiful." The words were forced through her tight throat. What did the necklace mean? Anything? Nothing? Would such an exquisite piece of jewelry look out of place on her?

"I noticed the other day that you never wear jewelry," R.J. told her quietly. "Then I saw the necklace, and the emerald is almost the exact shade of your eyes. It's not so fancy that you'd need a special occasion to wear it, and it's delicate—like you."

She stood frozen, her body vibrating with the force of her pounding heart. "It's too much."

He chuckled, pleased—or amused—by her. "Nonsense. I thought it was just right, and I have good taste. Ask anyone."

"Your good taste will be…wasted on me."

R.J. frowned. "What's that supposed to mean, Dana?" When she didn't answer right away, he touched her cheek. "Dana, trust me. The necklace will look perfect on you."

She did trust him, there was no denying that. She gave a small laugh of her own. "I have absolutely no idea what to say."

"You don't have to say anything. Let's put it on you, okay?"

Before she could begin to protest, R.J. had lifted the necklace from where it nestled in the velvet box. He opened the clasp with a sure flick of his fingers, proof positive that he was no stranger to women's jewelry.

He didn't look at her as he reached around her throat to hook it into place, but Dana was painfully aware of his nearness, of his rich, musky male scent, of the heat that seemed to pulse off him in waves, washing over her and making her skin tingle. If she leaned only a scant inch forward, her breasts would brush his hard chest. The knowledge teased and tantalized her.

Remaining still was very, very difficult.

His fingertips brushed her sensitive nape more than she thought should have been necessary as he hooked the necklace. Her eyes closed, and she struggled to regulate her breathing. After spending years dreaming of a moment like this, she had no idea what to think or do.

R.J. lowered his arms and she opened her eyes again. He

didn't look at her face, but rather at the small emerald, which lay just below the hollow of her throat. With infinite care he brushed aside the collar of her taupe blouse so that he could view the necklace more clearly. His hands touched her heated skin. One fingertip stroked there, smoothing the gift into place with a tender, almost tentative touch, making her pulse leap. Then his gaze met hers. His gentle breath brushed her temple as he whispered, "It looks beautiful on you."

Beautiful. That was a word that had never been associated with her in any way. Emotions swelled, exploded. Driven by a blind need she'd never experienced before, Dana slid her arms around his neck and hugged herself close to his big body. The sensation of hard muscle against giving softness, male to female, was enough to make her groan out loud. Her belly drew tight, as did her nipples.

She'd meant to thank him, to show her gratitude with a friendly hug. But she made the mistake of raising her face, and she saw his mouth so close to her own.

She kissed him.

CHAPTER THREE

R.J. CAUGHT his breath as Dana's mouth lifted to his with an innocent, instinctive curiosity. She was a very soft, feminine weight in his arms, her scent sweet and warm, unique. His eyes never closed; instead he watched her, saw the excitement on her features, the flush in her cheeks. He was acutely aware of her heartbeat drumming against his chest.

And he was aware of the fullness in his groin.

He couldn't believe Dana Dillinger had given him a hard-on, but there was no denying the truth. He wanted her, and it was only the novelty of the moment, his own enthralled disbelief, that kept him from carrying her to the desk and laying her across it to finish what she had unknowingly started.

Yet all she'd done was give him a chaste schoolgirl's kiss.

Her eyes were closed, and her breath came in ragged pants. She pressed her mouth more firmly against his, and her small hands tangled in the hair at his nape. She gave a soft, hungry groan, a low vibration of sound that proved she was as turned on as he.

The rush of unexpected lust threw him off balance—a feeling he didn't like and wouldn't accept. R.J. gripped her upper arms and moved her a few inches away, putting necessary space between their bodies. He could feel her trembling, and he could feel the pulsing excitement in his groin. "Dana."

Her lashes slowly lifted at the sound of her name. Almost immediately, she dropped her hands away from his neck with a gasp. Red hot color washed over her pale cheekbones, and she struggled to turn away.

He held tight, refusing to let her hide herself until she explained what had happened—though his body understood very well.

"I…I'm sorry!" She looked mortified, an expression he'd never seen on her face before. Dana was always cool and poised. His hands tightened in automatic reflex, making her wince. *"R.J."*

With a curse, he released her and paced away. Never in his adult life had he felt awkward with a woman. He had a very neatly prescribed place for the women in his life; they were either family, and therefore given his loyalty and protection without qualification, or they were lovers, kept at a distance, meant to share his bed but little else.

And then there was Dana.

He turned back to her, his confusion well hidden. He eyed her averted face. "Dana, are you all right?"

She was rubbing her arms, but stopped the telling motion the second he looked at her. Right before his eyes, her poise appeared like a velvet curtain, masking her dismay. He realized with sudden clarity that her coolness was as much a deliberate facade as his calm, and it enraged him that she could so easily deceive him.

He didn't give a damn how she presented herself to the rest of the world. But for him, he wanted honesty, and nothing held back.

With a patently false smile, she quipped, "I'm fine. Other than being a little embarrassed by my…overenthusiastic show of gratitude. I'm sorry about that."

He narrowed his eyes, watching her every nuance while looking for a chink in the armor. "Why did you kiss me, Dana?"

She looked him straight in the eye and said, "Because you've been so frustrated and withdrawn lately. I only meant to offer a little comfort, but I got carried away." He stared at her, trying to judge the truth of her words, and she waved a dismissive hand. "For heaven's sake, R.J., it was only a tiny kiss, hardly anything to get riled over. I realize I overstepped myself. It won't happen again."

A little kiss? Didn't she realize he was still hard? Her *little* kiss had hit him with incredible impact, and he instinctively rebelled against it. No woman affected him so easily, and certainly not with a chaste peck.

She stood there now, mild as a spring breeze, seemingly unruffled by the experience, and he just didn't know.

But he sure as hell intended to find out.

He stepped toward her, his gaze hard and intent. Her eyes opened, and she started to back up. Just then the phone on her desk rang, giving her a reprieve.

With an apologetic shrug, she turned away. He could have sworn he saw genuine relief in her eyes as she pushed the button on the conference phone. "R.J. Maitland's office. Dana speaking."

"Dana, it's Megan. Put me through to R.J."

R.J. stepped to the desk. "I'm here, Mother."

"I need you to come to my office, R.J. You, too, Dana."

R.J. saw that Dana was still holding herself stiffly, and there was an unnatural bloom of color in her cheeks, proving she wasn't as unaffected by the small kiss as she'd like him to believe. He frowned at the phone. "Now?" The last thing he wanted was to walk away from this situation without resolving things first. *What* things, he wasn't certain, but something had just happened, and he didn't like it worth a damn.

Megan's tone was half amusement, half command. "Are you too busy, son, to spare me a few minutes?"

R.J. glanced at Dana. She returned his look with one of polite inquiry, and he supposed there was little enough left to be said. Whatever reasons she had for kissing him, she had no intention of discussing them now. His interrogation would have to wait. "I can be there in two minutes."

"Excellent." The phone went dead, and both R.J. and Dana continued to stare at each other.

Dana cleared her throat and clasped her hands together. "Any idea what that's all about?"

Slowly he shook his head, still watching her. "Not a clue, but I guess we're going to find out."

He reached for her arm, and Dana quickly grabbed a steno pad and pencil. Since Megan's office was also on the second floor, they reached it only moments later. R.J. drew up short as he saw Chelsea Markum standing impatiently just inside his mother's door. She glanced at him as he entered, and her smile was saccharine sweet.

R.J. noticed Chelsea's eyes were a dark green, but not the clear, guileless green of Dana's. No, Ms. Markum looked devious, and he kept his own expression enigmatic.

Megan Maitland stepped forward with a smile. "We're all meeting in the reception hall."

"We?" He felt Dana standing stiffly beside him, but he had no idea how to reassure her since he hadn't a clue what was going on.

His mother, tall and slender, gave an imperious nod of her head. "I've allowed one reporter, Ms. Markum, and our own press staff to be present." As they started out of the room, R.J. holding her arm and leading the way, Megan added, "Oh, and, dear, Tanya will also be there."

He damn near missed a step. Staring at the top of his mother's regal white head, he wondered what the hell she was up to. Not once had he been able to reach Tanya, yet his mother had somehow gotten her to attend this impromptu meeting?

With an effort, he kept his tone merely curious. "Care to tell me why, or is this supposed to be some kind of surprise?"

She slanted him a look with her sharp blue eyes. "Oh, you'll be surprised, all right." Tilting her head over her shoulder to see the flagging Ms. Markum, she added, "You, as well, I think."

R.J.'s gaze briefly met Dana's. She was walking beside the reporter, and even now he felt her unerring support, her confidence in him. With a brief shake of his head, he pushed open the reception hall doors and met his ex-lover's startled gaze. Reining in his anger wasn't easy, but he had no doubt that if he displayed his true feelings for Tanya, Ms. Markum would have a field day with it. He wanted his private life to remain as private as possible, which meant he had to conceal his anger behind cold contempt. Tanya received no more than a brief, dismissive glance.

Looking restless and wary, she stood by the end of a long table. She caught her breath as he entered, panic washing over her features until she resembled a cornered animal. With feigned bravado, her gaze left R.J. and focused on Megan. "What's going on here? If you intend to try intimidating me—"

"Not at all," Megan said, her mouth tilted in a small smile. One of the hospital guards stood at the doors, blocking the way. Tanya couldn't have gotten far without causing a real ruckus. "I've decided we should get this entire situation dealt with, one way or another."

Tanya stared at her in wary defiance. "What does that mean? Are you going to try buying me off? Do you plan to offer more for me to walk away than 'Tattle Today TV' offered for me to come forward?"

Over my dead body, R.J. thought, but he didn't need to speak the words. Megan, looking highly insulted, said, "Never," in a tone that had Tanya backing up a step.

Chelsea Markum spoke for the first time. Her voice was shrill with excitement. "I think I should have a cameraman in here if you're—"

"You can either stay or leave, Ms. Markum, but I've had enough of cameras." Megan's voice remained quiet and calm, but there was an underlying steel in her words, and not for the first time R.J. admired this woman who'd overcome a very humble beginning and was now the matriarch of one of Austin's finest families.

Chelsea visibly suppressed her complaints, and instead pulled out a small tape recorder.

"Now then," Megan continued, scanning the audience, "as you are all aware, I've been given temporary custody of the baby. After spending so much time with him, it occurred to me that there's one positive way to identify the baby's mother."·

"But *I'm* the baby's mother!" Tanya blustered.

"So you've said. And you've also named R.J. as the father, but I admit I have my doubts. You see, R.J. simply isn't·the kind of man who could have done as you've claimed."

"Everyone knows we were lovers!"

Dana's hand settled on R.J.'s biceps. She didn't try to restrain him, which would have been a foolish effort, but her soft touch offered a measure of calm and helped him to maintain his control. He didn't acknowledge her in any way, fearful of the moment being misconstrued. He didn't want Dana drawn into this small war. But he did regain his casual stance, and that reassured her enough that she removed her hand.

"Very well," Megan said, unaware of R.J.'s fury, or else able to completely ignore it. "Since I've had the baby in my home, I've noticed one very obvious clue to his true identity. As his mother, you would immediately know what I'm speaking about, wouldn't you, Tanya? It's hardly something a mother would miss."

R.J., having no idea what his mother was getting at, watched Tanya's face blanch. Knowing Tanya and her conspiring ways, he could tell she was struggling, trying to come up with an answer that would appease everyone. Chelsea Markum hovered nearby, her tape recorder whirring away, her expression rapt.

"This is ridiculous!"

"Not at all, Tanya." Megan began to pace the room, but her gaze never left Tanya. "I think we all agree it's imperative for the baby's sake that we find the truth."

Tanya turned away, her hands fisted. She strode the length of the table, then turned. Finally she cleared her throat. "You're probably referring to the...tiny scratch the baby had on his arm."

Megan smiled, and the look was almost predatory. R.J. felt the first stirrings of satisfaction as he watched his mother in action. Beside him, Dana let out a shaky breath, and he knew she was feeling the same relief. He suddenly wanted to hold her, to take her hand. The idea disquieted him. He didn't need comfort from anyone.

And even if he did, he wouldn't dare touch Dana. The last thing he wanted was to give Chelsea new fodder for her audience, or to accidentally pull Dana into the scandal.

"No," Megan said, "there was no scratch."

"Then you're talking about the baby's...cowlick."

Megan merely shook her head.

Tanya's eyes narrowed as she tried furiously to think of something else, and R.J. made a sound of disgust. "Give it up, Tanya. You know damn well the baby isn't yours—*or mine*."

She flared at him, her chin shooting into the air. "Blue socks. The baby was wearing embroidered blue socks."

Megan's voice sounded almost gentle. "No, Tanya, he wasn't."

Dana gave a loud sigh of relief, moving infinitesimally closer to R.J. Deliberately, he let his arm brush hers, accepting her support. "The world knows you're a liar, Tanya." Then he glared at Chelsea Markum. "Of course, with that damn reward being thrown out there, it was almost a given that someone would crawl out of the woodwork, trying to lay claim."

Chelsea raised an auburn brow. "You're blaming me for this mess?"

"You've played your part in it."

"You know, it occurs to me, Mr. Maitland, that just because Tanya isn't the mother doesn't mean you're not the father."

Every muscle in his body bunched. "What the hell are you talking about now?"

"There was a letter claiming the baby to be a Maitland, don't forget. Everyone saw it, so you're not off the hook yet. As far as I'm concerned, until the real father owns up to his obligations, all the Maitland men are still suspect."

Tanya used the distraction to stalk out of the room. When R.J. noticed her, Megan put a hand on his arm. "She's gone, and good riddance." Then she turned toward Chelsea. "You'll print the truth?"

Chelsea shrugged. "That Tanya was a fraud? Of course. It's a great story. Even though I have to take your word about the so-called identifying clue."

Megan reached over and snapped off the tape recorder. With a glitter in her eyes that spoke volumes, she added, "If you want to continue to have first rights on this story, you'll make certain you print the *exact* truth."

Chelsea bristled. "Are you threatening me?"

R.J. thought she looked titillated by the possibility. He shared a quick, conspiratorial glance with Dana and almost smiled. They both knew Chelsea was no match for Megan, not when Megan was protecting her own.

Megan shook her head. "Of course not. I'm merely making my position on the matter clear."

Chelsea nodded and took her leave, seeing that all the grand news was over. Megan watched her go with a frown. "That woman is a barracuda."

R.J. stared at his mother, caught in a mix of emotions. In so many ways, he worried about her, especially with all the scandal of late. But every so often she managed to remind him what a strong, capable woman she was. He said simply, "Thank you."

"You're very welcome."

"Why the sudden disclosure?" He was curious about how she could have kept such a "clue" secret for so long, and why. If she'd had proof, why hadn't she used it earlier and spared them all?

Megan reached up for a hug, and R.J. readily indulged her. "I'm sorry," she murmured, leaning back to see his face. "I've been so distracted what with the baby, the clinic's anniversary and then with Connor suddenly showing up...."

R.J. scowled at that reminder. He wasn't too keen on this so-called long-lost cousin. Connor O'Hara had crawled out of the woodwork, and his timing couldn't have been more unfortunate.

"R.J. wasn't blaming you, Megan," Dana offered, automatically stepping in to smooth things over for him. She did that a lot, too, R.J. realized, kept his life organized and orderly even out of the office. She reminded him of family birthdays and holidays. She sometimes bought the gifts for the occasions, as well. He shook his head in dawning wonder as she added, "He's just been very worried himself."

Megan gave Dana an assessing look. "I trust you're taking very good care of him?"

Dana laughed, but it sounded a bit forced. "I'm doing my best."

R.J. eyed her determined expression, then smiled. "Her best is pretty impressive, as far as I'm concerned." He watched Dana blush as he said it, and knew she was thinking of the simple, sizzling kiss she'd given him. Since he hadn't fully recovered himself, he found it prudent to change the subject. "So, Mother, are you going to tell me what this mysterious clue is?"

Megan's smile turned impish. "I don't believe I will. This is our ace in the hole, possibly the only chance we'll have to sort truth from fiction. The real mother will know what I'm talking about, so it's best if I just keep it to myself."

Now that he was no longer being named the irresponsible father, R.J. didn't care enough to press her on it. Chelsea Markum could still make trouble, just as she'd promised to do. But now that Tanya was discredited, he really had nothing to worry about. He was so relieved to have that worry put to rest, he wanted only to get back to his office with Dana so they could talk.

The anticipation he felt annoyed him, and he forced himself to stay with his mother awhile longer, proving to himself, if no one else, that nothing had actually changed between him and Dana.

Everyone else had left the reception hall, including Maitland's press personnel and the security guard. For the moment, at least, they'd done all they could to suppress the scandal.

Only Megan, Dana and he lingered in the reception hall. "How is Connor settling in?" R.J. asked, trying not to let his suspicions filter through.

Connor claimed to be the son of Clarise Maitland O'Hara, Megan's estranged sister-in-law. Clarise and her husband, Jack, had had a falling out with the family and moved away from Austin a long time ago. There had been no contact between the families over the years, and now that both his parents were dead, Connor had suddenly appeared to mend the long rift.

Megan had welcomed him with open arms, disregarding her children's concern. Still, Connor was one more reason for R.J. to worry about her. Though he'd only met the man briefly, he'd wanted his mother to let him run a check on him, to verify his story, but Megan had insisted on taking care of the matter.

Seeing R.J.'s concern and hearing the words he hadn't spoken, Megan studied her son closely. He was worried about her, she knew, but for the moment, she could do nothing to reassure him. At least not where Connor was concerned. Only her daughter Ellie knew the whole truth about Megan's *nephew,* and Ellie had promised to keep her secret—at least for now.

Eventually she'd have to share the story of her tragic past with all her children, Megan realized. They had a right to know, especially now that she'd found out her baby boy hadn't died when she was seventeen, regardless of the lie her father had told her. Regardless of how they'd all lied to her. Connor was alive, and that was all that mattered—for now.

Standing a little straighter, Megan shook off the heartache of the past. Her family had their hands full tending to the scandal surrounding another boy. Her own past would have to wait. After all, forty-five years had passed, so what would a few more months matter?

Megan summoned her most motherly smile, the one that reminded her children she was perfectly capable of taking care of herself, despite how they liked to fret. "As you know, Connor has moved into one of the family condos. I thought that would be easiest."

Easiest, or cheapest? R.J. wondered, still not liking the situation at all. He rubbed his chin as he watched his mother's expression. "That's…very generous of you."

Megan lifted one brow. "I can afford to be generous, and you know it. Besides, he's family."

"And I suppose you've given him money?"

Her stern expression showed that she considered his question impertinent. "Don't fret over it, R.J. I know what I'm doing. If you recall, I've been handling my own affairs rather well for quite some time now."

With a reluctant grin, R.J. drew her to him for one more hug, then set her away from him. "Of course you have. And now you're handling mine, as well. I hope this newest disclosure about Tanya will stifle some of the speculation. I'm getting damn sick and tired of being gossiped about."

Dana shook her head. "Nothing will stop the gossip completely until the parents are named. You heard Ms.

Markum—the Maitland men are still fair game." Her brows drew down, and her slender nose wrinkled. "I wanted to trip her as she left."

Startled, R.J. stared at her a moment then burst out laughing. Megan seemed taken aback by his lack of restraint, then she smiled.

As she started out the door, Megan said, "I have to admit, Dana, the same thought crossed my mind."

R.J. chuckled again.

In some ways, he mused, Megan and Dana had a lot in common. They were both strong, proud women. Strange that he was just now noticing the similarities.

But then, he'd noticed a lot of things about Dana lately. And that, more than anything, made him very determined to get their working relationship back on track.

Two MORNINGS LATER, Dana stepped into the office, early again in the hopes of freeing up some time for R.J. But before she'd even turned the lights on in the dim room, she knew she wasn't alone.

R.J.

She knew it was him. She could detect his hot musky scent, feel the throbbing awareness of his presence. She also felt more, his emotional turbulence, the beat of his anger. What was wrong?

Quickly placing her purse in a file drawer, she rushed across the plush carpet in the outer office to R.J.'s inner sanctum. He sat behind his desk, staring out the window at the early morning traffic on Mayfair Avenue. Bright sunshine flooded through the window and illuminated the office. It reflected off his light brown hair and gilded his brown lashes, leaving shadows on his lean cheekbones.

His mood was disturbing, though he hadn't yet said anything. "R.J.?"

Very slowly he turned his chair to face her.

Since that awkward kiss where she'd made a total fool of herself, he'd been more distantly polite than ever. Dana had gone out of her way to reestablish their professional relationship, burying her feelings deep. R.J. had seemed to welcome her efforts, and returned them in kind.

But now, his eyes burned with a harsh light. "You're early."

"So are you." Dana surveyed his features and then turned briskly to make coffee. "First things first, R.J. I need coffee, and I assume you do, too."

Rather than wait for her, he unfolded himself from the chair and followed her out. "Thanks. I could use a cup."

Dana looked at him sharply. "Are you all right?"

"Just dandy." He shoved his hands into his pockets and leaned against her desk while she measured coffee and water.

Once she was done and the coffee machine had begun to hiss, Dana turned to him and crossed her arms over her sand-colored suit jacket. "What's wrong?"

R.J. dropped his head forward with a humorless laugh. "Shall I add mind reading to your repertoire of sterling qualities?"

There was more bite in his tone than usual. "It doesn't take a mind reader to know something's upset you. What's happened?"

"Hell, what hasn't happened? This infernal situation has gone from bad to worse."

"You want to explain the *worse* part?"

He gave her a cynical smile. "Sure, why not? Last night, one of our more high-profile mothers checked out of the clinic."

"The movie star?"

"Bingo." He shook his head in disgust. "And right now, three prominent families are packing up to go, too."

"But…I don't understand. I thought since you'd been

cleared, everything would have calmed down some. It doesn't make sense that they're leaving now—"

"Nothing has calmed down. Chelsea Markum made an announcement late last night that they're upping the reward from five thousand dollars to fifty thousand for an exclusive with the real mother. This morning, dozens of women showed up to lay claim to the title."

"Oh my God."

"Damn right." He gave her another cynical smile. "And guess who they're naming as the father."

Dana groped for her chair and then fell into it. "*Dozens* of women?"

"At least forty." R.J. managed a rough laugh. "Hell, I don't know whether I should be insulted or complimented. What kind of a Lothario do they think I am? My social calendar has never been busy enough to accommodate forty women. But does that concern Markum?" He snorted. "Right now, she's interviewing each and every one of them, hoping like hell she can nail me to the wall. We're losing patients because of this publicity. Every paper from the most respected to the worst rags are lobbying out in our parking lot, hounding everyone who goes in or out."

Dana shut her eyes. Several people had approached her when she'd arrived this morning, but at the same time, a limo had pulled up to the curb and drawn them away. She'd thought someone in the limo was checking in, but now wondered if it was someone preparing to pick up a patient and check out—a more likely possibility.

She swallowed hard. "I can't believe all those women are trying to name you—"

"Oh, it's not just my blood they're after. Since Jake isn't around to defend himself, he's become another prime target."

Dana had met Jake Maitland once, but she wasn't sure what he did for a living. She'd heard rumors of him being a government agent of some sort. She knew whatever he did was secretive and kept him away more often than not. "At least they're not singling you out."

"It doesn't matter." R.J. began pacing, his movements agitated and stiff. "All this attention is damaging the clinic and threatening the anniversary party. You know what that party means to my mother."

"Megan can hold her own, R.J." The coffee was ready, and Dana got up to pour R.J. a cup. She handed it to him, and he took several deep gulps before speaking again.

There was a spark of sardonic humor in his eyes as faced her. "You want to know what my mother is doing right now? She's questioning the women."

"Her secret clue?"

R.J. nodded. "So far, the guesses have ranged from webbed feet to mismatched eyes."

"Oh, lord."

"My thoughts exactly. Next thing you know, some ditzy woman will claim the baby has wings."

Dana hid a smile. R.J. could rail and curse and stomp all he wanted, but deep down, he maintained his sense of humor. He might not laugh or joke often, but neither was he an infernal grouch.

And his concern for the baby was evident, despite his frustration. "Maybe Megan will be able to send them all home this afternoon."

"I doubt it. Some of them are refusing to answer her question or even take a guess, claiming it's an insult to the love they feel for the baby, or that the baby's affliction is no one's business."

Dana lifted her brows. "So now the clue is an affliction? I suppose that's as good a cover as any."

"Even if Mother did get them all booted out, more would show up. I have to do something, Dana. I've been totally discredited as far as the public is concerned. First I'm accused of abandoning a defenseless infant, now I've been leaping from one bed to the next at the speed of light." He moved to stand directly in front of her. "All night long, after the 'Tattle Today TV' report, I've been thinking about this. I need to repair the damage done to my name, and hopefully in turn, that'll help the clinic's reputation."

Something in his expression warned her. He was watching her too closely, as if to judge her reaction. He did that often. R.J. was notorious for standing back and absorbing reactions and responses so he could use them to his advantage, a means to an end. It made him an excellent businessman and—by repute—an excellent lover.

She shivered at the thought, then quickly pulled her mind back to the problem at hand.

What could R.J. possibly want from her? Especially when she'd already promised she'd do anything in her power to help?

Dana sipped her coffee, refusing to be drawn in by his speculative scrutiny. He liked the effect he had on people, how easily he could rattle them, but she refused him the satisfaction of making her squirm. That was one reason she'd lasted so long as his secretary—she pretended to be immune. R.J. needed strong people around him to counteract his autocratic nature. Weaker people got trampled; strong people got his respect. "Do you have any ideas on how to handle this?"

He crossed his arms over his chest and stared down at her, his gaze hard and direct, unrelenting. "Yes. I'm going to get married."

CHAPTER FOUR

THE LOOK on her face wasn't encouraging, R.J. thought. She appeared caught between disbelief, nausea and hysteria. The disbelief he understood perfectly. Dana knew better than most how he felt about marriage.

The nausea and hysteria he hoped were from surprise. *Happy* surprise.

Then that serene curtain dropped over her features and her expression became blank. It annoyed him that she worked so hard to hide her feelings from him, especially now, when he needed to know what she was thinking.

She looked past him, not meeting his eyes. "I see. Are you sure that's the…right move to make?"

Her voice trembled the tiniest bit, and R.J. wondered how best to explain his plan so he could gain her cooperation.

With an edge of steel in his tone, he said, "I don't see too many other options, Dana. I thought about it last night, before Markum even offered the money for the exclusive. If I marry, I'll immediately represent the settled, domestic family man instead of a free-swinging bachelor."

Obviously agitated, she got up to pour herself more coffee. It struck him that they spent a lot more time talking lately than usual. When she'd come in, Dana had set a large stack of files on her desk. Work she'd taken home? His resolve hardened as he considered that possibility.

"Dana, have I put you behind in your work by bringing my personal problems into the office?" He wasn't used to sharing his worries so openly, so he hadn't even noticed the amount of time he'd kept her away from her desk.

She waved the suggestion away. "No, of course not."

She sounded positive, but he couldn't let it go. "You're the most industrious woman I've ever known. I can't remember a time when you haven't filled every available minute with work, but for some time now you've been coddling me while I sit here and grumble."

"That's not true!" Her head lifted with a brief show of temper, ready to defend him—even against himself. "You've had a lot on your mind and I've…I've enjoyed our chats."

He nodded at the stack of files. "Have you been working at home?"

Her expression turned wary. "Just a little."

"Then how have you been keeping up, because I know you too well to think you'd ever let yourself fall behind. You're as conscientious about work as I am."

Her eyes narrowed and her shoulders squared. "If you must know, I've been coming in earlier, getting things done before you arrive."

"Goddamn it." Filled with disgust for himself, R.J. sighed loudly. "That's what I was afraid of. But it's at an end right now, honey, you understand?"

At the use of the endearment, she froze, and her slender brows shot up a good inch. She turned mute on him, merely staring.

R.J. chuckled. "Well, that certainly got your attention, didn't it?"

"I—"

"No, don't start explaining things to me. I'm sorry if I took you by surprise."

She crossed her arms over her chest and he noticed how the gesture made the bottom of her jacket flare open, displaying the curves of her hips. Damned if he'd ever noticed before that Dana *had* hips! The discovery filled him with disquiet and a simmering curiosity, which he doggedly suppressed. "No more working before or after hours, understood?"

"Whatever you say, R.J."

Which meant she'd do whatever she damn well pleased, R.J. thought. He sighed again in massive frustration, then decided to let it go. After all, if things went according to plan, he'd soon be in a better position to know if she was working more than she should. "I think we need to get back on the topic."

That got her moving. She darted around the office, busying herself with everything and nothing. But instead of her usual smooth movements, every gesture seemed strained and jerky, as if driven by temper.

"Dana, will you settle down? I'm trying to talk to you."

She glanced at him as she bustled past. "About your marriage? Good luck. Oh, and congratulations."

He caught her arm and drew her to a standstill in front of him. "I'm not done explaining."

She glared at him, her eyes every bit as bright as the emerald just visible at her throat. She'd worn the necklace every day since he'd given it to her, and there were times when he wondered if she'd taken it off at all. Picturing it on her while she slept or showered had provided him with a few uncomfortable moments.

"What's to explain? It's an idiotic plan, but then I'm just the secretary, so what do I know?"

Her vehemence took him off guard. When she again tried to pull away, he gently maintained his hold with both hands. "I suspect you have quite a bit to say about it."

"Oh, no, you don't. You're not going to involve me in this farce." She struggled against him again, and when he didn't release her, went back to killing him with her eyes. "You want to marry some bimbo for the sake of your image, that's fine, but don't expect me to give my blessing. That's asking too much!"

He couldn't help but laugh at that, which made her

practically growl in response. She looked ready to inflict violence on him.

"Dana… No, just hold still a minute, will you?" As she settled mutinously in his grip, he added, "And please refrain from calling yourself a bimbo. Even if you know something I don't about your character, I'm afraid I can't tolerate that type of insult." He watched her closely as he continued, waiting for her reaction. "Not to my future wife."

He was taking a huge gamble, joking about it that way, but he thought it might make things easier for her if he set the tone up front for what their marriage would be. It wouldn't be a romantic alliance, so he'd be damned if he'd go down on one knee.

Dana became curiously still in front of him. Her eyes were enormous, her brows puckering her forehead with a look of guarded trepidation. "What in the world are you talking about?"

With a subtle pressure, he slid his hands up her arms, attempting to ease her tension. His thumbs settled into the hollows where her shoulders blended into her upper chest. She was so small-boned, his fingers spread easily over her back, nearly covering her shoulder blades. He felt a small quiver go through her and released her.

Apparently she had given up on running from him, so at least he'd get the chance to better explain his intent. He had no doubt he'd get her eventual agreement, but he wanted to make it as easy as possible, to avoid any major conflicts. The truth was, he had no real idea how she'd react.

He spoke in murmuring tones, not wanting her to feel pushed. "You and I have always understood each other, Dana. We work well together, and in all the years I've known you, we've never had a genuine quarrel."

"That's only because I learned early on how to get around your temper, R.J."

He held his smile in check. "Exactly. You're intelligent,

and you're quick." She looked far from complimented by his praise, so he cut to the heart of the matter. "I think we'll suit each other quite well. I need a wife who can counter all this nasty gossip and handle herself well under pressure. I need someone with a respectable background, with no outrageous secrets to uncover. You're quietly elegant, and you have a sophistication all your own."

Dana groped behind her for the desk, and still almost missed it when she went to lean her hip there. R.J. caught her before she could tumble to the floor, then kept one hand on her elbow until she was safely propped on the edge. Still, he stayed close because she didn't look at all steady. It wasn't like Dana to be clumsy, and he chose to see it as a good sign.

R.J. watched her with quiet intent, trying to decipher her thoughts, to gauge his next move. There were a lot of emotions flashing across her face, but gleeful acceptance wasn't one of them.

"Dana?" When her gaze lifted to his, he tried for a reassuring smile. "I realize you might not have been expecting this, but I promise you, I've given it a lot of thought."

She stared at him, not blinking, and a new possibility occurred to him, making him frown. "You're not involved with anyone."

He made it a statement rather than a question. He'd never heard of her seriously dating—hell, he'd never heard of her dating at all. But that didn't mean there wasn't someone hovering on the sidelines, and that possibility made him clench his fists with unwarranted anger. For all he knew, despite her reserved demeanor at work, she could be having a torrid affair with any number of men who—

Without a word, she shook her head, putting his mind, and his temper, at ease.

He told himself he didn't want his plans thwarted, but he knew there was another reason for his relief. Dana had been his for a long time. *His* secretary, *his* friend, *his* confidante.

He wasn't a man to share in any way, shape or form. "Good. That's good."

She still hadn't said anything, and annoyance gnawed at the fringes of his good intentions. "I want to assure you that things will go on pretty much as usual, if that's a concern."

One of her brows inched up higher than the other.

"We're friends and we'll remain so, " he went on. "That won't change. You won't be expected to sleep with me. My house is plenty large enough to accommodate two people. You'll have your own room and as much privacy as you might need."

Her look became so incredulous his temper snapped. "You could damn well say something!"

"I...I don't know what to say. You want a...a marriage of convenience?"

Hadn't he made that clear from the start? He gave one brisk nod.

She looked at him with accusation plain in her eyes. "But that's positively archaic!"

He kept his sigh to himself. He didn't understand this new show of temper, when he'd meant to reassure her. "It's a viable solution."

Shaking her head as if in wonder, she carefully edged around him and walked across the office. R.J. allowed her to think things through for a few minutes, forcing himself into an unaccustomed patience. Generally when he wanted something, he went after it with single-minded determination. This marriage was no different.

She kept pacing, and the silence got to him. "How old are you, Dana?"

She barely glanced at him, lost in her contemplation. "Twenty-nine."

Even though Dana had been friends with his sister forever, R.J. realized he knew little about her personal life. He frowned. "Have you ever been married?"

She cast him a worried glance. "No."

"Engaged?"

"No."

He nodded in satisfaction—and mingled relief. "That's what I thought. It's obvious to me that you're not some romantic dreamer who's waiting for a knight in shining armor to come along and put stars in your eyes. You're rock solid—"

"Be still my heart."

"—and mature and reasonable."

"Gosh, you make me sound just lovely. Like a decrepit old spinster."

She drew closer and he caught her, forcing her to look at him. He cupped her face, ignoring her sudden breathless reaction to his touch and his nearness.

Given the way he'd sprung things on her, she was justifiably on edge. He didn't mind her honest reaction, but he refused to let her shut him out. "Dana, honey, I don't mean to make those attributes sound like insults. The truth is, I like you a lot. There aren't many women I'd make such a proposition to."

"Uh-huh." She didn't look at all convinced. "You do mean proposal, don't you?"

"Semantics." His fingertips were in her hair, and he felt its softness, its warmth, without disturbing the careful arrangement. Again, he wondered about her hair, how it would look loose. As soon as they were married, that was one curiosity he'd put to rest. "I'm talking about a business arrangement. As my wife, new doors will open for you."

"I don't need any doors opened," she said quietly.

"Your life will be easier," he argued. "You wouldn't have to work if you didn't want to—"

"Whoa, just a minute."

Again she stepped out of his reach, moving a good two yards away then turning to face him. Her cheeks were bright red, but her eyes were direct and resolute, her shoulders squared as if for battle. R.J. thought she would refuse him, and already he was forming arguments to sway her to his way of thinking. She should know him well enough to realize he didn't give up his goals easily. She must also realize that a wife would be the most expedient way to repair his reputation.

And he hadn't lied to her; in fact, she was the *only* woman he'd be willing to make such an alliance with.

"First," she said, raising one finger in an imperious manner fit for a queen, "I'm going to work. There's no way I want someone else financially responsible for me."

His stomach muscles tensed as the meaning behind her words kicked in. *She was going to agree.* All that was left was the negotiation, and he had no doubt that would go his way. He struggled to keep his satisfaction hidden, not wanting to give her more reasons for anger. If she knew how triumphant he felt right now, she probably wouldn't like it.

However, he couldn't do a damn thing about his small smile.

"If you want to work, that's fine," R.J. murmured. He really didn't care one way or the other, but he hoped to change her mind once they were wed. As he'd explained, the marriage would be a business agreement, and he'd owe her for agreeing to it. Giving her some much-needed time away from work seemed like the perfect start to him. Dana had taken few vacations over the years, and to his knowledge, she'd never traveled far. She deserved to go anywhere she liked, maybe to Paris or New Orleans. And he'd gladly fund the trip. Or perhaps she'd like to buy herself more emeralds.

Strangely enough, he could easily picture her decked solely in emeralds, and the image was decidedly erotic. He would, he decided, make the arrangement for more jewelry himself.

He shook his head to clear it. "I knew you'd be reasonable about this."

"Don't get too cocky yet until you've finished hearing me out."

"More stipulations?" he asked, prepared to be indulgent. The color in her cheeks intensified, and he could see how difficult it was for her to maintain eye contact. Curiosity swamped him. What would she ask for? A new car? An expense account? He could easily afford either, so he waved away her concerns. "This isn't necessary, you know. I'm more than willing to give you whatever you need."

She drew a long, shaky breath and visibly braced herself. "I'm glad to hear you say that, R.J.—because what I want is a real marriage."

He took exception to her insinuation and with deadly calm explained, "Oh, it'll be real, all right, you don't have to worry about that. We'll be legally wed. I wouldn't ask you to do anything unethical—"

"You're not paying attention, R.J." She drew another breath and blurted, "I want sex."

Everything in him seemed to shudder and stall, then kicked into overdrive until his body fairly hummed with his racing pulse. Exercising extreme politeness, he whispered, "Excuse me?"

Her face was so red it was almost comical, only he had absolutely no desire to laugh. He felt the tension in the air, and the even more palpable tension in Dana. He waited in silence while she worked out her thoughts.

"I want us to be a regular married couple," she explained softly. "I want intimacy."

His eyes narrowed the tiniest bit, and she continued, her tone a bit forced, but filled with resolve. "I'm talking about the same bedroom, R.J., the same bed, every night. If I'm going to be married to you for however long it takes to repair the damage to the clinic and your own reputation, then I expect to be treated like a wife during that time—with all the privileges due a wife."

He stared at her, still trying to figure out how he was misunderstanding, because he was certain he couldn't be hearing her right.

She made a broad, nervous gesture with her hands. "Don't get me wrong, R.J. I'll do anything I can to help. Though I'm not sure marrying me will really improve your image, I'm willing to give it a try. We can have a few cocktail parties, get involved in some community activities, become the epitome of marital bliss for the media. Whatever it takes, whatever you want. I'll do anything you think will help. But in return, I want—"

"Sex," he finished for her, the single word laced with ice. "You're standing there demanding sex."

"With you," she clarified shakily, on the off chance he hadn't realized that much.

With a slow, measured stride, he stalked forward to close the space between them. "What game are you playing, Dana?"

She looked as though she wanted to retreat, but instead, she dug in, facing him squarely. "No game."

He gripped her shoulders and shook her slightly. It seemed he'd touched her more in the past week than in all the previous years combined. "Honey, I know you too well to buy this. Since when have you become so sexual? I've never even heard you say the word before now."

She appeared to resent that. Some of her embarrassment faded, and indignation took its place. "I'm as sexual as the next woman!"

He flicked the top button of her suit coat. "Yeah, right. You dress like a nun and you never date. When was the last time you had an affair? When was the last time you even had sex?" Her face paled, but he pressed on. "When was it, Dana?"

"That's none of your business." She trembled all over, and then abruptly turned away. "Just forget about it. If it's too much to ask, if it's a *hardship,* then there's nothing more to talk about."

R.J. pulled back, watching her walk stiffly away. He didn't

mind her anger. In fact, he'd set out to provoke it, preferring her anger over her insistence that he make love with her. But watching her retreat, he realized he'd gone too far.

It was obvious he'd hurt her feelings, and he wanted to kick his own ass. Things had seemed much more straightforward when he'd first come up with this plan. "Dana." She didn't look up. "I never said it would be a hardship."

The look she shot his way should have left him bleeding profusely on the floor. She threw herself into her chair and snapped open a file as if ready to forget the entire thing.

He couldn't let her do that.

Then he noticed her hands were shaking and her breath was catching in tiny pants. Good Lord, was she going to cry? Because she wanted to have sex with him and he'd pretty much refused? It boggled the mind. Of all the possible scenarios he'd figured might accompany his proposition, this particular one had never come up.

He went to her desk and sat on the edge. "Dana, you're a friend, sweetheart. That's all I meant." She didn't look the least bit appeased, and he floundered. He'd spoken the truth when he said sleeping with her wouldn't be a problem. Just the opposite, in fact. He was afraid he'd enjoy it far too much. That one simple kiss they'd shared had plagued his mind ever since, waking him too often in the middle of the night.

If he made love to her, nothing would ever be the same again.

Yet he'd always valued her so much as a friend, as a confidante. Her intelligence and kindness and loyalty had set her apart from other women, and he knew in his heart that once they'd given in to lust, their relationship would be irreparably altered. The qualities of their friendship that he valued most, the ones that had made the plan seem so ideal, might cease to exist. Sex had a way of muddying the waters, especially with a woman like Dana, a woman who didn't take physical relationships lightly.

He'd always gravitated to women who knew the score and expected nothing more from him than a good time in and out of bed. When he was with a woman, he treated her well, indulged her with expensive gifts and flattery. But that was as far as it went. When he tired of her company, or if she got too clingy, he moved on. He left himself free to do just that.

He didn't have to worry about forsaking his obligations, as his father had done, because he made sure there were none.

Tanya had tried to wheedle him into marriage, but he'd refused to allow her the upper hand. For some reason she'd thought she was special, though he'd been upfront with her from the start—as he always was. She hadn't agreed to go away easily. It had cost him an expensive gift to soften the blow, one she'd accepted with ill grace.

At the time, he'd considered the price little enough to pay. He'd appeased his sense of fair play, and still remained free.

Marrying for the sake of his reputation didn't put him at risk. He wasn't expected to offer love everlasting, and he wouldn't be obliged to start a family.

But if Dana expected a real marriage, that would change everything. What if it turned out he was more like his father than he thought?

"R.J.? I have a question."

Her tone sounded reasonable enough. Which he considered good cause for worry. "Go ahead."

"How long, exactly, do you expect this marriage to last?"

"There's no way I can predict that, Dana." And if he was truthful with himself, even trying to speculate on an answer was a lesson in keen frustration. Right now, he had all the frustration he could stand.

"But you do have a certain term in mind, don't you?" Her eyes were narrowed again, making the green brighter, more intense. Her pen tapped against the desktop. "Do you think things can be repaired in a week, a month, six months?"

He pushed away from the desk with repressed anger. "How the hell should I know? It took little enough time to destroy my reputation, but somehow I think it'll take considerably longer to mend it."

"You're probably right." Her gaze stayed glued to him as he strode across the room. "Which brings up another interesting thought. Do you plan to stay celibate during our marriage, or am I simply supposed to look the other way?"

He whirled to face her, thoroughly insulted at such a suggestion. "Being an adulterer would hardly improve my image."

"Oh? Then you do intend to remain celibate, even if it takes a year."

"I—" The protest died before it was spoken. He actually hadn't thought his plan through that far, so how could he take offense at her presumption that he wouldn't honor his wedding vows? When he'd come up with the idea to marry, it had been a near desperate decision. Though he didn't want the world to know it, it ate him up inside that the residents of Austin were beginning to see him as indulgent and reprehensible, an immoral reprobate who would blithely walk away from a woman carrying his child. The image sickened him and dredged up old feelings left over from childhood, from knowing his father hadn't cared enough, hadn't been responsible enough to fulfill even the smallest obligations to his children.

The turbulent memories were swept away as Dana once again stood, very slowly, to face him. "I've always known I was a plain woman."

R.J. glared at her. "What are you talking about?"

"It's just occurred to me. You don't want to sleep with me for the same reason you chose me to proposition."

He didn't like her tone or the direction of her thoughts. "Propose to."

Her grin was tight as she mimicked him by saying, "Semantics." She stalked out from behind her desk. "There must be any number of women who'd jump at a chance like this.

Even if the marriage only lasted a few weeks, as you say, the prestige exists. And everyone knows how generous you are. But then, most of the women you associate with are beautiful and sexy, and that might only reinforce your present image as a man who cares about superficial things and his own pleasure. If you marry me, a woman without extravagant looks or sex appeal and with an unremarkable background, they'll think it has to be for love, the kind of love that lasts."

"The *real* kind."

She totally missed his sarcasm. "You, on the other hand, have looks and money and breeding and background and sophistication. But my drabness will help to tone down your brilliance by comparison. That's it, isn't it?"

He stared at her, totally floored that she would come to such an asinine conclusion when those thoughts had never entered into his decision. "That analogy is a pretty good stretch, wouldn't you say?"

She shook her head, convincing herself she was on the right track. "I suppose it does make a bit of sense when you think about it. You can't exactly be seen as a playboy married to *me*. No one will wonder if you married me for connections, or money, because I have none."

"You have something much more valuable."

She quirked a dubious brow.

"You have a quiet dignity. And a generous soul, and an innate kindness. Those are all things that will reflect on my good judgment." And she was the only woman he could consider letting that close.

She sighed, then rubbed her forehead. "I do understand, R.J. But it's up to you. Will I be a real wife or not?"

She had no intention of backing down, he could see that now. She stood there in her innocence and naïveté and demanded that he have sex with her. Fighting for lost control, he nodded. "All right, Dana, you win."

Once she had her agreement, she seemed to wither before

him. Her eyes were downcast, and she nibbled on her bottom lip. "Are you sure?"

"Having second thoughts now?"

"No. I just…I don't want you to be angry."

Hell, he was far from angry. Turned on, maybe. His body had started to thrum quietly the minute she'd made her outrageous suggestion, and with each second the feeling had only gotten worse. The miracle would be keeping himself detached when they did have sex—but he knew he had to. He would maintain the upper hand, no matter what it took. "I'm not angry."

"Shall…shall I make the arrangements?"

One side of his mouth kicked up in humor as he registered the irony of her question. "The efficient secretary to the last, hmm? Still willing to handle all my affairs, even the more personal ones. Well, I think this time I'll arrange things myself. How does this weekend suit you?"

"So soon?" She couldn't hide her amazement—or her excitement. At least, he hoped it was excitement and not anxiety.

Very gently, he asked, "There's no reason to put it off, is there?"

"But…should I invite someone to be a witness?"

He enjoyed seeing her act like a nervous bride, which proved just how perverse he could be. "Of course. But I'd really like to keep it low key. My mother, two witnesses, but no more than that. I don't want the press to find out until it's over with."

She shuddered at the possibility. "They'd definitely taint the ceremony."

"And I've seen my face enough in the papers lately."

Her eyes widened. "I'll have to find a dress!"

Such a typically female consideration was a relief after her bout of sensual demands. "Your white suit will do just fine.

After all, it'll be a civil ceremony at the justice of the peace. And we'll want to keep the frills to a minimum."

The second he said it, he saw a small light go out in her eyes and belatedly realized that she'd wanted to make the occasion special. He had a sudden pang in his chest that he didn't understand, an ache that was unfamiliar but that he knew was centered around Dana and her happiness. He cupped her face with one hand, letting his thumb smooth over her temple. Now that he'd gotten used to touching her, he couldn't seem to stop. Her skin was so incredibly soft. "I'm sorry, sweetheart. Here I am, bulldozing right over you with no consideration for your wishes."

She shrugged, staring at his silk tie. "It was your idea, after all. You should certainly do things however you like."

He frowned. "There's no need for you to play the martyr."

"I wasn't!"

He shushed her by placing his thumb over her lips, which were even softer than her skin, prompting him to continue touching. She froze, her eyes huge. "What I'd like," he murmured, "is to make you happy. If you really want to wear a new dress—"

When she shook her head, he reluctantly removed his thumb so she could speak. "No, the suit will do. You're right."

He hesitated, not wanting her to look so fatally resigned. But he knew that the less fanfare the better—for his reputation and his peace of mind. He already felt far too involved. To make it up to her, he would buy her flowers, traditional white rosebuds to go with the suit. And another emerald for her wedding band. Knowing Dana, she wouldn't be expecting a ring; she wouldn't be expecting anything at all. He didn't want their bargain to be one-sided. He wanted to pamper her and he wanted to see her smile.

But he also wanted to protect himself, because he had a feeling he'd miscalculated his reaction to Dana Dillinger.

She'd changed things around so that now it was a marriage of *her* convenience. Her *sexual* convenience. And now that she'd insisted on getting down and dirty with him, he felt thrown off balance in a way he'd never experienced before.

He wanted her. And that had never been part of the plan.

CHAPTER FIVE

"HI, SWEETHEART."

Dana caught her breath as R.J. gently touched her cheek, drawing her attention. She'd been so preoccupied and nervous over the coming ceremony that she hadn't heard him enter. And this new habit of his of using endearments continually caught her off guard. She wondered if she'd ever get used to it.

His smile was teasing, as if he knew she was nervous and found it endearing. "This is for you."

Dana stared down at the large, square white box R.J. handed to her. She'd been surprised by the appearance of the judge's chambers moments before when she and her good friend Hope Logan had arrived. The large room had been fancied up with white satin ribbon and a white runner. And there were flowers everywhere, flanking a small altar, situated on either side of the door, in a row of pots bordering the floor and in every corner. The air smelled sweet with the combined scents of orange blossom, roses, carnations and orchids.

She wasn't sure what she'd expected, but it hadn't been wedding decorations, not when the wedding wasn't real, not when there was no love involved. Hope, one of her closest friends and the only witness Dana had invited to the wedding, had known for some time how Dana felt about R.J. Trusting her friend completely, Dana had confided R.J.'s motive for the wedding, and had been grateful that Hope hadn't tried to dissuade her from going through with it.

When they'd discovered the decorated chambers, Hope had squeezed her hand and whispered, "Dana, you know R.J. doesn't do anything halfway. You probably should have expected this." But she hadn't.

And now R.J. had another surprise for her.

Dana blinked at the box. "What is it?"

R.J. grinned and she privately thought he was the most charming, handsome man she'd ever seen. He looked stunning in his dark suit and white shirt, and there was a white rosebud in his lapel. "I promise you'll find out if you open the box."

Very aware of everyone looking at her with expectation, Dana lifted the lid on the cardboard box and carefully pulled apart tissue paper. Quietly she caught her breath. Lush, fully bloomed, creamy white roses and rosebuds, baby's breath and delicate orchids were framed by intricate white lace and long, dangling ribbons.

He'd bought her a wedding bouquet.

Tears threatened, and she struggled to subdue them. Ever since he'd made his proposition, her emotions had been on a roller coaster ride, winging high with excitement and an irrepressible, ridiculous hope, then soaring to the depths with stark reality. This was all for show, a complete sham. She wondered why everyone smiled. Did they truly not know? R.J. had always had his pick of beautiful women; why would any sane person believe he'd marry her for love?

Faint music started, startling her anew, and R.J. took her arm to turn her toward the altar. The judge stood in front of it, his face alight with pleasure. Hope had taken her place to the right of the judge, smiling despite the fact she knew this was all contrived.

Drake Logan, Hope's husband and R.J.'s good friend, stood to the left of the judge. Megan stood beside Hope, and Dana realized they all had flowers now. Hope and Megan wore corsages that matched her bouquet, and a white rosebud was tucked in Drake's lapel. Why had R.J. gone to all this trouble? Dana wondered.

But, of course, Hope had been right. When R.J. did something, he did it right, with no room for chance. He wouldn't want any speculation about the authenticity of the wedding.

"You're not going to faint on me, are you?" R.J. whispered in her ear as he gently urged her forward.

Numbly, she shook her head, though fainting seemed a very real possibility. "I'm fine."

He chuckled and gave her hand a squeeze. "A typical answer for you. Tell me, do you ever complain about anything?"

The question startled her. "Why would I complain to you? You're my boss, not my counselor or therapist."

"I thought I was your friend, as well."

They were keeping their voices low, barely audible over the music. Dana nodded. "A friend, but one with limitations."

His eyes glittered down at her. "I'm soon to be your husband."

Unable to hide her feelings, she gave him a stark look. "Not really." By this time they had reached the judge, who started in with the prescribed ceremony. Dana could feel the heat of R.J.'s annoyance beside her, but she refused to let herself be deluded. This wedding was meant to repair his reputation, nothing more. His gestures with the flowers and music were appreciated, but then, R.J. was always considerate of the women he associated with. His generosity was well known, but a smart woman understood that it didn't represent anything beyond superficial affection and a desire to please at best, an intelligent tactic at worst. Either way, it was a long, long stretch from love.

"If you don't answer him, sweetheart, I'm going to be mortified."

She heard the teasing in R.J.'s tone and saw the amusement on everyone's face. Her cheeks heated. She'd been so lost in thought she hadn't even heard the question. But the judge was looking at her expectantly, and she knew the appropriate answer. "Yes."

R.J. gave a rumbling chuckle and again squeezed her hand. In an aside to their small audience, he said, "I see she knows how to keep a man on pins and needles," and they all laughed softly. Dana forced a smile, but it fell away with a gasp when R.J. lifted her left hand and slid a wedding band into place on the third finger.

The ring was a narrow, polished gold circle with a glowing emerald embedded in the middle and surrounded by glittering diamonds. Though it was larger and somewhat more extravagant, it matched the necklace to perfection and left her utterly speechless. She stared at it, with no idea what to say.

Not once had she considered the idea of a ring. Her thoughts had centered on maintaining some sort of emotional balance, of taking advantage of the opportunity to be with R.J., to openly love him, without tossing away her pride by letting him discover her love. She had to protect her heart and at the same time feed the growing need to be with him, to touch him, to have all of him—even under false pretenses.

There'd been no room in her thoughts for the formalities of the wedding. R.J. had said to leave it up to him, and she had.

Hope and Megan oohed over the ring, leaning closer to see it better. Drake gave a masculine murmur of approval, prompting Dana to say simply, and somewhat breathlessly, "Thank you."

She hoped everyone would attribute her preoccupation to bridal jitters. R.J. had orchestrated such a convincing facade. He'd manipulated them all so skillfully, playing the doting bridegroom with the flowers and the music and the ring. Only Hope knew that beneath it all, Dana's heart was breaking.

Everything about the wedding shone—except the bride. When Hope had picked her up to bring her to the courthouse, Dana had wanted to run back inside and change. Her white

suit, which R.J. had suggested was perfectly suitable seemed
dowdy in comparison to Hope's classy silk sheath and pearls.
But of course, she'd had nothing more appropriate to change
into, only more suits and her casual clothes.

But now her businesslike outfit looked even more utilitarian against the beautiful flowers and the emerald ring. She
wanted to shout her frustration, she wanted to run away. *She
wanted R.J. to love her.*

And the judge, with a hearty smile, announced, "You may
kiss the bride."

Dana sucked in her breath and held very, very still. She
felt all the eyes watching her, Hope's with a sort of wistful
expectation, Megan's with joy, Drake's mildly amused.

Her thoughts and feelings fractured as R.J. smiled at her.
His rough fingertips, so warm and steady, touched her chin,
tipping up her face. The worries that had overwhelmed her
only seconds before disappeared at the prospect of kissing
him again.

Dana forgot to breathe. The kiss wasn't voracious, but rather
respectful and restrained. Through the ringing in her ears, she
vaguely heard Drake encouraging R.J. to do better, and before
she knew it, his mouth was back with new intent.

His hand slid from its gentle touch on her chin to grip the
back of her neck and to the sounds of loud cheering, he tilted
her over his arm and continued the kiss. Dana could do little
more than hang on to his lapels, inadvertently crushing his
boutonniere and dropping her bouquet to the floor, as his
tongue stroked hers. She actually felt dizzy, and when he
lifted his mouth, it was to grin down at her as she remained
balanced in his grasp.

Against her lips, he whispered, "Smile, or they'll all think
I'm blackmailing you into this."

Smiling was totally beyond her capabilities. Instead, she
leaned up the scant inch necessary and brought their mouths
together again.

Drake laughed out loud, and Hope and Megan applauded.

Dana was dimly aware of a flash of light, then another. In fact, there had been flashes all through the short ceremony, she realized. R.J. released her mouth and gently drew her upright, then placed one muscular arm around her shoulders. Hope, having rescued the bouquet before it got trampled, handed it to Dana, and they turned to face the photographer.

A small woman with short, straight blond hair and a Bohemian style wielded her camera like a weapon, turning this way and that with an excess of energy. R.J. didn't seem to mind, so Dana assumed this was another surprise, freezing the moment for posterity. She shuddered.

He had joked about the others thinking he'd blackmailed her, when in truth, she was the blackmailer.

And he was paying her demands. She'd insisted he give her all the benefits of a real wife, and evidently he was determined to do just that.

R.J. raised a hand and announced to the group, "Dana and I have arranged a celebration dinner and we insist you all join us, to allow us to show our appreciation."

Dana almost groaned. She wouldn't be able to swallow a bite, and she wanted this over with so she could relax. Then she realized where her thoughts had taken her. Once the celebration was over, they'd be alone—and R.J. would have to pay up, so to speak. She shuddered again at her own daring.

Among the murmur of agreements, R.J. leaned down and kissed her cheek, then whispered in her ear, "This will be the perfect time for our marriage to be leaked to the media. People will see us there, and it'll be reported. That way we won't have to break the news."

"I see."

He turned her to face him, still leaning close, holding her in a loose embrace. She knew it was for the sake of their audience and wanted to pull away. "Does that idea distress you?"

"No, of course not. I want to do whatever you think is best, R.J."

For some reason, her reply seemed to annoy him. Then his frown lifted, replaced by a look of chagrin. "You're not enjoying yourself at all, are you?"

She could tell the idea disappointed him. He'd gone out of his way to make things nice for her, and she was acting like an ungrateful wretch. Luckily the others were all standing a discreet distance away, giving them the privacy they needed. Dana tried to inch back, putting some space between them, and R.J. tightened his hold. She gave up. "Everything is lovely."

He searched her face. "If you're nervous about tonight—"

"No! I mean…" She glanced around. "I don't want to talk about that." Planning it in advance had been so much easier than dealing with it in the present.

He grinned, and then treated her to a swift, hard kiss on her lips. "You can still back out if you want, you know. I won't become a demanding husband."

He held her so close, the only way to avoid his gaze was to drop her forehead against his chest. And that treated her to the scent of his warm body and spicy cologne, the feel of his hard muscles and the rhythmic thumping of his heart. *God, she wanted him.* "I… I haven't changed my mind."

She felt his sigh against the top of her head, his hands coasting gently up and down her spine. "You are a determined woman, aren't you?"

There was no discernible inflection in his tone, which gave her pause. "Does that bother you, R.J.?"

His tight squeeze made her gasp. "Not at all," he said, without an ounce of conviction. "I just hope you know what the hell you're doing."

He stepped away from her, and they went about the formality of signing papers and discussing transportation. R.J. had rented a limo to take them all to the restaurant, and it was waiting in front of the courthouse when they exited. Dana assumed this was another measure to make certain the public took note of the wedding. And sure enough, speculation was rife as onlookers watched the small procession climb into the shining limousine.

R.J. seated Dana in the very back beside him, while Megan sat in the long seat to their right, Drake and Hope to their left. The privacy window was up, so the driver was invisible. Soft music played, and the leather seats creaked as everyone shifted to get comfortable.

"Drake, if you'll do the honors, the champagne is right beside you."

Without a word, the driver pulled away from the curb and Drake retrieved the champagne from the ice bucket and went about filling glasses. When he was through, R.J. lifted his glass in a salute. Smiling at Dana, he said, "To my very special bride."

There was a heartfelt round of, "hear, hear," and then everyone drank a toast to Dana.

Megan watched her son and his new bride. She still hadn't quite figured out how this had all come about, but she couldn't have been more pleased. R.J. was a recluse in many ways, so determined to prove himself, though it wasn't necessary at all. He'd become a total workaholic over the years, and her mother's intuition had often told her Dana was the right woman for him, maybe the only woman for him. Dana could stand up to him, meet him eye to eye, where others wouldn't dare. She supported him and believed in him even when he didn't believe in himself. Dana loved him unconditionally.

But R.J. had never seemed to realize it.

Megan had known for some time how Dana felt, though Dana didn't go about sharing that news with just anyone. But the people who knew her well could tell; it was there in the way she looked at R.J., the extreme effort she put out to be totally professional with him at all times. Like a drunk who carefully enunciates in an effort not to give himself away.

The horrid scandal with the baby had been hardest on R.J., and Megan couldn't help worrying about her son. Maybe, just maybe, Dana would be able to save him.

She tilted her head, smiling at them both. "I'm still amazed at how sudden this has been. Honestly, I'd suspected all along there might be more to your relationship than mere business, especially the way Dana has always been able to read you and manage your nasty temper. But marriage?"

Dana blinked, as if surprised by Megan's words, then she blushed. Megan's speculation doubled—and so did her satisfaction. She'd be willing to bet her son had met his match. "I swear, R.J.," she added, deliberately teasing, "I never thought to live to see the day. Dana must be a miracle worker."

Dana thought about sinking beneath the limo seat and hiding. Did Megan know what was going on? Had R.J. told her, despite his assurance that no one would know?

R.J. merely chuckled while Dana's face grew hot. He was sitting so close beside her in the plush seat, his hard thigh lying alongside her own, his muscled left arm draped around her shoulders.

He tugged her close, almost making her spill her champagne with clumsy nervousness. "There's not another woman in the world I'd have married."

"Then I'm doubly glad to have Dana around," his mother replied.

Dana had a horrible suspicion that they'd both been telling the truth. R.J. had told her many times that he wouldn't have propositioned any other woman, and Megan had never made a secret of her affection. Dana knew Megan liked her, and the feeling was well returned. R.J.'s mother was so different from her own mother, so lively and filled with laughter.

She shook off the disturbing comparison. The last thing she wanted to think about right now was her mother and her lifelong disapproval of her only daughter. But at the same time, Dana hated duping Megan. The woman deserved better from them both.

"Drake," R.J. said, "Next to the champagne there are some gifts I picked up for everyone. Would you pass them over to me, please?"

Surprised, Drake glanced around and located the tray of small packages. He handed it to R.J. with a grin. "I think I like this best man business."

R.J. laughed. "Then by all means, you should go first. Here, this one is for you." Drake took the package, and R.J. turned to the others. "Mother and Hope."

Drake opened his gift without hesitation, then whistled under his breath at the diamond tie clip. "Very nice! Thank you."

"Oh my!" Hope exclaimed when she opened her gift. "R.J., thank you, it's lovely." She held the small gold charm bracelet up for everyone to see. The charm, a golden rose, had a diamond set in the very center.

Megan shook her head. "You are outrageous, R.J. Now, let's see what you got me—oh, goodness. It's lovely, son." She lifted out the elegant diamond stick pin for everyone to see.

R.J. still held one box, and he pressed it into Dana's hand. "A wedding gift, sweetheart."

Dana swallowed nervously. This entire day seemed magical, and if any part of it had been real she'd be the happiest woman alive. Instead, she felt slightly hollow, as if she herself was a sham.

But she was also filled with expectation for the coming night. Conflicting, volatile emotions that made her feel totally off balance.

Her fingers shook horribly as she tore away the silver tissue paper. When she hesitated, R.J. sighed and took the long velvet box from her and carefully opened the hinged top so that Dana could see inside.

This time, the tears almost got her as she glimpsed the emerald bracelet. With a gasp, she launched herself at R.J., making him laugh and gather her close. Likely he assumed it was the costliness of the gift that had so pleased her, but her response had nothing to do with money, and his next words made her chest tighten with the effort to choke back her tears.

To the onlookers R.J. said, "I noticed earlier in the week that Dana looked very fine in emeralds. The color suits her. They perfectly match her eyes."

He didn't think she was too plain to wear such extravagant jewelry.

Dana continued to hide against his shoulder, then she got control of herself and pushed away. She would not continue acting like a complete ninny. One tear slipped down her cheek when she blinked.

Drake gallantly handed her a hanky, which made everyone chuckle again. "I'm sorry," Dana said as R.J. took the hanky from her and tenderly dried her eyes. "I don't know why I'm acting so absurd today—"

"Women are supposed to cry at weddings, silly, even their own!" Hope assured her, then dabbed at her own eyes.

Dana lifted the bracelet from the box. "This is so…so beautiful." She turned to R.J. "Will you help me put it on?"

He touched his mouth to hers in the lightest of kisses, but the emotional impact on Dana was almost more devastating than his blatant performance at the altar. She mustered a shaky smile, which he returned, then he deftly hooked the bracelet around her wrist. Unlike the pendant and ring, which each boasted a single emerald, the bracelet was a multitude of perfect square stones hooked together with gold links. Surprisingly, it wasn't heavy or too ostentatious, and it complemented the other pieces perfectly.

Dana met his warm gaze. "I didn't get you anything."

Given his reasons for marrying her, a gift had seemed out of place.

"You married me, sweetheart. Believe me, that's all I need."

Hope and Megan positively cooed, but Dana, determined to be more herself, snorted good-naturedly and poked him in the ribs. "You don't do humble worth a damn, R.J."

R.J. laughed and gave her another hug. Dana was stunned by how much physical affection he was showing her, but she assumed it was expected from a devoted groom on his wedding day.

"You may not be humble," Drake remarked as he surveyed his tie clip, "but you sure as hell know how to do it up right, don't you?"

"Small gestures, that's all. Dana and I appreciate the show of support, especially in light of all that's going on right now."

Hope leaned forward to touch R.J.'s arm. "That mess has nothing to do with you, R.J. We know that."

Drake shook his head. "It is a mess, though, isn't it? Who the hell could have abandoned the baby? And that damn 'Tattle Today' broad. She drives me nuts the way she fans the flames to make a more sensational story and improve ratings."

Megan sighed. "Did you know Lana has been bringing the baby a gift every day? And Michael can't even bear to look at the child. This is so hard on all of them, Shelby and Garrett, too, knowing that they were once abandoned themselves."

Dana knew about R.J.'s "cousins" and their past. The four siblings had been dropped off at Maitland Maternity shortly after it opened. No one had ever returned to claim them. Megan had found a wonderful home for them with good friends of hers, the Lords, and the children had been raised well. But Dana supposed being abandoned wasn't something you'd easily forget.

She looked at R.J. and wondered what he was thinking.

He'd been accused of abandoning a baby himself. R.J. was close to the Lords and knew they still struggled with their past. Because of his own father's desertion, his sympathy for them ran deep, and made even the suggestion that he would inflict the same pain on a child doubly hurtful. R.J. would never admit just how much the accusation had affected him, though. He'd stomp about and growl and put on a show of anger, but deep inside, Dana knew he was aching.

R.J. noticed her watching him and took her hand, though it was Megan he spoke to. "There haven't been any dull moments lately, that's for sure."

"You're the master of understatement." Drake settled back in his seat and lifted his champagne once more.

"Enough of that." Megan spoke with brisk command. "This is a day for celebration. There's no reason for us to dwell on all that unpleasantness. Let's change the subject, shall we?"

Dana noticed how R.J. suddenly focused on his mother, his gaze growing intent and purposeful. "All right, Mother. I have a topic for you. Connor."

Megan gave a look heavenward. "What would you like to know, R.J.?"

"Oh, I don't know. Anything. Everything. I'm sure the man has been fascinating since he's shown up."

The look Megan sent her son would have quelled most men. She plainly didn't appreciate his sarcasm one whit. But Dana saw that R.J. wouldn't back down. He was worried about his mother, and that was enough reason for him to butt in.

Megan needlessly twitched the skirt of her green silk dress, smoothing it out over the posh limo seats. "Connor is fine. And he seems to be enjoying himself."

R.J.'s laughter was brusque. "I'm sure he is."

"Don't be snide, R.J."

He didn't answer, choosing instead to take a swallow of champagne.

Megan sighed. "You'll feel better about Connor when you

see him again at Thanksgiving dinner." She turned to Dana. "Of course, you'll be there now, too. We're going to love having you in the family."

Dana gave her a wan smile. And just how long would she be in the family? a tiny voice asked her.

THE RINGING PHONE disturbed Janelle from her daydreams of wealth. A large home, a new car, vacations to the tropics—all the things that should have rightfully been hers since birth.

She pushed her hair away from her face and reached out with her left hand to snag the receiver. "Yeah?"

"What's up, sweetheart?"

Janelle bolted upright in bed, shoving aside the brochures spread out around her. "Petey?"

"That's 'Connor' to you, babe."

"Don't joke!" Janelle scooted to sit on the edge of the mattress, her heart racing. "It's all going well?"

"Like a dream. You wouldn't believe how easy it's been. The condo she set me up in is posh. I could get used to this."

"I'm worried, Petey."

His sigh was long and aggrieved. "All right. What is it now?"

Janelle rolled her eyes. The man could be so obtuse. "There's still been no sign of Lacy?"

"Nope. No word of any dead women being found."

"Damn."

"Relax, babe. I told you, it's not that big of a deal these days. Dead bodies turn up all the time." His chuckle grated along her nerves. "Besides, the Maitlands have had other things to occupy them, like the living, breathing bodies. You wouldn't believe all the ruckus over the baby. Every single male Maitland around is being accused of dumping that kid. They're all running in circles—it's pretty damn funny."

Janelle clutched the worn chenille spread with her free

hand. "Well, don't you dare act amused, Petey, do you hear me? You be humble and gracious and sincere." Why did she have to tell him how important this was? "When you all get together for Thanksgiving, make them believe the only thing you want is family. Once I claim the baby and explain our 'dire' situation, they'll get sucked in and we'll be on easy street!"

"I'm a born actor, sweetheart. I told the old lady how shocked I was to find out Clarise wasn't my real mother, that I'd been stolen from my rightful mother at birth, and she just ate it up. I told her I didn't want to cause her trouble, I just wanted to know her, since she was my ma." He laughed. "She's been real motherly ever since."

"What about the baby? Does anyone suspect anything?"

"With me? Nah. Not since I've told them it couldn't be mine."

"Still, Petey, keep on the lookout for any news about Lacy. Any bodies found with a head wound—hell, any bodies at all—I want to know about it. I can't quit worrying until I know she's been located. A dead woman in the alley that close to the clinic would make front-page news, regardless of what else is going on!"

"Stop fretting. I'll let you know the second I hear anything."

As she hung up, a cloud of misgivings loomed over Janelle's head. The color brochure of a luxurious Hawaiian vacation resort was crumpled in her fist. She threw the wad of paper across the room.

Damn it, she had as much right to the Maitland fortune as any of them. Just because her father had turned out to be the black sheep didn't mean she should be denied her fair share. R.J. and Anna were his kids, too, and they were being pampered, so why shouldn't she? But until that damned Lacy was found, she wouldn't be able to rest easy.

Things would work out in the end, she swore silently. She

and Petey would have the money, and they'd take the kid
for protection. They'd live the good life—she'd make damn
sure they did.

CHAPTER SIX

IT WAS SEVERAL HOURS later before the limo dropped Dana and R.J. off in front of his house. Dana had never been here before, and he wondered what she'd think of it.

Actually, he'd been wondering what she was thinking all day. She'd been totally closed off from him, playing the role of new bride to perfection while hiding any real emotion.

He didn't like it.

He liked his reactions to her even less.

Sitting in the limo, he'd taken special note of the way she crossed her legs—long legs, he had only recently realized. As she looked out the window, avoiding his eyes, he'd seen the way her chest rose and fell with nervous breaths and couldn't keep himself from imagining her naked.

Dana.

Somehow, the fact that he felt as if he'd known her forever, that she'd always been a friend, made the moment highly erotic. He'd bedded more than his fair share of beautiful women. Hell, even if he didn't have a healthy sex drive, he'd have been highly experienced. Women chased him down, drawn by his money, his power, his connections. Several times the papers had labeled him Austin's most eligible bachelor—a title he'd intended to maintain forever.

Yet here he was married. *To Dana.*

She certainly hadn't come on to him for money, or for any of the other motives women had shown in the past. He'd offered her money and she'd refused. She staunchly insisted on keeping her independence, on supporting herself. She'd looked poleaxed when she discovered he'd bought her a ring, damn her, which had made him feel like an ogre. She should have known him better than that, and probably did, but she intended to stick to their agreement, which meant she expected nothing from him.

Except sex.

That fact had been eating away at his control all day. Playing the diligent bridegroom, touching her, kissing her, had added to his strain. Dana hadn't noticed, but he'd been half-hard since the judge had proclaimed them man and wife.

He needed to get the upper hand again, and he might as well start right now.

"Dana?"

She glanced at him as if she'd forgotten he was there. "Yes?"

The chauffeur was pulling the limo around the curving drive to the front door. Lazily, R.J. leaned back in his seat and looked her over. "I had my housekeeper prepare your room for you. She's put away all your clothes and the things that you sent over earlier. Anything else you need we can get later."

"All right."

She was too agreeable, and he didn't like it. "It's not very late yet, but all things considered, I thought you could take a brief tour of the house to familiarize yourself, then change into something more comfortable. We can have a drink out on the veranda and relax…before going to bed."

He saw her slender, pale throat move as she swallowed, and he congratulated himself for taking her off guard. God knew, she'd kept him off guard since making her tantalizing demand. His head still reeled whenever he thought of it.

As she turned to look at him directly, he noticed that her green eyes were brighter than the emeralds she now wore. "I thought we agreed we'd share a room."

Persistent witch. He kept his expression impassive and

shrugged. "Our rooms connect, both by an inside door and the veranda. You'll be free to come and go as you please. I thought you might appreciate the privacy for dressing and bathing and doing your hair and—" he gestured with his hand. "—whatever else it is women do on a daily basis."

She nodded, again looking away from him.

He didn't like her lack of attention, and gently, deliberately, added, "You don't have to worry, Dana. I'll be available to you when you want my end of the bargain met."

Her gaze snapped back to his, and a rosy blush spread from her throat up. Intrigued, R.J. sat forward, keeping his eyes locked on hers, and slowly reached out to touch the emerald necklace with one finger. "Ah. Warmth. I did wonder if your blush was as hot as it appeared." His finger stroked beneath the small stone, then all around it. He smiled, and a slight tension invaded his muscles. "Even the gold is heated," he murmured.

Dana's breathing accelerated, but it was nothing compared with his own reaction. He enjoyed touching her, seeing her respond so freely. Her eyes drifted shut, and he looked at her pale skin where his rough finger slowly glided, going lower and lower.

As usual, her blouse was fully buttoned, but this one had something of a modestly scooped neckline. He wondered whether she'd chosen it to show off the emerald or to attempt to seduce him. He almost chuckled. Dana was reserved enough to think a small glimpse of collarbone might be enticing.

Strangely enough, she was right.

The limo stopped and the driver got out. R.J. straightened back in his seat and watched Dana struggle to regain her composure. She was still breathing a little roughly, still fidgeting when the door opened and the driver offered an arm.

With a mumbled thank you she got out of the car, then turned to stone as she surveyed his house. R.J. watched her from the corner of his eye as he dispatched the driver. She looked positively stunned, taking in everything around her as if in disbelief. It was fairly dark, but he had installed lighting along the path and at key points around the grounds to draw focus to a particular plant or tree. The lights gave off a soft, muted yellow glow.

Stepping up behind her, R.J. put both hands on her shoulders and whispered near her ear, "What do you think of your new home?"

"Oh, it's beautiful!" But she wasn't looking at the house, only the gardens.

"So it'll do?" he teased.

She stepped away to touch the feathery leaves of a young Chinese fan palm. R.J. had had several of them planted in staggered groups around the front of the property, to act as both a privacy fence and an ornamental border. There were also southern magnolia and crape myrtle trees, but it was November so they weren't blooming. He wondered what she'd think of his house in the spring when every tree and bush was fresh and new with budding life, ripe with color.

Except she wouldn't be here in the spring. By then, all the problems should be resolved, and he could resume his normal life.

A life without a wife.

"There are fruit trees in the back," he told her, "and several flower gardens. This isn't the best time of year to view the trees, but tomorrow I'll show them to you, if you like."

She turned to smile at him. "I'd love that. Thank you."

Taking her arm, he led her along the cobbled walk toward the front doors, pointing out some of his favorite plants. "I like things to take their own natural shape rather than be pruned into little squares or circles. Everything is bushier and softer that way. This is a Camellia japonica."

"It's beautiful. And so many flowers."

"The japonica has a very long season. And of course, those are hostas surrounding it. I prefer the halcyon for the bluish color. I just had them thinned out this fall, so they're not as full as usual. But it gives the day lilies more room to spread."

She stepped away onto another path lined with pansies of every color. "What's that tree?"

R.J. put his hands in the pockets of his slacks and followed along, enjoying her enthusiasm, the heavy darkness of the night. Her scent drifted back to him, noticeable even among all the fragrant flowers.

The evening was pleasant, around seventy degrees, with a bright moon and a multitude of stars. The lighting system gave the yard the look of early dusk, but it left deep shadows in Dana's bright green eyes. She looked…mysterious. "This one's a pink dogwood. The flowers are gone, of course, but the leaves turn such a brilliant scarlet in fall, as you can see, so it's always showy. One of my favorites."

She took off again, getting farther and farther from the house. "And that one?"

With a low, pleased chuckle, R.J. followed. Then he answered all her questions, which were numerous.

It was almost half an hour later when it dawned on him that Dana had effectively sidetracked him from his plans. Here it was his wedding night, and his new bride had him ambling around the grounds of his house looking at shrubs and trees and various types of mulch. Hell, they'd even discussed underground watering systems. He felt like an ass, and worse, he felt strangely vulnerable.

Damn her. He didn't like feeling out of control.

"Enough, Dana," he said when she started to question him on the homemade bench placed beneath a trellis of lush purple clematis. He managed, just barely, to keep the annoyance and inner turmoil out of his voice. "Don't you think it's time we went inside? I'd like to show you your room."

"Does my room have a view of the grounds?"

He caught her arm and started her back toward the path. Her French twist had begun to slip, and instead of being neatly anchored as usual, her hair looked softer and slightly tousled.

"Your room faces the back overlooking a fountain. There's a row or two of Sparkle berry, which you'll enjoy because they're loaded with bright red berries right now, and the birds flock to them."

She stepped away from him to turn a full circle, her arms outstretched, her face tilted to the endless sky above. "This is like a fairy-tale castle, R.J.," she said in a breathless whisper, "with so many gorgeous plants and colors and scents. I feel like I could get lost out here. I had no idea you knew so much about gardening."

That wasn't much of a surprise, since no one, other than his housekeeper, knew about his fascination with plants and his affinity for digging in the dirt. And he preferred to keep it that way.

Why in hell he'd opened up so completely to Dana, he couldn't guess.

She continued to stare into the star-studded sky, oblivious to his turmoil. If she'd been aware of it, he thought with a wry smile, he had no doubt she'd try to find a way to fix it for him.

For some reason, that thought perturbed him. She looked so happy and carefree, her fair hair glowing in the combined moon and lamp light, a few tendrils ruffled by the soft breeze, and suddenly he was restless, overcome by a vague longing. It was a wholly uncomfortable feeling, and he scowled. Snatching her hand as she twirled past once again, he pulled her against his chest and leaned down until their mouths were only separated by a breath.

"This is very private land, Dana. I know you haven't bothered looking at the house, but I chose it for its isolation. If you'd like, we could have our wedding night right here, beneath the weeping willow with the begonias all around us. Would you like that?"

Her eyes widened, looking dark and deep in the dim light, and her mouth fell open. He took advantage of the moment to kiss her, knowing it would distract her and embarrass her and most likely excite her. He felt as if he could deal with any one of those emotions far easier than he could the naked happiness he'd read in her expression.

It was the first time he'd ever seen her look that way, and the look was incredibly potent.

She was stiff in his arms for about three seconds, then her hands slid up his shoulders to his head and she gripped his hair hard as a groan escaped her, her mouth moving against his, her body pushing into his. She nearly pulled his hair out as she tried to get closer. She accepted his tongue, then went one further and sucked on it. R.J. gasped, her passion both astounding and seductive. He caught her wrists and gently eased her hands away before she could do more damage to his scalp.

"Easy, sweetheart. I like my head where it is."

She either didn't hear or didn't understand his teasing comment. Pressed full against him, she went on tiptoe and tried to find his mouth again. R.J. leaned back, laughing softly to himself. She was such a sweet surprise! As long as she was amusing him, there'd be no problem.

He cupped her face between his hands to gain her attention, then asked, "Is that a yes? Do you want to strip for me now and lie down on the soft grass? The air is a little fresh, but I think we'll manage to stay warm enough once we get things started."

Very slowly, awareness seeped back into her soft eyes. Her brows rose and her pupils flared. She scrambled out of his reach, crossing her arms over her chest in an oddly protective gesture that made him want to hold her again, gently this time, to comfort her.

"No." She shook her head, and her hair threatened to come completely undone. One long tendril dropped down across her forehead, fascinating him and making her huff with impatience. "I have no intention of…of…"

He wanted badly to smooth her hair and started to do just that. "Frolicking among nature?" He knew he was obsessed with her hair, like a pioneer male waiting anxiously to get a glimpse of a woman's ankle. Good God, it was only hair, and all women had it. It was just that Dana had always kept hers neatly pinned up, making his curiosity run wild.

She smacked his hand away before he could actually touch her. "It isn't funny, R.J.!"

Neither was his throbbing erection, but he was dealing with it the best he could. Which was evidently far better than she could deal with her own arousal. Dana had a tendency to get snippy when she was turned on or sexually frustrated. He'd found that out each time he kissed her. He wondered what would happen when she could let all that passion loose, rather than struggle to restrain it.

He wondered what would happen tonight.

Smiling, he looped his arm around her shoulders and again tried to get her on the winding path that led to the front door. "No doubt Betty, my housekeeper, heard the limo and is waiting for us. She'll have no idea what we're doing out here."

"That's a relief!"

R.J. was feeling just contrary enough to give her a squeeze. "We're married now, sweetheart. We can damn well cavort wherever we please." And soon, he'd be cavorting with her in *her* bed, where he intended to leave her. He liked his privacy, whether she valued her own or not. He expected to consummate the marriage with as little fuss as possible, pleasing her, pleasing himself, but no more than that. He'd remain detached and efficient and he'd fulfill her demands while still keeping as much emotional distance from her as possible. It could be done; he'd had sex with any number of women without feeling a single thing beyond physical satisfaction.

And afterward he'd hold her until she dozed off, then retreat to his own room.

He liked sleeping alone, damn it, and he expected to go on liking it. He was thirty-nine years old and he'd never before been inclined to share his bed. He didn't intend to start now.

If she wanted to repeat the procedure nightly, well, who was he to complain about an available lover? He'd always had a very healthy sex drive, and no doubt the arrangement would prove convenient.

She'd be happy with the bargain, damn her, and he'd still keep himself safe.

Betty was waiting at the door when they reached it, her large brown eyes curious, her hands clutched together at her rounded middle. She was more than twenty years his senior, but as spry as a teenager and as protective and bossy as a surrogate mother. When they neared, a wide smile broke out over her pleasant face.

"There you are! I wondered what happened to you."

"Sorry if we worried you, Betty." R.J. pressed Dana forward. "My bride showed an unexpected interest in the grounds."

Dana reached a hand out. "Hello, Betty. I'm Dana Dillinger."

R.J. made a tsking sound. "How soon they forget. It's Dana Maitland now, love. At least, if that's what you want."

"Oh." Dana looked almost bewildered as Betty took her hand in a warm welcome.

The housekeeper, who thought any outdoor activity was thoroughly heinous, gave Dana an inquiring look. "The grounds?"

"All the beautiful trees and shrubs," Dana clarified.

"Oh, yes. Mr. Maitland does like puttering around out-side." Her nose had wrinkled slightly, and then she ushered them both inside. "Come on in, now. I have everything ready for you."

To R.J.'s surprise, Dana didn't show nearly as much interest in the interior of the house as she had the gardens. Not that his home was a design showpiece. It was a modest two-story, situated in a quiet location. He was only one man and had no need for a much larger place. When he'd chosen the house, which had been built at the turn of the century, but recently renovated, it had been for the privacy, the abundance of land and the architectural charm. He loved the arched doorways and wooden floors and trim, the wide back veranda and original windows. The place had been professionally decorated, and many of his furnishings were antique, in keeping with the age of the house.

Dana gave a cursory glance at the entrance hall, peeked into the dining room at the right and the living room at the left, then peered at the curving staircase.

Betty started in that direction, leading the way up the stairs. "Your bags arrived earlier, and I've already put everything away." When they reached the top, she turned to the right to a pair of connecting bedrooms with private baths. To the left were two guest bedrooms and a hall bath.

"The kitchen is downstairs, just beyond the dining room," Betty explained, "and at the back of the house is a den with a nice library, and a workout room that's adjacent to an enclosed porch with a hot tub."

She turned and smiled at them both. "Dana, your bathroom is right through that door. I put all your toiletries away so you shouldn't have any trouble finding what you need. Here's the closet, and I've already arranged all your things." The door leading to R.J.'s room stood open.

He saw Dana bite her lip and knew she felt uncomfortable that Betty knew of the sleeping arrangements. He gave his housekeeper a hug and said easily, "Thanks, Betty, for staying late and for getting everything organized so well."

She sent a stern look his way. "It's not every day you get married, Mr. M., now is it? I was glad to stay and help out.

Besides, I had to meet your bride! Having a woman in the house is going to be quite a change."

"You're a sweetheart. But we can manage from here, so you might as well head home. And, Betty, take the day off tomorrow, all right?"

She winked at Dana. "I was planning to! I've already put a casserole in the refrigerator, and there's salad makings and a fresh-baked pie for dessert. The refrigerator is stocked with plenty of things for lunch, and I made sure no one else was set to come to work tomorrow." In an aside to Dana, she explained, "Mr. M. has a regular man to mow the lawn and another to tend the pool and the hot tub. All things considered, I figured that could be put off for a couple of days."

"Remind me to give you a bonus, Betty."

"Ha! I'll hold you to that." She squeezed Dana's hand again then bustled out the door, saying over her shoulder, "I'll lock up on my way out."

Betty was no sooner gone and the bedroom door closed softly behind her than Dana began to fidget. R.J. gave in to a private, very indulgent smile of satisfaction. Naturally she was nervous about being with him the first time, and that suited him just fine. He watched her walk to the window to look out into the garden below.

"How do you like your room?"

She jumped slightly at his voice, then glanced at him quickly over her shoulder. "It's lovely." She barely looked at the room, all her attention focused on the scene outside her window. "Who did it belong to before me?"

Ah. Was that a tinge of jealousy he heard? But that didn't make any sense, and in any case, he didn't want her to be possessive enough to feel jealousy. He decided it was no more than Dana's practical search for info. She always asked questions.

Slowly, R.J. approached her until he stood just a few inches behind her. He looked over her shoulder at the lighted fountain and flowers below, but he didn't touch her. Not yet. Let the tension build, he thought, knowing it would make things go that much smoother, and easier, when they got around to consummating their bogus marriage—as per her request. She wouldn't have the wit, or the interest, in insisting he stay the night with her, not when she was totally replete.

"This room was utilitarian. I had old files in here, a comfortable chair where I could read. Because of the other two guest rooms, I never felt I needed another. People don't visit me overnight all that often."

Dana stiffened somewhat, turning her head just enough that he could see her profile. R.J. touched the tip of her nose. "No, Dana, not even women. A woman who wakes in your house in the morning likes to assume things that don't exist."

Still slightly turned away from him, she asked incredulously, "You're telling me no woman has spent the night with you here?"

"That surprises you? You've seen how easily the media can turn against you, even though I've always been very discreet. Can you imagine how it would've been if I'd advertised my personal affairs?"

She waited a moment, then nodded, as if accepting the truth of his words. "Who decorated the room? You?"

That made him laugh. "Hardly. I have a knack for landscaping, and I know what type of furniture I like, but when it comes to matching flowered spreads with pastel curtains...."

She stepped away from the window. For the first time she really observed the room, and judging by the look on her face, it was only then that she realized the room had been done specifically with a woman's tastes in mind.

The carpet was a soft cream, as were the walls, which featured stark white moldings at the ceiling and floor. The furniture was light oak with a natural sheen, new, yet crafted with the care and detail of days gone by. The spread on the queen-size bed was a bright splash of pastel flowers with an abundance of velvety throw pillows in every shape and color. Feminine, but not overly so.

The dust ruffle was edged with crocheted lace. Fresh flowers were arranged in vases around the room, and the lightweight curtains had been drawn back to allow in the moonlight and the muted glow from the gardens.

R.J. spoke softly, watching the expressions flickering across her face. "I sort of judged what I wanted by looking at Anna's rooms. I hope you approve. I hired a designer, but specifically told her to style it for a woman with understated tastes and without a lot of fussiness."

Dana turned to gape at him. "Oh, my God! Your sister. Anna wasn't at the wedding."

R.J. turned to stone. "No, I didn't want Anna involved." His sister was very precious to him. Ever since they'd been dropped off at Megan and William's home when he had been only three and Anna little more than an infant, R.J. had been determined to protect her. That meant keeping her out of his lies and out of the public spotlight. He hadn't known for certain if the press would end up hounding them at the wedding, but it had been likely, and he'd wanted Anna as far from him as possible. He also hadn't wanted his sister to probe too closely into his reasons for his hasty marriage.

"R.J., she'll be hurt."

"Not after I explain." He wouldn't give Anna the full truth, but he would make her understand that he'd only been trying to protect her and his ten-year-old nephew, Will, from the relentless press. The thought of Anna's face ending up in some rag mag, as his own had been, filled him with a killing rage. He wouldn't let that happen.

Dana was watching him with a keen intensity, and he instinctively withdrew, concealing his thoughts instantly. He gave her a vague smile and kept his tone light. "I gather the room doesn't impress you."

"I like it very much."

She sounded far from sincere. "Honey, you live here now. You can feel free to change anything. I want you to be comfortable."

"The view is spectacular. Did I see a pond?"

His mouth quirked at her continued interest in the grounds. "Yes, filled with fat goldfish. I put it in over the summer. I'm surprised you could see it this time of night." The pond was a discreet distance from the house and was surrounded by lilies. It featured a small waterfall, as well as a few aquatic denizens, like the goldfish, frogs and some bottom feeders.

"Water is very reflective in moonlight."

More than ready to change the subject, he stepped forward and fingered a loose tendril of her hair. "So is your hair." He searched her face and found a touch of hesitancy, a little shyness and a dose of obvious eagerness. He grinned. "I think I'll go take a quick shower. I'll join you here in about thirty minutes?" That should give her plenty of time to prepare herself. He had a vague image in his mind of Dana with her hair falling free, a sexy negligee draped over her body and a smile of welcome on her face.

His hands shook.

"That's…that's fine."

R.J. touched her cheek once again, gave her a quick peck, then formed a strategic retreat before Dana could realize just how badly he wanted her.

She could never know the effect she had on him.

He didn't even like to admit it to himself.

CHAPTER SEVEN

R.J. WAITED thirty-eight minutes exactly, not wanting to seem too anxious. But the truth was, his body had been invaded by a fine trembling that wouldn't abate. He felt rock hard from his nape down to his toes, all his muscles tense, his movements awkward, his heart beating much too fast.

Never had he needed a woman this badly, but then, never had there been so much plotting involved. If he wanted a woman, he made an advance. She either accepted it or not, and the outcome had never been very important to him. He hadn't become the most eligible bachelor in Austin without being aware of the perks involved. If one woman refused him, he could always find another.

Somehow, Dana was different.

Wearing only a pair of slacks, he gave a quick tap at the door between their rooms, then quietly opened it. After her insistence that they see this through, he half expected to find Dana in the bed, provocatively posed, waiting for him. He half expected a shimmer of moonlight to drift over her partially clad body, highlighting some seductive detail of a sexy negligee that displayed more than it covered.

He did not expect to find her standing in front of the damn window once again, looking outside. Her hair was down now, but neatly braided, the pale rope falling just below her shoulder blades. She glanced at him over her shoulder, her face shiny clean in the moonlight, her eyes wide.

She wore a long white, granny gown.

It should have been the most sexless thing he'd ever encountered, given that it covered her from throat to toes. Even the sleeves were long, fitting to her wrists. It had no detailing that he could discern, just yards and yards of material that hid her body from him completely.

And made him pulse with need.

God, she looked so innocent and sweet. Never in his life had he seen a woman wear such a garment. The sheer novelty of it was proving to be extremely erotic.

Without looking away from her, he closed the door behind him. He hadn't meant to do that, wanting the return to his own room to be as inconspicuous as possible. But he'd needed something to do besides gawk, so he'd closed the damn door.

"Dana."

She turned completely to face him, her hands laced together in front of her, eyes glowing. She'd turned off all the lamps, but with the curtains wide open there was enough moonlight flooding over her for him to see. Not the small details, but her form and the bed, everything that was necessary.

"I'm a little nervous," she whispered.

He drew a slow breath that didn't do a damn thing to calm his galloping heart and forced the necessary words through his constricted throat. "You can still change your mind, you know."

She shook her head in immediate denial, causing the braid to swing over her shoulder, where it landed softly against her breast.

"All right." He reached out his hand. "Then come here."

She moved away from the window—and the moonlight— which left her body only a vague shadow. Taking tentative steps, she crossed the room until she stood before him. R.J. didn't dare touch her anywhere but her hand, which she offered to him shyly. Her fingers were cold and taken by a slight trembling that couldn't be feigned.

"You braided your hair."

"It tangles easily."

Amusement nudged at his lust-fogged brain. "Honey, most women would have left it loose, anyway. It's sexier that way."

He sensed more than saw her slight shrug. "For some women, maybe. I don't…don't do *sexy* very well. And my hair…it's just straight. And fine. It's not very sexy hair, believe me."

He swallowed hard, barely absorbing the meaning of her words. "I think I'd like to find out for myself, if you don't mind."

"You want me to unbraid it?" Her tone indicated that the prospect held little appeal for her.

He wanted her naked, spread out on the bed. He wanted to be inside her already. His muscles strained with the effort to reign in his urgency. *Absurd.*

"I'd like that very much." He'd have offered to do the deed himself, but he didn't think he could and still maintain control.

Dana released his hand and reached for the end of the braid. A cloth-covered band pulled free, and she placed it on the dressing table in a small dish. Her movements were only faintly visible in the dark room, a whisper of sound, a shifting shadow. Only her white gown, the glimmer of her wide eyes and her fair hair shone clearly, allowing him to track her movements.

With nimble fingers, she loosened the braid, separating each long tress until her hair was shining and free and he had to catch his breath. Not sexy? Who the hell had ever told her such a ridiculous thing?

Bent on seduction—hers, not his—he gathered a handful of her hair and caressed it. It was baby fine, just as she'd claimed, and very, very soft. It slipped through his fingers like warm water, and he wished very badly that he could see her better.

He imagined that hair trailing over his chest, his abdomen, his upper thighs. He barely bit back a groan, even as he trembled uncontrollably.

"You're wrong," he rasped.

She remained silent, and her wide eyes shone up at him in a sort of dazed confusion.

A gentle smile tugged at his mouth, despite his arousal. "Your hair," he explained in a gruff whisper. "It is sexy. Warm, silky. I can't believe you keep it put up all the time."

He could feel her restlessness before she asked, "Even…even if what you said were true, why would I wear it down?"

R.J. stared at her as the words sank in like a dose of reality. Why *should* she wear her hair down? Dana had never been a woman who tried to attract men. She didn't flirt, didn't pose, didn't indulge in casual banter. She was always perfectly attired and proper, her appearance neat and orderly, meant to draw male appreciation. She didn't wear clothing that accentuated any part of her femininity. If anything, her business suits tended to conceal.

The professional image she presented to the world pleased him immensely, both in her role as his executive secretary and as his friend and confidante. He didn't want anything to change, certainly not Dana. He didn't want to alter their relationship when it already felt so right.

He had to remember that. The last thing he wanted to do was convince her to change her look; he sure as hell didn't want any other man discovering how attractive she could be. She could keep her hair up, and it would suit him just fine.

He took her hand again and led her toward the bed, stopping right beside it. There was no moonlight here, just deep shadows and Dana's evocative scent. Taking her face in his hands, he bent low and whispered, "I suppose we should get things moving."

She stiffened at his words, as he'd known she would. But he needed to remind her—and himself—that this was part of their deal, not a love affair, regardless of how his voice shook when he spoke, or the way his hands trembled. They had a business arrangement, and he didn't want her to read any more into it than that.

First he kissed her cheek, then the very corner of her lips, before closing his mouth over hers. Despite her frozen posture, her lips opened softly beneath his. His heart drummed madly, confounding him and renewing his determination. Without preamble, he sank his tongue inside, then groaned aloud at the delicious taste of her. Her hands found his wrists and curled around them; her breathing deepened.

"Damn." He couldn't believe this was *his* Dana, his proper, restrained secretary who remained unflappable at even the most harried meeting, who faced disgruntled clients or upset contributors with cool poise and calm deliberation. The woman who'd confronted his temper many times without a single flinch.

Right now, she was simply a woman, shivering with need, low sounds of pleasure escaping her while he kissed her throat, her temple, her ear. He couldn't seem to make himself stop. He wanted, quite simply, to kiss her everywhere, to explore all the subtle fragrances and tastes of her body.

Yet she was still the same woman he'd always known but never regarded as a sexual being; his secretary, his friend, his Dana. *His wife.*

She pressed against him, trying to complete the contact of their bodies. Despite his resolve, it amazed and excited him that she had always looked so innocent. For all the time he'd known her, she'd seemed disinterested in sex, yet here she was, wriggling against him like a wanton woman.

He lifted one hand to close over her breast. R.J. was experienced in reading women, in picking up their nuances, knowing what pleasured them and when they wanted that pleasure. It was an awareness that made him a good lover. Dana wanted, needed to be touched, so he touched her.

Pure sensation shot through him at the feel of her. Her breast was soft and heavy beneath the fabric of her gown, and her small nipple tightened against his palm. He rubbed it with his open hand and she clutched at him, appearing both strangely bewildered and wildly excited. He heard her breath catch, felt her body shiver.

Kissing her voraciously, he forced her head to bend back to give him better access. The urge to tumble her onto the bed swamped him. He was so hard he hurt.

He pulled his mouth free to drag in a needed breath of air, his body awash in heat. Dana left her head tipped back, her eyes closed, as she gave herself up to his touch.

It was too much.

He hooked his free arm beneath her buttocks and lifted her against his pelvis, pressing her into him until her soft thighs parted and he could stroke the soft notch of her thighs with his pulsing arousal.

She cried out, her hands again clutching at his hair, trying to bring his mouth back to hers.

Instead, he raised her a bit higher and drew her cloth-covered nipple into his mouth. She went wild.

Her movements weren't smooth or practiced, and they fired his lust. Her legs closed around his hips, and he took two quick steps forward until her back came up against the wall. He pinned her there with his body, nearly beyond rational thought.

The damned floor-length nightgown was in his way, and he struggled briefly with it, jerking it above her knees and then sinking his fingers into her soft outer thigh just below her buttocks.

"R.J.!"

She wasn't wearing panties. His palm encountered the firm contours of her bottom, and he groaned again, caught up in a fog of raging lust. It had never been like this for him, but then he'd never made love with a woman like Dana before, a feminine paradox, subtle one moment, fiercely blatant the next.

He wanted her naked, but he didn't know if he could wait that long. He adjusted his hold, bringing his hand around the front to her smooth, silky belly. She stiffened the tiniest bit, her breathing suspended as his fingers stroked down and into her soft curls.

She jerked, but he held her tight, limiting her instinctive movements. He insinuated one finger between her delicate folds and touched her, overwhelmed by her heat, her wetness. "Oh, yeah." He squeezed his eyes shut. *"Hell, yes."*

His fingers stroked deeper, slowly, and she bucked against him, her breathing choppy, her fingers biting into his shoulders. "You want this, don't you, Dana? You're so damn hot." He pushed one finger into her and was amazed at the incredible tightness, the way her muscles spasmed, gripping his finger hard.

"R.J.?"

She'd gone still, but he wrote it off as expectant anticipation. If she was half as aroused as he was, he could understand her inability to move. He felt clumsy in his urgency to become part of her. He forced another finger deep and swallowed her groan with a long, devouring kiss.

There was a buzzing in his ears, a red haze blotting out the shadows in the room. Unable to wait a second more, he turned and lowered Dana to the mattress. Her legs hung over the side and she started to sit up, but he came down over her, between her widespread thighs. He kissed her quiet, until her arms were wrapped around his neck and her thighs moved restlessly alongside his.

"Don't move," he muttered, then levered himself up enough to shove the gown above her breasts. He couldn't see her in the darkness, and it frustrated him, but he was too close to the edge to start fumbling with the lights. He unzipped his pants and stripped them off, then hurriedly slid on a condom. The shaking in his hands enraged him, but thankfully it was too dark for her to see.

The welcoming softness of her body greeted him as he lowered his weight onto her. He almost growled at the exquisite sensation. In the back of his mind, he kept thinking, *Is this really Dana?* The reality of being with her like this was almost more than he could take. He'd always seen Dana as sexless, female efficiency in a suit. But the heat of her exposed body, the frantic beating of her heart and the soft cushion of her breasts beneath his chest proved she was very capable of indulging in even the most heated encounters. He'd been duped by her—and now he was learning the sweet truth.

Carefully he parted her with his fingers, struggling to go slowly, despite the urgency surging through him. He guided himself just inside, grinding his teeth at her heat, at her wetness as she closed around the very tip of him. Dana didn't move, didn't even breathe. He pressed forward with an effort, going a little deeper. She felt snug, unbearably so, tight enough to completely shatter his control.

With a rough curse he wrapped one arm around her trim hips, lifted her high and drove into her. He was met with natural resistance for a split second before her body opened to his and he sank deep with a raw groan of indescribable pleasure.

He had a single moment to absorb the pleasure of having his length wrapped tightly in moist heat, then Dana arched so violently she almost bucked him off. Her soft, nearly breathless gasp rang in his ears, and he realized several things at once.

Dana was no longer holding him tight. Her hands were pressed hard against his chest in an effort to shove him away. He didn't move.

Her breaths came in short, harsh pants, as if she were experiencing discomfort. Or worse. And he knew why.

She'd been a virgin.

Never in his life had he felt a woman so acutely. He'd been sexually active since his mid teens, but the tightness he felt now, squeezing him, nearly turning his mind to mush, was unique. He strained to hold himself perfectly still while his mind tried to assimilate all the facts. Her shallow, rapid breaths fanned his throat. Her small hands were hot against his chest. Her soft thighs encased his hips. And her body held him as if she'd never let him go.

"Dana?"

Several seconds passed in silence. He heard her swallow. "I…I'm sorry."

He couldn't begin to understand what she was apologizing for. "You're a virgin?"

She moved, shifting beneath him, and instinctively he used his hips to pin her down again, grinding into her softness in reaction.

"R.J.…." She moved again, lifting her legs so that her feet pressed flat against the mattress.

The position brought him deeper still, and his gut tightened painfully. He didn't know if she was trying to escape him or seduce him. All he knew for certain was that he was so deep, and the pleasure so keen, he was ready to explode.

His arms wrapped snug around her, his face pressed into her neck, he thrust hard, two times, three. He growled like a savage, thoroughly shattered, drained of all rational thought, his body balanced on an edge of pleasure so keen he'd never known anything like it.

Afterward he couldn't seem to do more than breathe—and even that required strenuous effort. They were still hanging half over the bed, Dana's legs now limp beside his. When they started to slip to the floor, he hefted himself onto his back beside her with a groan.

Like a shot, Dana was off the bed.

R.J., trying to regain normal breathing, watched as she hustled into the bathroom, her white nightgown a bright beacon as she dashed across the dark room.

He wanted to call her back, but he remained silent, listening to water run in the bathroom, trying to imagine what she was thinking while his heartbeat gradually slowed and his brain cleared of the fog that had taken over rational thought.

She hadn't found a bit of pleasure.

No, that wasn't true. She'd been every bit as turned on as he before he'd lost control and more or less attacked her. Shame washed over him. Damn, he'd been like a rutting animal.

He squeezed his eyes shut and silently called himself ten times a fool. Hell, he'd wanted to explore her entire silken body, yet he'd spent less than ten minutes on that particular pleasure, and had touched her only in the ways necessary to have her, without all the tenderness and detail he knew women wanted and needed.

He'd wanted to taste her everywhere, yet he'd barely kissed her, and certainly not in the ways and places he'd intended. She'd discovered the start of pleasure, the tip of the iceberg, but not the explosive conclusion.

And once he'd gotten inside her, he'd lost all claim to control.

It had never happened to him before and made no sense. She was Dana, for God's sake, not some femme fatale who'd deliberately seduced him. She'd done no more than stand there in her prim gown with her hair braided like a schoolgirl's, and he'd been as aroused as if he'd been indulging in hours of foreplay.

Hell, even when he *had* indulged in hours of foreplay, he'd never been that turned on.

Dropping an arm over his eyes, he groaned. There was still a pleasant buzz in his body, a sexual repletion that echoed. His muscles felt like mush.

And his bride was in the bathroom, hiding, maybe crying.

He couldn't stand it. He forced himself to his feet and staggered to the closed door. "Dana?"

The water shut off. Silence throbbed in the dark bedroom.

"Dana?" he repeated.

"Yes?"

Her voice was too high, too light. Very forced. He moaned low in his throat, thoroughly disgusted with himself. He felt like a defiler of innocents, and he didn't like the feeling at all. He hadn't lost control like that…ever. Spreading one hand on the wall, he propped himself up, still unsure of his shaky legs. "Honey, are you all right?"

A short, twittering laugh. "Yes, yes, of course. I'm fine."

His free hand curled into a fist, and his eyes narrowed in speculation. He wanted to see her, to judge for himself. She'd been in the bathroom a long time. "What are you doing in there?"

"Oh, nothing. Tidying up."

Tidying up what? Was she torturing her hair back into that twist? Or braiding it again? Surely it didn't take this long.

Another thought occurred to him, making him scowl. Her body had been so incredibly tight, had he hurt her? Would she tell him if he had? The answer to that was a resounding no. In all the time he'd known her, he'd never heard Dana complain, so he knew damn good and well she wouldn't start now, and certainly not over this.

R.J. rubbed his face and leaned against the wall beside the door, waiting. He liked to think he would have been more gentle if he'd known she was a virgin, but he couldn't force himself into that lie. He'd known. Not right away, of course, but the second he'd gotten inside her, realization had walloped him with the force of a sledgehammer. It made sense in so many ways. She'd always been reserved, dedicated to work. He'd never heard a single rumor of her dating.

But she was nearly thirty years old, and very, very special;

caring, comforting, intelligent. Surely some man somewhere had appreciated those qualities and given it his best shot?

R.J. shook his head in wonder, because he'd known her forever and he'd never even considered such a thing himself. He and Dana had a special relationship, and not once had he thought of risking that by introducing a sexual involvement. He could have sex with other women, but what he had with Dana couldn't be found anywhere else.

He turned his head and stared toward the closed bathroom door. Damn, but he'd blundered badly. The knowledge of being the first, the *only* one, obliterated everything else.

Sweat beaded on his forehead and he clutched the doorknob, rattling it once. He wasn't surprised to find it was locked. "Come on out, Dana. I want to talk to you."

Another lengthy silence, then finally, "I, uh, I'll be out in a bit. Why don't you go on to bed? You've had a long day."

He'd had a long day?

"We can talk in the morning," she added, sounding desperate.

R.J. started to insist, then caught himself. At this moment she wasn't his secretary, and he wasn't her boss. She was his wife, and due some courtesy, belated as it might be.

He couldn't really blame her for not wanting to talk to him. And he wasn't at all certain that now was the best time, anyway. She wanted to be alone.

Hell, he had wanted to retreat to his room, had planned to do just that. He'd wanted to maintain his privacy and stay detached. Now she obviously wanted the same thing. Here was his opportunity, yet he felt oddly reluctant to leave her this way.

"Dana, I think we should—"

The water came back on, drowning out his words. He didn't feel like shouting to be heard, damn it. So he'd goofed? He could explain things to her in the morning. He'd convince her he was a good lover and promise he'd make certain she found her own satisfaction next time. He'd tell her that she'd taken him by complete and utter surprise.

And he'd make damn sure she explained a few things, as well. Like how the hell an attractive twenty-nine-year-old woman had remained a virgin.

They could both use a good night's sleep to regroup. Then they'd talk, just as she suggested.

R.J. turned away, but he was followed by a feeling of foreboding. He glanced at the bed as he passed it, noticing how a shaft of moonlight danced just beyond the reach of the mattress, spreading out over the floor.

He'd made love to Dana, but she hadn't enjoyed it. He'd touched her intimately, yet he hadn't seen so much as that glimpse of an ankle he'd imagined earlier.

He'd had sex with his wife, but he hadn't even had the courtesy to undress her. Her nightgown had been bunched up under her arms, and her breasts had remained covered.

His eyes squeezed shut in disgust and self-loathing. He'd taken his wife with all the finesse and consideration of a sailor on one-day shore leave.

But he had seen her hair loose, he reminded himself, and that alone was enough to keep him tossing and turning for the rest of the night.

CHAPTER EIGHT

DANA HAD NEVER been accused of being a coward, but she felt very cowardly at the moment. She wanted nothing more than to stay in her room and hide all day, yet she'd heard R.J. go downstairs some time ago. He'd be wondering where she was, thinking he'd cowed her with his detached, emotionless brand of sex.

What had she been thinking when she'd made that horrendous bargain? She wasn't a woman who could indulge in meaningless sex. Especially not when it was with a man she'd loved for so many years.

She sat at her dressing table and brushed her hair, then expertly twisted it up at the back of her head. A few pins, and she felt more like herself.

Except that she had a hickey on her neck.

She stared at the small mark with appalled fascination, remembering R.J.'s mouth there, the heat of it, the nip of his teeth. He'd made a low, guttural sound of intense satisfaction as he'd come inside her, his whole body rigid, shaking, hot. She shuddered and squeezed her eyes shut.

Dana Dillinger, plain Jane extraordinaire, had a hickey from the most eligible bachelor in Austin, Texas!

She almost giggled. Then she remembered her name wasn't Dillinger anymore, and she groaned.

Her whole body bore signs of his lust—lust for *her*. Though they'd been covered by her nightgown, her breasts were tender from his hands and mouth and the press of his heavy chest after he'd climaxed. The insides of her thighs felt achy from the strain of opening wide for him, gripping him, and later, from trying to push away from him.

He hadn't hurt her, not really. In fact, for the most part she'd felt a pleasure beyond any she'd ever imagined. But the depth of his response had left her shaken.

Because it had only been physical for him.

Last night, all pretenses of the civilized businessman had vanished, replaced with ruthless determination and unrestrained desire. He'd shown no inhibitions, no reserve. She knew R.J. well enough to understand he could be that way, but she hadn't expected him to be that way with her.

And she knew she couldn't deal with it.

If he'd been suave and practiced and gentle, she could have held back her emotions and taken what he offered. But R.J. had been sensually intrusive, touching her in ways she hadn't been prepared for, ways that should have been about love, not just sex.

Knowing she'd had only part of him had left her feeling more alone than ever.

She shook her head at her fanciful, old-fashioned conclusions. No, it would be better if they went back to his original plan. Last night as she'd lain in her new bed, painfully aware of R.J. sleeping only a short distance away, she considered everything with new eyes. She loved R.J. enough to do anything in her power to help repair his reputation—anything except pretend she didn't love him while they were intimately joined. That was asking too much.

She couldn't feign an emotionless, loveless physical attraction that would allow them to sleep together. It simply wasn't in her.

And he hadn't even wanted her to. She'd been the one to insist.

Well, he'd be relieved when he found out she'd changed her mind.

Dressed in comfortable beige drawstring cotton slacks and a matching long-sleeved tunic, she left the seclusion of her room.

The house was eerily silent as she made her way downstairs. Surprisingly, the air conditioner wasn't on; instead, R.J. had opened all the windows. In mid-November, the air was cooler, refreshingly so, and she welcomed the breeze that lifted the curtains and filled the house with the scents of the flowers outdoors.

Hoping for coffee to clear the cobwebs, she found her way to the kitchen, glancing at the house as she went. It was cozy and well decorated, and it looked like R.J. If he'd had it done by an interior designer, she was certain he'd had a lot of input.

Smiling, she stepped into the kitchen—and stopped dead.

R.J. stood there sipping steaming coffee from a bright red mug. He was leaning against the counter next to the coffeemaker, ankles crossed, pose negligent.

He was wearing only a pair of well-worn jeans.

Her breath caught and held. Her heartbeat doubled.

R.J. looked up at her entrance, the coffee mug almost to his mouth, and his hazel eyes pinned her, gleaming with intent. "Good morning."

Though she didn't intend it to, her gaze moved over him. God, he was incredibly gorgeous, all hard bone and smooth muscle and visible strength. His dark hair was still damp from his shower, combed back from his forehead so that his angular face seemed more pronounced, more male than ever. His jaw was freshly shaved, and beneath the strong smell of coffee she could detect a spicy cologne. Her skin tingled with awareness.

He had one hand braced on the counter at his hip, and the other held the mug, which he used to salute her. Still she stared. His chest was broad, and she remembered feeling the crisp hair and hard muscle beneath her open palms last night. She wondered what it might have felt like on her naked breasts, tantalizing her nipples.

A rush of heat rose inside her and quickly spread outward until she knew she was blushing furiously.

R.J. chuckled. "Cat got your tongue this morning?"

She forced her gaze away from her fascinated study of his hard abdomen and reached for the empty mug he'd left sitting on the counter. The movement brought her close to him, and she did her best not to react to his scent, to his warmth, which she could feel enveloping her. "Good morning, R.J."

She turned her back to pour the coffee—a tactical error. R.J.'s mug clattered down beside her own, and his arms came around her from behind, his hands flattening on the counter, caging her in. She stiffened, the coffee carafe clutched tightly in her hand.

He nuzzled her nape. "Mmm. I've been waiting down here for you, hoping you weren't a slugabed."

"I…I never sleep late." Oh, my God, it felt so wonderful to have him kissing her neck that way, little kisses that were barely there, a soft brushing of his lips. It made her skin tingle and her insides curl. His thighs touched the backs of her own, teasing then moving away again. She caught her breath and held it.

He lifted his right hand from the counter and flattened it on her middle, making her gasp. His long, rough fingers moved idly. "I like what you're wearing. Do you realize I've never seen you out of a suit?"

"R.J.…."

"Last night," he whispered, his tone husky, "it was so dark, I could barely see you at all."

Thank God! She'd wanted it dark because she knew she wasn't the type of woman he was used to—sexy, self-assured, knowledgeable in how to please a man in bed.

His mouth paused, and he moved a slight distance away. He

drew his hand from her stomach, which gave her the chance
to breathe in a huge lungful of air, and then he reached up to
the neckline of her tunic. He found the chain on the necklace
he'd given her.

"You're wearing it."

She hadn't taken it off, not once. She didn't ever want to
forget the moment he'd given it to her, so gallantly telling her
it matched her eyes. Those were the sweetest, most romantic,
most meaningful words she'd ever heard, and she'd cherish
them always.

"Dana?"

"Shouldn't I wear it?" She'd kept the necklace hidden beneath her tunic, and the bracelet was concealed by the long
sleeves. But suddenly she had the feeling she'd made a mistake. She knew so little about jewelry, and even less about
gifts from men. "I mean, I know it's not exactly appropriate
with casual clothes…"

"Dana, it's appropriate for you all the time. I told you, you
look incredible in emeralds." His hands clasped her waist and
he turned her to face him. Bending his knees slightly so he
could look her straight in the eyes, he asked in a low voice,
"Were you wearing it last night?" His eyes were bright, intent.
His breath touched her lips as he spoke, and his fingers bit
into her waist. "And the bracelet?"

He was so close, his eyes searching. His bare chest beckoned her, and she wanted badly to touch him, to tangle her
fingers in the dark hair, to search out his nipples. Her heartbeat raced and she swallowed hard. Trying desperately to
control the aberrant urges, she kept her hands firmly at her
sides and tightened them into fists. "Yes."

His pupils flared and he drew in a quick breath. His gaze
lowered, and she knew he was looking at her breasts. She
looked down, too, and was appalled to see her nipples were
puckered tight, pressing against the soft fabric of the tunic,
clearly visible even through her bra. Her gaze shot back up

to R.J.'s, and she found him watching her with a calculating intensity.

He's trying to decide how to handle me, she thought. She'd seen him do it so many times in his business dealings, assessing the situation, planning his maneuver. She took several slow, calming breaths, sorting her thoughts. Probably he was as embarrassed about last night as she was, and searching for the gentlest way to handle things. Maybe he assumed the deal was still on. Just the thought made her shudder.

She should let him off the hook right now, before things got out of control.

R.J. tugged her slightly closer. "About last night…"

With a short laugh meant to hide her nervousness, Dana twisted away from him. "Last night was a mistake."

"What?"

"A total failure." The only place to go was to the other side of the small kitchen table, so she did, moving behind a chair and holding on to the back of it. R.J. tracked her every movement with his eyes, as if waiting for her to bolt, or to attack. She realized that for once, he had no idea what she was doing or thinking.

He turned to the coffeepot and poured her a cup, then reached across the table to place it close to her. A tray with sugar and cream was already there, but she couldn't quite deal with it.

He retrieved his own cup and sipped, and she could tell by his expression he was carefully gauging his next words, judging them for effect. Once again he took up his casual pose. "I'll admit last night didn't go quite as I'd planned—"

"I take full blame."

Both of his brows shot up at her blurted interruption, as if she'd said the unexpected. He watched her a moment, but when she only chewed on her bottom lip, he asked, "You do?"

"Absolutely. It was my idea, after all."

That caused one side of his mouth to twitch, and she knew if he laughed at her she'd throw the coffee at his head. But of course he didn't laugh. He was more calculating than that.

"What I recall," he said, his gaze probing, "is that you were a virgin, so any planning beyond the very basics seems pretty far-fetched."

She hadn't been R.J. Maitland's secretary all this time without learning a tactic or two of her own. She had no intention of discussing her virginity with him—there was no way to explain it, anyway—so she skipped it entirely. To give herself something to do, she began dumping sugar in her coffee.

"R.J., I was the one who thought up the ridiculous plan of…sleeping together in the first place."

"Ridiculous?"

"Absolutely." She gave a resolute nod and stirred her coffee so quickly some sloshed out. She snatched up a napkin and dabbed at it. "I thought I might enjoy a casual…fling." She nearly choked and picked up her coffee to take a sip. It tasted like syrup! "But last night," she continued, looking him in the eye, "proved me wrong. I think we should go back to your original plan."

"My original plan?"

She frowned at him. It wasn't like R.J. to parrot words or stand there looking dumbstruck. The man generally had something to say on everything. "Yes. During the day, I'll be the best wife to you that I can be. I have several plans that might shore up your reputation—though I'm still not convinced it's necessary—and I'm more than ready and willing to implement them. But at night…"

"Lovemaking isn't limited to the evening, you know."

His harsh statement took her by surprise. He looked annoyed, maybe even bordering on anger. Why? She was offering him what he'd wanted all along. Heaven knew he'd fought hard enough for it before giving in.

"I beg your pardon?"

Very slowly, he rounded the table. "Married people have sex whenever they want, or are you too much the puritan to realize it?"

Her mouth opened, but nothing came out.

"In fact," he continued, coming closer still, "I'd intended to make love with you right here, right now, on the kitchen table."

"R.J.!"

"It's sturdy enough. That's not exactly why I chose the style in the first place, but as I was making the coffee, it occurred to me it was strong enough to support us, and it's just about the right height for all kinds of *interesting* things."

He was too close to her now, and she could see the dangerous glint in his hazel gaze. Curiously, she eyed the small table. It was heavy oak with a slab top. And…it did look sturdy.

"R.J., you're being ridiculous." But she felt flushed and anxious—and very hurt. She didn't want to be a mere body to him. She'd thought she could, but she'd been so wrong.

"Don't you want to know what those interesting things are, Dana?"

"No." *More interesting than what he'd already done?* She didn't think she could stand it.

"I want to tell you, anyway." He reached for her, and she ducked away.

"Well, I'd like that tour of the yard you promised. It's a beautiful day for it." She stopped and faced him when she was again on the opposite side of the table from him.

R.J. gave her a speculative glance, his long fingers rubbing his chin. She saw the exact moment he came up with a plan.

"All right, Dana. Why don't we get some breakfast together and eat out on the patio? I can show you all the plant specimens I've brought in."

Relief flooded her. "That'd be wonderful."

"I knew you'd think so."

Was he laughing at her? Had her relief been so obvious? She frowned as she asked, "What would you like for breakfast?"

"Are you offering to cook for me? Is that one of those wifely duties you don't mind fulfilling?"

She'd spoiled him, she decided. He felt free to bait her because she'd always allowed him to as her boss. She'd waited on him, been the best secretary she could, because she loved him and wanted to make herself indispensable to him. But if they were going to get along during the duration of their bogus marriage, there would need to be some new ground rules.

Explaining things to R.J. wouldn't work. He'd instinctively balk at having rules laid out for him. So instead she'd have to show him by example. She went to the refrigerator and opened the door. "I'll do breakfast," she said casually "but then you have to do lunch. There's fresh fruit in here, and bagels. We can have that for breakfast."

R.J. was again watching her when she pulled the cantaloupe and fat strawberries from the fridge. He eyed her loaded hands and nodded. "I can toast the bagels. Do you like cream cheese on yours?"

He stepped close, then reached past her into the refrigerator and retrieved the bagels and cream cheese. His arm brushed her breasts, and his broad chest was teasingly close. Dana held her breath, wanting to move away but unable to get her feet to cooperate.

As he started to step past her, he dropped a hard, quick smooch on her open mouth and grinned. Dana stared up him.

"Dana?"

"Hmm?"

"Cream cheese?"

As if coming out of a daze, she shook her head and glared at him. "Yes, please."

R.J. chuckled and sauntered away. He thought he had it all figured out, she knew. And she'd just made it embarrassingly easy for him. Well, no more. She wouldn't get that close to him again.

This evening she'd start a campaign for improving his public image. That ought to keep them both busy enough to forget about last night.

Or at least to pretend to forget.

"I'M SUPPOSEDLY an excellent lover, you know."

Dana choked on her melon, nearly spitting it out on the table. It took her several gasping breaths and two sips of tepid coffee to clear her throat.

Damn him, he'd taken her completely off guard.

They were out on the enclosed patio, the beautiful sunshine reaching in through the open windows, the hot tub bubbling warmly at the far end. Birds flew around the yard, providing entertainment, while the flowers within the room itself continually drew her attention. They'd spent the past hour chatting about those flowers, and a dozen other innocuous topics. She'd started to relax, to let down her guard. But then he'd made that outrageous comment.

R.J. didn't smile at her shocked reaction. He simply continued to watch her as she wiped her mouth with a napkin and glowered at him.

When she made no reply, he pressed her. "You *do* know that, don't you, Dana?"

He wasn't going to let it go, so she shrugged, pretending an indifference she was far from feeling. "I'll take your word for it."

His eyes narrowed the tiniest bit.

She decided she needed to change the subject again, and quickly.

"Shouldn't you be getting dressed, R.J.?" No sooner had she spoken the words than she inwardly groaned. She couldn't have picked a worse thing to comment on. But then, his half-naked body was all she could really focus on. She'd made appropriate enough responses as he'd enthused over his flowers, telling her which ones did best indoors, which needed shade and which needed sunlight.

And she truly was interested—but not when R.J. Maitland was within touching distance and wearing only a pair of faded worn jeans that fit his lean body like a second skin.

She wasn't used to such close proximity to any man; breakfast after a night together was an aberration. But for that man to be R.J. was enough to keep her totally flustered.

R.J. leaned back in his wrought-iron chair and stretched. "Why should I pile on the clothes? There's only me and my wife present. And it's a weekend. After suffering suits all week, I prefer to relax on the weekend." He leaned forward, and in a conspiratorial tone admitted, "I actually hate suits. I prefer jeans any day."

Trying to maintain her dignity, Dana smiled. "No one would ever know. You wear your suits well."

"As well as I wear my jeans?"

The thought of throwing the rest of her coffee at him appealed to her greatly. However, she considered herself above such childish acts. "Actually, the jeans suit you better."

He settled back in his chair and tilted his head, his gaze thoughtful. "How so?"

Dana shrugged. If he insisted on playing this game, she'd do her damnedest to match him. But then, it had always been that way. R.J. would roar and stomp, and she simply kept pace with him. That was one of the reasons she had succeeded as his employee when others had failed. "You're a barbarian at heart, R.J. That much is obvious. The suits may hide it from some people, but not from me."

To her surprise, his mouth tightened. "Last night was no example of my character."

Her eyes widened. She hadn't been thinking of last night! Good grief, did he really think she'd deliberately bring it up? "As far as I'm concerned, last night is best forgotten."

That didn't appear to appease him at all, so she tried again. "I was referring to your controlling ways—at the office, with your family. You like to sit back and observe people, then force them to do your bidding without them even knowing it."

His face went blank with surprise. "What the hell are you talking about?"

"You think I haven't noticed?"

"I think you're damn well imagining things!"

"R.J." She made a tsking sound. "You do it all the time. You manipulate. Not in a mean-spirited way, because you're not a mean or petty man. You're just a man who likes things his own way. And you have very set ideas on what's best, for yourself and for everyone else. So you control things. You keep yourself apart from others so you can maintain that control."

His eyes were diamond hard, his jaw set. "I don't seem to have a hell of a lot of control over you."

"I have the advantage of being wise to your ways." A variety of expressions flickered through his hazel eyes, but mostly disgruntled resentment. He didn't like it that she had pegged him so neatly. Still, there was also a touch of admiration, and she basked in it. R.J. had told her many times that he greatly respected her intelligence. She'd valued the compliment each time he'd given it.

He chewed his upper lip a moment, deep in thought, then he smiled. It wasn't a smile to put her at ease. Just the opposite.

"So tell me, smarty-pants. If you're so attuned to me, what am I thinking right now?"

"Probably about some way to get the upper hand."

He slowly shook his head. "Wrong. But I'll tell you anyway."

She started to stand, using the excuse of carrying in their dishes. She didn't trust the iron determination in his voice and thought a strategic retreat was in order.

Before she could get completely out of her seat, though, he'd taken her arm and held her in place. "I'm thinking about how different you look in these clothes. Do you know I can see the shape of your behind? Well, almost. The top is too long and loose for me to get a good look, but it beats the hell out of those tailored suits you wear that reveal all the feminine curves of an army tank."

Appalled, Dana again tried to pull free. R.J. let her, but then stood to block her way. He wasn't being subtle in his domination, but then R.J. seldom used subtlety once he was set on his course. He walked his own path, and people generally got out of his way.

Dana stiffened her spine.

He stood very close to her, watching her intently, and she managed a smile, refusing to let him see how awkward she felt. "My behind is hardly worthy of all this discussion."

The tender touch of his hand on her cheek was shattering. "You forget," he whispered, "I may not have seen all of you last night, thanks to the darkness, but I sure as hell touched on all the important parts." He tipped up her chin, forcing her to meet his gaze. "I'm going crazy now wondering if you look as good as you feel. And let me tell you, your backside felt damn near perfect. Soft, round, just right for a man to hold on to."

If her face got any hotter she'd go up in a puff of smoke. "R.J.…." His name was spoken as a soft plea, barely heard— and R.J. answered by tilting his head and pressing his mouth to hers.

This isn't what you want, her mind screamed, but minds were easy things to ignore when the pleasure was so sharp. She'd been exceedingly preoccupied with R.J.'s chest and was now acutely aware of being pressed to it, of the steady, comforting thump of his heart, the silky-smooth hardness of his shoulders. Her hands crept over his biceps, thrilling at the thickness of iron muscle, before giving in and moving over his chest, exploring him as she'd so often thought of doing.

R.J. gave a deep groan of encouragement, his own hands idly coasting up and down her back, stopping just before cupping her bottom. Dana felt the crispness of his chest hair, the heat of his skin beneath. And the scents—R.J.'s scent was indescribably potent. She opened her mouth, wanting more of him, and his hot tongue slowly licked inside.

Oh…this was so different from last night. Now, with the sunshine bright in the cozy room, he could clearly see her. And though he didn't seem bothered by her unmistakable plainness, neither did he seem as carried away. He was moving too slowly, too…*methodically.*

Dana jerked away with a low gasp, knowing her eyes were round with distress. "We can't do this," she croaked.

He kept his arms around her, and she saw the fire in his eyes, the denial. "The hell we can't. We're married, remember?"

"No." She shook her head, and when she pushed against him, his arms fell to his sides. "You're doing it again—carefully figuring out how to get the upper hand. Doing whatever you need to do to keep it."

"That's what you think this is about?" His shoulder muscles were rigid, and his fierce frown carved deep grooves over his brow. "Control?"

His obvious anger didn't faze her. It never had. "Isn't it, R.J.?"

Moving too fast for her to avoid him, he snatched her wrist, holding her tightly but with careful restraint. His gaze locked on hers, he carried her hand to his groin and pressed it there. Beneath the denim she felt every masculine inch of him.

Her breath caught and held. Shock rushed through her, making her knees shaky, her chest tight. She'd never touched a man this way, and she couldn't help but react to it. Her palm tingled, her skin heated and her heart began to race.

R.J.'s chest lifted and fell with a deep, shuddering breath, and for a single moment, his eyes closed. Then he pulled her hand away. Rather than let her go, he slid his hand from her wrist and laced their fingers together.

His voice was little more than a rasping rumble, his eyes narrowed dangerously, when he explained, "Just so you know."

She blinked at him as he turned, then tugged her toward the house. Like a sleepwalker, she followed his lead. Their hands were pressed together, trapping the male heat of him against her palm.

He didn't look at her as they walked. "You may not know a hell of a lot about men, honey, but you've got to know enough to understand an erection. I want you, plain and simple. Remember that the next time you accuse me of something."

"I'm...I'm sorry." She didn't know what else she could say. She was still reeling from the realization that he'd wanted her and that he'd given up—at least for the moment.

R.J. groaned, then his muscles relaxed. He flashed her a crooked grin over his shoulder. "Don't be. Your first assumption was right, too. I *do* want control, and by God, I'll have it."

CHAPTER NINE

THEY FOUGHT all day long.

R.J. couldn't remember a time when he'd had this much trouble making someone—especially a woman—see things his way. Everyone tended to agree with him. Eventually. He had been raised, and was accepted, as the oldest son of the Maitland family. He was the president of Maitland Maternity, a world-renowned center. He was sought after by debutantes from miles around. Clout was his middle name, and he used it without thought whenever he deemed it necessary.

But Dana had spent the day defying him on even the simplest requests, which marked a complete turnaround for her.

She was usually so obliging with him, handling even the most monumental tasks with extra care just to please him. It was what he was used to from her. It was what he expected. Now she seemed to have developed an uncommon use of the word *no*. And it didn't matter what he did, she held firm.

Between wanting her and being flatly denied, and having everything he offered thrown back in his face, his normally healthy ego was badly battered. Women seldom told him no, and he couldn't recall the last time he'd had a gift refused.

He glanced at Dana's profile as he pulled the Mercedes into the drive and strove for a calm he was far from feeling. Dana, as usual, looked cool as an arctic blast. It was an expression he once appreciated but now resented. "You're being unreasonable."

She didn't look at him, just stared straight ahead at the house. "Because I don't want you to give me a credit card when I already have two of my own?"

Her look clearly said he was the one being unreasonable. Not that he cared. "That's hardly the point, Dana."

She pressed on, her tone irritatingly clipped and formal. "Because I don't want a joint savings account when we each already have our own?" She cast him a quick look. "And R.J., you pay me well. My accounts are not in need of padding."

She was being deliberately obtuse, but he didn't say so. A joint account would allow him to supply her with some of his own money, money he could well afford to spare. He needed to do *something* for her, to reciprocate her generosity in some way, but she turned him down every damn time he tried.

"Stop squeezing the steering wheel, R.J. You're going to break it in two."

R.J. glared at her and saw she was glaring right back. The cool detachment was gone. Her green eyes looked as if they were lit from within, something he'd never witnessed in Dana. There were a lot of things about her he'd never noticed before—muleheaded stubbornness, for one.

He'd thought the long ride would have given her time to think, but she hadn't calmed down at all. She was prepared to reject him on every level.

He took some measure of satisfaction in seeing the chain around her neck and the ring on her finger. She wore the bracelet, too, though he couldn't detect it beneath her sleeve.

She'd accepted precious little from him, but the possessive part of him was mollified to see that in at least some small way, he'd been able to please her.

He pulled into the garage and shoved the car into park. Now, if he could just get her to agree on a few more things.... "Having an account in both our names—"

"Will make you feel like you're paying me for marrying

you." Her words rang with outrage, which appeared to have shocked her as well as him. After a moment, she gave a melo-dramatic sigh and dropped her head back against the seat. "R.J., I've already told you it wasn't necessary to buy my help. I don't want your credit cards. I don't want your money."

She doesn't want me. He shook that thought off just as quickly as he realized it. He didn't particularly *want* her to want him; the marriage was temporary, and once it was over, he hoped things could go back—to some degree—to the way they'd been before.

He knew deep in his gut they'd never be exactly the same again. Not after he'd kissed her. And touched her. Not after he'd been buried deep inside her and found out he was the only one.

Not after he'd given her the impression he was a totally uncontrolled, bumbling fool in the sack. He felt disgustingly embarrassed every time he thought of it, and that made him angry, too.

He didn't really blame Dana for not wanting to give him a second chance. It had been her first time, and he'd totally lost control. He hadn't gently seduced her as he'd originally planned. He hadn't left her utterly sated when he walked away to go to his own room.

No, he'd left her hiding out in the bathroom after giving her nothing but a taste of how a wild man might behave.

Dana was controlled, always poised, always elegant. Sweaty, gritty sex likely repulsed her—especially since he'd been in such a frenzy to have her, she hadn't even gotten to climax.

R.J. swore softly, then threw open his door. Dana climbed out on her own, refusing to let him open her door the way a gentleman should, the way he wanted to. *Damn woman*.

The whole day was frustrating, and getting more so by the minute. After they'd tidied up the breakfast dishes together, he'd taken her on a tour of the house. She'd been woefully unimpressed, though she'd made appropriate noises of appreciation. But he knew her better than that. It was the plants, and especially the pond, that she found fascinating. They'd spent several hours outside, just walking and talking. Even in her enthusiasm, Dana had tried to remain impersonal. But he'd now met the woman beneath the suit. He knew what she tasted like, the way she sounded when she was sexually aroused. He knew the heated scents of her body.

Damn, if only he'd taken his time. She'd been satisfyingly close for a while there—until he'd botched it.

Dana headed into the house, oblivious to his heated thoughts, and R.J. made note of the gentle sway of her hips. Trailing behind her would become a new hardship, given she wanted a hands-off relationship. He was only too aware of how wonderfully touchable she was. He swallowed hard. "Where are you off to?"

"I'm going to make a few calls."

She kept walking, not bothering to look back. R.J. reached out and snagged the back of her shirt, pulling her up short. "What kind of calls?"

Looking over her shoulder, she glanced first at his face, then the fist holding her in place. One brow rose in the same imperious manner Megan often used. It was a command, plain and simple.

It wasn't easy, but R.J. managed to loosen his fingers and let her go. He shoved his hands into his pockets to resist the urge to grab her again.

"First I'm going to have my car driven over here."

That brought him up short. He hadn't even considered her car. "Why?"

"We have work tomorrow, remember?"

He remembered only too well. His mother had given him grief for not taking Dana on a honeymoon. She hadn't been impressed with his explanation of sudden decisions, bad timing and set schedules. Megan knew he could rearrange things if he chose to, just as she knew he'd damn well take a honeymoon if that was what he wanted to do.

But a honeymoon had never been the purpose of the marriage.

"I can drive you to work. We're going to the same place."

"I'd rather have my own car."

"Then we can get it later in the week."

She gave him a pensive frown. "Our schedules seldom mesh, R.J., other than arriving close to the same time. But I generally like to get there before you—"

"You don't need to do that now."

She shook her head. "Work is work, and I won't let our pretend marriage change that. Besides, you often stay later than I do and have meetings after hours when I go home. You're what we normal people call a workaholic. If you had to chauffeur me around, you'd resent it."

She had a point, not that he'd admit it. "I hardly think driving my wife somewhere could be called chauffeuring."

"Your *pretend* wife."

"To the world it's real."

"And to the real world, it makes sense for us to drive separate cars." Irritation edged into her tone. "I know for a fact you have meetings planned for lunch most of this week, while I usually meet one of my friends. We need two cars, so I might as well get mine here tonight. Besides, I've already made arrangements with my neighbor to have it dropped off. All I need to do is let him know."

R.J. ran a hand through his hair. Frustration gnawed at him, but he couldn't say exactly why. Two days ago, he'd have been insistent that she have her own car, because that would have guaranteed his freedom. Now he saw it as another tactic on her part to put distance between them. She wanted as little to do with him as possible, and his ego naturally rebelled. He'd expected to be the one fending her off, not the other way around.

He dropped his hands. "Fine. You want to drive yourself, you can use my Mercedes. I'll drive the Explorer—"

She stared at him. "You have an Explorer?"

"I use it when I travel or when I go to the lake."

"Oh." Then she shook her head. "R.J, I have my *own* car, thank you. I don't need yours."

A smart man always knew when to retreat, which meant he was losing his edge because he should have stopped ten minutes ago. "All right. Is that all you have to do now?"

"No. I'm going to set up some damage control. That's why we got married in the first place, remember?"

If he threw her over his shoulder and hauled her upstairs, would she fight him? Probably. Dana didn't appear to have an amicable bone left in her entire body—at least not where he was concerned. "It's Sunday. How much organizing can you do today?"

"Plenty. This is the best time to start because everyone will be home. I'm going to get the ball rolling on our public announcement, just in case the papers haven't gotten wind of it yet. And this coming week we're going to make the rounds visiting some of the places you regularly donate to. Like the One Way Farm for kids, the women's shelter, the various medical research facilities. You're very generous with your time and money, but no one reports on that."

He eyed her mutinous, disgruntled expression and knew she was feeling defensive on his behalf again. It was a unique experience having someone champion him, though he realized now that Dana had always done exactly that, so subtly that he'd barely noticed. He didn't like knowing that he'd taken her for granted, that he'd appreciated only part of the woman she was. "Don't get riled, honey. I doubt anyone even knows what I donate or to whom."

"Exactly." She raised a small fist. "But if the press wants to hound you this week, well, they can just follow us around and give some added publicity to the charities that need it. In fact, that'll be your stand, okay?"

Besides making him hot, she amused the hell out of him. "My stand?"

She began pacing as she pulled her thoughts together. "You want to turn all the bad publicity into some good. You don't mind being in the limelight if it will help someone. In fact, you welcome the press!" She nodded in satisfaction at her own conclusions, then turned away. "I'm going to get started on this right now."

R.J. stood there, speechless. Dana was in full work mode, so there was no point getting in her way. She went into *his* den and shut the door with a click, firmly closing him out.

Muttering a muffled oath, R.J. went down the hall. The night would arrive soon enough, and he'd try reasoning with her again.

It was a strange reaction on his part, because making love with a virgin had never appealed to him before. The few inexperienced women he'd known hadn't been very satisfactory lovers. They hadn't been virgins, but neither had they known enough to fully reciprocate his sensual advances. He'd done all the work, gotten little enough in the way of response, and there'd been no giving, no real sharing.

With Dana, it had been different. Her response had been first shyly open, then blindly feverish. She'd been more than willing to give and take, holding nothing back from him—until he'd lost control.

R.J. bit the side of his mouth, remembering the hot, tight clasp of her body as he'd pushed his way into her, the wetness, the seductive scent of her arousal. He got hard just thinking about it.

Damn, would he ever be given a second chance?

He thumped his fist against his thigh, cursing low and

making a silent vow. Tonight, he'd get started on wearing her down. He'd be honest with her, telling her that she'd turned him on, explaining why he'd lost control and promising it wouldn't happen again. No woman could resist a well-phrased compliment, especially when it was true. And just maybe she'd appreciate the fact that he'd found her so desirable he'd been pushed over the edge when no other woman had had that effect on him.

No, he decided abruptly, he'd keep that part to himself. No reason to leave himself so open or to make her think she had more influence on him than she did. Their marriage was temporary, after all, and he didn't want her to start imagining things that could never be.

All he really had to do was show her that he was no slacker in bed, that the rumors of him being a good lover hadn't been false, contrary to what she'd witnessed. He had to prove to her that her first plan hadn't been a bad one after all. And he had to make her understand that she could have incredible pleasure with him.

He had to have her, period.

DANA WAS SATISFIED with all she'd accomplished. She'd spoken to many of R.J.'s relatives, as well as some family acquaintances and closer friends. She'd given her humble apologies for not inviting them to the wedding, but claimed that under the circumstances, she and R.J. had wanted as little publicity as possible. Everyone had been gracious enough to say they understood, though she knew his sisters were hurt, especially Anna.

Though R.J. felt fully a part of Megan's family and was accepted and loved as the oldest brother, there remained a special bond between him and Anna.

Anna had only been a few months old when their father had abandoned the two of them. R.J. wasn't a demonstrative man, but his protectiveness and affection for Anna and her son, Will, were apparent to anyone who'd ever seen them together.

Dana had left the special circumstances of their marriage for R.J. to explain to Anna. He could tell her as much or as little as he decided was appropriate. Dana had never had any close relatives of her own except for her mother, who had passed away years ago, so she couldn't begin to fully understand, much less interfere with, their special relationship.

It was getting late when she finished making her plans for the week and had jotted down notes on things to do for the next day. She'd made a good head start on her intentions, but the week promised to be a hectic one. Since she was privy to R.J.'s schedule, she had taken the liberty of filling almost every available minute with an eye to repairing his reputation. That was the one thing she could do for him, and she was determined it would work.

Her car was dropped off and she paid her neighbor, who'd obligingly agreed to the service, before he took a cab home. Dana wondered about R.J.'s stubbornness concerning the cars, but little of what he'd done since the marriage could have been predicted based on what she knew about him—and she'd thought she knew him well.

Dana didn't see R.J. as she made her way upstairs to take a shower and get ready for bed. She was actually relieved. She didn't relish running into him again, rehashing all the reasons she couldn't accept his money. True, she didn't have his wealth, but she was comfortable. You didn't work as the executive secretary for R.J. Maitland without getting well paid for it. But even if she'd been a pauper, she'd never have let him pay her for their marriage.

Her pride, which he'd yet to discover rivaled his own, wouldn't allow for such a thing.

She went to her room, idly wondering where R.J. had gotten

to. Maybe he'd already retired for the night. Bone tired herself, she kicked off her shoes and stripped off her slacks, putting them neatly away. Then she turned to the mirror and pulled the pins from her hair. She was just reaching for the hem of her tunic to pull it over her head when there was a brisk knock on the dividing door and it opened.

Dana turned to stone.

A frozen, heavy silence filled the room. She could only imagine how she looked, standing there in nothing more than a long shirt, her hair disheveled, bordering on wild since she'd yet to pull a brush through it.

And R.J. He stood there staring, one hand still on the doorknob, one foot inside the room. His hazel eyes were fixed on her, not wavering the tiniest bit, and she could see the slow clenching of his jaw, could feel the strange energy gathering around him like a brewing storm.

Awkwardness swamped her, and she reached up to smooth her hair, though she knew it wouldn't do a bit of good. As if that movement had galvanized him, R.J. stepped the rest of the way into the room and shut the door behind him. He didn't say a word as he strolled barefoot across the carpet to stand directly in front of her.

There was an intense light in his eyes, turning the hazel to gold, and a frown marred his brow. His gaze slid with excruciating slowness over her, from the top of her head to the tips of her toes, lingering for long moments on her exposed legs.

Dana shifted her feet, pressing her knees together. Through the lump in her throat, she choked out the words that needed to be said. "I'd appreciate it if you didn't just barge in here."

It was as if she hadn't spoken. "Damn, you have beautiful hair."

She was too stunned to even blush. She simply wanted him out of the room before he felt forced to offer more outrageous compliments. "R.J., I'm in the middle of changing clothes." Her hands shook, and she tugged ineffectually on the bottom of the tunic, trying to stretch the material to cover her thighs.

His gaze met hers, and she felt seared by the heat. "I'm glad I didn't wait. You'd have never let me in, not looking like this."

"You're right." She started to step away, but she refused to be a coward. Situations such as this were bound to occur sooner or later. Though it was painfully awkward—at least for her—now was the perfect time to resolve them, so future incidents could be avoided.

The fact that he kept staring at her legs made it even more difficult. Men didn't look at her with such intensity, and certainly R.J. never had. In fact, she couldn't remember any man ever seeing her legs before. The skirts she favored were long, ending just below her knees. Besides, her legs were unexceptional. They were thin, long, pale. Not the shapely tanned legs of a beach bunny.

She did her best to stand still. "R.J., you promised me my privacy when I agreed to the marriage."

Other than drawing his darkened gaze from her legs to her face, he ignored her. She knew R.J. had a knack of forcing the topic any way he chose, and this was no different. Still, she was speechless when he reached out and tangled his fist in her hair.

"You look like a siren." His fist moved, his fingers caressing. "Your hair is so damn soft and sexy."

"R.J., please." This time she did try to step away, but since he didn't let go of her hair, she was drawn up short with a wince.

He didn't appear to notice. "And your legs." His free hand settled on her hip, his fingers gently squeezing as he looked down the length of her. "You have world-class legs, babe. I had no idea."

Her breath came too fast as she frantically tried to think of a way to get him out of the room.

"I keep thinking about last night," he continued. "How soft and sweet you were under me. I couldn't see you then. Damn, if I had, I wouldn't have lasted as long as I did, and we both know it wasn't nearly long enough."

As if that statement had reminded him of something, he jerked his gaze to her face. "You made me crazy. I hadn't expected that. Usually I'm controlled, and I can keep the love-making going for hours. I enjoy watching a woman climax, hearing her cry out, feeling her tighten around me."

His breath, coming in low, rough gusts, brushed her temple as he leaned closer, nuzzling against her. "That's what I meant to do with you," he whispered, the words a soft stirring of air in her ear, making her skin tingle and her toes curl. "You took me by surprise."

His hand tightened on her hip, and he drew her close so she could feel the length of his erection against her abdomen. "I put my fingers inside you, and you were so damn wet—"

Dana jerked away with a gasp, taking several steps across the room until she was safely on the other side of the bed. She hadn't known men talked this way, that they said things so bluntly. Or maybe it was just R.J., his natural arrogance in always speaking his mind.

"Don't," she rasped, the words raw and shaky. "Don't say dumb things just to manipulate me, to get the upper hand."

R.J. looked poleaxed. He stood there, one hand still out-stretched, his chest rising and falling, twin slashes of color high on his cheekbones. Very slowly, he lowered his hand to his side. *"Dumb* things?"

Dana felt close to losing her composure completely. She didn't want R.J. to see her like this, half clothed, vulnerable, behaving like a fool. If she expected to keep working with him after the marriage ended, she had to keep their relationship as normal as possible. He'd never wanted her emotions to interfere in the past. She had to believe he'd want it even less now.

She drew a deep breath and searched for control. R.J. had always liked and respected her for her reasonableness, her common sense. She dredged that up now, trying to sound cavalier. "I...I know what I look like, R.J. I'm levelheaded, not silly. And I've long since resigned myself to being plain. It's not something that bothers me."

His frown came slowly, not a frown of intensity, but one of building anger. His tone was low and rough, each word carefully enunciated. "You are not plain."

She laughed, though she felt far from amused. She refused to let him see how the topic of her very ordinary appearance hurt her. "I have mirrors, R.J. And I'm neither blind nor delusional. In fact, I'd say I'm rather astute."

"On occasion, usually with business," he agreed. "But this time you're dead wrong. Or are you going to stand there and call me a liar?"

She hadn't expected such a strong attack. She cleared her throat, wondering how to defuse this little disagreement—bizarre as it seemed—and get him out of her room.

"I wouldn't call it lying, exactly." She watched him, trying to calculate his reaction to her honesty. "More like outrageous flattery, something we both know you're an expert at when it suits you. But I'm not a woman easily fooled and the flattery is unnecessary anyway, since we've both agreed not to continue in any sort of...sexual intimacy."

"I didn't agree to a damn thing. And after seeing you like this, you can bet your sweet behind I want to get intimate. I want to get real intimate." He advanced on her, slowly circling the bed while keeping her pinned with his icy gaze. "I want to see the rest of you, Dana, not just your legs, which really are sexy as sin."

She shook her head, mute.

"I want you naked from head to toe. I want to see the breasts I held and touched and kissed last night. And your nipples. Do you know your whole body shuddered when I sucked on your nipples?"

Dana found herself speechless. She'd never dealt with R.J. in a mood like this and had no idea how to handle him. And she'd never in her wildest dreams imagined hearing anything so outrageous and bold said to her. She'd truly had no idea men spoke in such a way, not even R.J.

She bit her lip, more unsure of herself as a woman than ever before.

R.J.'s eyes narrowed when she remained silent, then focused intently on her mouth. His voice dropped another octave until it was so low she could barely hear him.

"I want to feel those long legs of yours around my waist. And I want to watch your face when I enter you, this time with no surprises. It'll be easier, you know. I'll make damn sure there's no discomfort."

Her heart beat so hard she felt it throughout her entire body.

R.J.'s smile was both gentle and predatory. "Most of all," he growled, "I want to watch your beautiful eyes when I give you your first orgasm."

"R.J." Dana tried to retreat a step. She bumped up against the bed and nearly tumbled onto it, only gaining her balance at the last second.

R.J. caught her arms in a gentle, unbreakable hold. "I have no idea why in hell you're so set on calling yourself plain or why you've tried to convince the rest of the world the same damn thing, but you're wrong." He gave her a slight shake to emphasize his statement. "Now that I've seen you, I don't intend to let you continue hiding from me."

"I was never hiding." She pressed against his chest, but he was as unmovable as an oak tree.

"Then what would you call it?"

"Being…being realistic." She took a breath and tried to explain before things got further out of hand. Had R.J. misunderstood and taken her actions as a challenge? She had to set him straight. "I've accepted who I am, how I look. I don't need you to dress things up for me."

R.J. seemed to consider that, his expression so piercing she felt herself squirm under his regard. His hands softened and began idly caressing her, then he lifted one hand to her cheek and smoothed her messed hair. "Let's sit down a minute and talk."

The only place for them both to sit was on the mattress, and she'd already determined never to find herself there with him again. "No, I…I want to get ready for bed."

His grin was fleeting. "Bed was uppermost on my mind when I came in here, at least until I understood just how damn confused you are."

He drew her down next to him on the edge of the mattress and kept hold of her hand, his fingers toying with hers, as if he needed the moment to measure his words. Finally he looked at her, and his smile was boyishly crooked and wickedly sensual. "If I'd seen you like this before," he said, "you'd never have lasted so long as my assistant."

"Why not?" Dana wasn't certain what to think, and with every word R.J. confused her further.

"Because I'd have had to make love with you. And office romances never last."

Her heart squeezed tight in pain. Was this his way of telling her that once the marriage was over, so was their business association?

"Is that why you hid from me? So we wouldn't get involved?"

Dana shook her head. R.J.'s eyes flared, and he caught her chin, halting her automatic protest. She met his gaze reluctantly. "I never hid from you."

"Then it's yourself you're hiding from." Taking her totally

off guard, he slid his hand from her chin to her breast, cuddling her softly in his palm.

Dana gasped, frozen in place, and R.J. gave a soft groan. "You see, you're very much a woman." He moved his hand to her other breast and treated it to the same torment, allowing his fingers to find and stroke her nipple. Even through her bra and shirt, the feeling was exquisite and she bit her lip hard.

"Shh. Don't do that. Don't freeze up on me. I'm not going to rush you, babe, I promise. Last night was a mistake, an aberration for me. Next time will be so much better. You have my word on that. But I've been going crazy wanting you again, and now I'm finally starting to understand a few things."

His fingers continued to tease and stroke, and she could barely think straight. "What things?"

"Number one, that you have no idea of your appeal. What I want to know is why."

"R.J., I—"

His hand gently squeezed her breast in sensual warning, his body going still. "Don't say it, Dana." His words were a muttered command, not harsh, but more compelling for their quiet. "Don't sit there and tell me how unattractive you are, because I won't let you lie to me or yourself."

It was difficult to breathe, difficult to form a coherent argument. Her breasts ached, as did other parts of her body. Without thinking, she leaned into his taunting palm and slowly closed her eyes. "I've always been plain, from the time I was a little girl."

He smoothed her breast without missing a beat. "Says who?"

At first she didn't hear the suppressed rage in his tone, she was so overwhelmed by sensations. His nearness, the heat from his large body, his heady, masculine scent. But she did hear it, and her reply was duly cautious. "My...my mother was a practical woman. She saw no reason why I should waste my time trying to be something I could never be."

His curse was low and filled with such fury she shuddered in response. Why was he so angry?

"Where's your mother now?"

He released her breast, making her sigh in relief—and disappointment. His hands tightened on her, one wrapping securely around her fingers, trapping her hand on his hard thigh, while the other slipped over her shoulders to draw her flush against his side.

Dana didn't dare look at him, too unsure of what she would see and of what she was feeling. "She passed away several years ago."

"I didn't know."

"There was no reason you should have. My mother moved to northern Oklahoma once I started to work, to a small town there." She peeked at him, then quickly away. She felt like a fainthearted ninny, but so much had happened that she'd never experienced before, she had no way of knowing how to deal with it. "We hadn't been close for a long time, but I saw her on holidays and during my vacations. In fact, I used one of my vacations to go home and take care of the arrangements after she died unexpectedly."

She could feel the tension emanating from him. "How did it happen?"

A vague uneasiness had filtered into his tone that she didn't understand. "She had a massive stroke. By the time I was notified, she was already gone."

There was a stretch of painful silence before R.J. asked, "Why didn't you tell me?"

She looked at him and said simply, "You don't pay me to involve you in my personal affairs. I asked for the time off, and you gave it to me."

He left the bed in an angry rush. "I've been a bastard."

"No!" Dana jumped to her feet and caught his arm. She held tight, though he didn't try to pull away. "That's not true,

R.J. You're one of the most generous, giving men I've ever known."

"Yeah, right. That's why after years of employment, after being friends with my family and with me, you never bothered to tell me when your mother passed away."

He sounded hurt, and she stared at him, bewildered. "I don't understand why you care."

He turned to face her. "Where's your father?"

Dana lifted one shoulder. She didn't know why he was pushing so hard on this. "I have no idea. I never knew the man."

R.J. looked her over, and she was acutely aware of her position at the side of the bed, her feet together, her knees together, her hands clasped at her waist. She was on the verge of pulling the spread from the bed and whipping it around her when he asked, "Will you explain that?"

"If you really want to know."

He crossed his arms over his chest, planted his feet apart and waited. He wouldn't leave her room until he was good and ready, she decided. "My father left my mother for another woman when I was still a baby. She said it was some awful floozy who was much younger than him."

"A pretty woman?"

"I suppose. Surely he wouldn't have run off with a homely woman."

R.J. worked his jaw in thought. "So you have no memory of your father at all?"

"No. There weren't even any pictures since my mother destroyed them all. But she told me often that I took after him in my looks."

His eyes narrowed. "How so?"

"He had the same washed-out hair color, the same thin, lanky build."

A savage sound escaped him. "I take it she was a bitter woman?"

She didn't want R.J. to know about her painful relationship with her mother, how hard she had found it to tolerate her mother's critical nature and jaded outlook. As soon as she'd been old enough, she'd put space between them, but she'd never shared the hurt with anyone and didn't want to start now.

Keeping all emotion out of her tone, she said, "Oh, yes, Mother was angry. To hear her tell it, my father was a loathsome creature with no scruples at all. I got the feeling the woman he ran off with wasn't his first indiscretion." Then she added, "He hurt her very badly, leaving her alone with a baby to raise."

"With *you* to raise."

She nodded. "Yes."

R.J. seemed to be soaking it all in, and he didn't look pleased. Dana decided it was time to change the subject.

"I called your family earlier to explain about our wedding."

His head jerked up and his eyes glittered. "You told them—"

"No! No, I didn't tell them that. How you explain things to your family is your business. I just told them that because of all the bad publicity that had been circulating and because you knew they all had plenty on their minds, you'd wanted to keep things as simple as possible."

He grunted, and she wasn't sure if it was a sound of favor or disapproval.

Dana nervously fiddled with the hem on her shirt. She was in a bedroom with the man she'd loved forever, her hair in wild disarray, and wearing only half her clothes. All things considered, she thought she was handling the situation well. "Do you know what Abbey told me?"

"That she'd have my ass for not inviting her?"

Dana chuckled despite her uneasiness. R.J. teased and bantered with all his sisters, but they knew he loved them just the same. "No. She said you were far too upstanding to shirk your responsibilities. It angers her that you've been put through this mess."

"It hasn't been easy for anyone involved."

"No, it hasn't. But you're the one the press has been pointing a finger at most."

R.J. had been pacing, and suddenly he stopped. Hands on his hips, head tilted, he studied her, then suddenly laughed. "I'll be damned. You did that deliberately, didn't you?"

She stared at him, surprised by his sudden mood shift. "What?"

"Changed the subject on me. We were talking about you and your personal misconceptions, not about me and this bloody scandal."

Dana laced her hands together and lifted her chin. "The scandal will die down once I get through pointing out—truthfully—what an outstanding person you are. I've got a busy week planned for you, and I trust you won't complain."

R.J. shook his head. "No, you don't. I'm not letting you lead me off the track that easily again. I'm on to you now, lady."

Dana didn't want him to be on to her. She didn't want him delving into her psyche, picking away at her painful past. Her childhood hadn't been an easy one, and now R.J. wanted to refute what she knew as truth. But it was so much easier to cling to her old beliefs than to take a chance on believing in him.

R.J. didn't appear willing to give her a choice in the matter. He looked her over once more and smiled. "Sometimes my own stupidity amazes me."

"You are *not* stupid, R.J."

"I'm not a bad lover, either, but I suppose I'll have to prove it."

"No!"

He started toward her again, this time with a purpose. "I

think the only way to make you understand just how attractive I find you is to show you. So that's what I'm going to do."

As he advanced again, she backed up. Only this time she moved too fast, and when she hit the edge of the bed she lost her balance and dropped back on it, bouncing twice.

R.J. was over her before she could even catch her breath.

CHAPTER TEN

R.J. LOOKED DOWN at her wide-eyed expression and smiled gently. "I'm not going to maul you, Dana. Relax."

She gave an audible gulp and stiffened even more.

"It's amazing," he half teased, "how different a woman can look after a man gets to know her."

"You've known me for years!"

"No, I've known the woman you've pretended to be, not the real you." And now he thought he knew why she'd always hidden herself. Dana had bought into her mother's angry words. Her mother claimed Dana looked a lot like her father—and the father was a total bastard. How had that made Dana feel?

"Is that what you think?" she asked, her voice unnaturally high. "That I'm now somehow different? Just because you've caught me with my hair loose and my..." Her words trailed off.

"And your pants off?" His grin was wicked, but then, he felt wicked. Wicked and eager. Patience had never been his virtue, but in this case he'd find a healthy dose of it somewhere. Dana needed to learn her own appeal, and he intended to instruct her on the matter. There'd be no reason for him to dent his pride, not when he had a perfect excuse for getting closer to her. "I'd like to get the rest of your clothes off, too."

"No!"

"I wish I could remove that damn word from your vocabulary." He wanted to reassure her, to help her relax. He had no intention of rushing her now that he realized how much care she needed, not only because of her virginity, but because of her fragile ego. "Regardless of my animalistic display of yesterday, I am capable of controlling my baser instincts. I want you. Ever since I stepped in here and saw your bare legs and your hair loose and the warm blush on your face, all I've thought about is making love with you. But I don't want you to be afraid of me—"

"I'm not afraid of you." She looked appalled at the mere suggestion.

"—and I don't want you to be nervous. I want you to trust me."

Very softly, she whispered, "I do trust you, R.J. That's not what this is about. It's…it's a lot more complicated than that."

R.J. felt a lick of dread go down his spine. He stiffened, feeling the tension gather in his neck. "You want me to have a paternity test done?"

Dana looked at him blankly. "What?"

He gently smoothed his hand over her hair, though he felt anything but gentle. "You're still wondering if maybe I'm the father of the baby, aren't you?"

He braced himself for her reply, but wasn't ready for her burst of anger. She shoved him, almost throwing him to the side. He caught her shoulders and held her still. "Dana?"

Hands pressed flat on his chest, she lifted her head and shouted an inch from his nose, "No! I do not think you're the baby's father. That's a stupid thing for you to say. For the last time, R.J., anyone who knows you knows it's an utterly ridiculous accusation."

The emotions that hit him then were too confusing to sort out. Her belief in him meant a lot, and he was grateful for it. But if the paternity issue wasn't the problem, then he'd been right all along.

He'd been a failure in the sack. He felt the heat of his

embarrassment climb up his neck. She didn't want to sleep
with him again not because she doubted his honor, but because
he'd been such a disappointment. His expertise in pleasing a
woman had never been questioned before now.

Of course, he'd never gone deaf, dumb and blind over a
woman before, either.

He clenched his teeth and resisted the urge to defend himself once again. Dana was simply too inexperienced and too
unsure of her own appeal to understand that it was his hunger
for her that had driven him wild. All she knew was that he'd
come after her with the finesse of a rutting bulldog, and she
hadn't found any satisfaction at all.

That thought made his muscles twitch. He couldn't wait
to bring Miss Dana Maitland—his wife—to completion, to
show her in explicit detail just how appealing she really was.
Once she found out what sex was all about, things would be
different between them.

But in the meantime, he needed to work at shoring up
her confidence. He had no doubt her mother had played a
real number on her, repressing Dana's natural sensuality as
something evil. After all, it was the sensuality of some other
woman that had taken her husband away.

It was ironic that Dana's father had abandoned her because
he didn't care about his wife, while R.J.'s father had walked
away because his wife had died, leaving him a man incapable
of caring about anyone or anything else.

He held her head between his hands, keeping her gaze
locked with his. He enjoyed looking at her, and his fascination
with her emerald eyes hadn't diminished one bit. He smoothed
his thumbs over her cheekbones, seemingly unable to stop
touching her. His sweet, efficient, orderly Dana.

She was by far the sexiest woman he'd ever seen.

"I've never in my adult life," he whispered, "treated a
woman the way I did you last night. But it was your fault too,

honey. You shocked the hell out of me. I didn't expect you to be so..."

"So what?" Her antagonistic tone proved she was going to fight him every inch of the way. "I'm just me, R.J. The same woman you've known for years, the woman you recognized for her secretarial skills. Not for anything else."

She was so defensive, he thought. He had his work cut out for him. R.J. rolled to the side and then hauled her up in the bed so they were lying against the pillows. "Let's look at this logically." He lifted a long strand of her hair and examined it. "You have beautiful hair, soft and pale. Not at all washed out. That's just plain stupid. Look at it, Dana, how the light catches it. It's the type of hair a man imagines spread out over his pillow while his woman smiles up at him."

"I already told you flattery doesn't affect me."

He hid a grin. Her voice had shaken just the tiniest bit as she made that statement. R.J. propped himself up on one elbow. Without moving a single inch, Dana looked at him. She had the appearance of a frightened doe, too wary to move but too cautious not to keep a close eye on him. Her body was rigid.

"What color was your mother's hair?"

"She had very thick, dark brown hair."

"I see." And he did. He could imagine her mother making all kinds of comparisons, but he held his anger in check. Dana didn't need his anger now.

Once again, he settled his palm over her breast. "Mmm. So soft. Those suits you wear make it impossible for a man to see what's beneath. But now I've felt you, and I've tasted you, and I know." He met her wide, unblinking gaze. "I won't ever forget, babe."

As he continued to touch her, her lips parted on a shuddering breath. He didn't want to overly arouse her, because he wanted her to know he'd wait for her. Until she told him she wanted him, until she began to believe in herself, he'd settle

for giving her all the compliments she hadn't gotten from him
so far.

"Do you want me, Dana?"

Her lashes fluttered as if she was trying to regain her wits.
"You didn't marry me for this."

He rested his hand on her silky thigh and wanted to shout
out how much he wanted her. But that sure as hell wouldn't
reassure her. "We could consider it an added benefit."

He said it like a question, leaving the ball in her court. Part
of him was so turned on he felt as if he could come with just
a touch. He couldn't recall ever wanting a woman so badly
or denying himself so completely.

But another part of him, the natural protector, wanted to
hold her close and dispel whatever ridiculous myth her mother
had perpetrated. Why would any mother make her daughter
believe such nonsense?

Dana shyly reached up and put her small palm on his chest.
Just that, such a simple touch, and his guts tightened in reaction. She looked at him, her eyes dark and soft, her lashes
leaving shadows on her cheekbones. He kissed her nose.

"R.J., I like my job."

"I'm glad." He was distracted by her small ears, tracing
the gentle whorls with a fingertip.

"If you and I...if we had sex..."

"Yes." Hell yes.

"...it would change everything."

R.J. stalled in the middle of licking her ear. Damn. That
had been his argument from the first, but he no longer cared.
Somewhere along the way his common sense had been side-
lined by other emotions, and they were totally different from
the physical wanting that had exploded inside him. There
was tenderness and curiosity and a deep caring. He'd known
Dana for many years and naturally felt a unique fondness for
her, built on in part by her loyalty and commitment to the
job. That fondness had suddenly altered into something else,

though, something he wasn't entirely certain of. All he knew was that he wanted her to be aware of her feminine charms, to know that he wanted her because of the woman she was, not because of a duty he felt from her initial demands or an enforced closeness.

Lifting his head to look at her, he asked carefully, "What if I promise you I won't let it interfere with your job?"

She snorted. "That'd be impossible, even for you."

He rubbed her thigh and felt her shift subtly against him. Damn, he wanted to rip that awful, baggy tunic off her and kiss her whole luscious body. He sucked in a lungful of air and said, "You're right, of course. I'm sorry." He took her hand and carried it to his erection, holding her fingers tight against him while watching her eyes widen. "I'm afraid a man's libido sometimes leaves no room for scruples. We'll say anything to convince a desirable female to see things our way, especially when in a state like the one I'm in now."

Her gaze remained glued to his face, and her fingers didn't move. She licked her lips. "Maybe... maybe it's that...um, state, that makes you think you want me."

He laughed, then groaned when her fingers tightened. "Sweetheart, you're the one who put me in this state, and I want you, not anyone else. Do you think I walk around like this all the time?"

"I don't know." Her expression turned serious, and her fingers started moving, gently squeezing him through his slacks, sliding the tiniest bit up and down his length, exploring. "I don't know much about this part of men."

He could barely talk. More than anything he wanted his pants off and her small hand on his naked flesh. His erection strained into her palm, and her eyes opened even wider.

"You moved."

R.J. choked. A fine beading of sweat touched his forehead. It took him a minute, but he managed to hold on to his control. He'd sooner become celibate than rush her again, and there was no way he'd stifle her curiosity. "You have your hand on me, sweetheart. It's driving me crazy. I moved."

"Oh." She started to pull away, but he caught her wrist.

"Crazy in an excruciatingly wonderful way." He saw the awareness dawn in her eyes, saw her eyes darken, the pupils expand.

"Like this?" She stroked him with a tentative touch.

R.J. bit back a moan at the pleasure of it. "Yes." Then he added, "Harder."

Dana levered herself up on one arm, her reluctance forgotten. Rather than meet his eyes, she looked down at her hand, which curved around him through his slacks. She clenched her fingers, and when he jerked, she let him go. "Did I hurt you?"

"God, no," he rasped. "But I think we'd better stop right here or I'm a goner. I can't take much more."

"You can't?"

He shook his head. "No, absolutely not. That is, unless you want to carry things to the natural conclusion."

She stared at him, then scrambled to sit up. Before she turned her back to him, he saw her expression of dazed amazement. "I...no. I don't want us to..."

"Have sex." R.J. sat up, too, though more slowly. He took advantage of her distraction to straighten himself, then sighed with minimum relief. "That's where we were headed, you know."

She rubbed her forehead in confusion. "I don't know what got into me. I hadn't intended any of that."

R.J. looked at her straight, proud shoulders, her mussed hair, and grinned despite his painful arousal. "You're a woman and I'm a man and we want each other. Things are bound to get out of hand now and then." Because he felt secure that she wouldn't be able to hold out against him for long, not with her natural sensuality, he said, "But don't worry. Until you make it clear that you want me, I won't pressure you."

She glanced at him over her shoulder, her expression one of complete disbelief.

Laughing, he flicked the tip of her nose. "I promise." But in the meantime, he'd also take advantage of his time with her to wear her down gently. He was thirty-nine years old; he knew women, and he knew how to get what he wanted. Before the week was out, Dana would be sleeping in his bed—where she belonged.

He gave her a swift, hard kiss good-night and forced himself to his feet. At the door, he stopped and faced her. "Good night, sweetheart. If you need anything, just let me know."

She still looked dazed by all that had transpired, but she managed a nod, and a polite, "Good night, R.J. Sleep well."

Ha. He'd be lucky if he slept at all with his body still on fire and the tempting knowledge that Dana, and relief, were only a few feet away. But while he lay awake, he'd have plenty to think on—like anticipating her surrender. He was a pro at getting what he wanted. Dana and all her silly hang-ups didn't stand a chance.

SHE WAS THE PRO—at sexual torment.

By Thursday, R.J. was wondering how much longer he'd be able to survive. He sat at his desk, ignoring the files Dana had just set before him. He wondered if it was his imagination or if she was deliberately teasing him. Lately, nothing with Dana was clear-cut. Oh, she still did the work of two people. More so than ever, in fact.

His mother had called just that afternoon to tell him he was once again in the papers. It had been that way every day, his face, his every word splashed across a multitude of papers from around the state. What wasn't a direct quote from a lucky source who'd been on the scene was taken from other reliable sources, because no one wanted to miss the story. He was big news.

The difference this time, of course, was that Dana had

engineered the entire thing so he'd come off looking like a saint. There were photos of him holding babies at the clinic. Photos of him speaking with women from the shelter. Candid shots of him writing out a check to the One Way Farm for children, checks that were usually taken care of by his accountant.

And in fact, they *had* been taken care of already, not that he minded donating twice. He'd chosen the charities himself and wanted to do whatever he could to support them. It amused as well as irritated him that Dana wouldn't accept a single cent from him, but she had no problem giving his money away.

Dana had worked things perfectly, and now Austin society didn't know what to think. Was R. J. Maitland a man capable of abandoning his own child, or was he the great philanthropist?

R.J. didn't know what to think, either.

At that moment, Dana bustled in—there was no other word for her irritatingly cheery disposition in the face of his disgruntled frustration—and refilled his coffee cup. She wouldn't serve him at home, and in fact seemed to take exceptional glee in refusing him even the most minor gratuities, but at the office, nothing had changed.

The confounded woman knew he couldn't strip her naked at the office.

Though the thought had singular appeal.

After the cup was full, she perched her hip on the side of his desk, making his pulse quicken, and said, "R.J., Chelsea Markum just called. She wants to interview you."

He made a rude sound. "That conniving little bitch. What's she hoping to do? Negate all the headway you're making?"

Dana lifted a brow. "The headway *you're making.*"

He eyed the length of her legs, one bent at the knee and the other outstretched. Damn, but she had long legs. Killer legs. Why the hell had it taken him so long to notice?

Because the long, sturdy skirts she wore and the flat, ugly

shoes on her feet conspired to hide that fact from everyone, including him.

He imagined her in a short, snug skirt—or better yet, no skirt at all. He took a deep, calming breath. "No one would have paid me the least attention these last few days if it hadn't been for you."

"Only because you're a private man and you consider your philanthropic tendencies no one's business but your own."

He leaned forward with a negligent lack of haste, his forearms flat on the desk, his hands close to her hip. One inch, he thought, and he'd be touching the soft curves of her behind.

She slipped off the desk to pace away.

R.J. swallowed his frustration. "My *tendencies* aren't anyone's business," he groused, "and if it hadn't been for Chelsea and her cutthroat newscast, things could have stayed that way."

Dana's gaze was suddenly solemn as she turned to him. "Oh, R.J." She searched his face. "Have I convinced you to do something you didn't want to do?"

After the miracles she'd performed, he felt like a cad. He left his seat and strode toward her. "Do you really think that's possible, babe?"

She blinked at the pet name he'd started to use and took one step back before halting and squaring her shoulders. "What?"

"For you to get me to do things I don't want to do?"

"Oh. Well, no, not really."

R.J. stood only three inches from her. Sunlight from the large window behind his desk poured over her, making her fair hair glint and gilding her eyelashes. Her skin, he found, was incredible. Not a single flaw, just soft and silky and smooth. He wanted to explore that skin everywhere, on her belly, her upper thighs, the small of her back.

He made a low sound and took her shoulders in his hands.

But as he lowered his head she ducked away, needlessly smoothing her hair as if he'd somehow mussed it.

"R.J., please," she whispered, glancing around, though they were alone in the big office. "We can't do that…here."

Evidently they couldn't do it anywhere. At least, not the *it* he wanted, which was everything. She let him kiss her occasionally and seemed to enjoy his attention. She even accepted the limited caress: a pat on the behind, a cuddle of her breast. The adolescent touches were enough to make him crazed. But if it went beyond that, if he started to breathe hard—which he seemed to do the second she responded to him—he'd see the haunting uncertainty cloud her big eyes.

His vow to wait until she was ready was wearing real thin.

She'd gone to his desk to straighten his papers, and he couldn't help himself. He stepped up behind her and slid his arms around her narrow waist, resting his jaw at the part of her hair on her crown. "Do you know what I've been thinking?" he murmured.

She was very still. "No."

"About you. And this damn enormous desk. And how easy it would be to bend you over it." Her gasp was loud, but he was learning to read her, just barely, and he recognized the sound as mingled excitement and persistent reserve. "Like this."

He pressed his chest against her back and she automatically braced her hands flat, supporting her weight while bending forward. The position put her buttocks at a very interesting angle. He slid his hands down her rib cage until they were holding her hips, then let her feel how aroused he'd become already.

The insanity of need almost claimed him as he felt the soft, firm cushioning of her derriere against his hard flesh. His fingers contracted, and only by force of will did he make himself go slowly. With a more experienced woman, he'd already be driving deep, easing the hot need for them both.

Feather light, he kissed along the nape of her neck, which he'd learned was ultimately sensitive to his every touch. She shivered and made a small sound of surprised pleasure—a sound guaranteed to make him throb.

"Just a few buttons undone at your jacket and blouse, and I could be holding your naked breasts right now. Are your nipples hard, Dana?" The words and accompanying image affected him as much, if not more, than her. He groaned, then found out for himself that indeed they were. She was ripe, aching.

She pushed back against him in an instinctive search for relief when he lightly tugged at her pointed nipples. His heart slammed against his rib cage. "Damn, but I love touching you, Dana."

She made a small sound, but R.J. couldn't be sure it was acceptance. He nipped her ear.

"If I pushed your skirt up high," he groaned against the side of her throat, "I could slide my hands between your soft thighs and—"

Straightening abruptly, she almost hit him in the head. She scrambled from between him and the desk. Chest heaving, eyes wide, face flushed, she stared up at him and blurted, "You have a meeting!"

"What?" Somehow that wasn't at all what he'd expected to hear. It took his sluggish brain a moment to assimilate the words.

Still panting, she closed her eyes as if that were the only way she could concentrate enough to speak coherently. Forming the words with care, she said, "You had a lunch meeting with Drake, remember?" She bit her lip, then opened her eyes. "He's…he's probably waiting for you right now."

R.J. stared at her, nonplussed, until the truth sank in.

Good God, he'd forgotten a meeting. The meeting had been penciled in on his calendar for over a week.

He remembered Dana putting the reminder note in front of

him—and he'd watched the gentle sway of her shapely rump as she'd left.

He even remembered confirming with Drake earlier that very day—but his mind had been on Dana sitting primly at her desk, a sight visible through the open office doors.

In fact, he thought in numb horror as he looked at his desk piled with files he hadn't touched, he hadn't done a damn thing all day except think of her and let his imagination go wild. To be honest, the entire week had been pretty much a write-off. A sick tightening of his throat made it difficult to breathe, and he swallowed hard, then met Dana's nervous gaze.

His hands curled into fists. He was responsible, reputable, a self-professed workaholic, and that was how he liked it, damn it. Unlike his father, he didn't take his duties lightly. And as president of Maitland Maternity, a lot of people relied on him.

Something had to change.

He stepped around Dana and snatched his jacket from the desk chair. "Get on the phone with the restaurant. Have them tell Drake I was detained but I'm on my way."

She didn't answer, and at the moment, he didn't care. He hunted through the stack of ignored files until he found what he was looking for, then shoved the papers into his briefcase and snapped the case shut.

He didn't look at Dana, didn't acknowledge her in any way. She'd become a weakness in his blood, and he'd have to deal with that. *Later.* Right now, he had business to take care of.

Dana rushed alongside him as he headed for the door. "What about Ms. Markum and 'Tattle Today TV'?"

"You can tell Ms. Markum to take a flying leap—"

"R.J.!"

They were in the hallway, almost to the elevators. He gave an impatient look at his watch and wondered what Drake would have to say about being kept waiting. A first and, most definitely, a last. "Tell her whatever the hell you want, as long as it's no. I don't want a damn thing to do with that woman."

"It might be good publicity—"

He stepped into the elevator and punched the button for the lobby. "I said no, Dana. And regardless of anything else, I'm still your damn boss."

She stiffened and her soft mouth firmed into a straight line. Just before the elevator doors shut, she gave him a sharp salute and chimed, "Yes, sir!"

R.J. found himself cursing violently to an empty elevator. He hadn't meant to hurt her, but he felt totally dispossessed of every value he held near and dear. His work ethic had always been uppermost in his mind. Not once since he'd been old enough to be responsible for himself had he shirked his duties. But now, having Dana in the office had become a distraction he couldn't deal with. One look at her, and all he could think about was how wonderful her body had felt beneath his. He'd been given to daydreaming, when all his life he'd disdained the fools who wasted their time doing just that.

Marrying Dana had done as he'd hoped. With all her efforts, his reputation was in repair.

But was it a reputation he was worthy of anymore?

CHAPTER ELEVEN

DANA HURRIED IN through the garage, noticing as she parked that R.J.'s car was there, also. She had hoped to beat him home. Home. What a strange word to use in connection with a house that wasn't hers and never would be. But she did feel at ease here. And she absolutely loved the grounds. Each morning she and R.J. took their coffee to the cozy back patio. The scent of flowers combined with gurgling water from the pond fountain nearby and the chirping of birds in the yard had worked to make her feel very relaxed and peaceful. She loved it.

Of course she'd kept her apartment. For now, she could enjoy his home as her own, but she'd be going back to her place once R.J. decided the marriage had served its purpose and was no longer needed.

He'd tried to argue about that, too, she remembered, as she retrieved her packages from the trunk. He'd been so unreasonable about so many things, but to even think she'd give up her apartment and all her furnishings when the marriage wasn't the forever kind…. Never mind that he'd tried telling her he'd get her another apartment—even a house if she wanted it— when the time came. You'd think the man would know her better than that.

R.J. must have been listening for her, because before she could juggle her keys to unlock the door from the garage into the house, he was there. He still had on his dress slacks, but he was in his socks and his hair was disheveled. His shirt was completely unbuttoned, hanging from his broad shoulders and displaying more than it concealed.

As usual, the sight of him did funny things to her stomach.

"R.J.," she said by way of a greeting.

He reached out and lazily relieved her of the bags, balancing them all in one arm. "Where've you been to?"

His tone had a slightly edgy sound to it, and she looked at him warily. "I went shopping."

He didn't reply, but waited until she'd stepped into the house then closed the door behind her. He followed her through the dining area to the kitchen. Dana pulled off her lightweight jacket and laid it over a chair. "What's wrong?"

"Wrong? I've been home for over an hour. The house was empty. No wife, not even a housekeeper."

"I thought your meeting might keep you longer."

His eyes narrowed. "After lunch, I got back on schedule." He lifted a glass from the counter and took a healthy swallow. Ice cubes chinked as he finished it off. "One blunder a day is enough. Besides, there was no way I could have been late for my last meeting. As it was, half my family was there and they gave me hell for not telling them about the wedding."

Dana eyed the drink in his hand. R.J.'s sister Abby was Maitland Maternity's finest obstetrician and one of Dana's closest friends. His sister Ellie was the hospital administrator and Beth, Ellie's twin, managed the day-care center. Dana had known they would all be at the meeting, with Megan, of course. Maitland Maternity was, for the most part, a very family-oriented business. Dana had wondered how R.J. would explain away their marriage.

But at the moment the reasoning he'd given for their marriage didn't matter. She remembered that Abby had confessed her concern over R.J.'s drinking habits of late. But to Dana's knowledge, he hadn't drunk at all since the wedding.

R.J. saw the direction of her gaze and shook his head.

"Don't start. Abby already gave me a earful. You'd think I'd turned into a damn lush the way she fretted."

"She loves you, so she worries."

"She has no reason. And as long as you're going to be the nosy wife, you might as well know it's only cola. I want to talk to you, and I intend to be dead sober while I do so."

That sounded far too ominous to Dana's ears. She tried for a lighthearted smile, though judging by R.J.'s frown, it wasn't effective. "Fine. Can you talk while I fix dinner?"

R.J. crossed his arms over his bare chest and scowled at her. "Why the hell are you cooking? I have a perfectly good housekeeper to do that sort of thing. Speaking of which, where the hell is Betty? She's usually here until after I get home."

Dana kept her back to R.J. as she pulled vegetables and pasta from the grocery bag then put a pot of water on the stove to boil. "I gave Betty the day off."

A beat of silence, then, "You did what?"

The low disbelief in his voice wasn't promising. Forcing a bright smile, Dana turned to head to the refrigerator. "I gave her the day off. I wanted to cook today, so I saw no reason for her to hang around."

"The reason for her to hang around is that I pay her damn well to do just that."

Dana tried to hang on to her own temper, but it wasn't easy. She'd so wanted tonight to be…special. R.J. had been so sweet all week. He touched her constantly and gave her outrageous compliments that she couldn't begin to believe but felt wonderful to hear all the same. She no longer felt so self-conscious about her looks around him. She'd even started to subtly change her appearance a bit. It wasn't much, because she'd never been the daring type, but she'd loosened her hair just a little, and had even gone so far as to let a few long strands hang free. Twice R.J. had gently smoothed them behind her ears, and she so loved having him touch her that she'd vowed to keep her hair a little less neat from now on.

And because he'd made such a fuss about her legs, she'd taken Hope's advice and bought a pair of shoes with a slight heel. They were far from being sexy, but they didn't look like orthopedic shoes, either.

She hid a smile, remembering the attention her legs had gotten at the office all day. R.J. had even forgotten his meeting, which was an absolute first.

She waved a hand at him. "Settle down, R.J. You're a big boy. I'm sure you can get your own drink."

R.J. caught her wrist and pulled her around to face him. His expression looked as if it had been carved from flint. "I can get my own drink. But I had laundry to go to the cleaners, as well, and I like to eat when I get home, not hours later. So don't ever presume to dismiss *my* housekeeper again."

He was ruining everything with his surly temper, and Dana didn't appreciate it one bit. She jerked her wrist free and poked him in the chest. Hard. "It won't be hours if you'll get out of my way and let me cook. Pasta takes all of about twenty minutes. And if we're going to be married, even for a little while, you better learn that once I leave the office, I stop taking orders from you."

She finished that sentence with another poke, and he grabbed her hand. He looked livid, though why, she couldn't guess. She met his gaze with as much bravado as she could muster, not giving an inch. Slowly, the look in his eyes changed to one of heat, but still he didn't release her.

"You won't let me give you a damn thing, and now you want to cook, too?"

Dana rolled her eyes. "R.J., is that what this is about? I keep telling you, I don't need you to give me anything, and I enjoy cooking." She glanced down at his large hand, which was wrapped around her much smaller one. "I wanted to cook— for you."

He took a slow, shuddering breath, then released her. Turning away, he ran one hand through his hair and cursed low.

"R.J.?"

"I'm sorry," he said abruptly. "I screwed up today and I'm taking it out on you."

"Screwed up?"

He turned to face her so fast, she jumped. "I almost missed my goddamned meeting."

It was starting to sink in just how much that had upset him. Dana knew R.J. was a workaholic, that he took incredible pride in the job he did. As long as she'd been with him, he'd never missed work, and he seldom worked less than fifty-hour weeks. It wasn't that it was expected of him; R.J. demanded it of himself.

Dana pulled out a chair at the kitchen table and pushed R.J. toward it. "Sit. You can talk to me while I get your dinner ready."

He sprawled into the chair. Dana thought he looked exhausted, but he asked, "Do you want me to do anything to help?"

Just to keep his mind busy, she handed him the package of prewashed romaine lettuce, along with a block of cheese and the shredder. "Tear the lettuce, and shred the cheese over it. Then toss on some croutons. You can put it all in this bowl."

Obediently he began tearing. As Dana began mixing up the creamy sauce for the pasta, R.J. said, "I can't be late for another meeting, Dana."

She glanced at him, worried at his tone. "I'll make sure you aren't, R.J."

"You didn't make sure today."

He wasn't casting blame so much as simply pointing out an irrefutable fact. He was in such a strange, almost dangerous mood, Dana chose her words with care. "You distracted me today. I'll be more careful from now on." He glanced up at her, and she added, "You don't have to worry about it."

He went back to shredding the lettuce. Dana didn't bother

to tell him he'd already prepared enough for the two of them. She threw in the angel hair pasta, then stirred it gently.

"Actually, I do."

She kept one eye on the boiling water, one on R.J. "You do what?"

"Have to worry. I've always had to be aware of the possibility that I was more like my father than I'd like to admit."

Dana closed her eyes a brief moment as the magnitude of what he was feeling sank in. She pulled the pasta from the stove and dumped it in a colander, then rinsed it with cold water. She moved automatically, her thoughts not on preparing the meal, but on R.J. "Your father…"

"Was the blot on the family name. He left his two children without a backward glance and hasn't shown his face since." He put the lettuce aside and rubbed his forehead. "I don't want anything in common with the man, Dana, do you understand that? There'll be no comparisons. I won't forget my responsibilities."

Without really thinking about it, Dana went to the back of his chair and wrapped her arms tight around his shoulders. He lifted his hands to hold her forearms and turned his face into her. She kissed his temple. "R.J., you're the most rock steady, dependable man I've ever known."

She moved her palm to his chest and caressed him, thrilling at the feel of his warmth, of the smooth flesh over hard bone and muscle. She kissed him again, then hugged him as tight as she could.

R.J. caught her and pulled her around to his lap. His large hand turned her face up, and he said against her mouth, "I don't want you to be hurt or angry."

Confused, she whispered, "I'm not." She kissed his chin, then tucked her face against his throat. "I'm so proud of you, R.J. And I know Megan and the rest of your family are, too."

His laugh was hoarse. "They weren't proud today. They

were ready to string me up for not telling them about our secret *torrid affair.*"

"Oh." She leaned back to blink at him.

"They all assume we must have been carrying on behind their backs since we up and married so suddenly."

Her face flamed. "Oh, God. What must they think of me?"

"I believe Beth said something along the lines of you being a saint, since you could tolerate me and my mercurial temper. And Ellie wondered if you'd be a good influence on me."

Dana chewed her lower lip as that sank in. "Will they be disappointed when we separate?"

His thumb smoothed over her cheek. "I don't intend to disappoint anyone. That's why I made a decision today."

Dana felt awkward now that he'd gotten so serious. It looked as if it was time for that talk he'd mentioned, but she was perched on his lap and she wasn't at all oblivious to the hard evidence of his arousal beneath her. The last thing she wanted was a lecture. "Maybe we should eat first."

R.J. pulled her head to his chest, held her tight and said, "I'm firing you."

"What!"

Easily subduing her struggles, he wouldn't let her up. "Shh. You can call it quitting if you like, but the fact of the matter is, I can't have you in the office all the time. It's too distracting."

Again she struggled, and again he tightened his hold.

"Just listen, babe, okay? I did something today that I've never done before, because all I could think about was making love to you."

Dana stilled. It shouldn't matter to her, but she liked the sound of that. Maybe R.J. was starting to care for her. Maybe, just maybe, she meant more to him than a secretary or a temporary wife.

"I watched you sitting at your desk," he murmured, "and

tried to imagine you there naked. You carried my papers and all I could think about was pulling you down on the carpet and opening your legs."

His words, which bordered on obscene, sounded incredibly sexy to her. Without meaning to, she knotted her hands in his loose shirt, pulling herself closer.

"I wanted you on my desk, or, hell, under my desk. Or standing up against the wall. I want you so bad, Dana. And I can't work because of it."

So she had to go. Dana hid a small smile of inconceivable joy. He wasn't manipulating her now. He had missed a meeting, and he had been distracted by her all day. Firing her wasn't just a ploy on his part to get her into his bed. He could have had her there at any point this week if he'd pushed her. But instead, he'd held back and he'd given her the most wonderful week—like a courtship.

No one would ever have accused Dana of being brazen, and now was no exception, regardless of what she was about to do. Keeping her face safely tucked against his body where he couldn't look at her, she whispered, "Then have me."

R.J. turned to stone. Dana wasn't even sure he was breathing. "Dana?"

It was a gamble, because the likelihood that R.J. would ever really care about her was remote. He'd had beautiful, sophisticated women after him his entire life, so why would he fall in love with her? But she wanted him too much to keep resisting. At least she knew his feelings, whatever they might be, were sincere. And she assumed once his frustration was taken care of, there'd be no reason for him to fire her.

She smiled and kissed his throat. "I want you, too, R.J."

He came to his feet in a rush, holding Dana close to his chest. "Right now."

Clinging to his shoulders, Dana took one quick look around the kitchen at the half-prepared meal. Reaching out, she turned off the stove, then dismissed the rest as unimportant. R.J. kept kissing her, her cheek, her hair, her ear. She almost giggled at his haste, and he squeezed her tight as he bounded up the stairs to his bedroom.

"Don't you dare laugh! Do you have any idea what I've been going through all week?" He strode down the hall, not the least winded.

Dana tangled one hand in his hair and kissed his jaw. "Since you put me through it, as well, I think I do."

"Ha. You have no idea what it's about yet. But you will. Before the night is over, you won't have a single doubt."

He stepped into his room and kicked the door shut, then stood Dana beside the bed. She watched him, caught between nervousness and dizzy excitement as he threw back the covers on the bed and leaned toward the light on the nightstand.

Dana caught his shoulder. "R.J...." She wondered what to say as he glanced at her, then muttered, "Let's leave the lights off."

He held her gaze a moment longer, then switched on the light and straightened. "No, you don't, babe." He threw off his shirt, then sat on the side of the bed. "You're beautiful and I want to see you, all of you."

Dana felt the first sick stirrings of dread. She wasn't beautiful and—

R.J. caught her hips and pulled her between his legs. "Look at me, Dana."

It wasn't easy, but she met his determined gaze.

"I want you to trust me. Forget our first time together. I was a fool and I've been berating myself over it ever since."

Wincing, Dana slipped her hand into his hair and explained. "It's...it's not about that first time, R.J."

"I gave you no pleasure at all."

"That's not true!" It was difficult to speak because R.J. had leaned forward and was kissing her belly through the material of her skirt. She realized a second later that while he'd kissed

her, he'd worked her zipper down. The skirt loosened. "R.J.,
I...I liked some of what you did to me that night."

R.J. reached beneath the skirt and caught the waistband
of her panty hose. "Yeah. You liked it so much you refused
to let me touch you again."

Her panty hose were around her ankles, and Dana, confused and off balance, stepped out of her shoes, then held onto
his shoulders as he tugged the stockings the rest of the way
off.

"It...it wasn't what I'd expected, R.J. That's all."

His laugh was hoarse. "I can believe that."

He reached for the buttons on her blouse and she blurted,
"It was more. It was...too much."

His fingers froze on her top button, then his hands slowly
lowered to her hips again. Gazing up at her with a burning
intensity, he whispered, "You want to explain that?"

When she fidgeted, he pulled her onto his lap, which made
it easier for her to concentrate. But the second she began to
speak he started undoing buttons again. Keeping her wits together enough to measure her words was almost impossible.

She assumed that was his plan.

"Since I'd never had sex before, I thought we could...you
know, do it and we'd stay detached. It would be nice but no
more than that. But you touching me, kissing me, it was so...
intimate. So personal. I felt overwhelmed and swamped with
feelings and—"

His hand slipped inside her open blouse and into the cup
of her bra, cuddling her naked breast. She gasped.

"Me, too, babe." His words were quietly spoken. "I felt
it, too." He bent down and kissed the upper fullness of her
breast, plumped up by his hand. "But part of the reason it
hit me so hard was this—your beautiful body totally took me
by surprise. I want to see you, Dana, and I want you to trust
me enough to know I'm not lying when I tell you how sexy
you are."

She didn't want to. She wanted to run away, to hide. But this was R.J., a man she'd loved since the day she'd met him and she didn't want him to be unhappy. He wanted her, and for now, that was all that mattered. "All right."

His squeeze nearly took her breath away.

Then he was lowering her to the mattress, and his hands were busy tugging away her clothes. Against her naked midriff he whispered, "This time I'll do it right, Dana. And we can both be overwhelmed."

CHAPTER TWELVE

BECAUSE she'd been so nervous, R.J. kept the light low, using only the bedside lamp. But it was enough. Soft light spilled over her nude body as she lay stretched out on his bed, highlighting the tilt of one full breast, the roundness of her thigh, the slight curve of her belly. Her skin was dewy, flushed a rosy pink all the way down to her restlessly stirring feet, and she was his.

He carefully circled one straining nipple with his tongue and heard the sexy, arousing groan Dana gave in return.

He'd been making love to her for an hour, and he wasn't at all ready to stop. He had a firm grip on his control this time, and he could easily have pleasured her, tasted her, touched her all night.

But judging by her increasingly frantic movements, the flushed heat of her skin and the silky wetness between her thighs, Dana couldn't take much more.

He hoped not. He wanted her to remember this night forever, and to know it was so special because of her, because of the incredibly feminine, sexy woman she was.

When she started to protest his lack of haste, he sucked her nipple deep into his mouth. Her hands gripped his hair so hard he winced, then switched to the other breast.

"R.J.," she groaned, "please."

His fingers had been teasing her belly, but now he dipped them lower, gliding through her soft curls to the swollen female flesh beneath. She was hot, enticing. She was his.

Dana. He pushed one finger into her, trying to determine exactly how ready she might be, and was surprised when she nearly climaxed, her hips jerking upward, her head arching back.

He lifted his head from her breast to look at her. "Beautiful," he breathed, and suddenly he wanted to watch her come, right now, with no more teasing.

He worked a second finger in next to the first, his mind going numb at the tightness, at the way she tensed around him, then he used his thumb to gently stroke her, finding a soft, deep rhythm. Dana strained against him, her eyes squeezed shut, her teeth clenched. Her reactions were real, with nothing held back, and he reveled in them.

"That's it, babe…"

He loved the sounds she made, without reserve or embarrassment, the sounds of a woman caught up in pleasure too intense to bear. He licked the nipple closest to him, watched her chest heave, and then she gave a low scream of pleasure.

He nearly came with her, it was such a turn-on watching *his* Dana in this way. He couldn't get over it, how innately sensual she was, yet he'd never known. She quivered, caught in the throes of her release for a long minute, before her body slowly began to go limp, relaxing against the mattress.

R.J. watched her through a nearly blinding haze of need. As soon as she'd quieted, he pulled himself over her and spread her legs wide. Again, he was struck by the realization that this was Dana, his quiet secretary, his loyal friend. His wife. It was as if her body had been made just for him. He couldn't imagine a woman any more appealing.

He lifted her knees to his shoulders, caught her buttocks in his hands and slowly pressed deep, groaning as he felt her silky, snug flesh surround him. *"Dana."*

Though she'd been utterly limp beneath him moments before, now she wrapped her hands around his upper arms and lifted her hips to meet his thrusts, giving a low moan each time.

"Am I hurting you?" he rasped, on the edge, but determined to make this as good for her as possible.

"No, no…please, don't stop."

Her breathless plea burned him. He lowered his chest to hers and kissed her, his tongue in her mouth, he was as deep inside her body as he could get.

She came with him this time, and R.J., who'd once planned to sleep alone, to maintain his privacy and his distance, locked her close to his chest as he drifted into sleep. Twice during the night she stirred, and each time he wanted her again as if the first time had never happened. She had to be tired, but not once did she complain. When she awoke to his hand stroking her breast, she reached for him and kissed him deeply.

When she rolled onto him during the night, R.J. used the moment to link their bodies and brought her fully awake by rocking into her. She bit his shoulder, then quietly succumbed to the pleasure.

Morning came too soon, but the sight of Dana sprawled in his bed, one of her slender thighs thrown over his hip, her pale hair spread out over his chest, did much to revive him. He smiled as he realized how insatiable he'd been, then smiled wider remembering how she'd reciprocated in full.

But she had to be sore, and he didn't want to be accused of being greedy, so he contented himself by stroking her awake, luxuriating in her silky skin and the fact that it was his to touch. The thought was oddly comforting.

He ran his hand down her back and over her firmly rounded behind, pushing the covers away as he did so. Dana stretched with a groan—then went abruptly still.

This was Dana's first morning after, he realized, and she looked startled, confused. As he thought about how wild she'd been through the night, he could understand why and couldn't resist teasing her a bit. "It's too late for modesty now, baby. I've already looked you over head to toe."

"R.J." She levered herself up and stared down at him as if she were totally surprised to be in his bed. Her slumberous eyes looked deep and dark in her confusion.

Then the blush came and she quickly sat up, jerking the covers to her chin. That left him completely naked, and she indulged in some shocked staring before belatedly turning her head. R.J. stroked her hair. "It's lucky for you I have to get ready for work, or I'd remind you of how useless that blush is."

He sat up and kissed one shoulder where the sheet drooped. Dana glanced back at him, and he saw the boldness come into her eyes before she said, "If we wouldn't be late, I'd show you that no reminder is necessary."

The grin came slowly, followed by a laugh. Damn, but he liked waking up this way. He cupped the back of her head and pulled her toward him for a hard kiss. "You can sleep in, remember? As of today, you're a free woman."

He stood beside the bed and ran a hand through his sleep-rumpled hair. It was a second before he realized Dana was rigid.

In precise tones, she asked, "What are you talking about?"

Uh-oh. He took in her cold expression and the tight grip she had on the sheet at her throat and gave an inward wince. Last night, he hadn't explained completely. Not after they'd gotten sidetracked with sex.

He decided to brazen it out, and with that plan, he sauntered to his dresser to pull out shorts and socks. Dana's gaze moved over his naked body in open fascination, but her frown didn't lessen one bit.

Another blow to his ego, he thought with wry humor.

"I told you, Dana. It's no good you working in the office

with me. Do you honestly think either of us will be able to keep our minds on work?"

Her eyes narrowed. "You said that was because you wanted me. Well, you've…had me."

He chuckled at her naïveté. "And you think that's an end to it? Honey, all you've done is whet my appetite. Now that I know what I've been missing, I wouldn't get a damn thing done with you sashaying around."

She shot off the bed as if someone had lit a rocket under her. "I do *not* sashay!"

R.J. lifted one brow. "Well, I've got news for you. Whatever it is you do, it turns me on, so we're not going to find a compromise here." He went to his closet to pull out a suit. "Besides, before I came home yesterday I contacted personnel and told them to send up some applicants today. I'm going to be interviewing for a new secretary during my lunch."

There was a lethal depth to her quiet words. "You did what?"

"Megan gave me a few suggestions of employees due for a promotion. I've arranged to meet with them today."

He could feel the explosive tension emanating from her, but he had no idea how to defuse it. He felt helpless, and that made his temper erupt. "Be reasonable, Dana. What happened yesterday can't happen again. I haven't worked this hard to be a damn good president just to throw it away because I have the hots for you. Too many people rely on me, and by God, I will not let them down."

She lifted her head like a queen and started toward the connecting door. "Fine. But you have absolutely no idea what qualities are necessary to handle your daily schedule. That's always been my job, so *I'll* pick the replacement."

"Dana…"

She whirled on him like a small tornado. "Don't you dare argue with me about this! I know the job, I'll find someone suitable for it. Period. And you can just deal with a little sexual frustration until I do." She stomped into her room and slammed the door behind her.

R.J. stood there, naked, confused, a little admiring. Dana had one hell of a temper when she let it loose. His ears were still rattling after the way she'd slammed the door. Another slow, perverse grin started. He was discovering new depths to her every day.

It made sense to let her choose her replacement; she did know the job requirements far better than he did. And now that he knew she was his at home, he could rein in his lust— *he hoped.*

Grinning, he went to the door and pulled it open and found Dana standing in the middle of the floor buck naked. She squealed and jerked a pillow from her bed to hold in front of her. "R.J.!"

Her modesty amused him, especially after how wild she'd been last night. "Hurry it along, honey. We never did eat last night, and I'm starved. We can breakfast along the way."

Her nose went into the air. "You go along without me. I have things to do this morning."

He scowled. "Like what?"

Keeping the pillow tight in front of her, she turned and headed into the bathroom, affording him a delectable view of her slender back and long legs.

"Like finding a new job, of course."

The bathroom door closed on his curse. Stubborn, obstinate, contrary—*sexy.* Why couldn't she just stay home and let him take care of her? And just who the hell did she think she was going to go to work for, anyway?

R.J. pictured another man ogling her the way he had, thinking the thoughts he'd thought, and he wanted to strangle the man without even knowing who he was.

He arrived at work that day in a bitter mood, and it only got worse as the day wore on.

MEGAN WATCHED R.J. brooding, and knew he wasn't hearing a single word she said. The moment she'd arrived, Dana had shown her into his office—an unnecessary formality, to be sure—then firmly shut the door. It wasn't often that door was kept closed, not the way R.J. and Dana had always worked together with an almost uncanny synchronization.

Megan lowered her gaze so R.J. couldn't read the speculation there and asked, "Trouble in paradise?"

He glanced at her sharply. "What was that?"

"You're hiring a new secretary, which I'm beginning to gather wasn't Dana's idea, and she's got you closed in here like a mummy. What's going on?"

"Nothing I can't handle."

Megan looked at her oldest son fondly. "I couldn't have asked for a better firstborn than you, R.J., but sometimes you can be very shortsighted."

He fiddled with a pencil on his desk, then threw it aside. "I'm not your firstborn. I'm your first stray."

Megan stiffened. "Don't you dare insult me that way, R. J. Maitland! No, I didn't give birth to you, but by God you're mine."

Whenever she lost her temper, it always amused her children, and R.J. was no different. His mouth quirked for just a moment before he repressed the grin. "You've never shown a difference, but that doesn't mean there isn't one. If my father hadn't been so worthless and self-indulgent, you'd be my aunt, as you should be."

"True." Megan stood and paced to the window, then added, "And I remember to give thanks often for the fact you were brought to me. Regardless of the circumstances, R.J., you're my son now."

He, too, stood, and put his hands on her shoulders. "Yes."

He kissed her cheek, but Megan knew he was still buried deep in the guilt of his father, in the knowledge that he'd been "taken in." R.J. had been born with an unusual amount of pride and self-determination. Nothing she could do or say would ever diminish it until he realized that he was fully his own man, with only the parts of his father that he chose to accept.

Megan turned to him, all business now. "I'd like you to call Dana in."

"Why?" He looked disgruntled at the thought of seeing her, but he was already headed to his intercom. "Dana, if you could join us, please?"

Her voice was cool when she replied, "Yes, sir, I'll be right there."

R.J. ground his teeth.

Shaking her head at the foolishness of young love, Megan waited for Dana. She came into the room within ten seconds, but she didn't look at R.J. She merely waited.

Two such proud, stubborn people. Megan wondered when R.J. would finally realize that Dana loved him. And when Dana would finally tell him. She saw a long, bumpy road ahead of them, but she'd made it a practice not to interfere in her children's lives.

"We've had two more women check out of the clinic."

R.J. cursed. Dana rubbed her brow.

"Dana, you've done an excellent job of showcasing R.J.'s more redeemable qualities, but the matter of the baby still exists. Until we find the father or mother, the clinic is going to be under suspicion. I'm not overly worried about that, but I've decided to call Jake home."

R.J. turned to her sharply. "Do you know how to reach him?"

"He always leaves me a contact number in case of an emergency." She tried to say it with more confidence than she felt. She had no idea what her younger son was involved in. They all teased him about being a spy, but sometimes Megan wondered if there was some truth to the taunt. "Since your marriage, much of the fire has been aimed at him. He has a right to be here to defend himself, and of course, though I wouldn't say it to anyone else, there is the possibility that he's the father."

Dana glanced at R.J. "Miss Markum asked to do an interview with R.J., but he refused. I think that's why she's turned up the heat again."

Megan drew a breath. "Well, you just go on refusing, R.J. That woman will only get what we choose to give her, and she'll learn the Maitlands can't be bullied."

R.J. put his arm around his mother and said, "Be sure to let me know how Jake feels about being accused of fathering a baby by fifty different women."

"You can ask him yourself," she said with a smile. "If I have my way, he'll be here for Thanksgiving. It'll be nice to have the whole family together and it'll give Connor the chance to meet Jake."

R.J. stiffened, as Megan had known he would. But she couldn't explain about Connor, not yet.

"Have you had him investigated, Mother?"

"Soon," was all she'd say on the matter. "Now, I need to get going. I'm meeting Connor for lunch."

R.J. was still frowning after his mother was gone, the door closed behind her.

Dana glanced at him, trying to keep her expression cool. "As long as I'm here and interrupting your day, could you spare the time to give me a recommendation?"

A shock of angry disbelief darkened his eyes. "A what?"

"A recommendation. I could use it for finding a new position. I spent the morning hunting up prospects—in between interviewing your applicants, who, by the way, all failed miserably—and I have a few possibilities that seem interesting."

He advanced until he was very near her. "Let's go over this a little more slowly, if you please. What the hell do you mean my applicants all failed?"

Dana shook her head with pity. "They were all anxious for the job, no doubt about that. But they didn't have the necessary skills. What they had was a healthy hunger to bag the boss. And if you think I'm distracting, you wouldn't have lasted a minute with any of them."

"Meaning?"

"Meaning they were all young and very attractive," she said with terse disdain, then started to turn away.

R.J. caught her to him, holding her against his chest. His gaze was probing, then his hazel eyes lightened, and though he didn't quite smile, Dana could see he was amused. "You're jealous."

Outrage bubbled up inside her because he was right. She'd taken one look at the women and dismissed them all, despite their qualifications. "Ha!" was all she could think to say.

R.J. pinched her chin and spoke in a husky whisper. "There's no need, you know. I've got a hunger for a prickly, up-tight, recently debauched virgin, and no one else will do."

Her face flamed at his description, but she thought with spite that he hadn't seen the women or he wouldn't be so positive about that. She pulled her chin free. "Well, your hunger will be safe soon enough, if you'll give me the recommendation. I have two positions to look at after work, and while you were in the conference with your mother, Mr. Brashear from the supplies office down the street stopped in. He heard I'd soon be free, and he offered me a job. With a raise."

R.J. took two steps back. "No."

Quirking her brow, Dana said, "I wasn't aware it was your decision to make."

"I know Brashear. You're not working for him."

Brashear had stopped by, but Dana had dismissed him as a possibility. The position was a good one, with excellent pay and benefits, but the man was a reprobate. "Stop grinding your teeth, R.J. I'll work for whomever I please."

"Not as my wife, you won't. Hell, the man's a lecher. If

he offered you a job, it's just so he can chase you around his desk!"

Dana went on tiptoe, which wasn't easy in her new shoes, and spoke straight into R.J.'s face. She was beyond furious, and the anger felt good, much better than the jealousy. "Maybe," she nearly shouted, "unlike you, Brashear recognizes my qualities as a first-class executive assistant! Did you think of that possibility?"

"No, and neither did he!"

Dana grabbed her head. "My God, you're a pigheaded man!" She stomped out of his office and into her own, this time refraining from slamming the door. It closed with a quiet click. She was in the office, after all, and as she'd just told him, she was the best executive secretary there was.

And she'd go on being that until R.J. actually forced her to leave. Not that he needed to know that.

She checked his schedule, then waited ten minutes before reminding him he had a few calls to make. She kept her tone polite—barely, and R.J. merely grunted a reply. When she inquired as to whether or not he'd written the recommendation, he slammed his finger down on the intercom button and disconnected her.

Dana grinned.

Poor R.J. He had his hands full right now, but she had to admit she enjoyed his display of jealousy. If she chose to see it as a promising sign, it was nobody's business but her own. She did feel horrible that all this was happening at such a bad time for him. His reputation was no longer being shredded, but apparently the clinic's reputation was still threatened, and she knew he was worried about Megan.

The sudden appearance of Connor was suspect, as far as she was concerned. Why would the man show up after all this time? And didn't he have any more pride than to allow Megan to pay his way?

Dana shook her head. She supposed they'd find some

answers in the next few weeks. Maybe then R.J. would be able to put at least that worry to rest. After all, if Connor was telling the truth, if he was Megan's nephew, then he had a rightful place in her affections.

The door between their offices opened and R.J. stood there leaning against the frame, looking at her. Dana glanced up with a silent question.

"I'm sorry."

She was so surprised, she blinked. "What was that?"

He gave a hearty sigh and shook his head. "You want your pound of flesh, huh? Very well, I said I'm sorry."

Dana came slowly to her feet. "For what—exactly?"

"For wanting to fire you. Hell, it won't matter if I can see you or not, I'm still going to want you. And I'm still going to spend far too much time thinking about you."

She gave him a steady look. "And you don't want me working for Brashear."

He gave a brief nod.

Dana smiled, then moved closer to him. "There's a solution, you know?"

"I'm ready to hear it."

She slid one hand down his tie, then slipped her fingers between the buttons of his shirt until she felt the hot silk of his skin. She felt incredibly bold. "We could spend all our time away from the office in bed, so that you'd get your fill. Maybe then you wouldn't have the energy to think about sex here in the office."

His look was so hot she felt scorched, but he kept his expression bland enough. "That's a very workable plan. I can see you truly are experienced in managing my office dilemmas."

She chuckled, but then gasped when he picked her up and carried her into his office, shoving the door shut with his foot. He set her on her feet then turned the lock.

"There's also another idea I thought we might try." His hand went under her skirt and lifted it even as he backed her into the door, wedging her legs apart with his knee. "It's called a nooner, and I think it'd go a long way to relieving my tension so I can quit slacking off and actually get some work done."

Dana, already feeling the effects of his seeking, stroking hand, said breathlessly, "I believe I could pencil that into your schedule." Then R.J. was kissing her and she didn't say anything else.

TWENTY MINUTES LATER, R.J. was whistling as he tucked his shirt in and watched Dana struggle with her hair. Her panty hose were ruined, lying in a heap on the floor. R.J. picked them up. "I'll personally see that you have a supply kept on hand."

She sent a teasing frown his way, still trying to catch her breath. "That won't do me much good right now."

His voice dropped, and he touched her cheek tenderly. "Shall I run down to the gift shop for you?"

"No!"

He laughed. "You know, another thing we'll need to keep on hand is condoms. I'm not in the habit of carrying more than one—and that has always been for emergencies."

Jealousy flared again, though he'd just finished loving her very thoroughly. Her eyes narrowed. "Emergencies?"

"Hmm. With you tempting me all day, I expect to have a lot of emergencies."

Dana considered that, then mentioned something that she hadn't thought of before. She straightened R.J.'s tie, just so she wouldn't have to look right at him as she said it. "You didn't use protection last night."

He drew a deep breath and caught her hands. "No, and I'm sorry about that. No excuse except that you do affect me in uncommon ways. But, honey, if there's any…problem, let me know right away."

"Problem?"

"I have no interest in being a father, Dana. Now or ever. I've told you that before."

She remembered him saying as much when Tanya had claimed to be the abandoned baby's mother. But that had been Tanya.

And what made her think she was special? Dana wondered.

Every wonderful thing she'd just been feeling seemed to dissipate like mist. "I want children someday."

There was no hesitation in his answer. "That's fine. And I wish you luck." His expression hardened and he added, "Just don't expect me to be the father."

She started to turn away, wanting only to be alone, to nurse her sudden overwhelming grief without fear of him seeing too much, but R.J. caught her arm.

"If you find out you're pregnant, you'll tell me immediately. I don't think there's much to worry about, since it was only the one night, but just in case—"

"I understand." And she did. Only too well.

As Dana sat at her desk, seeing nothing but the destruction of her own silly dreams, she wondered about the little baby Megan was taking care of. What if R.J. had been the father? She could understand now why it would have made him so angry. But that poor baby.

And if it wasn't R.J., who *was* the father?

CONNOR O'HARA walked outside his Montana ranch house, ambling around the empty, expansive grounds. The November wind whistled and howled over the trees in a mournful wail, reminding him he was alone. The cold sliced through his shearling coat like thin icy blades. This wasn't Texas, he thought with a shudder, where even now the temperatures would be mild.

He looked out at the brittle, winter landscape, but he

wasn't really seeing it. In his hand, the letter from the lawyer fluttered.

It was from Harland Maitland, his deceased grandfather.

His hand knotted into a fist against his thigh, crumpling the paper. He stopped to rest his back against a bare tree. So much had changed in his life. First his mother had confessed that he was adopted—a truth guaranteed to rattle anyone's foundation. But he could accept that. His mother had always been there for him, and he'd loved her dearly. Finding out she hadn't given birth to him wouldn't change that.

She'd known she was dying or perhaps he'd never have found out the truth. He'd wondered at the time who his real mother could be, but not once had he suspected the truth.

His grief and confusion had driven him to Lacy Clark, his young housekeeper. What a mistake that had been, he thought with the niggling remains of anger. She'd been so sweet, so ready to please him. And she'd seemed so wholesome, a child of nature with her long blond hair, her big innocent blue eyes. But after one night in his bed, she'd run off with someone else, or so Janelle, his mother's new maid, had claimed. He'd come home from a brief business trip to find Lacy gone. If Janelle hadn't still been there, he'd never have known what had happened to Lacy. Her betrayal had been the killing blow.

There'd been nothing left for him in Texas, so he'd dismissed Janelle, uprooted himself and moved to Montana.

But now, the lawyer's letter claimed he had a very valid reason to visit Texas again. Connor stared at the scrap of paper, more tattered than not, thanks to his bruising hold on it. That single piece of paper had affected a lot of people. He wasn't the only one involved.

The letter explained how Megan Kelly's father told a young Megan her baby had died when he'd really sold it to Harland Maitland for his daughter, Clarise—Connor's adoptive mother.

According to the letter, Megan, who'd become a Maitland

after her marriage to Harland's son, William, was his birth mother. She'd thought he was dead; he hadn't known she existed.

Now the big question was, what would he do with the information?

Should he look her up and explain? Or should he leave things as they stood? After all, if Clarise had known the truth, maybe there was a damn good reason she hadn't shared it with him.

Connor turned and headed for the house. Usually the quiet of his land gave him some measure of peace, but tonight there would be no rest for him.

CHAPTER THIRTEEN

DANA WAS too quiet, and he didn't like it. R.J. watched her as they stepped into his mother's home, trying to decide what the problem could be, but she was giving away no clues. She seemed fragile, and that brought out his protective instincts like never before.

He should have been well pleased with things, R.J. thought. Dana hadn't missed her period, as he'd first feared, and his relief had been monumental. She was still working for him, but true to her word, she scheduled private, very naughty meetings for the two of them whenever possible—and Dana was a whiz with his schedule. But it didn't stop there. Now that he'd gotten her over her skewed perception of herself, she was open, sometimes even extravagant in her desire, and she matched him perfectly.

He liked coming home to her. She insisted on cooking often, and though he'd always considered Betty an excellent cook, it was different when Dana was puttering around in his kitchen. He liked to sit at the table and help, or just talk to her. Or watch the graceful, feminine way she moved. He could easily imagine doing just that for the rest of his life.

They were mobbed as they stepped in the door of his mother's home, warm and filled with the scents of roasting meats, baking bread and sweet desserts. He glanced around the room and saw his twin sisters, Beth and Ellie, immediately heading for them. Beth's fiancé, Brandon, was in close conversation with Ellie's fiancé, Sloan Cassidy. R.J. thought to join the men, but his sisters pulled him aside, hugging him and chiding him for being late. Dana laughed as she was drawn in a different direction, welcomed by his family and their friends.

"I had a few last-minute things to take care of," R.J. explained to his sisters. "Is Connor here?" R.J. had met Connor earlier, but he hadn't had the opportunity to spend much time with him.

Ellie gave him a somber look. "He's in the living room with Abby and Kyle. Come on, we'll go together."

R.J. exchanged robust greetings with his various family members as he followed Ellie. His sister Anna was already ensconced with Dana in the corner, along with Hope Logan. The women made an austere group, not one of them smiling. R.J. naturally sought out Drake, and found him propped against the buffet, scowling at his wife from across the room. R.J. pulled up short.

"Just a minute, Ellie. I want to speak to Drake first."

"Good luck." Ellie gave Drake a pitying glance. "Mother had to practically twist his arm to get him to come this year. And he's done nothing more than brood since he arrived."

R.J. frowned. That wasn't like Drake. He and Hope always joined in the family get-togethers. Hope was close friends with his sisters, and Drake, as the clinic's VP of finance, knew the entire family well.

"Drake." R.J. clapped him on the shoulder by way of greeting and got a glare in return.

"You made me spill my drink."

Laughing, R.J. took the drink from him and set it on the credenza. "If you don't get rid of your black cloud, it's going to start raining in here and ruin my mother's rug."

Drake muttered an oath, then leaned his head against the wall, his eyes closed. "I shouldn't have come."

"Nonsense. We consider you one of the family."

Drake's eyes opened, and his gaze zeroed in on his wife. "It's getting harder and harder to pretend."

R.J. watched him with a frown. "Sorry, you lost me there."

Drake's expression grew even more sullen. "Hope and I are separated."

If R.J. had been drinking, he'd have choked. As it was, he nearly choked anyway. "When did this happen?"

With a vague motion of his hand, Drake said, "It's been a while. I haven't bothered to go shouting it to the world, but I have a feeling my wife has been more than willing to."

R.J. followed his gaze to the cloister of women in the far corner and saw they were all frowning in sympathy. Yep, they were commiserating. Then he noticed that Dana looked even more upset than the others, and wondered if she, too, had personal woes she intended to reveal to the female masses. The thought didn't please him at all.

But she met his gaze briefly and offered him a tentative, sad smile.

R.J., not understanding that look, turned back to Drake. "Is it something the two of you can work out?"

"Hell, no." Drake grabbed his drink and swallowed the rest of it in one gulp. Eyes glinting, he muttered, "She wants to have kids."

"Ah." R.J. shoved his hands into his pockets and rocked on his heels. "That's a tough one."

"Hope knew how I felt about it before she married me," he said, staring at nothing in particular. "I've always been honest with her."

"But?" R.J. could sense he had more to say, and he felt totally inadequate to help Drake figure this one out. Drake's parents were as wealthy as his own, but unlike Megan and William, they'd been cold and disinterested in their children. R.J. understood how Drake felt about having children, because he felt the same. Sometimes blood rang true, and you just didn't know if you'd be good at something, like parenting, or if you'd follow in your father's footsteps. Better not to put it to the test.

At the same time, he truly hated to see Drake in such torment. It had always been blindingly clear how much he and Hope loved each other. They were meant to be together.

Drake poured another drink. "But…nothing."

R.J. cleared his throat. He remembered when his nephew Will was born, the instant surge of love and protectiveness he'd felt, the overwhelming emotions. "One thing about kids, they can sure as hell throw you for a loop."

Drake gave him a bleak look. "I don't know much about kids, R.J. And what I do know is sure as hell not worth remembering."

R.J. lifted one brow, then again looked at Dana. She'd been speaking very quietly with Hope, but as if she'd felt his gaze, she looked up. Her smile was gentle, her green eyes soft. He saw the emeralds at her wrist and throat and his ring on her finger. "I haven't a clue how to help you, Drake. I just hope you and Hope can work this out."

Just then Megan called for everyone's attention. R.J. turned and felt his sister Anna slip up beside him, hooking her arm through his. Will, her son, who at ten liked to think himself very worldly, leaned against R.J.'s side. Because he'd done it so many times, R.J. ruffled his hair, then rested his hand on Will's head.

Everyone gave their attention to Megan.

"I'm sorry to tell you, but Jake phoned to say he won't be able to make it, after all. He'll be home by Christmas, but for today, we'll just have to get by without him."

Anna gave R.J.'s arm a squeeze. "I wish I knew exactly what it was Jake did for a living."

R.J. glanced at her, then shrugged. "Something with the C.I.A. or the F.B.I., no doubt. Or maybe he's really a street cleaner and just doesn't want us to know. That's why he pretends it's so hush-hush."

Anna laughed as R.J. hunkered down next to Will. "What about you, kiddo? You want to be a spy someday?"

Will pretended to think about that, his young face drawn in lines of concentration. "Nah. Mom needs me to stick around. She'd be lonely if I left."

R.J. gave him an approving hug. "That's the attitude!"

Will rushed off when the doorbell rang again, and R.J. watched him go with a smile. Anna smacked his arm. "You've got him acting as overprotective as you do."

R.J. sniffed in mock hauteur. "Grant the men in your life a little right to worry, all right?"

"Little would be the operative word there. You tend to hover in excessive amounts."

R.J. knew she was teasing. "Anna, can I ask you something?"

"Uh-oh, sounds serious. And here I thought you'd still be floating on a cloud of marital bliss."

"Actually, I am. Floating that is. Dana is…" He floundered, looking for the right words. Dana meant so much to him, and always had. He'd just never realized it before. He hated to admit it, but he'd taken her for granted when she was the most important person in his life.

"She's Dana. And you know she's loved you forever. Though I may never forgive you for not having a big wedding, I'm willing to cut you some slack for finally wising up and loving her back."

R.J. gave her such a blank look, Anna groaned. "Don't tell me you didn't know?"

He shook his head, then once more sought out Dana with his eyes. His heart was racing. He'd been so blind, so stupid. He'd almost ruined things between them. "You think she loves me?"

"Don't be a dope, R.J. Why else would she have married you?"

Why else, indeed? He thought of how she'd always doted on

him, how well she knew him and what he wanted or needed and when. The way she seemed attuned to his every thought. She was more than he'd ever imagined possible in a woman, and certainly more than he deserved. He continued to watch her. "I never thought I'd make very good husband or father material."

Anna put her hand to his cheek, gaining his attention. "I'll admit you're overbearing, and your temper is too quick, and you're autocratic—"

"Enough, brat!"

"But you're also one of the finest men I've ever met. I can't imagine any man being a better father or husband than you. Will adores you. Just look at how you've always been with him."

Just the word *father* made R.J. feel a little sick inside. He said, a touch of desperation in his tone, "I'm Will's uncle, there's a big difference."

"Not when there is no father. If it hadn't been for you, Will would have missed out on so much."

R.J. pulled her into a tight embrace and rocked her. He loved his little sister fiercely and would have challenged the world for her. "It's not your fault the marriage didn't work."

Against his suit coat, she mumbled, "But his own father took off, and *you* filled in. Not just as an uncle, R.J., though that's responsibility enough. But you have been a father to him, too. A wonderful father. And a friend and an excellent role model. How you've been with Will, the easy, comfortable way you've always handled him, says a hell of a lot about the type of father you'd be."

R.J. felt a loosening in his chest, a tiny crack in the stone wall of his resistance. He couldn't remember a single moment he'd spent with Will that hadn't been enjoyable. From the diaper stage to the teething stage to the repeating-every-curse-word-he-said stage, Will had been a joy. Because he'd been so aware of his possible shortcomings, R.J. had worked extra hard to make certain he offered the best influence possible. He hadn't wanted to screw up with Will.

Could Anna be right? Could he handle being a father?

He tried to imagine how he'd feel with a son or daughter of his own, and a lump the size of a grapefruit filled his throat. The idea scared him spitless, but it also brought about the image of Dana as the mother, and she fit that role so beautifully, he wanted to go to her then, to tell her, to admit…that he loved her.

He closed his eyes as the reality of it sank in. God, he loved her. She'd turned his world upside down and made him see things about himself he'd never suspected. Good things. And she did it all while asking for nothing in return except physical love.

Because she assumed she'd never have any other kind from him.

"You're crushing me, R.J."

With a muttered apology, he released Anna, then ignored the way she laughed at him. He wanted to pick up his wife and carry her out of there. He wanted to be alone with her, to tell her that despite his remaining doubts, he'd be willing to try fatherhood—for her. *With her*. Hell, he'd try anything to keep Dana happy.

But before he could make that decision, a man approached, and he knew without an introduction that it was none other than Connor.

R.J. eyed him closely. He looked to be around forty, with calculating bright blue eyes and dark hair. R.J. mistrusted him on sight, though he said nothing because of Megan.

His mother hovered nearby, and R.J. stuck out his hand, not wanting Megan to sense his reservation. After all, he'd once been a stray himself. "Connor. Good to see you again. Sorry it's been a while."

The man nodded, and his grip was a little too tight to be

called polite. "I just figured you didn't have any time to spend with your new cousin."

There was blatant challenge in his words and grip, and R.J.'s instincts went on alert. In the next instant Dana was there at his side. She always seemed to know when her calming influence was needed.

Dana was cool, poised, and she could defuse a situation with her mere presence. While Dana made social chit-chat with Connor, R.J. focused on his love for his wife rather than his distrust of this long-lost cousin. He felt full to bursting, and not even a hostile confrontation could dent his newfound inner peace.

Megan announced that dinner was ready. R.J., his arm around his wife, put his worries from his mind and enjoyed his family and friends and his newly realized love. The evening progressed smoothly. He watched Drake and Hope, and wished for some way to help them. Megan brought the baby down, and somehow R.J. ended up with the little scamp in his lap. Though his hands trembled and his heart raced, it wasn't a horrible feeling. He thought of how close he'd come to being named the baby's father, and suddenly, it didn't seem like such a horror. Holding the infant, he could understand Megan's feelings, how she'd immediately begun loving him.

Deliberately, R.J. carried the baby across the room, bypassing all the women with their outstretched arms, to place the little boy in Drake's lap, instead. Hope immediately settled beside him, her eyes soft with maternal yearning, while Drake went stiff as a poker.

R.J. laughed, surprising everyone. Love could work miracles; Drake didn't stand a chance.

He caught Dana's hand and announced to his family and friends that he was calling it an evening. Since the night was still young, he accepted the ribald comments tossed out about newly married couples.

He and Dana were silent on the ride home, but R.J. was

content. He parked the car and opened her door for her, then followed her inside. They climbed the stairs together, and already R.J. was hard with wanting her. The feeling was different now that he knew he loved her, that he'd make this marriage the forever kind, just as Dana deserved.

They stepped into her bedroom and he caught her shoulders, turning her to face him.

Before he could orate on his love, however, she beat him to the punch. She stared at him, her beautiful eyes solemn, and said, "I can't do this anymore, R.J. I'm moving back to my own place."

FOR A SINGLE HEARTBEAT, R.J. turned to stone. It felt as if the blood had frozen in his veins. Then determination set in. He'd be damned if he'd let her walk away after he'd just come to such a life-altering revelation.

Nodding slowly, his hands clasped behind his back in a pose that he hoped would hide his anger, he asked, "Care to tell me why?"

She paced over to the window, looking out on the grounds she'd always admired so much. "I love you, R.J."

"Ah." He thought he might explode with happiness. He felt taller, stronger. "Obviously a good reason to leave a man."

She toyed with the edge of the curtain, uncertainty obvious in the tilt of her head. "You don't understand...."

"You've never accused me of being a stupid man before, sweetheart. Let's not start now, okay?" That fragile look settled over her again. He wanted to hold her and decided there was no reason not to.

She looked startled when he strode across the room and scooped her up. "R.J.!"

"Shh. You're my wife." He laid her across the bed and sat beside her. The dress she'd worn was more feminine than her usual attire, and he'd remarked to her earlier how anxious he was to get her out of it. That urgency hadn't abated one bit, but first he had to take care of other things. "Did you know Drake and Hope are separated?"

Dana turned her head away, but quickly faced him again. His wife was no faint heart. "Yes. I've known for some time. Hope wants children. I...I thought about that, R.J. She's hurting so much, and I can't help but put myself in her shoes. Every day..." She swallowed hard, then continued. "Every day I love you more. I thought I could do this, thought I could play house, and wife, and enjoy the time I had with you, but every time we have sex—"

"Make love."

She paused, then nodded. "Every time it makes it so much harder to think of leaving. But you've made it plain you don't want this forever. You don't want kids, and—"

"I've changed my mind." He wanted to laugh at the way her eyes widened and her mouth fell open. Instead, he bent down and kissed her gently. "I have no idea what kind of father I'll make, Dana, yet Anna assures me I'll handle it just fine." His forehead touched hers, and he sighed. "I'm not my father, I know that, but as his son I was afraid I might carry a legacy of paternal disinterest."

"Oh, R.J." She looked equal parts amazed, sympathetic and annoyed. "For an intelligent man, that's not a very sound deduction."

He didn't take offense; he agreed with her. "I know. But I couldn't bear the thought of doing what he'd done, abandoning a child of my own, feeling no emotional tie or responsibility...."

"It's called love," she explained gently, "and you've already proven—to everyone but yourself, I guess—that when you love, you don't hold back. Anna knows that, as do Will and Megan and all the rest of your family." Her hand smoothed over his nape, and her smile was gentle. "You're an absolutely wonderful man, and I know you'd make a wonderful father."

R.J. accepted her words, then added, "But only with you. If you leave me now, Dana, well, then, I guess I'll just remain the most eligible bachelor in Austin, because I sure as hell won't settle for anyone other than you. Not after seeing how perfect you're suited to me."

She looked like a statue, staring at him, not moving, not even blinking. R.J. turned and pulled off her shoes, tossing them over his shoulder to the floor. He felt exuberant and excited. He was painfully aroused. "I think I may be ready to give fatherhood a try. The idea of you carrying my baby turns me on." He grinned at her. "But if you have any doubts..."

"No."

She sat up to regain his attention, and R.J. reached behind her to the fastenings of her dress. "Good. Your faith in me never ceases to boggle my mind."

"R.J.—"

The dress slipped over her shoulders, leaving her in her strapless bra. R.J. whistled. "Damn, honey, when did you get that?"

Distracted, she explained, "Hope and Anna bought me some things."

He fingered the lace edging the cups of the bra. "More things like this?"

"Yes. R.J., stop that." She pushed his hands away, then pressed on his shoulders. R.J. pushed back, and gently tumbled her onto the bed. "R.J...."

He kissed her ribs as he tugged the dress down. "Another thing, honey." The dress bunched at her hips, and R.J. lifted his head to look at her. Tears were in her eyes, ripping his heart out. "I love you."

She gasped, and the tears spilled over. "You love me?"

He settled at her side, then gathered her against his chest. "So much, Dana. Damn, I've been stupid." She stirred, and he squeezed her tight to keep her in place. "No, don't defend me."

"I was going to agree!"

He laughed. Much as Dana loved to defend him, she didn't pull any punches, either. She was, as he'd told her, perfect for him. "Good. Because I've been a blind fool. My only excuse is that you let me be blind. I'll trust in the future that you'll keep me better informed of things I should know."

Dana wriggled out of his hold to prop her elbows on his chest. The position did delightful things to her breasts and made the urgency beat at him. The emerald necklace hung free, the light glinting off it. "Tell me again," she said.

"That I love you? I do. And I need you. And I want you."

She pressed her hips down. "The want part I can believe. You've got proof."

He stilled her hips by gripping them in his large hands. "The love and need part you can believe, too. I don't want you to have any doubts, Dana. Not about me and what I feel for you. I've known so many women over the years, but none of them affected me like you do. I've been obsessed with you, but I didn't even know why."

"You've been obsessed with sex." She kissed him. "Not that I'm complaining."

R.J. pulled her back for a more thorough tasting that left them both breathless. "This isn't mere sex, woman. Sex I could have with any number of women. What we have together is special, and if you don't tell me you'll stay with me and love me and have my babies, I'll…"

"Fire me again?"

"Smart ass."

"Smart enough to know a good thing when I have it. I'm not going anywhere, R.J." She laid her head on his chest. "All I ever wanted was for you to love me."

"I seem to recall you demanding sex rather forcefully, too."

"R.J.!"

His grin was wicked. "As a businessman, I have to say that was the best deal of my life."

Dana met his grin with one of her own. "Then I think you should stop talking and start fulfilling your end of the bargain."

R.J. agreed. After all, regardless of his father's tainted legacy, he was no slacker. And he'd proved it.

* * * * *

MOLLY ALEXANDER EYED the spiffy-looking plane anew.
She'd never flown privately before. The plane was small
enough to make her extremely nervous.

Until they got on board.

"Wow."

Distracted, Dare Macintosh glanced down at her.
"What?"

"This is…decadent."

He gave a cursory look around the plane, but just
shrugged. "It's comfortable enough. Grab a seat."

However nonchalant he was, Molly thought as she chose
a seat toward the back, her rescuer knew how to travel in
style. She only hoped it wouldn't break her bank account.
She had no idea what something like this might cost.

He joined her a moment later. "Want a drink?" He indicated the fancy lighted bar she'd already noted.

"No, thank you."

"You sure? Might steady you a little."

"I'm plenty steady, thank you very much." How many
times did she have to tell him that she would not fall apart?
She couldn't afford to. If she wanted to survive this, she
had to keep her nerves steady. Later she could give in to the
panicked hysteria that still gnawed at her facade of calm.

Shrugging, Dare sat beside her and fastened his seat belt.
"Buckle up."

She scowled at the order, but still connected the seat belt

around her.

Lifting his armrest and turning in his seat, he leaned forward with his elbows on his knees and studied her.

"What?" Just then the pilot started the engines, startling Molly. She grabbed for the armrests. "We're taking off?"

"It'll be easier to get home that way."

She scowled again. "Sarcasm is unnecessary."

He said nothing. Molly cleared her throat. "Where is home and when will we get there?"

"Kentucky, and it'll be late."

As the plane rolled forward, she sucked in a breath, and then swallowed hard.

Dare eyed her. "So you're one of those people who panic at flying?"

"No." But she was, sort of. That the plane was so small didn't help matters. Rigid from her head to her toes, she repeated, almost by rote, "I'm fine."

"So you keep saying."

He took her hands, and it reminded her of the differences in their sizes. Dare was huge, and she was not. His big rough hands totally engulfed hers, making her feel extra small and delicate.

She didn't quite know what to make of that.

"Molly, look at me."

When she did, she got snared in his bright blue gaze. He had the most amazing eyes…

"Tell me why you haven't contacted your sister to let her know you're okay."

The pilot announced something over a speaker system, and the plane moved, jarring her heart. She clutched Dare's hands and when she spoke, her voice was a little too high and squeaky. "Natalie might be younger than me, but she's a teacher—meaning she's used to governing with ultimate power."

Dare didn't smile at that small jest. "Yeah, so?"

"So if I had called her, she'd be grilling my dad and my ex-fiancé and anyone else she thinks could be responsible for having me kidnapped. If either of them is involved, they might be clued in. They could hide evidence or, in my ex's case, maybe even skip town."

Dare looked a little stunned at her reasoning, but damn it, she couldn't take chances.

"Whoever did this, I want him to be taken by surprise when he sees me free and unharmed. I want to blow his mind and then maybe he'll give himself away."

Consternation lowered Dare's brows. "Not a bad plan, really. But you do realize that whoever arranged this must already know that you're free. That's what those thugs we saw earlier were about. People are still after you."

"I know." She shivered, and then shivered some more when the plane began lifting. She squeezed Dare's hands as tightly as she could. "Oh, God."

Dare searched her face, looking resigned and…maybe a little expectant. Then he leaned forward and kissed her.

Molly was so shocked she leaned away from him—until he pulled his hands free from hers and cupped her face, bringing her back.

His hands holding hers had been startling; his hands gently framing her face were more so.

This kiss wasn't hard and fast. It was warm and easy, slow, lingering and oh-so-distracting. When she didn't retreat again, he turned his head to better fit their mouths together, and deepened the kiss.

A rush of heat chased away her icy fear. Her rigid muscles went liquid. Wow.

Molly caught his wrists, but not to pry him away; she

held on for dear life. Being thirty, she'd been kissed many times, but never had it felt like...*this*. When she made a small sound, a cross between a moan and a purr, Dare stroked his thumbs over her cheeks.

A second later, he touched his tongue to hers.

Heart pounding and skin burning, Molly forgot about the plane, about unscrupulous men who meant her harm. Right now, for this moment, there was only Dare and his warmth and intoxicating scent, his strength and the security of him, the way he tasted and felt and how he touched her.

He smoothed a hand over her face, over her hair and, to her regret, eased away.

Molly got her eyes open, only to find that the blue of his looked incendiary. He glanced down at her mouth, eased his thumb slowly over her bottom lip and, with a frown, settled back into his seat.

She, on the other hand, perched as far forward as her seat belt would allow, still straining toward Dare. With a gasp, she realized how that looked and flopped back. Again, she clamped her hands over the ends of the armrests.

Her heart continued to thunder and her body burned in select places. She could feel Dare looking at her and it made her both uncomfortable and more excited. Was he waiting for her to react?

Well, this was not something she could ignore. The first kiss, maybe. But *that* kiss? No way. "Dare?"

He watched her like a hawk watched a mouse, his gaze unflinching, ready and alert, almost as if he expected her to bolt. "Hmm?"

"That's, uh, the *second* time you've kissed me."

His gaze went back to her mouth, his voice deepened. "I can count."

She bit her lip, saw his eyes narrow and quickly relaxed

her mouth again. "You were distracting me, because the flight—"

"No."

No? But of course he was. Wasn't he? She shook her head. There was so much she didn't know about him, but she didn't want to cross the line and intrude in his private life. "I don't understand what it means."

He looked over her entire body, oh-so-slowly, before his gaze lifted back to hers. "Yes, you do."

Don't miss WHEN YOU DARE,
in stores May 2011 from HQN Books.

And for the story of Natalie Alexander, Molly's sister,
be sure to check out THE GUY NEXT DOOR,
a sizzling new anthology featuring
Lori's all-new novella "Ready, Set, Jett."

On sale in March 2011!

REQUEST YOUR FREE BOOKS!

2 FREE NOVELS
FROM THE ROMANCE COLLECTION
PLUS 2 FREE GIFTS!

YES! Please send me 2 FREE novels from the Romance Collection and my 2 FREE gifts (gifts are worth about $10). After receiving them, if I don't wish to receive any more books, I can return the shipping statement marked "cancel." If I don't cancel, I will receive 4 brand-new novels every month and be billed just $5.74 per book in the U.S. or $6.24 per book in Canada. That's a saving of at least 28% off the cover price. It's quite a bargain! Shipping and handling is just 50¢ per book.* I understand that accepting the 2 free books and gifts places me under no obligation to buy anything. I can always return a shipment and cancel at any time. Even if I never buy another book, the two free books and gifts are mine to keep forever.

194/394 MDN E7NZ

Name	(PLEASE PRINT)
Address	Apt. #
City	State/Prov.	Zip/Postal Code

Signature (if under 18, a parent or guardian must sign)

Mail to The Reader Service:
IN U.S.A.: P.O. Box 1867, Buffalo, NY 14240-1867
IN CANADA: P.O. Box 609, Fort Erie, Ontario L2A 5X3

Not valid for current subscribers to the Romance Collection
or the Romance/Suspense Collection.

Want to try two free books from another line?
Call 1-800-873-8635 or visit www.morefreebooks.com.

* Terms and prices subject to change without notice. Prices do not include applicable taxes. N.Y. residents add applicable sales tax. Canadian residents will be charged applicable provincial taxes and GST. Offer not valid in Quebec. This offer is limited to one order per household. All orders subject to approval. Credit or debit balances in a customer's account(s) may be offset by any other outstanding balance owed by or to the customer. Please allow 4 to 6 weeks for delivery. Offer available while quantities last.

Your Privacy: Harlequin Books is committed to protecting your privacy. Our Privacy Policy is available online at www.eHarlequin.com or upon request from the Reader Service. From time to time we make our lists of customers available to reputable third parties who may have a product or service of interest to you. If you would prefer we not share your name and address, please check here. ☐

Help us get it right—We strive for accurate, respectful and relevant communications. To clarify or modify your communication preferences, visit us at www.ReaderService.com/consumerschoice.

MROM10R

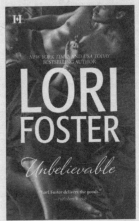

LORI
FOSTER

77491	UNBELIEVABLE	___ $7.99 U.S.	___ $9.99 CAN.
77444	TEMPTED	___ $7.99 U.S.	___ $9.99 CAN.
77382	SCANDALOUS	___ $7.99 U.S.	___ $7.99 CAN.

(limited quantities available)

TOTAL AMOUNT		$_____
POSTAGE & HANDLING		$_____
($1.00 FOR 1 BOOK, 50¢ for each additional)		
APPLICABLE TAXES*		$_____
TOTAL PAYABLE		$_____

(check or money order—please do not send cash)

To order, complete this form and send it, along with a check or money order for the total above, payable to HQN Books, to: **In the U.S.:** 3010 Walden Avenue, P.O. Box 9077, Buffalo, NY 14269-9077; **In Canada:** P.O. Box 636, Fort Erie, Ontario, L2A 5X3.

Name: _____
Address: _____ City: _____
State/Prov.: _____ Zip/Postal Code: _____
Account Number (if applicable): _____

075 CSAS

*New York residents remit applicable sales taxes.
*Canadian residents remit applicable GST and provincial taxes.

HQN™

We *are* romance™

www.HQNBooks.com

PHLF1110BL